THE

BRIDAL RING;

OR,

THE MAIDEN'S SACRIFICE.

A Domestic Romance.

BY THE AUTHOR OF

"LOVE AND MYSTERY; OR, MARRIED AND SINGLE."

LONDON:

PUBLISHED BY E. LLOYD, SALISBURY-SQUARE, FLEET-STREET.

THE
BRIDAL RING;
OR, THE
MAIDEN'S SACRIFICE.
A ROMANCE OF GREAT POWER.

CHAPTER I.

THE PROPOSAL.—A SCENE IN A SHRUB-
BERY.—THE RUINED FARMER.—A
TRUE FRIEND.—"ALL FOR LOVE OF
THEE, AMELIA."

SUNSET was lending the image of its
beauty to one of the loveliest landscapes
that the picturesque county of Devonshire could produce, and the twitter of
innumerable birds was making the still
air vocal with harmony, when a young
and beautiful girl, whose general appearance betokened haste and grief,
made her way with hasty steps down a
lane that was rich in it shadows, its

glimpses of sunshine, and its floral beauties.

The young girl was simply, but yet elegantly attired; that is to say, there was all the elegance of style, but none of the costliness of material about her apparel. She was a lady of nature's own making, and her simple muslin dress became dignified when associated with the delicate and gentle being to whom it belonged.

Her sunny hair floated about her neck and shoulders in more disorder than it was wont to be allowed to assume, and the heightened colour upon her cheek showed that she had been, or was going, upon some errand which strongly interested her feelings.

At first she sped down the beautiful lane with great rapidity, but as she neared a stile which was at the farther end, and which partially defended the verdant meadow that was beyond, she paused irresolutely.

"Another hope gone," she said, despondingly. "Alas, my poor father, how will he fight up against the misfortunes that have come over him? Indeed, I did think that my old rich godfather might have, at such a time, opened his heart and his purse; but no—no—there is no hope."

She dashed some tears from her eyes, and ran on for some short distance further, until she was in sight of the stile, and then she paused again, but it was to dash aside the hair that came clustering about her eyes.

"I can scarcely bear," she said, "to look at the dear old house that so soon may be taken from us. The house where I was born, too; where my poor father hoped to live his life long, and where my dear mother——"

Sobs choked the utterance of the young girl, and for a time those sounds of grief from her breast mingled strangely with the chattering melody of hundreds of forest birds, seeking shelter for the night in the thickly interlacing boughs of the elm and the sycamore, which lined the lane on either side.

"I must let them know," she said, at length, "I must let them know, I promised Julia Anderson, who has been so kind to us, and who has done so much to soothe and support the spirits of my father, that, if I were successful in get-ting some help from my godfather, I would, from the top of this stile, wave my handkerchief; but if unsuccessful, this blue sash would let her know, and she could prepare father better than I could for either chance. I must keep my word, or she might awaken in him false hopes."

She loosened from her slender waist the blue sash she wore, and mounting upon the stile, she, in a slow, dejected manner, waved it in the light, balmy air, that was gently floating around her.

From her present position she could well see her father's farm and homestead.

The house was one of those large, irregular-looking buildings, the architecture of which owed something to every age, although the prevailing character was Elizabethan. It was surrounded on all sides, except the south, by fine timber; and extending for a considerable distance in that southerly direction were the fertile fields that belonged to Riversdale, which was the name of the place.

She who now tearfully gazed upon the well-known old place was Amelia Revis, the only child of Farmer Revis; who, from a variety of circumstances, some within and some without his control, had fallen at length under pecuniary difficulties which threatened to drive him from his old patrimony, and make him and his beautiful child wanderers upon the face of the earth.

It was to raise a small sum, which would have warded off the immediate danger, that Amelia had been to her godfather; but a stern refusal had been the result.

She was now returning, full of grief and despair, to narrate the ill-success of her mission.

"Why do I look upon the old house?" she said, in a tone of deep pathos. "It will soon pass away from us for ever. My father is yet twenty pounds short of the claim that, if not satisfied by twelve o'clock to-morrow, will drive him from his farm. How strange it is that this ruin should have come so suddenly."

It was strange, indeed. There was a mystery about the whole affair which Amelia had no means of fathoming; but that there was a mystery, she felt confident.

She certainly had known that her

father's affairs were not prosperous, and that there was some constant claim upon his resources which prevented the possibility of his doing well; but she had no idea that they were so near ruin as they turned out to be.

"Alas—alas! what will became of us?" she said, in a low, plaintive tone, as she descended from the stile.

"What should become of us, my dear?" said a voice close to her, and upon starting at its proximity, and looking in the direction from whence it proceeded, she saw one who was particularly the object of her dread and aversion.

This was a Captain Strachan, who belonged to a marching regiment which was stationed in the immediate vicinity of the village, on the outskirts of which the farm of Mr. Revis was situate.

There was an air of insolent assurance about this man, which was particularly abhorrent to the feelings of Amelia, and she shrunk from the contamination of his touch, as he stretched out his hand towards her.

"What, my village belle," he cried, "still in the sulks? Come, now, tell me what it is that has put you in the pouts this fine evening."

Amelia disdained to make any reply to this insolent speech, and the captain, fearing that she would escape him, adroitly stepped between her and the stile, where he stood with a smile of triumph upon his lips.

"Well, my beauty," he added, "so you won't make a friend of me?"

"Sir," said Amelia, goaded now to say something, "he who is cowardly enough to insult an unprotected girl, can be no friend to any one."

"Indeed! Where did you read that, now? In some play or novel? It's very fine, indeed, but not quite appropriate to your situation or mine. Amelia Revis, I love you."

"Captain Strachan, I despise you!"

"A fair beginning; but if you listen to me a little longer, I shall, perhaps, be able to convince you that policy would dictate another course."

"Let me pass, sir. I will not hold further converse with you. Let me pass, sir."

"Wherefore so anxious to leave me? You have nothing to dread from me. On the contrary, you should have everything to hope. You must, after all, think but lightly of your father's distresses and approaching ruin, if you haughtily refuse a hearing to one who has the ability, and perhaps the will, to save him."

Amelia was astounded that he, a perfect stranger as she considered him to be to her and to her family, should actually be aware of the state of things at the farm. He fancied that her surprise was an indication of some change of feeling, and he advanced a pace or two nearer to her.

The manner in which she on the instant recoiled from him was quite sufficient to convince him that he was mistaken if he fancied he had made any advance in her esteem.

"'Tis well," he said, with bitterness. "Now listen to me, Amelia Revis. I am seldom prophetic, but when I am, you may be assured that I will stir Heaven and earth, and the other place besides, to fulfil that which I promise. The day will come when you shall kneel at my feet and sue for one of those looks of favourable regard you now affect to shrink from with horror."

"Never—oh, never!"

"Well, we shall see, unless you accept from me at once twice the sum which will make up the amount your father has to pay to-morrow; and in return, all I ask of you at present is, that you will wind those fair arms around me, and say, 'Henry Strachan, I love you.' An easy way, methinks, of earning forty pounds."

Amelia felt sick at heart. The strange knowledge that he had of the exact amount which her father was deficient in was confusing; but at the touch of his hand upon her shoulder she immediately recovered, and with a shriek bounded from him.

"Think you to escape me?" he cried. "No, Amelia, you do not leave me now until I have kissed——the devil!"

A large dog belonging to the farm, and of the true English mastiff breed, had quietly crossed the meadow—made his way under the stile, and without giving the remotest sign as indicating his presence, he fastened his teeth in the ankle of the captain, and held him as fast as though he were in a vice.

"Help—help—curses!" shouted the captain.

Amelia took the opportunity of surmounting the stile, and when she was safe on the other side, she called to the dog—

"Prince—Prince!"

In a moment he released the captain, and with all the composure in the world crept under the stile again, and rejoined his young mistress, as if he had done nothing to speak of.

The countenance of Captain Strachan was perfectly livid with rage. He shook his clenched fist in the direction of the farm, as he exclaimed—

"Be it so. Revenge or love is my motto. You have scorned me, Amelia, and twenty-four hours shall not elapse ere you will feel the consequences of my hate."

Prince, seeing the clenched fist of the captain, appeared to consider it a sort of defiance, so back he bolted to give battle to the captain, who no sooner saw the movement than he roared out—

"Call off the dog! Murder! Call off the dog!"

A word from Amelia brought Prince to her side again, and without casting a glance behind her, for she knew now that she was effectually protected, she made her way hastily towards her father's house.

Captain Strachan stood in the lane, watching her for a few moments, and then he muttered—

"Be it so. I have power, and I shall not scruple to exercise it. Well, I can guess why it is that my proffered affection is scorned. The schoolmaster's son, Arthur Wilton, is the favoured lover of this young beauty; but it shall go hard with me if I do not yet find some means of bending her stubborn haughtiness to my will, and of likewise being revenged upon him."

He stepped back from the stile, and taking a small silver whistle from his pocket, he blew it with a peculiar thrilling sound.

In a few moments it was replied to by another, and then there was a rustling in the hedge to his right, and a man sprang on to the pathway.

A more ferocious-looking being could scarcely have been imagined than this fellow, who now, with an air of equality faced Captain Strachan.

His attire consisted of a ragged military undress coat, with trowsers, down the sides of which a faded broad gold stripe showed that they had belonged to a regimental costume. It was quite clear from his manner that he considered himself to be no whit forced to humble to Captain Strachan.

"Oh, you are there Clinton," said Strachan.

"I am."

"Well, did you overhear what passed?"

"Yes, to be sure I did. What of it? I don't care."

"I know you don't care; but there is this result of it, that the blow must be struck to-morrow."

"Be it so."

"The farm must be seized to-morrow morning after twelve. The money will not be paid, and Mr. Huncks, the attorney, here, will be my agent to take care of it. You had better reside in secret upon it, for which proceeding I will make to him some sufficient excuse, and when old Revis and his daughter leave, which they must do, I will keep an eye upon their movements."

"And do you mean to tell me, Strachan, that your only motive in all this affair is your love for Amelia?"

"And revenge."

"Against whom?"

"Everybody who has thwarted me. Listen to me, Clinton. You know that by my means I have saved you from death."

"Pshaw! How often do you go on saying that! You know as well as I do that it's the old man's means that has done it all."

"By my contrivance."

"Well—well."

"Say no more, then, about it. I was only going to remark, that having conceived such an affection for Amelia as I never yet felt for woman, I hate most naturally and completely the person who opposes me."

"Young Wilton?"

"Yes. The son of the village schoolmaster. And when I have concluded matters at the farm, it shall not be long before I find some means of revenging myself upon him."

"I have seen him."

"Curses on him!"

"Ay, curses break no bones."

"But he shall have broken bones for all that."

"Be careful, captain; when I said I saw him, I was about to add that I saw as sturdy a young fellow of his inches as one may see upon a long summer's day. He is more than a match for either you or I, and perhaps for both of us put together."

"Bah!"

"It's the easiest thing in the world to say, 'Bah!' but I don't know that it ever overcame an enemy yet."

"But I will overcome Wilton for all that. You shall see that come about."

"Shall I?"

"Be assured you shall."

"Well, settle matters your own way. I flatter myself I have achieved a height of philosophy that makes me tolerably indifferent to all things, except good eating—plenty to drink—a dry bed, and personal safety."

"All of which, you know, I have made yours for some considerable time now."

"Granted."

"And all of which you shall have for a continuance in the farm of Riversdale, which will be mine to-morrow. You have kept a strict watch, I hope, to be certain that nothing was removed from the farm for the purpose of raising the money?"

"All's right."

"Well, you are quite unknown now in this part of the country, except to a very few; and all you have to do is to keep most carefully out of the way of the old man to-morrow. His pride, I think, will induce him, when he is turned out of his farm, at once to leave the neighbourhood."

"Very likely. What's that?"

"Only a drum or fife, belonging to the recruiting party of the regiment. Men are so scarce now, and the war rages upon the continent so fiercely, that Colonel Percival, in order to complete his complement of men, intends offering twenty pounds to any approved recruit."

"Indeed!"

"Yes; and in the course of a few days he hopes by such means to get sufficient to march to the next depot with. I, however, shall still be kept in England, until the regiment is one of a few months' older standing."

"Ah, well, it don't matter to me. I'm out of it."

The clear, inspiriting sound of a drum and fife, playing a martial air, came upon their ears, as they scrambled up the bank on one side of the lane to catch a glimpse of the recruiting party.

CHAPTER II.

THE RECRUIT.—THE FARM SAVED.— THE THREAT.

"My child," said Farmer Revis, on the morning following the events we have just recorded, as he parted the fair hair upon the brow of Amelia, and kissed her tenderly, "my child, we must be resigned to our fate. All is lost!"

"But father—father!—this mystery —this strange affair, which no one can understand ——"

"Hush—hush!"

"It was but yesterday I heard Robert, Mr. Angand's gardener, say there was not in the whole of Devon so fertile a little farm as Riversdale, or a better farmer than you, father, and yet you say all is lost."

Farmer Revis rose and paced the room for a few moments; then he said—

"Robert was right."

"And you are careful, father, and just to all, and yet all is lost."

"As you say, my child, all is lost! I—I cannot tell you! I dare not tell you how it is that we are beggars; but this I can do—I can ask you to trust your father's honour, and to believe that the mystery, be it what it may, is not one that before heaven will be his disgrace."

"Is this kind, father?—is it necessary?"

Amelia flung herself upon her father's neck, and burst into tears.

A fast foot approaches—she rose, and tried to smother her emotions. The handle of the door is turned, and then, as if the person approaching had only done so from eagerness, there came a low tap upon the panel.

"Arthur—it is Arthur!" said Amelia.

"Come in," said Mr. Revis. "Come in."

Arthur Wilton stepped into the apartment with a smile of pleasure upon his face.

"Good morning, Mr. Revis," he said. "I hope you are well, sir. Amelia, I have brought you some of the last blossoms of your favourite flowers. What —what is amiss?"

He saw tears in the eyes of Amelia, and that the countenance of Farmer Revis expressed trouble and anxiety. Before any reply could be made to him, a door at the opposite end of the room opened, and old Dame Revis, the aunt of Amelia, hobbled into the apartment by the aid of two sticks.

"My dream—my dream!" she said. "My dream! Where's the child—the child?"

She always called Amelia the child.

There was a strange, unearthly look upon the old woman's face, which terrified and grieved Amelia, who ran up to her, and placing her arms around her, assisted her to a seat.

"You are not well, dear aunt."

"My dream—my dream!" added the old woman. "My dream! How came I to dream it? Bury the lady deep—deep—deep. There—there, don't chop the hand off with the spade, though it does project above ground. Hush—hush! Tramp down the earth harder—harder still. How pale she looks—how very pale!"

"She raves," said Farmer Revis.

"Alas—alas!" moaned Amelia.

"Poor lady, her mind is gone," said Arthur Wilton. "Some dream has completely disturbed her faculties. Is it upon her account that I see you so distressed?"

Amelia shook her head, as she said faintly—

"No, Arthur. My aunt's state is a new trouble, only of this morning's growth—I—I thank you for the flowers. Good-bye, Arthur, good-bye—good—"

She burst into tears.

"Amelia—Amelia!" cried Arthur. "What is this?"

"Hush—hush! Bury the dead," muttered old Deborah Revis. "Bury the dead—deep—deep—while the clouds flit over the fair moon's face."

"Father—father, tell him all," cried Amelia. "You may trust him, for now in times of trouble, difficulty, and distress, I declare to you that—that he loves me; and—and why should I blush

to own an honest passion? Father, I love him."

"Oh, joy—joy!" cried Arthur.

The uplifted hand of Farmer Revis restrained him.

"Hold!" he cried. "You shall hear all. Arthur Wilton, I have not been so blind or so negligent of my child's happiness as not to see that you were looking upon her with eyes of affection, and that she was not indifferent to the manifestations of a feeling which had already found a place in her own bosom. I knew that you loved each other."

"Sir, I——"

"Hear me out. Various circumstances have combined to surround me with grief and difficulty; my worldly circumstances have suffered, and —and——"

"Go on, sir. Oh, go on."

"For years past I have been paying away large sums—the last of them is due to-day; I—I cannot meet it, and by the conditions of my debt, the farm and all that I possess in the world becomes forfeit to my creditor. I am twenty pounds short of the amount required, which is one hundred pounds."

Arthur drew a long breath.

"Twenty pounds only, sir? Why—why, surely there are friends?"

"Who have been tried and found wanting. Twelve o'clock to-day is the last hour at which the payment can be made."

"But—but, sir—the farm produce—the furniture — the freehold itself — surely there is abundance of means of raising so small a sum."

"It would, indeed, seem so, Arthur," replied Mr. Revis; "but the same power which binds me to pay it all, likewise binds me to touch nothing here under a heavy penalty. I dare not, and have not dared to sell a load of hay for the last two years without written permission given me, of whom I wish not to speak further."

Arthur looked staggered and amazed.

"I see," continued Revis, "that this tale is almost revolting to your understanding. I dare not render it more clear. Young man, I bid you farewell. We shall be far away to-night from here."

"No, no, no! Twenty pounds, say

you, only wanted to preserve you in the farm?"

"But twenty pounds."

"Alas—alas! and we cannot boast of the possession of so many shillings! Is this, indeed, the last sum that this extortionate, unknown, mysterious wretch can demand of you, sir?"

"It is the last."

Arthur clasped his hands, and looked wistfully at Amelia, while Revis walked to a window and gave a shudder, as he heard the church clock strike ten.

"Farewell, Arthur!" said Amelia, holding out her hand to him. "Farewell! God bless you!"

"Amelia—Amelia! For the love of Heaven, tell me is all this real, or merely some phantom of your father's brain? Oh, speak to me!"

"You know, Arthur, all that I know."

"Can it be possible?"

"Indeed, yes, Arthur! Go—oh, go from me at once! It is a pang, now, to look upon you, because it can but tell me of the pang to come in parting from you. All that could be parted with has been already parted with, to make what my father already has paid to I know not whom. There is some mystery hanging over our house, which I dare not further inquire into."

"There are two hours yet."

"What mean you?"

"There are two hours until twelve, Amelia, I will try what can be done. Be of good cheer! Twenty pounds, you say—only twenty pounds? I—I will try."

"Arthur—Arthur!"

"Amelia, do not unman me by those tears. Hush! nothing of this to your father. Mr. Revis."

"Sir?"

"I wish you good-morning, sir."

Revis merely inclined his head slightly in acknowledgment, and then sunk into a chair, and covered his face with both his hands, appearing to give himself completely up to painful reflection.

Arthur made two steps towards him, as though he would have spoken to him, but he changed his purpose, and after one more glance at Amelia, he hastily left the room.

"How now?" muttered old Deborah, placing her fingers upon her lips. "Now or the box. Take it out. Where's all the blood?—where's all the blood? A strong man should have some blood in him. Is this a fit task for such hands? Wait till the moon peeps out again, Amelia, my child; and then stamp—stamp upon the face of the dead! It's all my dream—all my dream!"

Amelia shuddered, and Farmer Revis, looking towards the old woman, cried—

"What in the name of Heaven does she rave about now? Alas! what will become of her?"

"Father, have hope."

"Hope?—hope? No, my Amelia! Even hope, that I have, I scarcely know how, contrived to cherish for these last two years, has at length deserted me."

"That dreadful secret!"

"Hush! It must continue one for a time. My Amelia, the day will come when I, perhaps, may tell you all, but not now—not now, darling."

"Oh, father, father, how pale you look! Your eyes are fixed upon something. Father, what is it?"

Revis pointed through a window, which commanded a view along a gravelled walk, conducting to the house, and by following that direction with her eyes, Amelia saw that three men were approaching.

She knew them all. One was Mr. Huncks, the village lawyer—another was the beadle of the parish, a general constable, whose name was Flummery, and the third was no other than Captain Strachan, whose coming to the farm was as great a surprise to her as it was an affliction.

She could not imagine in what possible way he should become mixed up in her father's affairs, although, certainly, in his interview with her in the lane he had shown an intimate knowledge of them, which it completely baffled her to account for.

"Behold! behold!" cried farmer Revis, bursting into an agony of grief. "Behold! They come to wrest from me my only possession! Amelia, my child—my Amelia, we shall be beggars!"

He sunk upon a couch that was in the room, and seemed to be incapable of making any effort to save himself.

Amelia fixed her eyes upon the advancing men, and with breathless anticipation of what their message was, she stood an image of despair.

The keen, gray eyes of old Deborah, too, seemed to scan the intruders with a strange and preternatural scrutiny.

CHAPTER III.

MALICE DEFEATED.—THE GENEROUS SACRIFICE.

ALL was silent in the apartment, so that the sound of the footsteps without upon the crisp gravel came plainly upon the ears of the ruined farmer and his daughter.

Suddenly Revis rose and clutched Amelia by the wrist, as in a hoarse, half-choked voice he said, pointing at the same time through the window at Captain Strachan, who was the foremost of the group—

"My child! my child! do not—do not anger that—that man—fiend I should call him.—Do not allow any natural feeling of resentment at what may be said or done to-day to tempt you to a reply that—that—hush!—no more! The causes—you understand me, my child ——"

Amelia was confounded. She had not entertained the remotest idea that Captain Strachan was known to her father, and now to have him pointed specially out as an object of dread—a fiend, and yet one who must not be angered, passed all comprehension.

It seemed to her as if gradually all that had held her to life was slipping from her. Home—Arthur Wilton—her father—all were not as once they were, and she was herself commanded to stifle her natural feelings—feelings admitted to be natural—lest she should anger a fiend!

A low growl came from Prince, who had been sleeping that delicious sleep of a watchful dog upon the ample hearth.

The huge creature rose and gave himself an angry shake, as though he prepared far action, and his ears were inclined towards the garden path.

"Down! down!" cried Revis.

"He knows an enemy, father, is coming," said Amelia. "Oh, father, you have told me too much, or you should tell me more."

"Hush! hush! Down, Prince, down!"

The dog crouched to the floor, but he till kept his eye upon a window, which opened as doors from the floor to the ceiling, and towards which now the approaching party was rapidly making its way.

And in a few moments more they all stood only separated from the room by the window. Mr. Huncks rapped upon it with his knuckles.

Revis, with a strange, staggering gait, made his way towards the window, and although his hands trembled so that he could scarcely do so, he managed to undo the fastening.

The window opened, and the three unwelcome guests entered the room. Prince made a short dart towards Strachan, but Revis restrained the dog, who, at the command of his master, crouched down, whining and dissatisfied, under a large table that was in the centre of the room.

"A-hem! Good-morning, Mr. Revis," said the attorney, assuming the office of spokesman, "this is the twentieth time, then, that I have called upon you for instalments of a total sum of two thousand pounds in all. There remains but one hundred pounds due to-day. A-hem! I hope that, like all other occasions, this will pass off with that peculiar pleasantness which — A-hem! a-hem!"

"Keep His Majesty's *peas*," said Flummery, the beadle; "above all *varsal* things keep, His Majesty's *peas.* How dare you, Miss Amelia——Lord bless you! I ——"

"Silence!" cried Huncks. "Really, Mr. Flummery, I wish, sir, you would recollect that you are merely brought here in case there should be a breach of the peace; and the less you say the better, Mr. Flummery."

"Lord protect us, Mr. Huncks! what have I said?"

"Mr. Huncks," said Revis, in a tremulous tone, "I premise you still act as agent for that—that—person?"

He pointed to Captain Strachan, who affected to be looking at a print that was upon the wall.

"Yes, Mr. Revis. Two years ago a bond given by you to that gentleman was confidentially placed in my hands. The money was to be paid in twenty instalments, running over the two years; and I must say that you have always been ready—A-hem! I, too, have kept the business quiet—A-hem!"

"And the penalty——"

"The penalty, Farmer Revis, of non-payment by twelve o'clock on the day due of any one of the instalments, is the forfeiture, absolutely, of the farm, with all that it contains."

"Sir," said Revis, and he thrust his hand into his bosom as he spoke, "sir, I have paid one thousand nine hundred pounds of this debt, how contracted, Captain Strachan well knows. To do that, Heaven only knows what exertions I have made. I have exhausted the means and the patience of every friend I had in the world. There is not a common acquaintance of whom I have not attempted to get money. I am considered as a perpetual borrower, and I lie now under the stigma of being either a gambler or a cheat, for no one but yourselves knows what I have done with the money."

"Is this to the purpose, Mr. Revis?" said Huncks.

"Yes, sir."

"A-hem!—well—a-hem!"

"Yes, sir, it is to the purpose. I thought all means would have failed long before this—they have failed at last. I have waded through every species of humiliation that a man could wade through. I and mine have submitted to every privation that can be conceived short of absolute starvation, and the result is this!

He threw upon the table a small canvas bag containing money, and Captain Strachan, with a face pale with passion, suddenly exclaimed—

"You have raised the amount?"

Revis shook his head. The colour returned to the cheeks of Strachan, and in a voice of bitter irony he said, as he laid his watch upon the table—

"One minute past eleven, Mr. Revis."

"Eighty pounds," said Revis, "are in that bag. If I were willing to coin my very heart's blood, I could not raise more. I have got to the end of all efforts."

"Indeed!" said Strachan.

"Yes, and well you know it. By the condition of the bond, my hands are completely tied. I dare not raise one sixpence in a proper and legitimate manner. I dare not touch an article upon the farm, or encumber the land with a loan, which I could procure in a moment without subjecting myself to the same absolute forfeiture which a non-payment of any of the instalments produces."

"Remarkably clearly stated," said the attorney. "Strictly true—a-hem! very right. Mr. Flummery and I have kept the secret, so that if you could have struggled through with the affair, no one in the parish would have ever known anything about it—a-hem! But if you cannot——"

"I understand you, sir."

"A-hem!"

"Ten minutes past eleven," said Captain Strachan.

"Sir," said Revis, approaching him. "You and I—and—and God only know for what I gave this bond, which for two years has crushed and blasted every energy I possessed. You are nearly paid the full amount. Be generous in a trifle, and forego this miserable twenty pounds of your claim."

"Not a farthing!" cried Strachan, as he dashed his hand upon the table. "Not a farthing, by——"

"Hush! add not the impiety of using the name of your maker, young man, as a witness to your hardness of heart. Beware!"

"Ah! do you threaten?"

"No—no Oh, no, Captain Strachan. No—I—I—It was only a word. I submit—I submit."

"'Tis well."

Amelia had looked upon this scene in silent amazement—a species of terror seemed to freeze up all her faculties; and as word after word was spoken to show how onerous had been the task that for two years her father had had to perform, and how great was his dilemma now, it seemed to her as though she was wading through the intricacies of some fearful and confused dream.

Now, however, much as she had cause to hold such a man as Strachan in abhorrence and contempt, she could not see her poor father perish without making an effort to save him.

Approaching Strachan, she said, in a low voice—

"Sir, you boasted that the day would come when I should be humble to you. It has come much sooner, probably, than you expected."

Strachan's eyes glanced again with satisfaction, as he looked in the fair face of the humbled girl.

"I pray you, sir, to take what my father has to offer you, and give up the bond."

"You will be mine?" he said, in a hissing whisper, as he projected his bloated, animal-looking countenance close to her angelic-looking face. She recoiled with horror.

"Never—never—never!"

"Twenty minutes past eleven," shouted Strachan, in a voice that rang again through the apartment.

"A-hem!" said Huncks, "it is evidently twenty minutes past eleven, and at twelve, Mr. Revis, it will be necessary that I and Mr. Flummery, as witnesses, should see you fairly off the farm. If, then, Captain Strachan chooses to give you the management, as his agent, or to invite you and Miss Amelia back again as his guests, why—a-hem!"

"His agent?" cried Revis. "His guest? No—no, I may have sunk low, but I have not sunk so low as that. Amelia, my child, they are almost reconciling us to absolute beggary."

"Quite, father—quite. But I can work for you. Heaven will not desert us. Come away, now, and let us for the future depend upon God and our own honest labour."

Both father and daughter advanced a step towards each other; but as they did so, their eyes fell upon old Deborah, who till this moment they had really forgotten. There was a strangeness about the old woman's face that rivetted their gaze.

Slowly she rose, and tottering forward a few steps towards Strachan, she pointed with one of her shrivelled fingers at him, and in a low, although clear voice, she said—

"I know you!"

He shrunk from before her like one dazzled suddenly by a pencil of sunshine in his eyes. He writhed and shook as though the pointing of that palsied finger had some strange power over his system.

"I know you," she said again.

Slowly she approached him, still pointing in his face.

"What does the old hag mean?" he cried.

Step by step he went back as she advanced upon him, until he reached the wall; and then, when he could get no further, he laid his hand upon the hilt of his sword, and cried—

"Keep her off—keep the old hag off, or I shall do her a mischief."

"I know you," she said again—"I know you."

"D——n! will nobody drag her away?"

"Not till I have told you my dream," said the old woman, as she placed her finger upon his breast, and appeared to hold him as if by some talismanic influence—"not till I have told you my dream, for you are, after all, the man for whom I dreamt it, and who must hear it. Listen."

"Not a word—not a word. Take the old hag away, lest I do her a mischief, I say!"

He trembled as he spoke, and it was quite clear to all that he had not the power, however he might have the will, to do any harm to the old woman, for spell-bound he certainly was by his own conscience, if not by the finger placed upon his breast to hold him.

"Listen," she added. "Listen to the dream. There was a sea of blood, and only one strong swimmer in the midst of its gory and horrible waves, and even he was at times faint as thou art now; for his conscience, like thine, was not wholly stifled. He spoke but once that I heard him; and then his cry was—'Blood—blood! shed by me, but expiated by the innocent! The time is coming. Bury the body deep—deep—deep!'"

"She's mad—mad!" cried Strachan. "Away with her! She is mad!"

"But I heard another voice," continued Deborah, "and it said, as a hand thou couldst not see held over thee a flaming brand, 'The death of despair and horror shall be the death of the false witness!'"

She removed her finger from off the breast of Captain Strachan, and he breathed more freely, as though some most grievous weight had been lifted off him.

Then turning to Revis, he said, confusedly—

"What—what has happened?"

"Nothing — nothing," he replied. "Be at peace—be at peace."

She sat down in the chair from where she had arisen, and in a faint voice, she said—

"Crop the long field to-morrow."

"Alas! I shall never crop field again in Riversdale," said the ruined farmer, with a deep sigh.

"A quarter to twelve," said Captain Strachan, making an effort to recover his composure, but looking askance from his watch to the old woman.

CHAPTER IV.

THE YOUNG RECRUIT.

"Relent—relent!" cried Revis. "Surely you cannot, you will not tear from me my only home on such a ground as this, Mr. Huncks? Have you no word to speak to your friend and client for me?"

"My client, if you please, Mr. Revis, but not my friend. We know nothing of friends in law, although lawyers are all each other's learned friends—a-hem! It is not my business to interfere."

"Stop a bit!" shouted Flummery—"stop a bit! I ain't a pig, or a hippopotamus, or a helephant. Look at me, Mr. Revis, and just ask yourself if so be as you thinks I'm a kindervidel as 'as no bowels?"

"What do you mean, Flummery?" said Revis, gathering some hope from the beadle's manner.

"Just this here: I never knowed so much about this business as I've heard to-day, though I have always had half-a-crown to come here as a wet nus."

"A what?"

"A-hem! a witness he means," said Huncks.

"Well, a witness—I said a witness—didn't I? But, as I was saying, I'm stunnified now at what I hears, and I tells you what, Mr. Revis—I've got twenty pounds at home, and you shall have it."

"Oh, Mr. Flummery," cried Amelia, "Heaven will bless you for this noble act."

"Have I, indeed, at last found a friend?" said Revis, as he grasped the hand of the beadle. "Strachan, you are defeated."

"Bless us and save us!" said Mr. Flummery, as he wiped his eyes with the sleeve of his capacious coat, "what a spear we lives in! I saved up that twenty pounds, saying to myself, 'Napoleon Flummery'—you must know, Miss Amelia, my poor mother called me Napoleon, 'cos I had a heagle eye—'Napoleon,' says I, 'there be twenty puns to spend at any time in something that will please;' but I never thought I should be so pleased as this here.—Oh, dear, no! What a rogue you is, Mr. Captain!"

"Well, Mr. Flummery," said Huncks, "if you will make up the money for Mr. Revis, of course he relieves his bond. You know the distance to the village, and all the shortest cuts. It is my duty to inform you that you have just seven minutes and a half in which to fetch the money."

Flummery's countenance fell. Farmer Revis uttered a deep groan, and Amelia burst into tears.

"Let us be correct," said Captain Strachan. "I think it is even now seven minutes and three quarters. You had better go at once, Mr. a—a—Beadle."

"Dash my cocked hat, why it's a good quarter of an hour's walk, at any time, from here to my house; but so as you has the money, what can half an hour or so matter? Come with me—"

"Seven minutes to twelve," said Strachan.

"Lost—lost!" moaned Revis.

"Father—father," shouted Amelia, as she flung herself into his arms, "even yet do not despair. We are in the hands of heaven. Oh, father, do not look so wild. You will kill me. Oh, speak—speak to me."

"You shall not beg, my child. I will do all—all that."

"Blow my bellows!" cried Flummery, "if you can stand all this here, Mr. Captain, you are a paving-stone with a polish on it!"

"Five minutes to twelve," said Strachan.

"Crop the long field to-morrow," murmured the old woman. "Crop the long field to-morrow, betimes. All is well—all is well now. We shall all die in the old house."

"God send we might!"

"You may cut your throats within the next three minutes, if you please," said Strachan. "I don't know of any other plan you can adopt of verrifying the old hag's prediction. Produce the bond, Mr. Huncks! We will do things regular. It shall be read in the presence of all concerned, at twelve o'clock."

"A-hem! Certainly, captain, certainly. Here is the little document quite safe—a-hem—with all its endorsements upon it quite regular—a-hem!"

"No—no!" cried Amelia. "I will not believe anything so monstrous as this. It cannot be. Captain Strachan, you have pushed your poor debtor far enough. It is time to show that you are at least human."

"Four minutes to twelve!" was his only reply, and then he gave a slight start and assumed an attitude of listening. All present heard as distinctly as he did the sounds which at that moment arrested his attention.

The peculiar, clear, piercing music from a drum and fife came upon their senses. The tune was a lively one, and it was evident that those who played it were at a quick step approaching the window at which Captain Strachan and his subordinates had entered the farm-house of Riversdale.

The steady and measured tramp of feet, too, was now heard, and amazement sat upon the countenances of all who were in the house, for the gravel path, which was now evidently being trodden by a party of military, led to nowhere but that window, at which no one could suppose they had any business.

"Confound this interruption!" exclaimed Captain Strachan. "I will quickly——"

He made a movement towards the window, when the word "Halt!" was heard from without, and a deep, rich voice cried—

"Go in, my boy, and we will give them the Rogue's March as they come out."

The front window was impetuously dashed open, and Arthur Wilton, accompanied by a corporal of the same regiment to which Captain Strachan was attached, rushed into the room.

"Arthur?" cried Amelia.

"In time!" shouted Arthur. "Mr. Revis, where is your eighty pounds?"

"There—there."

"There, then, are twenty pounds more to make up the amount. To whom am I to pay it?"

"One minute to twelve!" cried Flummery, catching up Captain Strachan's watch and holding it at arm's length. "Hip—hip—hip, hurrah! hurrah!"

"I won't take the money—I can't count it in one minute!" cried Mr. Huncks. "How do I know it's good, either? It won't do—it's too late."

"So, Mr. Huncks, you are a party concerned in this transaction?" said Arthur, as he took up the bag with the eighty pounds and poured into it his own twenty sovereigns. "Now, sir, I happen to know enough of law to show that this is a legal tender. Here are one hundred pounds. Before these witnesses I hand you that amount on account of Mr. Revis, here present."

"But—but——"

"Corporal Steady, you are attending?"

"Eyes right, my boy—right as ramrods."

A faint flush came over the face of the attorney, as he said—

"I—I suppose, then, I may as well take the cash?"

"No!" cried Captain Strachan, suddenly advancing, and for the first time showing himself to Corporal Steady. "No!"

"Whew! my captain!" cried the corporal, as he drew himself up and saluted his superior.

"Keep the bond," shouted Strachan. "I contest the payment, and will contest while there is legal delay to be purchased for money."

"Ah, that, indeed," said Huncks, as he proceeded to fold up the parchment bond he had previously laid out upon the table to read.

"Thank you," said Arthur Wilton, as the moment the folding was concluded he snatched the bond out of the hands of the lawyer. "The money is yours, but this is an acquittance."

"Go it, my boy!" cried the corporal.

"Villain!" cried Captain Strachan, advancing fiercely upon young Wilton, and half-drawing his sword.

"Villain in your teeth," said Wilton, "and coward at the back of it; for drawing that weapon you disgrace by wearing upon an unarmed man."

"Go it, my boy," said the corporal in a whisper.

As the captain still advanced upon him, Wilton glanced around him for some weapon, and seeing nothing more handy than the poker, he possessed himself of it, and struck Strachan a blow upon the side of the head that staggered him.

"Just struck one!" cried Flummery.

"Steady! Eyes right," said the corporal.

"I—I think I'll go," said Huncks. "Ladies and gentlemen, I have the honour to wish you a remarkably good morning."

"Hold!" cried Strachan. "You are a witness that I was assaulted by this young man, and you, likewise, Corporal Steady?"

"Yes, your honour, I saw it all."

"Very good!"

"I saw your honour draw your sword upon him, and I saw him take up the poker in self-defence."

"So did I," said Flummery, "and it served you right, you humbug."

During this scene, which passed in much less time than it has taken in the telling, both Farmer Revis and Amelia seemed too much astonished to speak or move ; but now Amelia clasped her father's hands, crying—

"Father—father, it is to Arthur we owe all."

Mr. Revis walked forward and embraced the young man, but his feelings would not allow him to speak. Amelia, too, made her way up to Arthur, and held him by the hand, while the tears coursed each other down her cheeks.

"We shall be happy, Arthur, now—oh, so happy."

"Yes, my Amelia. Yes. This is the happiest moment I have ever known, and when I return——"

"Return ?"

"Return ?" cried Mr. Revis.

"Return ?" shouted Flummery. "Where is you going ?"

"Steady—steady," said the corporal. "Tell 'em, my boy—tell 'em all about it. Steady ! Eyes right !"

"Time was so—so very precious," began Arthur—"there was no other resource. Amelia, your father must be saved, so—I—I——"

"You pause, Arthur ! Speak—oh, speak ! My heart tells me you have made some dreadful sacrifice."

"No, my Amelia, do not call it by such a name. Rather reflect that in having saved your father's house for him I have saved a sacrifice instead of making one."

"God of Heaven, what has been done," cried Mr. Revis, "to get this money ? To what consummation—what climax have my miseries brought me ?"

"Steady, boy—steady," said the corporal.

"The war wages," continued Arthur. "Men are scarce, and—and as twenty pounds bounty were offered this morning, I—I enlisted."

A scream from Amelia echoed through the room, and clinging wildly to Arthur, she exclaimed—

"Oh, no—no—no ! They shall not tear you from me, Arthur. Arthur, you shall not go. Father, take back the m ney. Each piece of gold of that twenty pounds may be a drop of Arthur's best heart's blood, coined into the dross that is to give us a delusive peace."

"Amelia—Amelia," said Arthur, "you know not what you say. Be calm—be calm. For my sake—for the sake of all who love you, be calm."

"So !" said Captain Strachan, advancing with a smile of devilish meaning upon his face. "So, to raise this twenty pounds to fail me, you have enlisted, young man, into my regiment. Better had you leaped into a boiling cauldron, for I can and will make that regiment to you a hell upon earth."

"Steady, boys, steady !" said the corporal.

"Silence !" cried Captain Strachan. "Silence, corporal, on your peril ! Is this young man a soldier ?"

"'Listed, yer onner, and got the twenty pounds."

"Ha ! ha ! ha ! Recruit, recruit, I

say !—attention !—right about face !—march ! Ah ! you dare to disobey !"

"Sir," said Arthur Wilton, "it is true I have enlisted—it is true I have taken the bounty—God knows I little thought that the heartless oppressor of Farmer Revis would turn out to be my captain ; but as it is, if I do my duty, surely you will have honour enough to spare a soldier to his country ?"

"Steady ! Eyes right !" said the corporal.

"March !" shouted Strachan. "Do you disobey the orders of your officer ? The halberts to-morrow shall be your portion."

"No, sir, you have no power as yet," said Arthur, proudly. "I am unattested, and, therefore, not yet under martial law."

"True, by God !" said the corporal. "Steady, boys, steady !"

Captain Strachan knew well that he had no power over an unattested recruit, and for a moment he looked like some wild animal, between whom and its prey a sudden chasm has opened, and baulked of its fatal spring. Then, turning fiercely to Huncks, who was close to him, he cried—

"Come away. You shall have ample satisfaction. I am baulked, but not defeated."

"All's right !" said Flummery ; "it's just the same, old cock, which way your nose has been brought to the grindstone." Huncks was so anxious to get away that he quite, in his progress from the room by the French window, impeded Captain Strachan ; and the drummer and fifer without, according to their previous instructions from the corporal, struck up the Rogue's March before, to their astonishment, they saw that one of the delinquents was an officer in their own regiment.

"Put it off to another time," whispered the corporal. "Steady, boys, steady ! Eyes right ! March !"

CHAPTER VI

NEW HOPES AND NEW DISAPPOINT-MENTS.

FOR a moment or two Captain Strachan paused, as though at the instant he meditated some species of revenge which should strike down with terror those who had so signally defeated him.

His clenched hand and contracted brows gave sufficient evidence of the storm of passion that was in his breast ; but his malignant and passionate feelings did not altogether blind him to the consequences of any sudden ebullition of rage, nor to the fact that a cautiously matured revenge would be much more likely to be complete and successful.

"No," he said ; "no, not now. I bide my time."

"But, captain," returned the attorney, "I was to have had the management of the farm, and—and —"

"I have no farm to manage."

"But —"

"Fool ! why am I tormented by your ravings ?"

"Sir ?"

"Tell me, you, who boast yourself to be a most cunning practitioner in the law—you, who have over and over again assured me that there is no twist or quibble that you are not familiar with, can you suggest no means of diminishing the triumph of those people, or of changing it into a defeat ? Speak, trickster, speak !"

"I must confess, Captain Strachan, your language is scarcely civil ; but the fact is, all the power of action was the other way."

"What do you mean ?"

"You never let me into your confidence, sir, sufficiently to allow me to know upon what grounds Farmer Revis was frightened into signing that bond, and acknowledging a small debt of two thousand pounds."

"Nor don't mean !"

"Very good, Captain Strachan, very good ; and, perhaps, as I am most unexpectedly, at the last moment, deprived of what was to have been my reward, namely, the management of Riversdale Farm, you will be so good as to think of some other means of recompensing me."

"Now, is not this monstrous ?"

"What, sir ?"

"That you should be so graspingly selfish—that for mere filthy lucre——"

"I beg your pardon, Captain Strachan. You hardly supposed, I fancy, that in this transaction I served you for lucre ?"

"Sir ?"

"Well, sir?"

"You seem to wish to threaten."

"Not at all. But the infernal hypocrisy of a man taunting me with a love of lucre, after, by some diabolical means, no doubt, he has robbed another of two thousand pounds, is rather too bad."

"Mr. Huncks, you don't know your own danger."

"Yes, I do. There is none."

"My anger—my vengeance——"

"Pho! You are a coward."

"A coward?"

"Yes, to be sure you are, and you know it. Now, Captain Strachan, you have always carried matters with a high hand as regards me. That must be over. We are two rogues, and we both know it. What am I to have?"

Strachan looked thunderstricken. He had always fancied the attorney to be a supple, timid, unscrupulous man; but he never had the least idea that he could or would turn upon him in the way he now did.

But Mr. Huncks knew his man well, and waited, with all the composure in the world, the result.

"Mr. Huncks," at length said Captain Strachan, "you made a remark some time ago to the effect that all the opportunities were on the other side."

"I did—as regarded the bond."

"Yes. What did you mean?"

"Just this: that the bond would have been deemed to be invalid by the Chancellor upon its demerits."

"Indeed!"

"Yes. If Mr. Revis had applied to any attorney, and stated to him the conditions of the bond, he would have laughed at them; and an application to the Court of Chancery would have made you powerless."

"Mr. Huncks!"

"Captain Strachan!"

"You can keep that last one hundred pounds."

"Of course."

"Sir!"

"Of course."

"What do you mean by that?"

"A professional man never thinks of giving up money belonging to a client upon which he has a lien. I will keep it on account, and send you in my bill another time."

Captain Strachan bit his lips.

"I must think over this business," he said. "One revenge I certainly have in my power, and this young man, Arthur Wilton, as they call him, shall live to feel that, perhaps, he has made a greater sacrifice than he dreams of. Mr. Huncks, will you call upon me at my quarters to-night, half an hour or so after sunset?"

"I will."

These worthies then separated, and we hasten back to the farm, where a very different conversation was proceeding.

It seemed, when Captain Strachan was gone, that the atmosphere was clearer and better. A gleam of sunshine shot into the apartment, and the noble, frank countenance of Arthur was radiant with satisfaction.

Amelia was lounging upon his arm, and looking with admiration and fondness in his face. Her father was vainly endeavouring to hide the tears of acute feeling that would force themselves into his eyes, and Corporal Steady was at the window, keeping a wary eye upon the movements of the captain as he walked down the path, gesticulating with violence during the brief conversation we have recorded with Mr. Huncks, the attorney.

When the captain was fairly out of sight, the corporal shook his head.

"Bad business—eyes right—no idea the captain was the man—don't know what to make of it."

"Fear nothing," said Arthur. "I shall return."

"Don't you think it!" blubbered Flummery "You are a lost mutton. I have heard often enough during the wars of a return of the killed and wounded; but I never saw any of 'em, nor nobody else, either."

"Hold!—A happy thought!" cried Revis, springing forward. "The power that held me down and crippled my resources is no more. Here is the bond which, for two years—two long and weary years—has prevented me from having the use of that which was mine own. I am now free, and I dare do what I please with my possessions."

"Yes, father—yes!" cried Amelia. "I begin to see."

"The farm and all that is on it is now

fairly mine own again. Arthur, my gallant boy, what difficulty can I now have in raising ten times the amount that will be sufficient to purchase your discharge in the army ?"

"Yes — oh, yes !" cried Amelia. "Joy—joy ! You will stay with us, dear Arthur, and be a son to my father."

"A son !" gasped Revis.

He sank into a chair, and so sudden a paleness occupied his face, that all present crowded around him, fancying that some serious indisposition had come over him.

"Father — father !" cried Amelia, "Look up—look up ! Help !—help !— Oh, Arthur, he is dying !"

"No—no !" said Revis. "It was only a slight spasm—a—a faint feeling, that was all. The excitement of this morning has been great. I—I am quite well again. What is the matter ?— Who spoke ?"

"Oh, father—father !"

"Nay, my child, do I not say that all is well now—quite well ? Arthur, your home must be the old farm. Bless you, my Amelia — bless you ! You have made, indeed, a worthy choice. Arthur, your discharge shall be purchased of your colonel within the day. I—I surely shall find some one who—Yes— yes. Send somebody to Farmer Hutch- ings to say that I am willing now to part with the three wheat ricks at the price he mentioned yesterday. All will be well.—Corporal !"

"Eyes right ! Here you are, yer honour."

"What will be the course to adopt to procure the discharge of this—recruit ?"

The corporal whistled wofully.

All eyes were turned upon him in consternation, and what he was about to say was waited for with breathless impatience by every one.

"All wrong," he said. "Canton- ments broken up. Orders from com- mander-in-chief—Steady !"

"What—what order ?'

"No smart money to be taken till further orders—no recruit, once accept- ing bounty, to get off on any terms whatever. Eyes right — must serve now."

Amelia trembled excessively.

"Gracious Heaven !" she exclaimed,

"is it so ?—No—no ! It surely cannot, cannot be ! They will not tear you from us, Arthur. What can the loss of one single soldier affect the service ? Oh, Arthur, we will make the effort to keep you with us."

"Is there no hope ?" said Mr. Revis to the corporal, who, after a moment's consideration, said—

"The colonel might do it. Are you sure there is nothing the matter with you, Mr. Wilton, that the surgeon did not find out ?"

"The matter ?— no — I—I am not aware of anything."

"Humph !— Steady, boys, steady— Don't think there's any chance myself.'

"Do not say so," cried Amelia. "You spoke of the colonel just now, did you not ?"

"All's right—I did, miss. But colonels must obey orders from head-quarters as well as corporals."

"My Amelia, and you, Mr. Revis, whom I hope I am justified in calling my best friend, next to my own father, I beg of you to be resigned to this necessity of my completing the course I have begun. I did not, when I took the bounty for en- listing, anticipate for one moment that there would be any chance of escape from the duties devolving upon me as a con- sequence of that act."

"And you would leave me, Arthur ?"

"To save you, Amelia. The thought in leaving you was full of sorrow ; but to see you and your father turned from your home at the fiat of a merciless vil- lain was positive distraction."

"Alas ! how dearly is this home now purchased !" said Revis. "But I will at once wait upon Colonel Percival, and acquaint him with the whole particu- lars."

"Stop a bit !" said the corporal. "Cockles, Cockles !—Left face !—quick march !"

A drummer-boy immediately made his appearance in the room, and would have walked right across it, unless stopped by the opposite wall, if the corporal had not cried—

"Halt !"

Cockles stopped abruptly.

"Where's the colonel ?"

"Lodgings is a-holding on him," re- plied Cockles. "He's a-packing up like

smoke, cos of a large piece of seal m-
wax with a bit of paper."

"What does he mean?" cried Revis.

"All up," said the corporal. "The
colonel is packing up at his lodgings,
in consequence of orders to start with
the regiment. Eyes right!—All up!
Cockles, beat a retreat."

Cockles immediately commenced such
a banging upon the brass drum that hung

DEBORAH RELATES HER WILD DREAM TO CAPTAIN STRACHAN.

before him, that every one was nearly
stunned.

"Silence!" cried the corporal. "1
didn't mean that. Right face! March!"

"Oh, that dreadful drum!" sobbed
Amelia.

"Eh!" said Cockles, "eh!—dreadful
drum?" He looked narrowly all round
his drum to see what had happened to it
that it should be so stigmatised, and
then muttering to himself—"Dreadful
drum!—Well, I always thought it about

as good a drum as there wasn't in the service," he marched out of the room.

"There is no other chance," cried Revis. "I must have an instant interview with the colonel."

"No," said the corporal. "No."

"Why not?"

"Colonel won't hear you."

"Not hear me?"

"No! Tell you to mind your own business, and leave him to mind his to himself. Let the young lady go to colonel's wife."

"A happy thought!" cried Amelia.

"No, no," said Arthur. "You will expose yourself, my Amelia, to the bitterness of a new disappointment."

"Very likely," said the corporal. "Worth trying, though. Show you the way myself in a moment. Quick march! —no time to lose. Only a chance, that's all. Steady, boys—steady!"

"I am ready—quite ready," cried Amelia, hastily wrapping round her a cloak, and snatching her bonnet from the wall. "I am quite ready."

"Amelia, Amelia!" cried Arthur, "do not ——"

"My child, go and prosper," said Revis. "Do not attempt to stay her, Arthur. She may succeed, and if so, will it not be some slight return for that which you have done for me? Go, my child, and God bless you in the going."

"I'll go, too!" cried Flummery. "Bless everybody; and if any money is wanted, only think o' my twenty *puns* at home. Oh, lor!—oh, lor! I shall remember this here morning as long as I live, and two days after. I never was so upset since once when I fell in Dame Goodenough's great cream pan, and fourteen Tom cats held me down to lick me before I had got half way through the village."

Amelia kissed her father tenderly; and then, with an amount of resolution no one would have thought she possessed, she turned to the corporal, saying—

"I am quite ready, sir."

"Mr. Arthur must come," said the corporal. "Don't lose sight of recruit till attested."

"Then we will all go," said Revis; "and may we all come home happily together Amelia, call some one to attend to your aunt—she is sleeping, I think."

The old woman had dropped off into an uneasy doze; and when one of the women servants of the farm arrived, in obedience to Amelia's summons, the little party sallied out by the window.

The drum and fife preceded them, and struck up the tune of "See the conquering hero comes."

"Let them play it," said the corporal. "It's right enough; for, as my old captain, as had his head blowed off last year in Spain, beautifully used to say— 'Cupid is the conqueror,' and ain't you, Mr. Arthur, a wearing of the laurels?"

"You are quite poetical, corporal," said Arthur.

"Quite what, sir?"

"Poetical."

"Oh, thank you. I try to march as well as I can, and turn my toes out like another man, I hope. Forward! Quick march! Steady, boys, steady!"

CHAPTER VII.

THE APPEAL.—THE REGIMENT'S DE-PARTURE.

"Halt!" cried the corporal, as they reached the door of the colonel's lodgings, and confronted a sentinel who was there stationed—"halt!"

They came to a stand-still, and the corporal passed into the house. In a few moments he came out, and gave one of those peculiar whistles of his which always indicated that things were not going on as he wished them.

"What is amiss?" said Amelia.

"Colonel's wife gone away in advance of regiment half an hour ago."

"Return, Amelia—return with your father," said Arthur.

"The colonel?" said Amelia.

"Upstairs."

"Then him will I see, Arthur. By the love you bear me, I desire you not to stop me. Let me go and make this effort, and, successful or unsuccessful, I shall be all the happier with the knowledge that I have made it. Do not— oh, do not, I implore you, Arthur, say one word to stay me!"

Arthur shrank back with a sigh, and Amelia entered the house at once.

"A credit to any regiment that girl," said the corporal. "Let her go—Who knows but the colonel may hit upon some scheme to do what she wishes? Don't despair. Many a man goes on a forlorn hope, and comes back to his canteen again, while a fellow who smirks and dodges very likely gets the things reserved for him."

When Amelia had got half way along the passage of the house, she met an orderly sergeant, who looked at her as though he would have said—

"What on earth do you want here?"

"Is Colonel Percival within?" she said.

"Yes, but very busy."

"Announce to him that a lady wishes to speak to him"

"Well, I really don't know."

"I know, sir. Do your duty."

There was an air of great command about Amelia that awed the sergeant, who at first was disposed to put on a degree of familiarity, which she felt it was absolutely necessary to check.

"Certainly, miss," he said, in a more subdued tone. "What more shall I announce?"

"A lady—a stranger to the colonel."

The sergeant went up the stairs upon his errand, and in a few moments he returned, and said—

"The colonel presents his compliments, and says, unless it is very urgent business he would be obliged if you would go away again; but if it is, will you please to walk up?"

Amelia ascended the stairs without one word of reply to the sergeant, who called after her—

"It's the first door opposite the landing, miss."

Amelia's feelings were wound up to a pitch of intensity; but yet as she neared the door she trembled, and her heart beat so violently that she was compelled to pause. She saw a half-opened door immediately opposite to her, and from within the room she heard some one bustling about as though getting ready for immediate departure.

She felt that there was not a moment to lose, and yet she could not sufficiently command herself to advance into the room.

The strong conviction, however, that this was not only, in all probability, the last, but, likewise, the only effort that could be made to save Arthur from the sad necessity of leaving friends, home, kindred, and love, aroused her, and she hastily stepped into the room.

When there, however, she was compelled to hold her hand upon her heart in a vain endeavour to still its wild, tumultuous beating.

In the room was a tall, gentlemanly-looking man, in an undress military uniform. He cast a keen glance upon Amelia, as he said—

"What is it? Pray inform me as shortly as possible what are your wishes?"

"Do I speak to Colonel Percival?" faltered Amelia.

"Yes, surely; but I see that you are not very capable just now of speaking to anybody, so sit down, my dear, and compose yourself a little. Don't mind me—I'm only packing up. You can go on speaking whenever you like."

There was an odd mixture of singularity, harshness, and kindness about the tone of the colonel. He tilted up a chair, so as to throw off an assemblage of miscellaneous articles, and then pushed it towards Amelia, who was in truth glad enough to sit down upon it.

"Confound that Jackson," muttered the colonel. "He knows just about as much of packing a trunk, as——Well—are you going to speak?"

"Yes, sir. My name is Revis."

"Ah!"

"A Captain Strachan, for reasons best known to himself, prosecuted my father for a debt."

"Ah!"

"He could not pay it, and a young—young—gentleman——"

"Ah!"

"Sir?"

"Go on—go on. D—n the trunk, it won't hold the epaulette box now. Go on."

"A young gentleman, sir, enlisted, to raise the money, which was twenty pounds, just the amount offered for a recruit, you see, sir."

"Ah!"

"But, oh, sir, only consider how hard——"

"D——d hard," said the captain, as he gave the box he was trying to pack a kick. "Here, I only tried to squeeze in an odd sword hilt, and the lid is as wide open as —— Ah! go on—As you were saying—

"Oh, sir, pity me!"

"Pity you? Pity me, rather."

"But, sir, consider the motive which influenced the young gentleman. His name is Arthur Wilton. Will you——"

"Stop!"

"Yes, sir?"

"Will you just do me the favour of coming and sitting upon this box to try and punch the lid down, while I lock it, or stand upon it? That's right! Stamp hard!"

"Yes, sir."

"Stamp as hard as you can."

"I am, sir."

"Stamp a little harder, then!"

"But, sir, will you save us all from such grief—such agony of spirit?"

"Eh?"

"Will you let the recruit go?"

"Let the what go?"

"The young recruit. Oh, sir, my prayers will cling around you in the hour of battle, and ——"

"Stop!"

The colonel rummaged about for some few moments among a heap of papers upon the table, and at length he took up one to which was appended a large official-looking seal, and handing it to Amelia, he said—

"Read this, my dear."

Amelia saw through her tears that it was headed, "Horse Guards," and she read enough of it to find that it was the very order to which the corporal had referred, when he spoke of the utter hopelessness of getting Arthur Wilton bought off.

"Read it," cried the colonel.

"Yes, but ——"

"Good-morning. Row de dow, dow de dow, row de dow, dow!—D—n the boot-jack! I have forgotten that, after all. Good gracious! my dear! by all that's abominable, did you ever, when you were packing up, forget your boot-jack?"

"Is there no hope?"

"How should there be? If I unlock the box again to put it in, everything will roll out, I know."

"But about the recruit, sir? Captain Strachan is so bad a man. He has threatened to prosecute him."

Colonel Percival drew himself up to his full height, and looked at Amelia

"Hark you, my dear," he said, "you might as well ask me to give you the commander-in-chief's eye-tooth just at this juncture of the war, as a soldier out of the ranks; but as for any man in my regiment being prosecuted for petty spite by any officer, I'd have his epaulettes off, and make him swallow them in the face of the army, if I knew it."

Amelia trembled.

"Row de dow, dew de dow, dow de dow, dow!" sung the colonel, as he bustled about the room.

Amelia saw that there was not the shadow of a hope remaining of a favourable issue to her suit, and she rose and moved slowly towards the door of the room.

"Sir," she said, "I believe that the impossibility of your granting my suit is the reason it is not granted. I thank you for what you have said about the—the prosecution."

"Row de dow, dow!"

"I bid you farewell, sir."

"By, by, my dear! Never fear—your lover will come back to you, safe and sound. Look at me—I'm all right, and been in so many engagements that I left off counting them."

"You think, sir, there is not much danger?"

"Lots!"

"Then—then he may be killed?"

"And then—then, again, he may not. Row de dow dow. The idea now, after all, of forgetting the boot-jack! The devil take it. What's to be done?"

"Farewell, sir!"

"Good-by. Stop—stop!"

Amelia bounded back. Hope once more sprang up, phœnix-like, in her heart, and she listened with bated breath and clasped hands to what the colonel was about to say.

"My dear, if you meet a fellow on the stairs with red hair, and eyes staring half way out of his head, don't say anything about my leaving out the boot-jack. He'd only laugh, the rascal, when he was by himself, about it."

Amelia turned away with a deep sigh.

How she descended the staircase and gained the street she scarcely knew, but when there, she almost fell into her father's arms, as she said—

"All is in vain!"

"Steady—steady," said the corporal.

"Oh, Arthur—Arthur!"

"Cheer up, my Amelia—cheer up. Time will soon soften down the rigour of my absence. At every opportunity you shall hear from me. I shall return to you with honour."

"Eh—eh?" cried a voice from the window above. "Hilloa, there—hilloa!"

They all looked up, and the corporal immediately saluted the colonel, who was looking from the window, and who, seeing Amelia, added—

"Arthur, what did you call him, my dear?"

"Arthur Wilton."

Bang! went the window down again, and they were all left to draw their own conclusions from the singular conduct of Colonel Percival.

CHAPTER VIII.

THE FAREWELL.—THE PROMISE.

THE corporal gave one of his whistles when the colonel had closed the window, and appeared for a few moments to be lost in thought.

"Beats me," he said. "Can't make it out. What did the colonel say, Miss Amelia?"

"No hope."

"Humph! He means something. However, you must come along, Mr. Wilton, to the nearest magistrate and be attested. I can't let that affair wait any longer, and then we must away to barracks."

"Oh, no!" cried Amelia. "Surely for some short time he may yet remain with us?"

"Hush, Amelia—hush," said Wilton. "Farewell! God bless you! In the conviction that I leave you and your father in safety, I am happy. It is well known to all the village that my own father, although a just man, is a stern one. I do not think that this will be much of a blow to him. At all events, I shall obtain leave to see you all to-morrow morning, I dare say. Eh, corporal?"

"You will, unless you are actually placed in the company of Captain Strachan, and he should be present."

"Can that not be avoided?"

"It is an affair of the colonel's. He inspects the recruits, and drafts them into what company he likes. Eyes right—march!"

Amelia clung to Arthur for some short distance, and her father followed her with a look of consternation, while Mr. Flummery muttered something about having a good mind to go and offer the colonel his twenty *puns* to let Arthur go; but the corporal stopped him by saying—

"Don't be a fool. No go! Stiff as a ramrod. All right!"

Arthur Wilton was evidently struggling very hard indeed with his feelings, and it was wonderful how he succeeded in keeping down the manifestation of those sensations which must have found a home in his bosom; but he thought that an exhibition of firmness upon his part would be a something for Amelia to fall back upon when he was gone, while if he were to give way to a feeling of regret, she would lose all power of controlling her grief.

"To-morrow, dear Amelia," he said, "to-morrow we shall meet again, and after to-morrow for many and many a happy day."

She allowed her father to take her arm, and Arthur walked away with the corporal.

"Well," said Flummery, "what a thing it is for a man to have twenty *puns* and not be able to make anybody comfortable with 'em!"

"We thank you all the same, Mr. Flummery, and shall be always glad to see you," said Revis.

Flummery tried to speak, but it was quite evident that his feelings got the better of him; so he walked rapidly away, making a ludicrous attempt to whistle as he went down the street.

* * * *

That evening, at one hour after sunset, Mr. Huncks and Captain Strachan met according to previous agreement.

They had matters to look about which could not be kept too secret. Accordingly, they proceeded together to a place in the immediate neighbourhood of Riversdale, bordering, in point of fact, upon its grounds; and there, amid a solitude which few often intruded into, they held their guilty council.

This spot, which had been before pointed out to Captain Strachan by Huncks, was a long-since deserted quarry of marble. A rich vein of that desirable material had been there found, and it was worked until it was discovered that as they proceeded in depth, the quality of the stone degenerated; so that shortly it became of no marketable value sufficient to pay for the working and the great expenses of transit.

The quarry was, therefore, given up, and it remained a gigantic evidence of former industry.

There was one immense excavation, and down the sides of that ran many strange, gloomy, cavernous openings deep into the bowels of the earth.

Time had done much to give this deserted quarry a picturesque appearance. The heavy rains of the last twenty years, during which it had been neglected, had washed down a quantity of alluvial soil into the hollows, where all sorts of stray seeds had generated; so that at the period when Captain Strachan and the lawyer, Huncks, chose it as a place to meet in, it presented an appearance of rich and varied vegetation.

But little of the rough, jagged outlines left by the quarrymen was visible; and so completely had creeping and other plants covered up every point and hollow, that one might look a long time without being able to come to an opinion concerning so enormous a depth among smiling meadows and luxuriant cornfields.

But then it was at some places partially railed in, and at others yawning open, as if ready to engulph in its dark and mysterious recesses the unwary traveller who should be hardy enough to approach too near to its treacherous brink—and its brink was, indeed, treacherous.

Vegetation was very thick and massive close to the edge of the quarry at some points, and long tendrils of ivy had crept up from below, and then spread out into the open air, interlacing in each other; so that when it would appear to be safe enough walking, it was, probably, nothing but a tangle of ivy, convolvulus, and various other creeping things.

This, then, was the place to which Captain Strachan and the attorney wended their way.

There were several winding paths which led down into the depths of the excavation; but they were known to but very few persons in the neighbourhood: inasmuch as the presumed danger kept many from the exploration; and idle tales of strange sights and sounds, at times said to exist in the quarry, had kept a large class from even approaching its brink.

"You are well acquainted with the quarry, I think you said?" remarked Captain Strachan to Huncks, as they neared it.

"Tolerable. But, permit me to say, that I think I am not better acquainted with it than some one else."

"Who mean you?"

"Yourself, captain."

"I?—Impossible! Have not I come here merely with my regiment, which has been in Canada for eight years? How should I know anything of the neighbourhood, further than my few opportunities as a stranger, with a moderate store of curiosity, should enable me?"

"How you should," replied the lawyer, "it is not my business to inquire; but that you do, I am certain."

"You rave."

"Do I? We shall see, captain. And now here we are, and we must descend as cautiously as possible."

"Descend here?"

"Yes. How else?"

"Oh, the other side, surely, by the firs is—is——"

"Ha!—ha!—and yet you know nothing of the place?"

Confusion showed itself upon the face of the captain; but the rapidly-increasing darkness saved him from the scrutiny of his companion, who preceded him to the other side of the quarry, where, sure enough, by some gigantic old fir-trees, there was a tolerably safe and easy descent to the depths of the excavation.

The village clock struck nine.

"So late?" said Strachan.

"Yes. It is nine. But a lighter

night I never saw, not to be actually moonlight."

"It is light."

They descended into the quarry, and when they had got down sufficiently deep that it was not at all probable their dark dresses could be distinguished against the rank vegetation that was everywhere, Huncks paused, and resting his hand against a projection of rock, he said—

"Now, captain, at the onset of this interview let me tell you, that unless you make a free and unreserved confidence to me, I shall, after to-night, abandon the further conduction of your affairs in this part of the world."

"Confidence? You surely know enough."

"No. Enough will be all. Short of that will be anything but enough. While I am ignorant of any part of this affair, or of any of your hopes and wishes, I may do something which may baulk you at a time when your triumph might be made certain."

"Dare I trust you?"

"Yes. I dare not betray you. What should I get by it? People pay for roguery; but honesty is a free virtue, and a man may practise it a life-time, and yet get but that negative advantage which arises from silence. I am not what I seem."

"Indeed?"

"No. The world thinks me a garrulous fool; but I am something far deeper than that. You are perfectly safe entrusting me with any secret which involves a condition that I shall make money by it."

"And you would not be tempted to betray it?"

"For what?"

"Any feelings of remorse?"

"Remorse? Ho! ho! ho!"

"Ho! ho! ho!" ejaculated a startlingly vivid echo from the quarry. Captain Strachan started with alarm

"Psha!" he said, after a moment, "I ought not to have forgotten that there was here such an echo. The folks used to say that it was the marble king of the quarry laughing."

"Oh, you know that, do you?"

"Yes. I will confide in you, Huncks. You shall know all."

"'Tis well resolved."

Captain Strachan whispered in the ear of Huncks for the space of about five minutes, and then he said, in a louder tone—

"Are you satisfied?"

"I am; and yet ——"

"Yet what?"

"No matter, no matter. The prize seems a small ones to take so much trouble to come at; but, I suppose, the addition of a great boast of revenge enhanced its value?"

"It did, indeed."

"Then, I understand that you are resolved at all hazards to become master of Riversdale Farm, and of ——"

"Amelia Revis!"

"Which is much more difficult. If ever there was in this world deeply-rooted affection, it is to be found in the feelings of that girl for Arthur Wilton."

"It may be so, but his doom is fixed."

"You will murder him?"

"No. I am above such a poor and vulgar mode of treating those whom I most heartily hate. I must have some more refined and accomplished revenge against him, for he has baulked me in every way. I will think of some mode by which he shall suffer some of the pangs which he has made me suffer; and I think I shall raise a barrier between him and Amelia Revis, such as she will never pass. I have a scheme."

"What is it?"

"When more matured, you shall know all. The regiment marches to-morrow morning, but it will not leave the country, as I am credibly informed, so that I shall easily be able to communicate with you. You must keep an eye upon the Revis family for me."

"Be assured I will. But what on earth is to be done with this Clinton?"

"That puzzles me most of all."

"Puzzles you?"

"Yes."

"Puzzles you?"

"Why do you repeat those words? There is a significance in your tone. What do you mean?"

"Oh, nothing, nothing!"

"By Heaven you do!"

"Indeed! I was only surprised that a man of your resources should be puzzled to know what to do with such an encumbrance as Clinton. What good is he to you or to any one else upon the face of the earth?"

"Ah! I understand. You would have him beneath the earth, Huncks: is it not so?"

"I leave it entirely to yourself, captain. Only understand me; I decline being put into communication with such a man on any account. Remember that."

"Well, well!"

"And then you can do what you like."

Scarcely had the attorney uttered these last words than a stone came bounding down the side of the quarry, dashing from rock to rock, and startling several wild birds from their coverts ere it reached the bottom of the excavation and was at rest.

"What's that? what's that?" cried Captain Strachan.

"Hush! hush!"

Huncks listened attentively for some few moments, and then inclining his lips to the ear of Strachan, he said—

"We are watched."

"Gracious God!"

"Hush! What have we to do with Gracious God? I don't like such remarks. But, I say again, we are watched. There is some one hidden among the herbage, or in some hollow on the side of the quarry."

"We are lost!"

"Why so?"

"May not all we have said have been overheard?"

"Not all, but sufficient, perhaps, to be mischievous. You are, no doubt, armed, captain?"

"I have my pistols here. They never failed me yet; and, among the idle accomplishments I possess, that of killing what I aim at may be reckoned."

"A very useful peculiarity. Look up."

"Yes."

"Do you see where the brink of the quarry just cuts the night sky?"

"I do."

"Keep your eyes fixed upon there, and if the intruder ascends, you will be sure to see him, while I bend all my attention watching the side of the steep, and listening for any sound that may be indicative of the presence of a stranger."

"Yes, yes!"

"I will creep forward and alarm him, so that probably he will be compelled to ascend."

"I will watch."

"Do so, for more may depend upon this than either you or I are aware of."

The lawyer moved slowly in the direction of the spot from which the stone had accidentally been dislodged, and where he felt certain some one was concealed.

The event fully justified his suspicions and his sagacity, for, as he approached the spot, he clearly heard some one making efforts to scramble up the side of the quarry.

It was by no means his intention to go too close. All he wished to do was to alarm the intruder, not to make him desperate by thinking he was too closely followed to admit of a chance of escape.

Suddenly Captain Strachan called in a whisper—

"I see him! I see him!"

"Where?"

"There—there! Do you not see the dim and dusky outline of a human person slowly rising out of the quarry against the night air?"

"Fire!" cried Huncks.

CHAPTER IX.

THE MURDER.—CONGRATULATIONS.

CAPTAIN STRACHAN heard Mr. Huncks say "Fire!" and yet he hesitated a moment, for he thought he would be quite certain that it was a man whose dusky form was rising up out of the quarry before he fired.

"Look! look!" he cried to Huncks; "look up, and tell me what you think of it. Look up a moment."

"Fire!" said the attorney, "or your opportunity will be lost. Fire, I say! Are you mad?"

Bang! went the pistol, and the echoing noises it awakened almost terrified Strachan himself; but he felt certain that the skill he had boasted of possessing with the pistol had not deserted him, for mingled with the thundering echoes that came from the depths of the quarry came one sharp, sudden yell of mortal agony.

"Where is he?" cried the lawyer; "where is he?"

"I don't know."

"Don't know?"

"No. The smoke from the pistol blew down upon my face. I did not see where he went to."

"Hush!"

They were both silent, and then distinctly upon their ears came the lumbering sound of some heavy body falling from crag to crag, and rock to rock. It passed them about twenty yards from where they stood, and went far down be-

THE REVIS FAMILY ON THE MORNING OF LEAVING RIVERSDALE.

low the level on which they were into the depths of the quarry.

For a few moments they were both silent, and then Huncks said, in a drawling tone—

"Was that the body?"

"It must have been," said Strachan. "I know well that I hit him, whoever he was."

"And I heard a cry."

"Yes ; one unmistakable cry of pain. It must have been the body. What else could it be ?"

"Well, I suppose I must subscribe to the opinion that it was, for want of further evidence to the contrary."

"Further evidence ? Do you doubt it ?"

"My feeling in the matter scarcely amounts to a doubt ; and yet I confess it did not sound to me like the fall of a dead body. The object, whatever it was, seemed smaller. But we can resolve all these doubts by descending lower, perhaps."

"No—no !"

"Of what are you afraid ?"

"Nothing ! Cowardice is not one of my feelings ; but I know, for I caught a sight of it, that what rolled past us was a human form. I have no doubt. If we had a lamp, we might, perhaps, be able to look down without descending actually ourselves.—I must say that, although I dread nothing, I would prefer not going any deeper."

"I have a lantern here, and matches."

"That will do. But yet there may be danger of the light being seen by some one."

"No, we are much too far below the level, and I'll warrant there is no one in this neighbourhood courageous enough to peep over the edge of the quarry. To be sure, there must have been one, but he is, I take it, beyond the temptation of further curiosity."

The attorney soon managed to light his lantern, but it had no sort of effect in enabling them to look below. In fact, it only cast a halo of dim light around it for some short distance, which made all beyond that darkness of the blackest and most impenetrable character.

"Worse and worse," said Huncks.

"Stay, what is that ?"

"What ?"

"There, upon a furze-bush. Something seems hanging that is not the colour of the rest of the bush."

"I see it—I see it."

"What can it be ?"

"I think there will be no great difficulty in ascending. I can scramble so far, I fancy. Perhaps it may let us know, too, something confirmatory or otherwise of the fate of our inquisitive friend. Wait here while I make the attempt to reach that object."

Captain Strachan was quite willing to wait where he was while Huncks went on the voyage of discovery. The fact was, that the quarry at that time of night, with all its concomitants, had rather alarmed him.

In the course of a few moments Huncks called to him, saying—

"It is a cap."

"A cap ?"

"Yes, a military cap. Wait a bit, I will bring it to you. I think there can be very little doubt now but that its owner is at the bottom of the quarry, where there is water enough, even at this season of the year, to hide a hundred bodies piled one upon another."

Huncks had scrambled back and handed the cap to Captain Strachan, who, after looking at it for a few moments, said, in a voice of exultation—

"Chance fights for us. The head that wore this cap is one which you and I have no objection should lie at the bottom of the quarry."

"Indeed !"

"Yes. 'Tis Clinton's."

"Is this possible ?"

"I know the cap well. I cannot be mistaken. Behold !—do you not see where the initials of his name have been only partially erased ?—I am as certain this was Clinton's cap as I am of my own existence. Who else could feel any interest in watching us ? You may depend, Huncks, that we have been dodged by this Clinton to this place."

"No doubt."

"And there he concealed himself for the express purpose of overhearing our conversation ; but he has paid for his folly."

"Well, that's a relief, at all events," said Huncks. "It's a lucky presage in our future operations that the very man of whom we were conversing as most likely to be in our way, should fall so securely."

"Securely, indeed ! If we had taken his life anywhere else, there is no place so secure to cast the body in as this where he has himself fallen."

"None, none !"

"What a relief this is to me."

"The death of Clinton does, indeed,

Captain Strachan, place you in a much easier position."

"Wonderfully easier."

"Yes; and yet ——"

"Yes what?"

"You will never be satisfied that he is really dead, unless you go there and see him."

The attorney pointed downwards to the depths of the quarry as he spoke, and Captain Strachan appeared to be for a few moments engaged in deep reflection. At last he said—

"I really should like to make assurance doubly sure as regards this matter."

"And I."

"Well, do you think that, without much risk, we might venture a short way further down?"

"Do I think so? I know so. Follow me, and I will take you to the waters that for years have congregated, and lain stagnant at the bottom of the quarry. Come on! I know the path well—a path which is beset by no dangers, except those with which a weak head chooses to meet it."

"Then I will meet it with none."

"Follow me."

The attorney commenced the descent, and it was astonishing with what precision he led the way. Captain Strachan was quite surprised; but he said nothing, although he had an opinion that a tale he had heard of some smuggling transactions being conducted on the coast through the means of the quarry and some subterranean passages connected with it might, after all, be true.

"Stop!" said the attorney, suddenly.

"What for?"

"In a few moments more the moon will rise, and we shall have as good a view as we can have of the quarry."

"Need we go no further?"

"Not a step, if our only object be to obtain a good point from which to observe the pool beneath us. See, the moon rises. It is a young one, but it will give us light enough."

As Huncks said, a young moon was just rising high enough now in the heavens to cast the beautiful magic of its silvery rays into the quarry; and as Captain Strachan, and his bold, bad companion looked around them, they could not but admire the gradual soft lighting up of that gloomy place, as the moon's rays fell upon each tree and plant.

"Behold," said Huncks, as he suddenly pointed to a dark object in the still water beneath them, "there is certainly something that, if it be not a portion of a human form with clothes upon it, I never saw one yet. Are you now satisfied, captain? Is it Clinton?"

"Come away! come away!" said Strachan. "I am, indeed, satisfied."

They walked on for some time in silence, until, in fact, they were quite clear of the quarry.

"Now," said Huncks, "there remains one important point to arrange between us, Captain Strachan."

"What point?"

"You know well that this whole affair is to me a matter of pounds, shillings, and pence, and therein lies your great security."

"Well, well?"

"How and in what way am I to be paid?"

"I will be frank with you, Huncks. The whole of my resources comprehend my pay, and the money which has been wrung from Farmer Revis."

"The two thousand pounds?"

"Of which you have already one hundred pounds."

"On account."

"Well, well—what do you want?"

"Half."

"Half?"

"Yes. You are astonished at my moderation. There are, I know, many professional men who would want two-thirds; but I always found liberality the best policy in the long run; and although I will be paid, nobody shall be able to accuse me of grasping."

"Liberality?"

"Yes, liberality."

"One-half, you say?"

"Yes, I credit you for one hundred pounds, and you owe me nine hundred. Short reckonings make long friends, you know; and before you go to-morrow morning, I shall be obliged if you will hand me the amount."

"You are jesting."

"I never joke about business matters. They are much too serious, I can assure you. Have you the money about you? If not forthcoming to-morrow morning, I shall be compelled to——"

"What?"

"Be virtuous."

"Which means, betray me?"

"Call it by what name you please, captain. I have a positive rule in my practice always to be honest when you can make as much by it as by roguery, and always to be virtuous, if I am not paid for the contrariwise."

"You shall have the money, Huncks."

"Certainly I shall."

"I hope, then, that you will consider yourself as well paid, and that you will aid me, in all the means within your power, to carry out my ultimate schemes."

"I pledge myself to do so."

"Then, Mr. Huncks, permit me to say that I have that opinion of your talents that I don't think you dearly purchased for one thousand pounds."

"Say you so?"

"Indeed I do, and I think it, too."

"Then, Captain Strachan, you and I from this moment have a better understanding with each other than ever we had. I am agreeably surprised by your liberality, and you shall find that by paying me a good price, you shall have good service done you in return for it by me."

By this time these two consummate scoundrels had reached the village again, and they separated for the night, perfectly satisfied with each other, and with the prospects before them.

"This lawyer will be a great help to me," thought Strachan. "I don't know what I should do without him."

"This captain will be the making of me," thought Huncks. "I don't know what I should do without him."

CHAPTER X.

THE MORNING.—THE BUGLE CALL.

THE morning—beautiful and heart-cheering morning—came at last; but, alas! never had such a morning dawned upon Amelia Revis—for it was the morning upon which she was to take a farewell of Arthur Wilton for an indefinite period of time.

It was the morning upon which he was to leave her to encounter dangers; perhaps, all the more appalling to the imagination on account of the vague hopes they aroused.

Nevertheless, to the fancy of a man, such things are, indeed, of small amount compared with what they are to a young and timid female; and the idea of him whom she had so fondly loved, and whom she would have had free from even the most ordinary and accidental perils of existence, exposed to the chances of warfare, was agonising in the extreme.

No sleep, but such as had seemed rather to increase fatigue than to remove it, had visited the eyes of Amelia during the night; and at an early hour she waited anxiously for some message from Arthur.

She and her father sat together at their morning meal in the same apartment in which the marked and peculiar events of the day before had taken place.

"My child," said Revis, "I see well that you feel most acutely the amount of the sacrifice that Arthur has made for us. But you cannot suffer more upon that head than I do. If anything that it was possible for me to do in this world would save him from the necessity of a departure, I would most gladly this moment do it."

"I know you would, dear father—I know you would."

"Hush! Some one comes. Prince is alarmed."

The dog had risen, and was looking uneasily towards the French windows. In another moment Revis and Amelia both heard the sound of an approaching footstep.

"'Tis some one from Arthur—perhaps himself!" cried Amelia.

She rose on the moment, and drew aside the blind that was before the window, for the bright sunshine had made it necessary to close it, when immediately outside she beheld Arthur Wilton's father.

Mr. Wilton was a man who never had associated pleasantly with his neighbours. There was about him a stern coldness of manner which had always expelled everything in the shape of familiarity; and now, if possible, there was upon his face an additional aspect of sternness, mingled with a look that really might almost be called fierceness.

Amelia was somewhat alarmed at his sudden and most unexpected presence at the farm-house, and she drew back in alarm.

"Who is it, my child?" said Revis.

"Mr. Wilton, father."

Revis rose and opened the window, not that Mr. Wilton had said or done anything to indicate a wish to be admitted; but as he stood there, they presumed that such was his desire. He walked into the room with a slow and measured step.

"Will you be seated, sir?" said Revis.

"No, sir," was the brief reply. "I am come to ask a few questions, and I can ask them and hear the answers quite as well standing as sitting."

"Sir," said Revis, "you are in my house, and, therefore, I shall not quarrel with you for playing the churl as much as you please."

"The churl, sir?"

"Yes, the churl. Surely it is churlish conduct to come to any man's house unasked, and then refuse the commonest civility."

"Your house, sir," added Mr. Wilton, "would have been perfectly free from any intrusion of mine, except peculiar circumstances had called for it."

"Well, sir?"

"Is it true that you have, to free yourself from some real or fancied difficulty, induced my weak son to enlist?"

"No, sir."

"No?"

"I said no."

"Then I am deceived?"

"Very probably."

"Do you mean, then, to tell me that my son has not enlisted?"

"Now, Mr. Wilton, I understand you, and my answer is—'Yes;' but most emphatically do I deny that your son was induced by me to take that step."

"You draw some fine distinction, sir."

Before Revis could reply to this insinuation, the door was thrown open, and Cockles, the drummer-boy, whose duty it had been the day before to accompany the recruiting party, made his appearance.

"If you all pleases," he said, "the regiment marches at ten, and he's a coming on a half hour's leave."

"Who—who?" cried Amelia.

"202," said Cockles.

"Who do you mean?" said Mr. Revis.

"That's his number in the mess. 202—you'll recollect that? I mean Arthur Wilton. Here he is."

In an undress military uniform, Arthur at that instant made his appearance. His father had stepped back, so that at first Arthur did not see him, but rushing to Amelia, he clasped her in his arms, as he said—

"Courage—courage, my Amelia! Believe me, that there will come some happy day of meeting, when we shall part no more."

"Your father, Arthur."

"My father! What of my father, Amelia? I shall snatch time to see him before I go. I will call as I return to the barracks."

"You may spare yourself that trouble," said old Wilton, advancing towards him.

"My father here?"

"Yes, I am here. What have you to say for this desertion of your duties to me? Young man, this is a step which has my entire and most unqualified reprobation."

"I am sorry for it, sir."

"For the step you have taken?"

"No, sir, for the reprobation."

"'Tis well. I do not expect that you feel much regret about parting thus from me; and I leave your new friends here, towards whom you seem to feel so much enthusiasm of feeling. to make the best of a disobedient son."

"Disobedient, father?"

"Yes. I commanded you to abstain from visiting this house, and to entertain no further thoughts of this young person."

"Father, I suppose you loved my mother?"

"Arthur!"

"I say, father, I suppose you loved my mother? I now ask you, if you had been coolly ordered not to love her, what would have been your reply?"

"I disdain to hold an argument with you. I cast you off for ever, and, consequently, desire to see you no more."

Arthur merely bowed.

Old Wilton marched to the window by which he had entered the room, but he paused before reaching it, and turning, he said—

"Money, I suppose, will set this matter in its former state? What in the name of all that's—No, no—I am calm, quite calm. What amount is required?"

"That has been tried," said Arthur. "No money will now buy off a recruit, or Mr. Revis would not have permitted me to leave my home."

"Go, then, and—No—I am quite calm!"

Mr. Wilton dashed open the window, and stepped out upon the gravel path, down which he sped with great haste.

"And that is a father!" said Revis, as he looked after him.

"Forget him! forget him!" said Arthur. "He is my father; but from the earliest dawn of my recollection I do not remember to have heard one kind or affectionate word from his lips. He has always, when I would have approached him with the feelings of a son, chilled me by a harsh word or a look."

"'Tis strange."

"Think no more of it.—Amelia, my time is short. You shall hear often from me."

"Yes, Arthur—yes."

"And—and you will be happy in my absence. You will not suffer yourself to be cast down by imaginative fears, nor will you suffer every idle story that may reach your ears to alarm you. Remember that it may yet be a considerable time before the regiment leaves England for foreign service."

"Yes, Arthur; yes."

"I—must go now, dear Amelia."

"No—oh, no, Arthur!"

"Nay—yes! yes! Mr. Revis, Mr. Revis! this, indeed, is a moment of agony! Say something to her."

"No, no, Arthur. I thought that I had firmness," cried Amelia, "but, alas! I have none! I will make yet another effort to get your freedom."

"I implore you not to do so, Amelia. You but expose yourself to the pangs of fresh disappointment. I must now leave you."

"Time's up, ' cried Cockles. "Hark!"

The faint sound of drums beating at a distance came upon all their ears.

"There it is," cried Cockles. "That's to bring in all stragglers. In a quarter of an hour the regiment must be formed in line of march."

"Farewell, farewell, dear Amelia!"

Amelia still clung to Arthur, while Mr. Revis sat with his hands over his face, unable to speak.

"For goodness' sake come on," cried Cockles. "You know, 202, that you are in Captain Strachan's company; and if you had seen the look he gave you last night, you would not exactly like to come under his power for anything wrong."

"In the power of Strachan!" cried Amelia. "Oh, surely, no perverse fate cannot have placed you, Arthur, in the power of such a villain? You are lost!"

"Not so, Amelia. I shall do my duty!"

She wrung her hands and wept bitterly.

"I tell you what it is," said Cockles, "the only way to get 202 into trouble is just to keep him here for a few minutes longer, that's all."

"'Go! oh, go!" cried Amelia.

Arthur caught her to his bosom for a moment, and then tore himself away. He approached Mr. Revis, and spoke—

"Sir, dear sir, farewell!"

"This is all my fault," said Revis.

"No, no!" cried Arthur; "do not say that, sir. All is for the best. Those who are innocent of evil notions are in the hands of one who will lead them to glory. Shall we quarrel with him for choosing his own path? Farewell! You see I am full of hope. Farewell, my Amelia! Ah, Prince, my boy, good-by!"

The dog sprang upon him, as if knowing that he was going from them. Amelia sank into a chair, half dead from emotion, and Mr. Revis stood pale and inanimate by the open window.

"I tells you what it is," cried Cockles; "another minute, and you won't have time to reach the parade, if you runs like a Frenchman with an English bayonet behind you."

"Stop—stop!" cried a voice, and Flummery appeared at the window. "Stop! here it is."

"What—what?"

"My twenty *puns*. I won't have 'em any more. Here they is. For the love of vengeance, somebody take 'em!

Wha 's the use o' having twenty *puns* if they ain't no use to nobody ?"

Cockles ran outside the door in a fit of desperation, and seizing his drum, which he had left there, he commenced beating the roll-call upon it with a vehemence that effectually put an end to all further conversation.

Once—only once more did Arthur turn to Amelia, and clasp her in his arms. Then he rushed down the avenue, followed closely by Cockles, who continued beating the drum at a furious rate.

When they had got about half way to their place of destination, Cockles gave a groan, and stopped his attack upon the drum.

"What's the matter ?" cried Arthur.

"We are too late."

"Too late ?"

"Yes. The regiment is in marching order, and all the recruits ought to be in time."

"And what will be the consequence ?" said Arthur.

"Don't know. The captain of the company can say something or nothing, as he pleases."

"But if something ?"

"Then it's a case of extra drill and black hole as soon as we come to quarters, and, perhaps, more. Your captain, you know, ain't over-disposed to be friendly."

Arthur's cheek slightly flushed at the idea that he was, by the force of circumstances, committed to the tender mercies of such a man as Captain Strachan; but let what would happen, he determined to bear himself manfully, and not gratify the savage hatred of Strachan by anything in the shape of humbling to him.

"I tell you what, 202," said Cockles, 'there's only one chance of getting out of this trouble."

"And that ?"

"That is just this here : when you come on the ground, go bang up to the colonel and ask him to look over it. If he says ' Very well,' go into the ranks— you are all right, and Strachan can't interfere; but if Strachan interferes first, you see, the colonel won't."

"I understand."

"That's what they calls the *hitty-kit* of the service."

"The what ?"

"Well, perhaps I haven't got it quite right. It's a rum word rather, and in early life my blessed parents were very forgetful o' many things, and among others, it quite slipped their memories to send me to school, you see, 202.'

"Etiquette, I suppose you mean, Cockles ?"

"Ah, that's it. Well, you see, it isn't etiquette for the colonel to interfere after the captain has given an order; but if the colonel says anything first, the captain might as well try to cut his own head off as to say anything as is contrariwise."

"I thank you kindly for the hint, Cockles. It shall not be thrown away upon me, I can assure you."

"All's right. Come along, 202— come along."

The distance was now but short to the ground where the regiment was already formed in marching order, and upon abruptly turning a corner, formed by a clump of gigantic chestnuts, Arthur found himself close to the troops.

He eagerly cast his eyes around the place with the hope of seeing Colonel Percival, but he was disappointed. A soldier was leading his horse to and fro, but he was not present. Before, however, Arthur could take half-a-dozen steps forward, the colonel came out of a house close at hand. His horse was brought to him, and he at once mounted.

"Now for it," whispered Cockles. "Don't mind anybody, but march right up to him. Any soldier may do so before the word, to march is actually given."

Arthur at once adopted Cockles's suggestion, and in the face of the whole regiment marched up to the colonel, who, by this time, had several officers round him. Among those officers was Captain Strachan, and he seemed to be the first to see Arthur advancing, and bent upon him a look of anger.

It was fortunate for Arthur that in a moment after, and before Captain Strachan had time to do anything, the colonel saw him, and turned his horse's head towards him.

Arthur saluted him, and said—

"Sir, I have committed a fault."

"A fault ? Of course, you are, all of

you, always committing faults. What is it now? Apply to your captain."

"Yes—yes!" said Strachan, eagerly.

"I have kept a drummer over his time," added Arthur, "and I would respectfully hope for your indulgent forgiveness for him, sir, as it was entirely my fault."

"But if you kept him you must have exceeded leave yourself," said the colonel.

"I did so."

"To your ranks, sir!" cried Strachan. "I—I——"

"A little patience," said the colonel. "It is for the drummer you ask my indulgence, young man, and not for yourself?"

"It is more important, sir, that I should screen him, as he repeatedly urged me to come away."

"And why did you not?"

"I—I was taking leave of some who are very dear to me."

"To a soldier, sir, the thing dearest to him should be his duty. I am bound to set an example to every regiment—"

"Yes—yes! Oh, certainly!" said Strachan.

"Of kindness," added the colonel, "whenever my duty will allow me to do so. You are excused, and the drummer likewise."

"I thank you, sir, with all my heart."

Captain Strachan looked daggers.

"What is your name?" said the colonel. "I like to know a man in my regiment who comes boldly forward to take a fault properly upon himself."

"Arthur Wilton, sir."

"Arthur Wilton? Oh, indeed! Humph! Arthur Wilton! Come to my quarters to-night. To your rank, now."

CHAPTER XI.

ARTHUR'S NEW SITUATION WITH THE COLONEL.

THE events connected with those persons whom we have introduced to the reader which we have now to relate, are of that astounding character, that, previous to commencing upon them, we are anxious to state that they are literally true.

To be sure, it might be possible enough, in the extensive realms of fiction, to find something which might match with such events, but certainly nothing that could exceed them in their absolute horror or painful interest.

The situation of Arthur Wilton was one which gave rise to feelings of hope in his breast, inasmuch as what the colonel had said amounted almost to a positive promise of protection against Captain Strachan.

Amelia and her father, he well knew, were both in comfort, so that upon that head he could have no uneasiness; and, taking one thing with another, the situation of affairs at present, and their future prospect, was anything but intolerable.

The march during the day was rather a fatiguing one; but when Exeter was reached, the regiment halted for the night, or probably for a longer period. That, however, was known only to the commanding officer himself.

Quarters were soon assigned to the troops, and it was about nine o'clock in the evening that, in pursuance of the order he had received to present himself to him, Arthur Wilton set out in search of the colonel's quarters.

The house was found without any difficulty; and after sending in his name by the orderly sergeant on duty, he was desired to walk into a parlour upon the ground-floor of the house. This parlour looked into a pretty garden at the back, and adjoining to that garden further on was a cross-road leading directly into the public highway.

The colonel sat with papers before him, and his personal baggage was in the room.

"Shut the door," he said to Arthur, and when that was done, he added—"Now, Mr. Wilton, take a seat, and tell me how it is that you have thought proper to leave the peaceful pursuits you were engaged in to become a common soldier? Conceal nothing from me, but speak to me frankly."

"It would be an ill requital, sir, for this great kindness," said Arthur, "were I to be otherwise than most candid with you, although how, sir, you obtained information that I was engaged in peaceful pursuits I cannot tell."

"Some one called upon me and interested me in your favour, and then I made further inquiries. Now go on."

Arthur, upon this, told him the whole story as related to the reader already, and when he had concluded, the colonel said—

"And so, Captain Strachan would have really turned this family of the Revis's from their home by the mysterious power he had managed to acquire over them?"

"No doubt of it, sir."

"It is a singular affair altogether. No

STRACHAN DETERMINES TO FORCE REVIS TO KEEP TO THE BOND.

doubt, then, you are an object of his greatest hatred?"

"I cannot question it, sir; and he will do me all the ill he possibly can, by the power he, as my officer, can exercise over me."

"Oh, I can stop that. You will be always under my private orders, as my secretary; and so you will have no regimental duty to perform whatever, and you will be quite independent of Strachan."

"How can I thank you, sir?"

"Oh, nonsense. I expect you will be useful to me. If there be anything more than another that I detest, it is writing— Now, you can do that for me. The colonel of a regiment has necessarily many letters to send off. Besides, in these times, every colonel is in constant communication with the war-office."

"Sir, I shall strive my utmost to please you."

"You will rank as a sergeant, and receive the pay of one; and you will come to my quarters every morning at nine o'clock for my instructions concerning what is to be done during the day. So now, Mr. Wilton, I hope you feel more comfortable than you did this morning?"

"You have, indeed, altered my position from gloom to sunshine."

"I'm glad to hear it; and now, I think, I can guess that you would like to write to your friends ? There are materials upon the side table, so you can do so at once, and let those who are interested in your fate know that it is not quite so bad as they may think."

Tears of grateful feeling rose to the eyes of Arthur, and he could not thank the colonel in words, but going to the table, he employed himself for the next quarter of an hour in writing to Amelia.

When he had finished his own epistle, the colonel gave him some writing to copy, and likewise dictated some letters to him, after which he gave him the whole packet to take to the post.

Before he left the room, however, Colonel Percival called up his orderly sergeant, and said to him—

"You will always admit Arthur Wilton. He is my private secretary, and ranks as sergeant in the regiment."

The orderly made a military salute and left the room, followed by Arthur, to whom he said, when they got down stairs—

"I congratulate you very much, Mr. Wilton. You have had a very narrow escape, for Captain Strachan would certainly have sacrificed you upon the very first opportunity. I have good reasons to believe so."

"I believe," said Arthur, "that it is an escape. Can you come with me to the post-office?"

"Yes, certainly. By George, there he is!"

"Who—who?"

"Strachan. Salute him and pass on. Don't give him any excuse for a complaint against you."

"I salute the captain," said Arthur, "while I despise the man."

He drew himself up, and proudly saluted Captain Strachan, who paused a moment and looked at Arthur. Then he said—

"To your quarters, sir!"

"I am on business for Colonel Percival," said Arthur.

"Colonel Percival! And, pray, what business can you have to do for Colonel Percival?"

"Beg pardon, captain," said the orderly. "But the colonel has made Mr. Wilton his private secretary, constantly under orders, and released from regimental duties."

Strachan staggered back as though he had been shot.

"And he gives him the rank of sergeant," added the orderly, as he again saluted the captain and moved on.

Arthur did the same, and before Captain Strachan appeared to have recovered from the surprise into which the communication had thrown him, they were some distance from him.

"Don't look back," whispered the orderly.

"You may depend I shall not pay Captain Strachan the compliment of doing so," said Arthur. "Is he liked in the regiment?"

"Liked!"

"I am answered."

"Liked! Well, that is certainly a question that sounds oddly, when asked concerning Strachan. He is simply detested."

The post-office was duly reached. The letters were given into the hands of a foolish, giggling girl, as is too frequently the case in country towns, and Arthur went to the house at which he was quartered.

When Captain Strachan was left behind, he certainly stood still until he saw Arthur and the colonel's orderly turn a corner, but then he came on and watched them to another corner, and then another, until he fairly dogged them to the post-office.

When they were gone, he stepped into the shop, for it was a shop, and addressing the girl, he said—

"My dear, I'm sure you are too pretty and too kind to refuse me a slight favour."

"Oh, sir. Really——"

"I know it is against the rules, but I want to add something to a letter that I have posted, before it goes off; and then— then only one kiss!"

"Sir ?"

"Only one."

"Really, you officers are so—so—I could not think of such a thing. No, sir. Virtue may well be—be—and, besides, somebody might see. Where is your letter directed to ?"

"To Riversdale."

The girl soon found Arthur's letter, which was so directed, and then, of course, she could not hand it across the counter, but must come round with it, and Captain Strachan saluted her glowing, fiery-looking lips with the promised kiss.

"It was a cheap mode," he muttered to himself, "of getting hold of Arthur's letter."

In the course of ten minutes Strachan was in his own quarters, and had carefully removed the envelope from Arthur's letter to Amelia, which he read without the least compunction at the deliberate baseness of the act.

He then took from a small travelling trunk that was in his room, carefully removed from his regular luggage, writing materials and paper of a great many varieties.

"I should never have succeeded in a variety of little matters," he muttered, "which have advanced my views, if I had not had an almost marvellous facility in copying any handwriting that I pleased."

He now sat down, and with the most elaborate care he copied Arthur Wilton's letter. When he had finished and compared his copy with the original, he said—

"A most successful effort, indeed. The copy shall go, while the original remains in my hands. I think if I carry out my present industrial idea with regard to this Arthur Wilton, I shall make a good thing, after all, of his joining the regiment. Ha—ha! There are folks who would call it providential."

Having duly made up the letter again as like as possible to the original, he hurried back to the post-house, and informing the girl that he had made the necessary addition to his letter, he got her to re-deposit it in the box.

After the same necessary compliment upon her beauty, he left her, and proceeded to his quarters again.

"Well," he said, as he flung himself into a chair, "I feel that I am now at the commencement of a chain of events that will either make me and accomplish all my revenges, or destroy me; but I have a faith in my own genius that it will do the former."

He smiled ferociously as he now pronounced the name of Amelia; and after a few moments, he added—

"Not only shall she be mine, but, I think, a large amount of treasure likewise, that no one but myself dreams of."

The feelings of revenge which had found a home in the mind of Captain Strachan were rendered, in reference to such a man, quite understandable enough; but what he meant by these last words, time alone will develop.

That night he slept a sort of sleep which a successful villain flatters himself is serenity, and proper repose; but Arthur it was who, in the fitful dreams of slumber that were his, really enjoyed serenity, for the image of his Amelia was ever present to him.

Even when he awoke and found that the morning had not yet come, he found a solace to the weariness of waking hours in thinking upon her, and telling himself that they should surely be happy yet.

Ah! little did he guess what a web of deceit and horror was being wound around him by the arts of Captain Strachan, and how much he and those whom he loved had yet to go through on their mortal pilgrimage.

And she, too, Amelia, that young, innocent, and beatiful being, she slept in grief; but it was not that grief which is like the agony of sin, and without all hope. It was the grief of virtue suffering for the virtuous and the noble. But there were angel hopes yet in her breast, as she thought of Arthur, and she, too, amid the calm stillness of the night, said to herself—

"Yes, surely, we shall be happy yet!"

And in all the village of Riversdale there was but one person who slept the sort of wild dreamy sleep that those whose minds are steeped in the depths of iniquity may be supposed to sleep, and that was Huncks, the lawyer.

Twice he arose in the night in his dreams, and cried—

"Thieves!—thieves!"

The thousand pounds that he had had from Captain Strachan were bringing with them their own retribution.

CHAPTER XII.

THE PARADE.—AN AUDACIOUS PROPOSAL.

ON the following morning Arthur Wilton, with his mind more cheerfully at ease regarding his prospects of safely and speedily returning to Riversdale, took care to make his appearance in good time at the quarters of Colonel Percival.

The orders of the day were given him to write out, and then the colonel told him he should not want him until after the parade, which was to take place at eleven o'clock.

"You can attend," he said, "but it is

more as a spectator than anything else. Of course, your position is merely a nominal one in the regiment. By-the-by, have you encountered your enemy, Captain Strachan?"

"Yes, sir."

"Ah!—when?"

"Last evening, when I think I should have suffered some inconvenience from his resentment, had I not possessed your powerful protection."

"Well, I should advise you to be upon your guard concerning him; and if he should say anything to you, report it to me as soon as you have an oppportunity."

Arthur bowed and left the colonel.

The parade of the regiment took place punctually at eleven, and a very brilliant affair it was, for being the first morning that the regiment was in Exeter, both officers and men were anxious to make a favourable impression upon the lower people.

At that period, when the war with Napoleon was raging, the army was extremely popular in England, so that a large concourse of people assembled and greeted the regiment with loud cheers.

The band played a martial air, the colours were unfurled to the breeze, and as the bright sunshine glittered upon the martial array, Arthur Wilton at the moment felt something of that enthusiasm for the life of a soldier, which animates so many hearts, even in the dread hour of mortal conflict.

"I do not wonder," he said to himself, "at this being a profession which turns the heads of thousands. It is the very romance of existence."

As he cast his eyes towards the colonel, he was rather surprised to see him in earnest conversation with Captain Strachan, and when the conference was over, the colonel nodded his head and smiled, as if satisfied, and Captain Strachan, having respectfully saluted him, made his way towards where Arthur Wilton was standing.

"What on earth," thought Arthur, "can be the meaning of this?"

The captain approached closer to him, and Wilton saw that the eye of Colonel Percival was upon them both. He was much puzzled to account for the whole proceeding. He did not like, however, to seem to avoid Strachan, so he remained quite quiescent until Strachan was close to him.

"Well, sir," said Strachan, after glancing around him, and being quite satisfied that no one was within hearing. "Well,

sir, you fancy, I daresay, that you have got the better of me?"

"Sir," said Arthur, "I desire no sort of communication with you."

"No doubt. But it suits me to seem to have some sort of communication with you."

"Sir?"

"Bluster as much as you like. You are now playing for me my game, although you don't know it. I have a proposition to make to you."

"I desire no proposition from you, and I give you fair warning that whatever you say to me I shall communicate to Colonel Percival."

"Indeed? Ho—ho—ho!"

Arthur felt his cheeks flushing with anger, but the idea uppermost in his mind was that Captain Strachan, for some special object of his own, wished at that time to pick a quarrel with him, and, therefore, he resolved to avoid indulging him so far, if possible.

"Well, sir," added Strachan, "you are silent."

Arthur made no reply.

"Very good. I will, then, at once make to you a proposition which, I think, you will accept. I daresay, while you were in Colonel Percival's quarters, you noticed a small box—a band-box?"

Arthur would not reply.

"Well, be silent if you like. It will answer my purpose just as well. In that box there is a large sum of money—in fact, there the colonel keeps all his valuables. Now, what I propose to you is, that you should take your opportunity of cutting the colonel's throat and carrying off that box, when you and I can go to America easily with it."

Arthur was perfectly astounded. The idea of such a proposal being made to him by any man, was sufficiently confounding, but that it should come from the lips of Captain Strachan to him, transcended all belief.

The villain saw how completely Arthur was taken by surprise, and with a low, sardonic laugh, he said—

"I told you you should play my game for me, and you shall this day commence it. Ha—ha!"

"Villain!" exclaimed Arthur.

"Beware! I am an officer, and you are under martial law. Raise your hand against me, and death is your portion."

He turned away as he uttered these words, leaving Arthur perfectly bewildered by the scene. In a few moments, however, calmer reflection came to his aid, and he then felt quite certain that in the whole proceeding Captain Strachan had some ulterior object, which in time would develop itself; for that he really intended the proposal he had made, was not to be thought of for one moment.

"No—no," said Arthur to himself, "he is spreading the net of some plot around me. He is making some elaborate and most laborious attempt at my ruin, and Heaven only knows how far he will succeed."

An anxious question now arose in Arthur's breast, as to whether or not he should detail to the colonel what had just passed. He had an indistinct, but still a growing feeling that Strachan wished him to tell the colonel; but yet how could he consistently keep it from him?

True, he could, by not telling it, defeat some plan of Strachan's; but by such a course, did he not lay himself open to a charge of concealment of an important, or seemingly important matter from the colonel?

"My difficulties have begun," he said. "This Strachan is in truth a most wily and dangerous villain."

Had such a circumstance occurred to any one whose conduct was based upon less certain and correct principles than Arthur's, the trouble to decide what should be done would probably have been immense; but he adopted the course he always adopted when in anything like a complexity of circumstances, and that was, to conceal nothing, but to travel onwards upon the broad path of truth, and trust to it in the end making its way.

"I will tell the colonel," he said, "let the consequences be what they may for the present."

There was, however, no suitable opportunity of doing this until after the parade; in fact, unless he, Arthur, made a point of marching up to the colonel, and disturbing him in the midst of his military duties, he could not speak to him at all. Besides, it was, at all events, sufficient to vindicate his consistency and his truth, if he told Colonel Percival what had happened on the first opportunity he had fairly of doing so.

But now, all the manœuvring of the regiment was, to Arthur, dreadfully tedious, for his mind was no longer in a fit state to receive agreeable impressions, but was thrown back again, by the conduct of Strachan, into a complete chaos of conflicting thoughts and opinions.

It seemed to him as though the parade and inspection would never be over; but the most tedious things in all the world must have an end, and so had the marching and countermarching of the regiment.

At length all was over, and Arthur Wilton hurried to the colonel's quarters as quickly as possible.

"Well, Arthur," said Colonel Percival, as he came in, "so you have had some talk with your old acquaintance, Captain Strachan?"

"I have, sir."

"Don't trust him too far, that's all."

"Trust him, sir?"

"Well, well, I am glad he has not deceived you by his glossy tongue. Remember, you may muzzle a bear, but it is still a bear, Arthur, for all that."

"Sir, I wished to tell you what Strachan said to me."

"A treaty of peace, eh? He expressed his regret to me for ever harbouring the idea of tormenting you, and said he would make friends with you; but, as I say, be wary, Arthur; do not trust that man."

"You bewilder, me, sir."

"Ah, how?"

"Permit me to tell you what passed between me and Captain Strachan, and then judge for yourself whether I have not ample cause to be bewildered."

"Say on—say on."

"He proposed to me to rob you of a small brass-bound box you have, in which, he says, you keep money and valuables."

"Rob me—of that box?"

The colonel's eyes wandered to the identical box in question, and which Arthur observed for the first time in a corner of the room.

"Yes, sir. And he thought, he said, the best plan was to cut your throat. Indeed, he absolutely proposed to me to take an opportunity with him of cutting your throat, robbing you of the box, and going off to America at once with it."

"Cut my throat?"

"Yes, sir."

"And go off to America with my brass-bound box?"

"Precisely."

"And Captain Strachan, your avowed enemy, proposed this to you on the parade-ground?"

"He did, sir."

"You are fond of a joke, I see, Wilton."

Arthur uttered a deep groan. A new light broke in upon him. The words of the colonel had opened his eyes to a new aspect under which the affair was to be viewed. The truth of his communication was doubted, and, hence, the confidence which the colonel had in him was at once shaken.

Truly, the diabolical plan of Captain

Strachan was already beginning to bear its fruits.

"Oh, sir," said Arthur, "it never until now struck me that this would seem too monstrous and improbable for you to believe."

"Indeed," said the colonel, coldly, "you should have thought of that."

"But if I had, sir, the truth remains the same."

"Oh, yes; truth, Arthur Wilton, may, for a time, be trodden down; but it never can be wholly trodden out."

"I hail the sentiment, sir."

"It does, indeed, seem something beyond all human probability that such a man as Captain Strachan should, upon the parade-ground, walk deliberately up to one whom he knew to be his enemy, and make to him a proposal for robbing and murdering me, when he must have been certain the thing would come to my ears immediately. Arthur, this, I say, transcends all belief."

"And yet it is true."

"Why—why—what motive could he have? Come—come! What object could a man in his senses hope to achieve by such a course?"

"That, sir, which he has fully succeeded in achieving."

"Succeeded?"

"Yes, Colonel Percival, fully succeeded."

"And, pray, what my that be?"

"Striking a severe blow at your confidence in my truth and integrity; and that he has succeeded in that is but too apparent."

The colonel seemed rather struck by this remark; and after a few moment's pause, he said,—

"This may be so, Arthur, as you say. I will not judge hastily or harshly of one to whom I have held out the hand of friendship. Your solution of the difficulty may be perfectly true, and I will endeavour to think of some mode by which I may arrive at the truth, which, I hope, will be as honourable to you, as it will, in finding it so, be satisfactory to me."

Arthur was much affected at this change in his position, for that his position was changed he felt most truly, although the colonel was not a man to decide hastily, especially when the decision might be against some one. Yet, the manner in which he spoke to Arthur was constrained, and as different as possible from that which in the early part of the morning had characterised him when they were conversing together.

"I shall not want you," he said, "until the evening, a little before the post closes for the day."

Arthur left the room. But, oh, how different were his feelings as he did so, to what they had been upon the last occasion before the parade. Then he felt that he had the full confidence of an honourable man; but now, by the arts of a villain, that confidence was shaken, never, for all he knew to the contrary, to be renewed again.

It is a sad and awful thought to consider how much mischief a really unscrupulous man can do, if in the doing it he chooses to throw aside every other consideration but how he may best accomplish it. One would hardly have supposed that Captain Strachan, after all that had passed, possessed so much real power over the fate of poor Arthur Wilton.

CHAPTER XIII.

AN OCCURRENCE AT RIVERSDALE.

THE letter which the villain Strachan had been so successful in getting possession of, as we know, still remained in his hands; but the copy he had made duly found its way to Riversdale.

Amelia was much too delighted at its reception at all to be in any way critical regarding the handwriting of it, and if she had, it is not at all probable she would have entertained any suspicion upon the object, for Captain Strachan did notf boast of his cleverness in the particular o copying the handwriting of other persons without good grounds of so doing.

Of course, the contents of the much-hopeful epistle were shown to Mr. Revis by Amelia, and there was more of real happiness in the farm of Riversdale on that day, than there had been for many months previously.

It seemed to Revis, as if evil destiny was really at last tired of persecuting him, and as if a period of peace and contentment was now to arise, as a good set-off against the very different state of things that had existed for so long previously.

"My Amelia," he said, "these are surely the trials—grievous while they last—through which we have to pass before we reach anything in the shape of real and perfect happiness. Something tells me that Arthur Wilton will soon return to us; and is it not a joy to you, my child, to know that he will be as welcome to me as he will be to you?"

"It is indeed a joy, father!"

"We shall be very, very happy."

In such blissful anticipations of a future that seemed to be full of sunshine, did the farmer and his daughter pass the remainder of the day; on the morning of which the most welcome letter from Arthur Wilton arrived; and as the evening advanced, Amelia found that without a pang she could visit some of those spots about the little estate which were endeared to her by many recollections of long rambles and loving discourses with Arthur.

It was just as the sun was touching the horizon, that, hastily wrapping a shawl around her to protect her from the evening air, Amelia passed through the flower garden, and entered a shady walk that led to a little wilderness that bordered the farm on the south.

All was beauty and serenity. The slant rays of the setting sun lent a beautiful glow to all objects; and the songs of the birds, as they retired to roost, had never to her seemed to be so full of melody as upon that occasion.

It was her heart that was translating everything to music.

"Ah, Arthur," she said to herself, "how true is it that we often murmur at those things which are the direct means by which our dearest happiness is to be achieved. How could my dear father, now, have ever known your real worth if circumstances had not occurred as they have? But now he indeed feels how worthy you are of being cherished in his heart of hearts; and I, too—have not I discovered that there are virtues and excellences in you, Arthur, of which I was before ignorant?"

She advanced quite into the little wood, fearlessly; for, although she had certainly not been in the habit of visiting so lonely a place by herself, yet her mind was too full of happy thoughts of him who was absent from her to harbour any ideas of danger.

But the sun was rapidly sinking, and the bright and beautiful tints that had settled upon all objects were departing, leaving but on esombre hue of gray in their place.

Amelia began now to think of returning to the farm, but still she lingered in those spots, each one of which was full of some tender recollection.

There was the old chestnut, were she and he had once taken shelter in a storm, during the continuance of which he had told her how long and how truly he had loved her; and how hopeless, at one time, to him, had appeared the task of winning one whom his partial imagination invested with so many charms.

Could it be wondered at that she should linger long in such a spot as that? The very tones of Arthur's voice seemed still to dwell upon the soft evening air, as it wantoned among her tresses.

"Love him!" she exclaimed. "Who could not love him?"

Almost before these words were well uttered, a sound as of some one making way through the thickets near to her came upon her ears, and she started for the first time in that place with a feeling of alarm.

Her heart beat violently, as she asked herself—"Who is this?"

To listen intently for some repetition of the sound, and then to laugh at her own folly for being terrified at what was, perhaps, nothing of the smallest importance, were her next acts.

"Oh," she said, "it is only, after all, some stray animal—most probably a rabbit, a hare, or perhaps a pheasant—rustling in the thickets, and I so foolish as to be alarmed at it!"

The sound came again.

Notwithstanding she had made such valorous and indifferent remarks as we have stated, she now felt the blood forsake her heart with a painful gush, and for the moment, although she certainly wished to flee, she found herself quite incapable of doing so.

A deep, sepulchral voice, said—

"Amelia Revis!"

The tone was quite unknown to her, but she held by a low branch of the chestnut tree, as, after a few moments, she recovered sufficient resolution to say—

"Who speaks?"

"Amelia Revis!" said the voice again.

"Yes," she said. "I am Amelia Revis, what would you with me? Speak—speak."

Her eyes were intently directed towards the thicket from whence the sound proceeded, and there she saw a horrid, grizzly-looking head and face, with eyes that seemed like pieces of burning coal, glaring at her from amid the foliage.

Terror took possession of her. She felt paralysed, and all she could do was to utter one loud scream, and then hold by the bough of the tree with convulsive energy.

The rustling of the branches of the thicket increased, and in another moment a man appeared before her. He was without a coat, and the rest of his attire was stained and travel-worn, being torn likewise in many places. His unshaven visage gave an appearance of much ferocity to his countenance, and enabled his eye to shine up with that preternatural lustre which had so much alarmed Amelia when first she saw his face in the thicket glaring at her.

"Amelia Revis be not alarmed," he said; "no harm is intended you. All I require is, that you should listen to me."

"Who, and what are you?"

"That I may find a time to tell you, but not now, Amelia—not now. First, you must promise that you will say nothing to any one breathing of this meeting."

"I cannot promise."

"You cannot?"

"No; wherefore should I keep secret from my father such a circumstance as this? I cannot do it."

"Without a reason, you would say. Well, I will furnish you with one. Your father has just escaped a great danger, and, for a time, he certainly holds the villain Strachan at bay."

"Ah! you know——"

"More than you know, for I know the secret reason why the bond was given to Captain Strachan by your father."

"You do?"

"I do."

"And you will tell me?"

"Why should you ask me to tell you that which your father desires should be kept from you?"

"You are right," said Amelia, "be you whom you may, and I am justly rebuked. I will not ask you again."

The stranger was silent for a few moments, and then he said—

"Amelia Revis, I am starving."

"Starving? Alas!"

"Yes. I have not looked forward for mercy, because I am a bad man—my whole career since I threw off the trammels of childhoood has been one of wickedness—there are few crimes I have not stooped to commit : and yet, I ask you to have compassion upon me."

"Heaven help you! It is not for us to judge of each other. You shall not starve, were you worse than all you have said you are."

"Indeed?"

"Yes. Come to the farm, and I am sure my father will not send you away without food."

"Your father? Oh, no—no—no!"

"You speak of my father with horror. Oh, you know him not?"

"Know him not? Alas! I know him too well. Amelia, once more I charge you to say nothing of this meeting. If you do it, may chance that all the sacrifice ur father made to the villain Strachan

may be in vain, and you may plunge him into grief."

"What fearful mystery is this?"

"It is a fearful mystery. For the present, Amelia, it must remain one. I am starving, and cannot well determine upon what course of action to pursue. Be assured, however, that it shall be one that will save Arthur Wilton from the machinations of Strachan."

"You know Arthur, too?"

"I do. I am acquainted with the circumstances in which he is placed, and it shall be my task to rescue him; but again I say to you, that if you acquaint your father with this meeting, and describe me to him, you will spoil all, and plunge him into grief."

"What can I do?"

"As I bid you."

"But—I know you not."

"Have faith in me."

"I am distracted by different emotions."

"Your decision is important to your father's happiness. Be quick."

"I—I will say nothing."

"'Tis well. And now I will hand to you one weapon, which in case of necessity you can use against Strachan"

"A weapon!"

"Yes; but not what you suppose. Take this slip of paper. If you hear from Arthur Wilton that Strachan is injuring him, write boldly to Strachan the words you see there written."

There was just a faint twilight sufficient to enable Amelia to make out the following words:

"Beware of the secret of the quarry pool!"

The words were written in print upon a soiled scrap of paper, that looked as though it had been torn from the inside of some old hat."

"You have read it?" said the man.

"I have."

"Keep it safely then."

"I am far from comprehending how such words can have any effect upon such a man as Strachan. "

"You will perceive, should you have occasion to use them, and most assuredly you will, that they will have a great effect indeed. Have faith in them, Amelia Revis."

The idea flashed now across the mind of Amelia that, after all, this might be some lunatic, and she said—

"Remain here quietly, and I will bring you some food. Remain here quietly, and do not follow me."

There was a something in Amelia's tone which probably gave the man an idea of what was passing in her mind, for he said, earnestly—

"Do not, I pray you, fall into the fatal mistake of supposing that all this is a result of insanity. Believe me, it is not so. Madmen might look as I look, but it would not give me a knowledge of your father's affairs. Remember, I know more about the bond than you do."

"Yes—yes; I do remember."

COLONEL PERCIVAL DOUBTS THE TRUSTFULNESS OF ARTHUR WILTON.

"I know why it was given—you only know that it was given, and with what difficulty it was paid and redeemed."

"Forgive me!"

"No more; and, now, in good truth, I do pray you to give me some food."

Amelia persuaded him to come with her some distance up the shady lane, and there he waited while she hurried back to the house, and hastily filling a basket with what provisions she could, without observation, lay hold of, she took it to him, and left him well provided.

"This shall not be the worst hour's

work in all your life, Amelia Rivers," he said. "You have done your father more service than you will be aware of for a long time."

CHAPTER XIV

ARTHUR WILTON WRITES AGAIN TO AME-
LIA.—THE COLONEL IS STILL DIS-
PLEASED.

It was strange, that each moment the mysterious being who was indebted to the charity of Amelia Rivers for a meal's victuals, seemed to be ever upon the point of saying something to her which should have the effect of clearing up some of the mysteries by which she was surrounded; but as often, with a shudder, he desisted, and in a low moaning voice he would say—

"No—no; I cannot!"

Amelia had lingered with him as long as she thought there was a chance of his being communicative; but finding that at length there was really no chance of getting from him the secret of who and what he was, she had left him in peace.

It was upon Amelia's return to the farm-house that she found the following letter from Arthur awaiting her:—

"Exeter.

"MY DEAR AMELIA,—It is a relief to me to write to you, although I feel that it is a selfish one, inasmuch as I am about to make you a participator in my fears and sorrows. Notwithstanding the kind protection of Colonel Percival, I fear that Strachan is at his devilish work, and that it will not be long ere he shows me that he is far from not venomous still. Oh, Amelia, I have but one hope, and that is, that, through good report and evil report, you will still love me; and ever believe that I am now, and shall be to the end of time, your own   "ARTHUR WILTON."

It is quite clear that the letter must have been written while poor Arthur was in the greatest distress and perplexity on account of the doubts Colonel Percival had of his truth. If Arthur's mind had not been deeply affected, he could not have penned a letter which could have no other effect than that of reaching the heart of Amelia, and making her full of unknown fears.

With the letter in her hand, she hurried to her father, and while the tears coursed each other down her cheeks, she held it out to him in silence.

James Rivers could see, by the expression of Amelia's countenance, that the letter was not a consolatory one, and he took it with trembling fingers and read it in silence. He then looked in the tearful face of Amelia, but still he said nothing. He felt what a fearful price, in the sacrifice of the happiness of his child, had been paid for the continued possession of his ancient home; and what could he say in the way of consolation to her who had been the sufferer?

"Father, you have read the letter," said Amelia; "what am I to think? From your extended experience, I ask what interpretation I am to place upon the letter?"

"My child, it has been written in a mind of depression. The next letter that you receive, will, in all likelihood, breathe a more hopeful spirit."

"Alas! alas! Arthur is not one to despair without cause, father."

"You must remember, my Amelia, that Arthur is placed in, to him, novel circumstances, and that many incidents, that in a little time will appear as commonplace, now deeply affect him."

"Yes, but—but he suffers!"

Mr. Revis rose; and pacing the room in silence for a few minutes, in evident agitation, he suddenly turned upon Amelia, and in such a voice as he had never yet addressed her in, he said,—

"Girl—girl! do you wish to drive me mad?—Do you think that I have not felt—ay, and felt most keenly, too—the frightful sacrifice that that young man has made for me and mine?—Do you imagine that it does not haunt me, night and day, that I am the roof that is above me, to what may be called the destruction of Arthur Wilton? I do not weep.—I do not show, by my manner, that I nurse to my heart the great affliction; but still it is there."

"Father! Father!"

"Amelia, you do not know what I suffer. You only look into your own heart, and there seeing cause for sorrow, you are content."

Amelia burst into tears. Those tears were more than the father could bear, and approaching her, he flung his arms around her, saying—

"My child, my own Amelia! forgive this little burst of impatience ; but, oh ! you do not know, you cannot guess, and Heaven forbid that you should, what I suffer."

"Father! I feel how much I have been to blame. Indeed, I do feel now that I have been very selfish."

"Selfish? Oh, no."

"Yes, father ; quiet grief was so new a thing to me, that it has made me selfish."

"Dear Amelia, say no more. Only when you brought me that letter, and in silence placed it in my hands, and when I saw your beautiful face, it seemed like a cruel rebuke to me for what is entirely out of my power to aid or alter, and the thought at the moment half maddened me."

"Say no more, father. It is I who was to blame."

"No, Amelia, there is no blame—none whatever. But now listen to me, my child, and from this time we shall understand each other better. When Arthur Wilton brought at the last moment the money that disappointed that fiend, Strachan, of his frightful purpose, I felt a degree of joy and exultation that banished all other thoughts; but that feeling soon subsided."

"Yes, father?"

"And then came the abiding one, which told me at what a sacrifice to poor Arthur all this had been accomplished, and from that time I have taken no joy in the old house, nor in the garden that I beloved so well, nor in the songs of the birds, nor in the sighing of the soft summer winds amid the ancient trees of this little domain. All has been a blank to me, and I am wretched. Well I know that it is for the true love he bore to you that Arthur did what he did; and that act is sufficient only the more to let me see what a dear companion you have lost, and what a friend in my advancing age he might have been to me."

Amelia wept bitterly.

"Father," she said, when she could command her voice sufficiently to speak, "we will say no more upon this subject."

"Be it so, my child. It is a theme that only distresses us deeply, and leads to no practical result. You may rest assured that the matter is never absent from my mind, and that I am ever thinking of some mode of relieving Arthur from the situation he is in. Should any practical plan occur to me, then, Amelia, I will at once take you into consultation regarding it."

"Yes, father."

How she longed at that moment to say to him—"But why did you give a bond to Captain Strachan for two thousand pounds?" The words were almost upon her lips, but she dreaded to pronounce them, and she did not utter them.

"Now, my dear Amelia," added Revis, "this painful conversation is over."

He kissed her tenderly, and she left the room. Amelia dried her tears as best she could, and murmured to herself—

"I must keep Arthur's letters now to myself, and show them no more to my father."

But for the little ebullition of painful feeling upon the part of her father, no doubt, Amelia would freely enough have told him what had passed between her and the mysterious man in the garden; but she dreaded now to increase the eccentricity of a temper that seemed to be already taxed almost beyond its powers.

If Amelia had told Revis of the circumstance of her meeting such a man in the neighbourhood, it might have had the effect of very materially modifying the circumstances that shortly took place; but it was not to be. The affair was kept a secret by Amelia, and she little suspected that by so doing she was effectually screening the crimes of her enemies, and of the enemies of her father and Arthur Wilton.

The principal pleasure that Amelia now had was, accompanied by Prince, the dog, who was an able defender, and all but a companion to her, to wander about the spots in which she had been in the habit of meeting with Arthur Wilton, and in recalling every word and look of his that at the time had not seemed so precious to her as they did now that he was away from her, and that the period of his return appeared to be dim and dubious, indeed.

More than once in the course of a few days Amelia had met Mr. Hunks, the attorney, hovering about the old homestead, with a greedy kind of look, as though he longed to call it his, and had got an idea that, in the course of time, he might cross the threshold as a master. The looks of that man caused Amelia to shudder when she encountered them, and yet she knew not how it could be that Hunks could be at all dangerous, now that the bond upon which he and Captain Strachan had based all their guilty thoughts of possessing Riversdale was duly paid.

Amelia little knew that with such men the wish to do mischief generally brings with it the power; and, indeed, what may not any one do against the peace of another if he be unscrupulous enough to adopt any course that will complete his object, without reference to right or justice?

We must now, however, leave Riversdale for a space while we return to the regiment in which Arthur Wilton was a soldier.

It will be remembered that the colonel, while he was too just a man wholly to disbelieve the strange statement of Arthur respecting what Captain Strachan had said to him, yet could not help having his doubts upon the subject; and he was that open, frank-hearted man, that, for good or for evil, what he thought generally quickly enough made itself apparent, and to Arthur's perception there was now a coolness in the colonel's behaviour to him that was inexpressibly afflicting.

On the day following that upon which the ill-omened dialogue had taken place, Captain Strachan passed Arthur and eyed him with such a look of triumph that it was with the utmost difficulty that Arthur could keep his hands off him; and as it was, it is highly probable that he would have committed the indiscretion of assaulting him but for Corporal Steady, who very opportunely appeared at the moment.

The honest corporal saw the looks upon both sides, and drawing himself up as stiff as a ramrod, he saluted Strachan with punctilious ceremony, and then, when he had got out of sight, the corporal marched up to Arthur.

"Mr. Wilton," he said, "for God's sake be careful."

"Careful of what, corporal?"

"Of yourself, sir. I saw you look at Strachan, and I saw Strachan look at you. Now, Wilton, do recollect that you are a soldier, and if you so much as wag your finger at Strachan, it is a crime of no small degree of magnitude in the service. It won't do, Mr. Wilton."

"He is a villain!"

"Hem! that word is as round and strong as a bullet; but he is your officer, I tell you, and it's a foolish thing to run your head against a brick-wall. You know his power, and you know that you can keep out of it if you like; but if you will bring ruin upon yourself, I can't help it."

"Steady," said Arthur, as he held out his hand to him, "I am much beholden to you. I know that the caution you give me is dictated by the kindest of motives, and I feel all its force."

"That'll do—March!"

"But, Steady — listen to me a moment."

"Eyes right! I listen."

"I feel that I ought to make some kind friend acquainted with what is taking place around me. Will you accept the office of confidant and adviser?"

"Humph! I ain't much good at advising about anything that don't belong to regimental duties; but if you think you would like to tell me anything, Mr. Wilton, I will hear it, and keep it as secret as a surprise party going to take a battery."

"I will tell you all, corporal, for I do not know how soon the time may come when I may be glad of some honest heart to come forward and say that I made such a statement."

"Halt! I begin to understand now."

"How do you mean?"

"I mean, Mr. Wilton, that something is going on that you think you ought to tell some one about, in case somebody should say to you, why didn't you tell somebody?"

"That is about the truth, my good friend."

"Very good. Then I tell you what I'll do, I'll speak to Cockles."

"To Cockles?"

"Yes; you know young Cockles? There isn't a better hearted fellow in the regiment than Cockles, though he does get through the world by banging on sheep-skin. To be sure, Cockles is only a drummer, but I know him, and he has the heart of a general."

Arthur considered for a few moments, and then he said with alacrity—

"Be it so, Steady. I shall be glad to take both you and Cockles into my confidence, my friend, and I make no doubt but that I shall feel easier in my mind after saying to you both what I wish; and if anything should come of the affair, concerning which I am very anxious, it will be in my favour to have spoken to you."

"Very good. Where shall we meet? If I might advise, you would come at about six o'clock to a little garden that is just outside the town, called "The Flora," where Cockles and I go and have a glass of small ale, and some fruit. There you will find us both, for we shall be off duty from six to nine, you know, and it ain't at all likely any one will interrupt us."

"I shall be punctual," said Walter, "always provided the colonel does not require my services. If I do not come to you, you will be so good as to put that construction upon my absence."

"All's right. March."

Steady walked off, for he felt how awkward it would be if Captain Strachan should happen to discover him in close conference with Wilton, as it was no doubt concerning the captain that he, Walter, had to speak to him.

"Yes," thought Arthur. "In these two honest fellows, Steady and Cockles, I shall find willing witnesses that I told them all; and thus, come what may, it will be seen that I did not keep secret the villanies of Strachan."

Even as he spoke, for he uttered these words to himself in a low tone, he saw Captain Strachan returning. To get out of his way was impossible, and Arthur had no resource but to salute him, as he came by. This was certainly a sore strait to Arthur to salute, with even the show of respect, such a man, and it required all his philosophy to convince himself that it was the officer, and not the man whom he so saluted. In fact, Arthur, in touching his cap to Captain Strachan, went upon the same principle that people uncover to the queen in public. It is the queenly office, and not the individual who by the accident of birth fills it, that they respect, although there is always an attempt in this country to confound the two, and to try to insinuate that it is the queen or the king for the time being, and not the office, that is of importance.

With this feeling, then, was it that Arthur Wilton saluted a captain in the army, and did not salute Strachan as an individual.

Captain Strachan smiled as he came up to Wilton, and said—

"Well, have you considered about cutting the colonel's throat? I think that it might easily be done some night."

The flush of indignation came to the cheeks of Arthur, and he said—

"I have communicated to the colonel your words upon that subject before. You are a villain!"

"Ha! That is very good. But the colonel won't believe you. Tell him that you called me a villain, and hear what he will say. Ha! ha! Now, I tell you what it is, Arthur Wilton: I will cut the colonel's throat, and rob him, if you do not. Only I intend to leave you to take the consequences of the crime. I'm tired of a military life, you see!"

"Wretch, why do I not strike you to the earth?"

"Because I am your captain, and you would then be shot, which would gratify me very much indeed. But as regards the robbery, and the murder of the colonel, you hear, Wilton, that can easily be done, as he is not a suspicious man. A pistol fired into the lock of the box, I mentioned to you, would break it open easily. Good day. Think on it, my dear fellow."

The captain walked off with the greatest nonchalance in the world, leaving poor Arthur groaning with indignation at his villany, and yet so interested that it was quite out of his power to resist it.

"Oh, Heaven," he said, "what shall I do? What can I do in this dreadful dilemma? Is this fiend to destroy me with my eyes open to all his villany?"

CHAPTER XV.

AN UNEXPECTED CHANGE TAKES PLACE IN THE DESTINY OF THE REGIMENT.

THE reader will not fail to perceive, that whether or not Captain Strachan really meditated the dreadful crime that he mentioned with such cool effrontery, he was taking the most effectual mode of destroying the confidence that had subsisted between Arthur Wilton and the colonel.

Had Arthur, in the first instance, said nothing to Colonel Percival about the most extraordinary words of Strachan, his situation would have been better; but, then, nothing was more impossible than that he should keep secret such a communication, and then, if he had done so, and any such crime had been committed, or attempted to be committed, how would he have looked to have had subsequently to state that he had heard of it, and said nothing?

No, Arthur was fairly in the toils, and he could not avoid being placed in the difficulty that surrounded him. With regard to this second communication of Captain Strachan's, Arthur trembled, and finally he made up his mind that he would not volunteer the intelligence to the colonel, but that, if he should ask for it, he should have it, let the consequences be what they might.

This was but a gloomy state of things, and in the midst of it, just after the colonel had dined, he sent for Arthur Wilton.

Colonel Percival was pacing his room when Arthur entered, and turning abruptly to him, he said—

"You will write from my dictation."

"Yes, sir."

Arthur was ready in a few moments, and the colonel dictated a letter to a friend of his, named General Brotherton. The letter contained various matters, some of rather a puerile character, but none that required great secrecy. When it was concluded, Arthur rose, and saluting the colonel, was upon the point of retiring, when the latter called to him.

"Wilton?"

"Yes, colonel."

"I have been thinking over the singular conversation you say you had with Captain Strachan. Do you still adhere to that statement?"

"Adhere, sir?"

"Yes; do you still assert it to be true?"

Arthur felt at that moment as if his heart would burst; but, by a great effort, he controlled his feelings, although he became as pale as marble, and said—

"Yes, colonel, I cannot tamper with the truth, while my name remains to me."

The colonel paced the room to and fro in silence for some moments; and then he suddenly pointed to the small box that Strachan had mentioned, and said—

"In that box is a rich treasure for any one to possess. It is strange that any person but myself should be aware of the fact, but it is true, that there are jewels and valuables amounting to a very large sum indeed."

"Sir," said Arthur, clasping his hands as a sudden idea struck him, "let me implore you to remove that temptation. Take it from here, sir—send it to your bankers—to your lady—anywhere but here !"

"Temptation !" said the colonel.

"Not to me," added Arthur, as his eyes flashed with the conscious pride of rectitude. "It is no temptation to me, but it may be to others. Oh, sir, let it go, and then the villain Strachan cannot even threaten your destruction. You do not know him, sir—indeed you do not. He has spoken to me again, and says, that a pistol shot would at once break the lock, and that he is tired of the army, and is quite resolved to rob and murder you, and then quit it, but that he will lay the imputation of the transaction upon me."

"What! again?"

"But an hour since, sir."

"Oh, impossible — impossible. I tell you, Arthur Wilton, that it was only this morning Strachan said to me, that he feared the only way in which he could prove to you that he harboured no malice against you, was to interest himself on the very first opportunity to get your discharge; and he asked me if I likewise would use my good offices for such an object. He said he loved the young lady to whom you likewise are attached, and that jealousy for a short time blinded him ; but that feeling she loves you, and not him, he is ashamed of his passion, and only anxious to see you both happy."

"Oh, God !"

"Why, what is the matter with you?"

"Sir, I declare with indignation, that that man is a fiend, and is playing with you and with me."

"I beg your pardon there, Wilton. He would find it rather dangerous work to play with me, I can tell you. In a word, Wilton, I cannot believe your assertions regarding what he says to you. They are too monstrous."

"They are, indeed."

"Why, do you admit that they are untrue?"

"Oh, no, sir. I only say that they are too monstrous. I do not expect you now to believe me, nor does Captain Strachan. I have but one duty, and that is to tell the truth. I tell it, and then I have but to suffer. It was never intended, Colonel Percival, that you should believe what I tell you."

"Wilton, there again you stagger me. You have one argument that I cannot but admit the full weight of, and yet my judgment goes against your story. Leave me, now. I will consider further of the affair."

With a heavy heart, Arthur left the apartment, and then it was that he wrote the despairing note to Amelia that we have seen she received. A wild idea that the best thing he could possibly do, would be to desert, and so, by committing that venial offence, put an end to the possibility of his being suspected of a greater crime; or if Strachan contrived aught against the life of the colonel, the absence of Wilton would at once exonerate him even from suspicion, came across his mind ; but he resolved to meet Cockles and the coporal first, and to make them thoroughly acquainted with the whole of the circumstances of the case ; so that, even if their advise and judgments should fail him in any useful suggestion, they would both be witnesses that he had told them all, and that he was in a state of mental tribulation regarding the words of Captain Strachan.

The garden which Corporal Steady had mentioned as the place to which he would bring their mutual friend, Cockles, and where they might uninterruptedly enjoy a little private conversation, was about half a mile from the outskirts of the city, and, accordingly, as it would take him some time to get there, Arthur set off rather earlier than the appointed time. He rather assumed than knew that the colonel would not require his services again that evening, for he was painfully anxious to make his purposed confidence with Steady and the drummer.

A very little inquiry enabled Wilton to find the place, and he had the satisfaction to see, seated in a little summer-house or rustic arbour, the corporal and drummer, enjoying the delights of a pipe each and a pot of small ale.

"All's right," said the corporal; "there he is."

"Steady," said the drummer, "I see him."

"Ah! my good friends," said Arthur. "you are beforehand, I see, with me. I hope that I am something near my time?"

"All's right," replied the corporal; "military time it is. That's how we beat the French. We were always a quarter of an hour too soon for them, you see, Mr. Arthur Wilton, and that bothered them a little."

"I should think so," said Cockles. "Take a drop of this, Mr. Wilton. I think I can promise you that it won't get into your head."

"Thank you," replied Arthur. "And now, my good friends—for I may, in truth, call you such since I have had kind offices from both of you—I am going to tell you something that will astonish you. I do not expect for one moment that you will either of you be able to advise me anything that can get me out of the fearful circumstances in which I am placed, but the time may come when I may have to call upon you both for your testimony, simply to the effect, that I told you the story that I am now about to relate."

"March on," said Steady. "We are all attention, Mr Wilton."

Cockles opened his eyes very wide, and Corporal Steady placed his hand over the ale jug to prevent the flies from getting into it, while Arthur Wilton related the extraordinary words that Captain Strachan used towards him upon the two occasions that he had spoken to him. When he had concluded, he paused with some degree of anxiety for their reply. The main part of that anxiety was to devise if they, like the colonel, should think the story too monstrous for belief. It was an immense relief to him when Cockles dealt the table a thump, and said—

"It's as clear as a drum-stick that that Strachan means mischief."

"He does," said Steady, "he does. It's a mine, and a regular mine, that it is, and the blow-up is a-coming."

"Tell the colonel," said Cockles. "Drum it into his ear. and blow the captain afore he can blow his mine."

"Why, yes," added Steady, "that will be about the way to do it. Countermine the fellow, and send him star-gazing. Confound it, what a fool he must be, too."

"No, my friends," said Arthur, "he is no fool, He meant me to tell the colonel, and I have told him; and he meant the colonel not to believe, and he does not believe me. That was Captain Strachan's calculation from the first, and so far he has succeeded, that the colonel now looks upon me as one who, for his own private purposes and vagaries, will invent the most outrageous stories."

Corporal Steady blew a long whistle, and Cockles, with his knuckles, beat a march upon the little table, that made the ale jug move gradually along in little starts, till it fell into the corporal's lap, and deluged him with the remains of the small ale.

"The devil!" said the corporal.

"No, it's the ale," said Cockles. "Steady, never mind, old friend. What's ale and a brown jug, to be compared to this fix of Mr. Wilton's?"

"Why, nothing at all ; only my trousers are not quite so comfortable as they were before, that's all. But never mind that. Mr. Wilton, you were right when you said that we were not likely to advise you any good in this affair; I confess it gets the better of me altogether. We can only do one thing, and that is, to keep such an eye on the captain, that he shan't move hand or foot without our knowing it. Cockles is the fellow to watch him. The captain will be clever if he keeps much out of his way."

"Rather," said Cockles. "I'll be down upon him like a bat-wing morn and night. He don't like me, I know; but as long as I do my duty, I don't care for him. The colonel will protect a man who beats his drum as he ought to do."

"Now, there is one thing," added Wilton, "that I had a thought of, and that was desertion."

"Eyes right!" said the corporal.

Cockles beat a fierce march on the table, now, with his double fists, and the corporal had to shake him well to stop him, for while that noise was going on he could not say a word to Wilton. Having, however, at length obtained silence, he spoke with more feeling and real dignity than any one would have thought him capable of saying.

"Mr. Wilton, you are a gentleman, though circumstances have made you a soldier and our comrade; but still I say you are a gentleman now you have enlisted, and done a brave thing by enlisting, because you got the twenty pounds' bounty, and put it to such a use, that as sure as there is a heaven above us, that deed will yet be rewarded. I say it was a brave thing, Mr. Wilton; but it would not look like a brave thing to desert for fear of Captain Strachan. No, no, Mr. Wilton, you mustn't do it."

"I should not," said Cockles. "Don't you go for to fancy that's the sort of work to do you any good, Mr. Wilton. You trust to our watching the captain, and who knows but we may find out something that will rid you and the regiment of him at once. But the man who deserts is—is—What is the man who deserts, corporal?"

"A deserter, Cockles."

"No; but I mean he is—a kind of— I'm sure I have heard some fine things said about the man who desert his colours, but I can't recollect them."

"You have convinced me, both of

you," said Arthur. "I promise you, on my honour, I will not desert."

CHAPTER XVI.

THE COLONEL TRIES A LITTLE EXPERIMENT UPON CAPTAIN STRACHAN.

MAJOR CUTHBERT and Captain Grant, two officers in the regiment, took coffee with the colonel, while Arthur Wilton was with Cockles and Corporal Steady at the Flora Gardens.

The colonel had told them the whole of the rather mysterious affair between Captaid Strachan and Arthur Wilton, and he added—

"Now, Cuthbert, and you, Grant, likewise, I confess to you that this matter puzzles me. I like the young fellow, and there is about him such an air of gentlemanly sincerity, and so much natural candour, that I dread to be convinced he is a heartless hypocrite."

"You dread it, colonel!" said the major. "Why do you dread it?"

"Just because it will shake my confidence in human nature for ever."

"Well, that is rather an uncomfortable state of things."

"Very," said the captain; "but—but——"

"Go on, Grant,"

The captain reddened a little, as he added :—

"I am going to say something, colonel, that I feel I ought not to say, and, therefore, you will oblige me by not asking me."

"Grant, answer me one question. Don't you feel that you ought not to say it, on account of your military position in this regiment?"

"Exactly so, and on account of yours, likewise."

"Then let me tell you, that I hope and consider, when I am at my own table with you or Cuthbert, that I forget, and wish you to forget that we are anything but private gentlemen, and old acquaintances; and, therefore, I beg you will say just what you like, and let our public positions or offices have nothing in the world to do with our private intercourse."

"Then," said Grant, "I was going to say, that I had an opinion, founded on facts, as the novelists say, that Strachan is rascal enough for anything."

The major smiled, as he said—

"Come, there is no mincing the matter, then, at all events; and just in a mild way, as we are quite alone, I may add my opinion, that he is a disgrace to the regiment."

"Go on, gentlemen," said the colonel. "Go on."

"Is not that enough, my dear sir?"

"Well, indeed, and in truth, it ought to be. But come now, be fair, and give even the devil his due. Upon what do you specifically found this opinion?"

"I am bound," said Captain Grant, "after saying what I have, to be prepared with my reasons, and I should hardly have consented to make so strong a speech, if I had not the means quite ready at hand. Captain Strachan, then, wherever the regiment is quartered, brings disgrace and discredit upon it by his low intrigues. Then, again, he always makes low acquaintances in every town he comes to. He lends money, too, at usurious rates of interest, and he is a liar."

"Humph!" said the colonel.

"Now," added Grant, with animation, "having said all this, I am quite prepared to give evidence of any of these charges."

"And then," said the major, "there was that affair of Clinton's."

The colonel shook his head.

"Heaven send the fellow would leave the regiment; but of that there seems to be no hope."

"Except by the means he proposes," said Captain Grant, "and that is, as you have heard, by cutting your throat, eloping with your strong box, and throwing the guilt of the transaction upon the shoulders of Arthur Wilton."

"Tell me, Grant, in all seriousness. Do you believe that Arthur Wilton has reported to me the truth?"

"Yes, colonel."

"There, now, I am lost again in a complete maze of conjecture. By Heaven, I would give five hundred pounds cheerfully to be assured of the truth, one way or the other, as regards this affair. But that is impossible."

"I don't know that," said Major Cuthbert. "If you do not shrink from the means of coming at the truth, there is a means."

"What are they? Speak at once, Cuthbert."

"To arrange so that this young man, Wilton, and Strachan shall meet, thinking that they are alone, while, in reality, every word they say is overheard by yourself, colonel."

The colonel was thoughtful for a minute, and then he said—

"I do not see why I ought to shrink from any mode of discovering the truth.

It is the object with which such a thing is done, that sanctifies or damns it, and Heaven knows my object is a good one. I will do it, Cuthbert—I will do it."

"Allow me to say," cried Captain Grant, "that while I highly approve of your determination, I should not think that experiment decisive."

"Indeed, Grant?"

"No, for it is just possible either that Strachan might suspect something of the sort, or he might upon that occasion alter

THE SORROW OF THE FATHER AND DAUGHTER ON READING WILTON'S LETTER.

his tactics, and so involve poor Wilton in ruin."

"You are rather an advocate for this Wilton."

"I hope not, colonel, if by an advocate you mean one who upholds a cause or an individual right or wrong; but I do own that, from what I have seen of the young fellow, I have a high opinion of him."

"Hang it, so have I; and that girl that came to me to beg him off, and so obligingly helped me to pack a box, by standing on the lid, gave me a still higher opinion of him; for, mind, it is not the crafty rascal who wins the heart of a high-spirited and elegant young girl."

"Bravo, colonel! It was rather a cool thing of you, don't you think, to make the girl stand on your box?"

"He wanted to look at her ankles," said the major.

"No—no, gentlemen," said the colonel, "you know me better than that. But we will drop that portion of the subject, if you please, and I will arrange so as to bring Captain Strachan and Wilton together in my room. It will be quite easy for me to do such a thing, as I can set Wilton down to writing something and then send for Strachan, and then have him shown into the same room with a message that I will be with him in about five minutes. I hope that you will both aid me by lending me your ears upon the occasion."

"We will."

"Very good, gentlemen. The door of the adjoining room can easily be left open to such an extent that you can listen through it without the possibility of being observed, I think."

"Night will be the best time," said Captain Grant, "as then the inner room can be in positive darkness, which will prevent the possibility of a discovery of the ambuscade, which would be an uncomfortable circumstance for all of us."

"To-night, then, it shall be."

Having made this arrangement, the gentlemen began to talk about other matters, although it was quite evident the colonel's mind was very full of what might possibly be the result of the trial he was about to make of the honesty of Wilton. The remark of Captain Grant that, after all, the trial could not be possibly satisfactory, did not escape him; but yet it might be so, for if Strachan committed himself in any way during the interview between him and Wilton, it would be sufficient to establish the innocence of the latter, while a different line of conduct upon the part of Strachan could not establish his guilt.

Arthur Wilton had been home, if we may call the barracks by such a name, as far as he is concerned, some half hour from the Flora Gardens, when a message came to him that the colonel wanted him.

Hastily leaving Steady, with whom he had been conversing, he went to the colonel's quarters, and was shown into a room with one light burning upon a table. The colonel was there, and Arthur thought that his manner was rather strange and wayward.

"Where have you been, Wilton?" he said.

"To a garden, sir, called the Flora, with Corporal Steady and a drummer named Cockles."

The truth came so naturally from the lips of Arthur Wilton, that he would have told it upon the impulse of the moment, let the consequences to himself be what they might.

"Do you not find the company of a corporal and a drummer rather irksome to you?"

"No, sir. The fact is, that I have received kindnesses from both of them, and that has endeared them to me. I believe they are both kind and good-hearted, and high-principled persons; and for those qualities, how easy it is to overlook any little defects in education."

"Yes, yes, it is. Well, Wilton, you will write a fair copy of this despatch, you understand; it will take you about half-an-hour, and so I will come to you in that time, as I have some business that requires my attention now."

"Yes, sir."

The colonel left the room, and for a few minutes after he had gone, Arthur Wilton rested his head upon his hands, and said to himself—

"Is this returning confidence, or what is it? There was a kindness in his tone, and yet I tremble, I know not why. How weak and nervous I have been of late, to be sure, and yet I am not conscious of any bodily ailment. Well, well, I can but do my duty, and trust in that heaven which surely, unless providence be a fable, will not desert me."

Arthur then set about diligently copying the despatch, while Colonel Percival sent an orderly to say that he wanted to see Captain Strachan, and when he come, the orderly had directions to show him into the room where Arthur Wilton was writing, and to say that he, the colonel, would be with him in five minutes' time.

After all this was settled, Colonel Percival, by another door that opened from the staircase, went into the room adjoining that where Wilton was writing. In that room to which the colonel repaired, there were already the major and the captain, his two friends, and in a very low whisper the colonel said—

"Has he made any remarks?"

"Only one," said the major.

"What was it?"

"Something about providence being a fable, I think; but as we did not hear the context, it would be unfair to draw any inference from it."

"Oh, yes, yes. But it is a strange saying, for all that."

There hung a military clock just inside the door of the inner-room, so that, partially shaded by that, those who were intent upon listening to what might pass between Wilton and Captain Strachan, could get very close to the narrow opening of the door. About ten minutes elapsed before they heard a footstep upon the stairs, and then another following it, and then they heard the orderly say—

"The colonel will be with you in five minutes, sir, if you will walk into the room and take a seat."

"Very well," said Captain Strachan. "You had better let him know that I am here, in obedience to his summons, orderly."

"I will, sir."

The orderly sergeant flung open the door of the room in which Wilton was sitting, and Captain Strachan entered it, little suspecting who was there. The door was closed behind him, and even then, by the dim light that was in the apartment, he could not for a few moments tell who it was that sat at a table writing. Wilton, however, looked up, and then their eyes met, and each became aware of the presence of each other.

Strachan staggered back for a moment, and then a glance of suspicion shot from his eye, and contracting his brows, he glanced around him, tremulously. Arthur Wilton was asking himself the question— "Ought I, in the course of my duty, now to rise and salute this man?" and then he decided that as he was upon other duty for the colonel, there was no occasion. Arthur was wrong, though, for Captain Strachan was his officer, and was entitled to the salute ; but what was Arthur Wilton's surprise, when Strachan stepped up to the table, and in a clear voice, said—

"Wilton, I am glad of the opportunity of seeing you alone, to tell you that I sincerely pity the sacrifice that a young man of education must feel that he is evidently making, by being in such a situation; and I assure you that I will do all in my power to procure your discharge."

"Sir?" said Wilton.

"It will be a difficult thing to do, I fear," added Strachan, "at this time, when the whole of Europe is so convulsed with war, and rumours of war; but I will try it, as well for your own sake, as to rid you of the foolish idea that I harbour towards you any ill-feeling."

"You monstrous villain!" said Arthur, rising from his seat.

"Sir?"

"I say, you monstrous villain! What new device is this? What other crafty idea, full of devilish ingenuity, has now found a place in your heart?"

"Alas!" said Captain Strachan, "you surely at each interview that we have together are more and more intemperate ; you are either a little deranged, or your passions are so fearful that they for the time being overcome your reason entirely. I will not remain in the room, but will leave you to yourself; and all I can say is, that I shall be glad when the day comes that you quit the regiment."

Captain Strachan walked quite to the door of the room, and then he looked with a fiendish grin at Arthur Wilton, who was too much confounded now to make a ready reply to him. In another moment the crafty villain was gone, and he had done all the mischief possible to Arthur, who sank back in the chair again with a deep groan.

The orderly sergeant was below, and while Strachan was speaking to him, the colonel descended, and said,—

"Oh, Strachan, by the by, I sent for you concerning some despatches to me, you see;" and then he engaged him for about ten minutes in a conversation about some military routine matter, which sufficiently excused and accounted for the sending for him, and then he dismissed him.

"Ha! ha! I am not quite sure," muttered Captain Strachan, as he went towards his own quarters— "I am not quite sure, but I suspect there is something more in this affair than meets the eye. If so, I have met it well; and if not, why, it does not matter a jot. If this is a trick of yours, Master Wilton, you'll see that it has failed most signally. You may strive how you please, but you are my victim, I tell you, and you will be my victim to the last."

CHAPTER XVII.

CORPORAL STEADY TELLS THE STORY OF CLINTON.

It was with the utmost difficulty that Arthur Wilton could sufficiently command his nerves to enable him to copy the document that the colonel had set before him; but he felt the importance of carrying out the task, and he did contrive somehow to do it. Oh, how little did he suspect that the colonel and the two officers, of all others, in the regiment had been listening to the scene that had just taken place!

To be sure, there was something that was rather inexplicable to them all three in the affair, for it seemed so odd that Arthur Wilton should so plainly call Captain

Strachan a monstrous villain, and that the captain should not appear to lose his temper as his officer under such opprobrious terms. But yet there was the fact, that instead of saying anything about murdering and robbing the colonel, Captain Strachan had only promised to try to get Wilton's discharge, and the reply he got was one that showed much passion and ill-will on the part of Arthur.

The three officers left the room by the door opening upon the staircase, and went to another apartment on the ground floor of the house, where the colonel, with great anxiety, asked his two friends to give him their candid opinion about what had just taken place between Strachan and Arthur Wilton. The major spoke first.

"Colonel, I don't know what to think. There is much to be said upon both sides; but as far as positive evidence goes, the bad feeling was all upon the side of Arthur Wilton."

"And yet, if we suppose for a moment," said Captain Grant, "that Strachan had a suspicion that he was overheard, the case assumes quite a different complexion, and is altogether in favour of Wilton."

"All of which means," added the colonel, with a look of perplexity, "that we are as much in the dark about the affair as ever, does it not?"

"That is about it," they both said.

"Then I will give myself till to-morrow morning to think of it. I am much vexed and distracted by the matter, because I dread to do an injustice; but I will make up my mind by to-morrow."

It was quite clear that neither the colonel, the major, nor Captain Grant, could find evidence sufficient to come to any decided opinion one way or the other; and the only thing the colonel could make up his mind to, would be some course of action which would just as likely be right as wrong.

Poor Arthur little suspected that his fate hung in such a balance, and that it was so likely to preponderate against him.

Being dismissed from further attendance upon the colonel, he sought out Corporal Steady, to tell him what had transpired in addition to what he had already told him. The corporal was cleaning his musket, and in a little room in the barracks by himself, so that he closed the door and asked Arthur Wilton to be seated, and heard him with attention.

"Ah!" he said, when Arthur had finished, "that Strachan is a regular fox. You may depend that nowhere, except in the open air where he is quite sure, by

eyes right and eyes left, that no one can steal a march upon him, will he say to you anything ugly."

"It seems so, corporal."

"Lor bless you, yes. The fellow found himself between walls, and, therefore, you see, he wouldn't say a word that wasn't all soft and nice, that all the world might hear, and do him no harm."

"The crafty villain!"

"Hush! Don't say anything, Mr. Wilton, but stick to the colonel. As long as you have his good-will, you know, after all, you needn't be much afraid of Captain Strachan."

"But have I that good-will?"

"Why, yes. He wouldn't send for you to write a dispatch, if you hadn't. He isn't that sort of man, Mr. Wilton. The colonel may be a little posed by what has taken place, but that is all, you may depend."

"Well, you give me some comfort, Steady. But now that we are alone, I wish to ask you some questions, as it is as well that I should know all I can about my enemy."

"Ask away; I can go on polishing the stock of my musket and answer you at the same time, you know."

"Are you sure that there is no one within hearing, as I am well aware that it might get you into trouble, if it were known that you spoke freely of your officers."

"Oh, it's all right, Mr. Wilton. There's no one overhead, and if any of the men heard a word or two about Strachan, they would add a curse or two, and never say a word to him about it, you may depend."

"Then, corporal, how long has Strachan been in the regiment?"

"About five years, or so."

"What sort of character does he bear? Has he ever done anything that has brought him particularly under notice?"

"Did you never hear about the court-martial business?"

"Court-martial! No."

"Well, then, he has been once tried by a court-martial; but we don't like to speak of these things in a regiment, if we can help it; but as it may be as well for you to know, I will tell you how it all happened."

"Do so, Steady. I shall be much beholden to you."

"Well, you must know that about three years ago there was a young fellow in the regiment of the name of Clinton. He was a wild, harum-scarum sort of a fellow, and we thought that carelessness was his worst fault, but it turned out that it wasn't, as you will hear. We were all of us quartered at Winchester, and Captain Strachan, whose servant this Clinton was, occupied a very old house near the great cathedral; for, although the officers might have apartments in the barracks, they, somehow, for the sake of the change of society, always took lodgings in the city. When I say he occupied the house, of course, he only had a few rooms. I was only once in them, and they were the oddest, gloomiest-looking rooms ever you saw in all your life. They had been built at the same time as the cathedral, and were for some great Catholic priest to live in. They looked like a part of the cathedral themselves, with their great carved chimney-pieces, and their heavy doors, all covered with carvings of little fat angels and clouds."

Rub-a-dub-dub—rub-a-dub-dub! came upon the door of Corporal Steady's room at this moment, with the fists of some one.

"Ah!" said Steady, "that is Cockles."

"I guessed as much," said Wilton.

"He generally comes and sits with me for a little in the evenings, and we then talk over old times together, for we have both been a goodish while, you see, in the regiment. Shall I tell him to march off, Mr. Wilton?"

"By no means. Call him in."

The drummer had just begun a fresh hammering upon the door in his odd way, when Corporal Steady cried out,—

"Forward! March!"

The drummer opened the door and marched in.

"Hilloa! Mr. Wilton, I didn't know you were with Steady, or I shouldn't have interrupted you; but all you have got to do, is to say, right about face—march, and I am off."

"By no means, Cockles," said Wilton. "I am always glad to see you."

"Then sit down," said Steady; "but shut the door first, Cockles. I am just going to tell Mr. Wilton about that odd affair of Clinton's."

"Hem!" said Cockles, placing his fingers by the side of his nose. "It has come over me, do you know, that now's the time that it would be just as well to tell him that; so, I am glad to hear you are going to do so. It was an odd affair."

"Very; so you be quiet, Cockles, while I go on."

Cockles sat upon a little stool that had only two legs to it, so that it required some dexterity to keep it up at all, while Steady went on with what he was saying.

"Mr. Wilton, I was just telling you what an odd sort of lodging Strachan had in the old house close to the cathedral at Winchester. The house was in a kind of paved yard or passage, divided by the great grim walls of the cathedral, too; and there was always a dingy, damp sort of feel about the air in that place, for the sun, you see, couldn't get at it morning, noon, nor evening; and everybody wondered why Strachan lived in such a gloomy place, for he was always rather inclined to look after his own comforts."

"So he was. Row-de-dow-dow," cried Cockles.

"Will you be quiet, Cockles?"

"Yes, Steady. March on with the story."

"At last, Mr. Wilton, it got whispered about, that it was a beautiful young girl, of only fifteen years of age, the landlady's daughter, that proved the attraction for Strachan to the dismal old house; and you must know, that the only two people in the house were the landlady and her daughter, for though they had an old servant that was there all day, it turned out that she was accustomed to go home to her own child and husband at night; so that, as they had no other lodger, there was no one but Strachan and the two females in the house."

"And this Clinton?"

"Oh, he, as I told you, wore the regimental suit of Strachan, and he used to be to and fro all day till night, when he slept in the barracks, unless Strachan, as any officer could do as regarded his servant, got leave of the colonel for him to be out all night, and then it is supposed that he slept in the old house by the cathedral."

"And the young lady," interposed Cockles, "was a real pretty creature. She was as straight as a drum stick, and as blooming as a peach, she was; and the captain, he had an eye upon her, he had. Oh, yes.

"Silence!" cried Corporal Steady. "How can I tell the story, if you go on in that sort of way, Cockles?"

"March on, then, yourself. I only put in a slight remark, that's all."

"Then don't put in another."

"Very good. Go on, corporal, go on; it's all right, old friend, and tight. Row-de-dow—no, I mean go on."

"Well," added Steady, "you will be so horrified Mr. Wilton, at what I am going to tell you, that I almost feel as if I oughtn't to tell it to you at night; but here goes."

"You need be under no apprehension of its taking too fearful a hold of my fancy, Steady; I have so much mis of my own to think of, that I'm qui roof against that of other people's which has gone by, and become historical."

"Then I'll go on. You know that we were to leave Winchester in a week, and we were all on the look out to know where we were to go to, for although we knew we were to break up our quarters, we didn't know exactly where we were to go to, when one day there came, just about sunset, such a rattling shower of thunder and lightning, that the old city seemed to shake again, and there was no end of damage done all over it; and when the thunder was at its height, old Mrs. Nunn, for that was the name of the lady who kept the house that Captain Strachan lodged in, rushed into the street with a brass hand-box in her hand, crying out—

"'Oh! the house will fall down—the house will fall down, and I shall lose my thousand pounds! The house will fall, and I shall be ruined!'

"Well, it was only the hail rattling in the old chimneys, after all, and Captain Strachan coming up at the moment, got her to go in doors again; but from what she said, everybody found out that she had a thousand pounds, though nobody suspected it before, notwithstanding they always said the old lady was well to do, as her husband many years before had been verger to the old cathedral, and made no end of money by showing it to the curious. Well, the storm died away, after nearly splitting the drum of your ears by such a clap of thunder for the last as never was heard before by any one in the place."

"Row-de-dow-dow!" said Cockles.

"Will you be quiet?"

"Oh, yes; but didn't you say drum?"

"No."

"Well, I'm sure I thought I heard you say drum; so I drummed on the table, you see, at once."

"I said the drum of your ears."

"Well, that's the same thing. I should like to know, Mr. Wilton, what would be the use of a drum if it didn't come to your ears? But go on Steady—Steady you is, and steady you are; and if you don't want any more drumming, don't mention it, that's all."

"Really, Cockles, you are — Well, never mind. I will now go on with my story, if Mr. Wilton is at all interested in it."

"I assure you I am, indeed!" said Arthur, "and I beg that you will continue it."

"Very good, sir. Well, then, you must know that several people ran into the house after Mrs. Nunn but Captain Stra-

chan soon cleared them all out again, and that night he didn't ask for Clinton to be out of barracks; but he was out of barracks for all that, and a pretty night's work he made of it, by all accounts. What has become of him now? I often and often wonder in my mind if he is dead or alive."

"So do I," said Cockles. "They do say, though, that he has been seen by some one."

"Oh, stuff!"

"Yes, but only listen now. You know Sergeant Gallathy of Captain Grant's company. Well, he declares, upon his honour, and you know a sergeant oughtn't to say upon his honour unless he means to act upon his honour, that he saw Clinton once at our last quarters."

"Oh, he was drunk."

Cockles looked taken all aback at this rather abrupt statement of Corporal Steady's, and after a few minutes' consideration, he added—

"Well, I won't take upon myself to say that he wasn't; for, between us all and the post, it's a state of things that the sergeant is rather given to, than otherwise."

"To be sure it is. The man's dead long ago, I should say; and if he isn't dead, why——"

"There he is!" shrieked Cockles, as over he fell, stool and all, right into the corner of the room. "There he is! Murder—murder! Row-de-dow! Clinton—Murder!"

CHAPTER XVIII.

THE MYSTERIOUS APPEARANCE OF THE MURDERER IN THE BARRACKS.

THE exclamation of Cockles, as well from the manner of it as from its suddenness, had quite a startling effect upon both Corporal Steady and his friend, Arthur Wilton. They both sprang to their feet, and turned towards the door, and there they just saw something like a human head disappear through the slight opening of it, and in an instant it was banged shut again.

Now, it had unfortunately happened that both the corporal and Arthur Wilton were sitting with their backs towards the door of the little room, so that they had not had an opportunity of seeing the first of the strange appearance at its entrance; but Cockles, who was partly, although not quite facing the door, had had a tolerably good opportunity of observing who it was who had opened it.

The corporal did not wait for any further explanation from Cockles regarding the appearance, for he had seen quite enough of the strange, shaggy-looking head of some one to convince him that it was neither a joke nor a matter of imagination upon the part of the drummer.

The musket that he, Steady, was cleaning was in his hand, and although the lock was off it, so that it could not be of much use as a weapon, he rushed with it in his hands into the passage on the outside of the room, shouting as he did so, in a loud voice—

"Who goes there?"

All was still, and rather dark, too, for, by some means, the little oil lamp that usually lit the barrack staircase after dark was out, or it had not been lit, so that the corporal might have been tolerably close to some one without knowing it. With a courage that under the circumstances might fairly not have been at the sudden call of most men, considering the preternatural-like character of the occurrence, the corporal sprang to the staircase and ran down to the next floor of the barracks, where the officers' quarters were, and again he cried—

"Who goes there?"

"A friend," said a voice, and the corporal heard a footstep approaching up the staircase.

"Speak, friend, who are you?" he shouted.

There was a lamp upon this landing, and as the figure that was approaching came slowly on up the stairs, the corporal saw, to his wonderment, that it was no other than Captain Strachan.

"What is the meaning of all this?" said Strachan. "Are you posted here, sir?"

"No, sir," said the corporal, as he saluted Strachan; "I—that is—no, sir."

"Why did you challenge me?"

"I did not know it was you, sir, or, of course, I should not; but—but——"

"But what? Why you tremble, man. What is the matter with you?"

The corporal felt that it would be better to tell the truth to the captain, without saying anything about the suspicion that it was Clinton, so he said—

"I and a friend, sir, were sitting quietly talking, and I was cleaning my musket in my quarters above, when the room-door was opened, and a strange head was popped in for a moment, and then, before we could move, it was off. I followed it, as I thought, down here, sir, but have missed it."

"A strange head!" said Strachan. "What do you mean by a strange head?"

"The head of no one in the regiment, sir."

"But—but—" Strachan turned very pale as he spoke—"but how could you tell it was the head of no one in the regiment? How could you tell that, corporal?"

"Why, sir, there isn't such a head of hair in the whole regiment. It's quite contrary to all regulations, sir. It was more like a great, dirty mop, than a head of hair."

Captain Strachan fairly staggered a step or two, and had to lay hold of the balustrade of the staircase for support.

"I came in by the open door, just now," he said, "and walked leisurely enough up stairs, and I met with no one in my progress, whatever. Tell me. Did you see the face?"

"No, sir."

"Then you did not," added Strachan, drawing a long breath of exquisite relief, "you did not recognise, or fancy you recognised, the face as one you knew, or had ever known—eh, corporal?"

How well Corporal Steady knew what the captain was trying at! But he stood the keen gaze that was bent upon his face with unflinching nerves, and said coolly, as though the question did not in the least disturb him—

"No, sir."

"Oh, it was all imagination, corporal."

"Hilloa!" cried a voice.

"Help! No—hush!" said Captain Strachan. "Who is that?"

"Cockles, sir."

"D—n him!"

Captain Strachan opened the door of his own room, that was close at hand, and disappeared, uttering other nice little expletives, which were rather more fearful than ornamental, and with which we would rather have nothing to do, as our readers can easily imagine for themselves what a passionate and unscrupulous scoundrel like Strachan might feel inclined to say when he was thoroughly angry with himself or with any one else about him. It was, indeed, Cockles who called out "Hilloa!" and gave Captain Strachan such a start, when he thought no one was near but the corporal.

"Have you got him?" he cried. "Have you got him, Steady?"

"No—no."

"Well, I could take my Bible-oath, any day, do you know, that it was no other than our old acquaintance——"

"Who?" roared Captain Strachan, dashing the door of his room open at that moment, and confronting Cockles, who nearly fell down the stairs, in his surprise at seeing Captain Strachan with a candle in his hand, and his face as pale as death, while his very lips had lost, too, their colour.

"Who?" roared the captain again. "Who will you swear it was?"

"Clinton!" gasped Cockles.

"Ha! ha!" laughed Captain Strachan—but what a hideous, unmirthful sort of laugh it was ; "Clinton, was it? Do the dead, then, come to life? Do they look up from their bloody rest to—to——Curses! No no !"

Bang went his door shut again, and Corporal Steady and Cockles looked at each other in silent dismay. The corporal then made up his mouth as if he meant to whistle, but emitted no sound; and Cockles used his fists as though he were beating a roll upon his drum, but took care to be equally noiseless as the corporal.

"I say," began Cockles, after rather a long pause, "I say, Steady, I think——"

Corporal Steady placed his fingers upon his lips, and pointed to the door of Captain Strachan's room. He thought he saw it shake a little. Cockles understood him and nodded, and then they both crept up stairs again quite gently, and they did not exchange a word till they got into the little room again.

To be sure, they met Arthur Wilton on the landing, reaching his neck over the balustrades of the staircase with the hope of seeing what was going on below; but Corporal Steady took him by the arm and led him back to the room again, before he would say a word.

"What on earth," said Wilton, "is the meaning of all this, Steady?"

"Hush!"

"Yes, but——"

"Cockles, my boy?"

"Here you is," said Cockles.

"Take the light, and go to the bracket by the stair head, and see if the oil lamp has been alight at all to-night."

"Well, but how can I tell?"

"Feel if the wick is soft and warm, Cockles. That will let you know at once."

"To be sure, it will."

Cockles left the room, and Arthur Wilton was again urgent to say something, but the corporal interposed, with— "Wait till Cockles comes back, and then we will all talk the matter over. Here he is. Well, Cockles?"

"It had been alight, but blown out by somebody. I have lit it again."

"That's right, Cockles. Now, I don't think we shall be interrupted again in a hurry, for there goes as good a bolt into its socket as ever was shot. And now let me tell you, Mr. Wilton, that there is more in this matter than either Cockles or myself can possibly explain to you. Now, Cockles, there is only one thing that I wish you to be quite positive upon, my boy. Was it really Clinton that you saw?"

"How can I tell? Lor! corporal—how am I to take upon myself to say which is a man, and which is his ghost? But I will say it was one of the two."

The corporal nodded.

"It wasn't his ghost, then, Cockles."

"Ghost!" cried Arthur Wilton. "Surely at this time of day none but those with a decidedly dismal imagination will believe for one moment such an absurdity as a ghost."

"No," added the corporal. "Besides, I don't think a ghost would have blown the oil lamp out on the stair-head, do you know, Cockles; and if you saw the face—"

"I did."

"Well, then, if you saw the face, and satisfied yourself that it was the face of Clinton, I saw his head, and his hair had wonderfully grown since he left the regiment; and, you know, ghosts' hair don't grow."

"You know best," said Cockles. "They may, or they may not. But Clinton it was, and, as I say, I'll take my oath of it. There's the stool, and here was me, and there is the door, and I was just going to say a something that I don't know anything at all about now, when I happened to cast my eye to the door, and there I saw him, and down I went—Murder!"

Cockles gave such a vivid description of the occurrence, that down he went again with the two-legged stool, into the same corner that he had shot into when the apparition at the door made its appearance.

"All this is very strange indeed," said Arthur Wilton. "I certainly myself saw a human head, with a quantity of black disordered hair upon it; but that was all. I was coming down stairs to you, corporal, when I heard the voice of Strachan, and I so dislike meeting with that man, that I hesitated at once."

"It was better you didn't come, Mr. Wilton. But now I suppose you will be more than ever anxious to hear the end of this story about Clinton and Captain Strachan, that I was telling you very quietly when all this hubbub took place?"

"You are right. I shall, indeed, be most anxious to hear the ending of this story; and if you will oblige me with it now, I shall thank you."

"It is to be told in very few words, now, Mr. Wilton; and if Cockles will only be quiet, you shall soon know all about it."

"I will," said Cockles.

"Well, then, where was I? Oh, just after the great storm that happened at Winchester. Well, you must know, that several of the non-commissioned officers had had leave to stay until a late hour, as they had been invited to a sort of party, and a dance, that an old sergeant, who lived retired from the army in the town, had chosen to give upon some family occasion and they were coming home to the barracks through the old churchyard in which

THE CONFERENCE BETWEEN COLONEL PERCIVAL AND HIS TWO FRIENDS.

the cathedral stands, as it was the nearest way to the High-street, and so on to the barracks.

"Hardly had they got half-way through the churchyard, when they saw in a remote corner a dim light, and they thought they saw the outline of the figure of a man hard at work, as though he were digging. The light, they said, looked more like a kind of Will-o'-the-wisp than anything else, and they were all a little panic-stricken at first, as they had been talking all along of how the old churchyard was said to be haunted.

"Now, Mr. Wilton—four sergeants ought not to have been afraid, but they were, and the man who was showing them the way ran off at once in a regular panic. After, then, a few minutes' delay, the sergeants made up their minds to go quietly up to the spot, and see what was going on; but as they neared it, they saw a man in a cloak, crouching down among the tomb-stones, and they heard the other, for they still saw the figure working as if at a grave, call out—

"I can't bury her! By Heaven, I can't get her into the ground. Her head! Her head!"

"Chop it off with the spade," cried the man in the cloak.

Well, upon this the sergeants made a rush to catch him, but he was off, and out of sight in a moment, and the noise alarming the other man at the grave, he too, after flinging his spade at the foremost of the sergeants, and wounding him very badly in the shoulder, made his escape."

"So he did," said Cockles, "But he left behind him, his——"

"Hold your tongue, will you, Cockles?"

"Oh, dear, yes. Row-de-dow—Row-de—Hush! I forgot."

"He left behind him," added Corporal Steady, "his jacket and his cap. That jacket and cap were proved in a minute to belong to Clinton."

"But what was he doing?" said Arthur Wilton. "What was he doing in the churchyard, Corporal Steady?"

"You shall hear, Mr. Wilton. You shall hear what he was doing. The sergeants made a great outcry, and alarmed the watch in the city, as well as a patrol of military that was going the rounds, and they came with torches, and found a rough grave half dug in the churchyard, and the dead body of Miss Nunn, the young girl who lived at Captain Strachan's lodgings, half in the grave, and half out of it, and mutilated, as if by blows with the spade, in a dreadful manner about the face."

"Good Heaven!" said Wilton.

"The watch, and the patrol, and the sergeants, were all panic-stricken at the sight; and it is not too much to say, that in ten minutes, not only was the whole barracks in a state of commotion, and every man was under arms, and every officer that could be got at up and dressed, but the whole city was alarmed. Some rushed one way, and some another. Parties were sent out in search of Clinton in all directions, the instant the jacket and the cap were proved to be his; and as the door of Mrs. Nunn's house was forced open some of the officers and men rushed in and called aloud for Captain Strachan. No one answered them."

"Ah, but"——began Cockles.

"Silence!" cried the corporal. "They found old Mrs. Nunn lying dead by the foot of her bed—she had been killed by a blow upon the head; and they found Captain Strachan in a profound sleep in his room, from which they had some trouble to awake him, and only succeeded in doing so by giving him a good shaking, and flashing lights in his eyes."

CHAPTER XIX.

THE CORPORAL CONCLUDES HIS HORRIBLE NARRATIVE.

ARTHUR WILTON had hardly expected that the circumstance that Corporal Steady had to relate to him was of so awfully tragic a character, and he listened to it with breathless interest, for it seemed to him like a foreshadowing of something of a similar character in which he might, or would be involved.

"Go on Steady," he said. "What was the result of all this?"

"Why, the first result was, that Clinton was found in the cathedral itself, he having managed to climb into it through one of the old windows, and, of course, being secured, he was placed in confinement at the barracks. As for Captain Strachan, his story was that he supped with Mrs. Nunn and her daughter, and that they all separated, and that he went to bed at eleven o'clock, and that he saw nothing of Clinton since five on that day; and from the moment that he went into his bed-room to the moment when he was roughly shaken to awake him by his brother officers, he knew nothing at all."

"But the man in the cloak," said Arthur Wilton. "It appears by your statement, that there were two men in the churchyard."

"Exactly so; but no clue to that part of the mystery was ever found, and people thought that the sergeants must have, in the excitement of the moment, been deceived, and that there was no such person. Some shadow among the old tombs, it was thought, would be likely enough to lead them, at such a moment, into error."

"But Clinton was clearly guilty?"

"You shall hear. Captain Strachan was on guard at an early hour that morning, on account of the officer whose turn it was becoming suddenly seriously ill, as if he were poisoned; and a long time he was, too, recovering from the indisposition of that night."

"That was Captain Grant," said Cockles.

"So it was. Well, on account of his sudden illness, it came to Captain Strachan's turn to be upon guard, and when the morning came, that is to say, at roll call, at half-past eight, the prisoner was gone."

"What, Clinton gone?"

"Yes; he had escaped during the hours of from four in the morning till about six, it appeared, and how he got away no one could make out."

"Suspicious it was, and suspicious it is," said Cockles.

"It was, indeed," said Arthur Wilton, in a low tone, as though he were pondering with himself upon the strange events of the tale that had been told him. "I now see the whole affair clearly, and can understand how Captain Strachan came to be tried by a court-martial. It was for the escape of the prisoner while he was on duty?"

"Just so," said the corporal.

"And how did he escape? for, as he retrieved his neck, escape he did."

"To be sure he did. Honourably acquitted, and his sword returned to him by General Brotherton, who commanded the district, with a handsome speech. The story of Captain Strachan was very simple. He visited the prisoner four times during the night or early morning, and on the fourth time he was gone, and that was all he said about it; so what could they do?"

"But the sentinel, Jack Adams," said Cockles; "you recollect him, Steady?"

"To be sure I do. The sentinel on duty was, of course, arrested, and his story was, that Captain Strachan visited the prisoner to see that all was safe, four times or five times, he couldn't say which, as the countersign was given to him each time, and he did not take notice whether it was four or five times; and that no one but the captain going to and fro passed his post while he was on duty between the hours of four and six."

"And what was the end of it all?"

The corporal shrugged up his shoulders.

"Nothing," he said. "The people in Winchester offered a reward of five hundred pounds for the murderer; and there the matter ended, and now, I suppose, it has quite blown over."

"But the thousand pounds," said Cockles, "Mrs. Nunn's thousand pounds. They do say, that not above a few shillings

were found in the house, and that the brass-bound box was quite empty, and it had been opened by a pistol shot having been fired into the lock."

"A pistol shot?" exclaimed Wilton.

"Yes, that was it."

"Why—why, I told you both, if you recollect, I told you both that such was the plan of opening the colonel's chest that Captain Strachan proposed to me."

"Yes," said Corporal Steady, "no doubt it had made an impression upon him at the time as the way poor Mrs. Nunn's box was opened by Clinton."

The corporal looked at Cockles, and Cockles looked at the corporal, but they were both silent; and then Arthur Wilton, in a subdued tone of voice, spoke—

"I know what you both think—I am certain it tallies with what I think myself of this occurrence—but it is not safe to whisper such a thought to the very air."

The corporal nodded, and Cockles beat a ringing march on his knees.

"I will not compromise either of you," added Wilton, "by saying what inference this story has got up into my mind; but tell me how it was that you came to think that Clinton was no more? for that appeared to be your decided impression awhile ago."

"It was, Mr. Wilton. But we had no reason to think so, except that nothing was heard of him, and it seemed quite impossible that he could so thoroughly escape all observation unless he had gone into his grave."

"Yes, out of the air," said Cockles. "Food for worms. But, after to-night, I shan't take upon myself to believe any such thing."

"Nor I," said the corporal.

"And I," said Wilton, as he rose to leave the place, "would not have the conscience of Captain Strachan to be Emperor of the World. I thank you heartily for the recital. I seem awake after it. I know Strachan better than I did. His character and grand projects seem to me to be more apparent than they were before, and I hope that the effect will be to enable me to guard myself against him."

"Hope so, too," said the corporal. "All you have to do is to go through the world easy, and do your duty."

"And attend to your drum," said Cockles. "Whenever anything goes wrong with me, it all gets right again with a roll of the drum, and I say to myself, Cockles is himself again!"

Wilton, after heartily shaking hands with his two friends, left the little room in the barracks and walked down the stairs. As he did so, he saw that the door of Captain Strachan's room, upon the first floor, was ajar. That was a circumstance which, however it might annoy Wilton, was not one that he could take any notice of, so he passed on, and would not look behind him, although he thought he heard the door creak upon its hinges after he had got down a few stairs past it.

Arthur was quite right. The door did creak upon its hinges, and Captain Strachan, still pale and disordered in his appearance, looked out. He saw Arthur, and he shook his clenched fist at him, as he uttered,—

"Ah, my enemy—no, my victim!—the time for your destruction has not quite come; but it will—it will! Oh, yes, it will!"

Arthur Wilton walked across the square of the barracks, and went towards the quarters of the colonel. He wished to devote the remaining time he had before retiring to rest in writing to Amelia. It was an anxious relief to him to converse with her pure spirit, and to make her the depository of his hopes and fears. The letter that he dispatched to her had rather a gloomy character about it, but still it was not altogether so desponding as the last he had written, for there was a feeling of holy faith in the mind of Wilton, now, which the silence of the rather advanced time of the evening, no doubt, seemed very much to foster.

He could not think that Heaven, whose behests he had endeavoured to fulfil to the best of his power, would abandon him to the villanous devices of such a man as Captain Strachan; and as he prayed, for he did pray before writing his letter, he felt how petty must be all the artifices of Strachan, if the fiat of the Almighty were against their success. He rose from that prayer in a much calmer state of mind than he had been. Indeed, after the frightful narrative of the corporal, he had found it necessary to apply some sedative to his nervous system, and what so efficacious for such a purpose as prayer?

The letter that Arthur Wilton wrote to Amelia upon that night, was as follows. We transcribe it, because it is afterwards alluded to, and forms a rather important part amid the singular and most unprecedented train of circumstances that was to surround Arthur in the time to come.

"Exeter.

"MY OWN DEAR AMELIA,—It is night —nearly midnight; but I feel that I could not sleep until I had written to you, if it were only a few lines, to tell you that I still live, and that I still hope that we may be happy.

"The colonel, after being so very kind to me as he was at the first time of my appearance in the regiment, now evidently suspects me, and treats me with coolness, for which I have to thank Strachan—that arch villain.—I thought when I sat down to write, that I should have been able to give you in detail some of the circumstances that now surround me, but my heart fails me as I think of them. Oh, Amelia, if I were but free from the army, and, with a small amount of means, able to call you my own, how happy we should be in the quiet and serenity of some cottage home, with free hearts and consciences at ease, and nothing but the season's difference to cost us a thought.

"But for the present, Amelia, such thoughts are but dreams, and should not be indulged in. Let it suffice that I feel my fortunes are upon the verge, as it were, of some crisis, and what may be the result I cannot even guess; but I dread it, Amelia. Do you, however, my own dear one, keep up a good heart, and expect to hear from me soon again; and in the meantime believe me to be

"Your own, ever and ever,
"ARTHUR WILTON."

There is not much in this letter—perhaps less by a great deal than there should be, and probably there are some things that Arthur would have done well to omit; but then the state of mind that he was in when he wrote it is to be considered.

Arthur Wilton was smarting under the sore of the unjust nature of the colonel's suspicions of him. The coolness that he spoke of in the letter as subsisting on the part of the colonel towards him, cut him to the quick; and then his imagination had been very much excited by the story of Captain Strachan and the soldier, Clinton, and the frightful double murder at Winchester; so that, upon the whole, we may say that poor Arthur was not in a fit state of mind then to write to Amelia, although, no doubt, the doing so had the effect of cooling him down a little.

The hour was indeed a late one by the time he had his letter finished, but he knew that there was a letter-box open all night at the post-office, so he sallied forth to avail himself of the convenience it afforded, by slipping in his letter.

Now, Arthur Wilton had not the remotest idea that Captain Strachan had carried the audacity of his enmity to such a height as to induce him to tamper with his, Arthur's, letters, so that he by no means went at such an hour as this to post his note to Amelia because he was suspicious of its safety; but Captain Strachan thought otherwise, and dogged his footsteps.

It was quite impossible that Strachan, at such an hour, could get at the letter again, but he resolved to make the trial so to do in the morning, and the unsuspecting Wilton was dogged home again by the villain who had determined upon his utter destruction in this world.

When he, Strachan, had seen Arthur to his room again, he repaired to his own, and there he was heard for the greater part of the night pacing to and fro.

The fact, or the apparent fact, that Clinton had been in the barracks, had had a great and distracting effect upon Captain Strachan, and he could not rest. It was about four o'clock in the morning, that, unable to attempt even to retire to rest, he stepped down to the barrack-yard, with the hope that some exercise in the open air would restore his mind to its usual state.

The sentinel challenged him, and Strachan, after giving the word for the night, asked him if any one had crossed his path.

"No, sir," was the reply, "but——"

"Ah, what do you mean by but?"

"I did think, sir, about half an hour ago, I saw a shadowy kind of figure by yonder wall, but it wasn't a man, sir."

"What was it, then?"

"Why, sir, it disappeared in such an odd way, that it looked, begging your pardon, sir, for saying so, like a ghost!"

"Like a nonsense! How do you know what looks like a ghost? Did you ever see one?"

"Why, no, sir, I hope not,"

"Then, how came you to take the shadow you saw, for, I suppose, it was nothing more, for a ghost?"

"Don't know, sir."

Captain Strachan turned away with an exclamation of anger; but how his coward lips quivered at the idea, and how his knees shook under him, as he went to his own quarters again.

"What can all this mean?" he muttered. "Am I to be haunted by that man? Surely he is really dead! I shot him in the marble quarry! I surely shot him there, and Hunoks was a witness that I did. His dead body lies where we saw it fall. Yes, he is dead—dead; but his ghost—this appearance, first in the room of Corporal Steady, and then in the barrack-yard—What does it mean?"

Captain Strachan reached his own room. He had locked the door, but had the key with him; and now he shook like a coward, as he was at heart, as he entered the suite of apartments appertaining to him, and closed the door after him. He had left a cheerful light burning, but, to his surprise, it was now out, and all was darkness in the room.

"How is this?" he said; "the light out? Oh, the closing of the door has done it. The sudden draught and—and the concussion of the air has done it."

He searched for a box of matches, and having found one, he lit it, and turned round to light the candle again, when he saw, sitting on a chair in the middle of the room, no other than Clinton, looking ghastly and care worn, and with blood upon his face.

Captain Strachan uttered one shriek, and fell senseless to the floor.

———

CHAPTER XX.

A CHANGE OF QUARTERS TAKES PLACE.—
THE MARCH.

SEVERAL people about the barracks thought that they heard a strange cry during the night, but no one paid much attention to it; and it was not until broad daylight, when Captain Strachan did not make his appearance, that the sergeant of his company knocked at his door, but receiving no answer, went and communicated the fact to the major.

"Oh, he has over-slept himself, I suppose," said Major Cuthbert. "Let him be."

"Yes, sir."

This was quite sufficient for the sergeant, and Captain Strachan was let be for another hour, and then, as he made no appearance, a feeling of alarm began to get wind in the barracks, and finally got to the ears of the colonel, who at once ordered the door of the room to be broken open, and blamed those who brought him the intelligence of the non-appearance of Captain Strachan for not having resorted to that means before.

"Where is Wilton?" asked the colonel.

"Writing below, sir."

"Very well. Break open the door of Strachan's room, and bring me a report if anything is amiss with him, and—and——"

The colonel was going to say, "Keep an eye upon Arthur Wilton in the meantime," but he didn't say it. We regret to have to state that the result of the colonel's experiment had been unfavourable to Wilton, and that he looked upon him now with more suspicion than ever. The fact was, that Colonel Percival was too fair-spoken and heartless a man to comprehend the deep-laid villanies of such a man as Strachan.

Upon arriving at the door of Captain Strachan's room, the couple of pioneers who were sent for burst it open in a moment, without any ceremony, and the first object that presented itself was Captain Strachan lying upon his face on the floor.

"Dead!" said the sergeant. "Pick him up."

A couple of officers walked into the room as the soldiers lifted Strachan, and placed him on a chair. He was breathing slowly, but his eyes were open.

"Fetch the surgeon," said one of the officers. "He is ill."

The surgeon was quickly upon the spot, and he was rather puzzled at the condition of Strachan. "Apoplexy, possibly," he said, "may be the cause; but he is in a very strange state. Bring in some cold water."

They dashed cold water in the face of Strachan, and then the surgeon gave him a slight stimulant, and he was evidently recovering very rapidly from the state in which they had found him. The first words he spoke, were—

"Is it gone?"

"What gone?" said one of the officers.

"The apparition. Where is it now?"

"Oh, he has been frightened at something," said the surgeon. "Some dream, I dare say. Why, Captain Strachan, rouse yourself; it is broad daylight now."

"Clear aside. Don't choke me up so, all of you. Stand aside. Yes—ah, there is the chair! There is the chair!"

He pointed, with a shudder, to the chair upon which he had seen the figure sitting, and they all looked at the chair with curiosity, and the sergeant lifted it up, and looked underneath it, and then shook his head with a puzzled look.

"Nothing there, sir," he said.

"You have had a bad dream, I dare say, Captain Strachan," said the surgeon, "arising, no doubt, from indigestion. You had better lie down, sir, for a few hours, and I will prescribe for you a sedative."

"No—no, I want air, that is all. I don't know what has happened, but I saw something, I don't know what it was—but there was something here last night in that chair—I can't tell you what it was; but now I want air—air!"

He rose, and snatching up his cap, he left the room. The soldiers looked at their officers and the surgeon, as much as to say, "Shall we stop him?" but as neither interfered, Captain Strachan was allowed to take his own course, and they saw him leave the barracks at a fast pace.

"Well," said the surgeon, "if he can take it, exercise will do him as much good as anything else, and perhaps more. Let him go."

The officers thought it was very odd, and one of them went to the colonel to tell him what had taken place. Colonel Percival listened with surprise to the narrative, and then he said,—

"Well, I cannot make it out. There is something the matter, I am sorry to say, in the regiment with some persons, and this, I suppose, will show what it is. Be so good, sir, as to send my orderly to me, if you see him below."

"Yes, colonel."

The orderly attended the summons in a moment, and Colonel Percival, in a slow and deliberate tone, as though it was rather a labour for him to say the words, said,—

"You will tell Arthur Wilton that it is my order he goes into the ranks—I do not require his services any further; and you will give the necessary orders concerning him, as he will take his place in his company in the regular way."

"Yes, sir."

The orderly sergeant felt a pang of anguish at being the bearer of the order; but the idea of making any comment upon it never entered his head, although it is possible that, wavering as the colonel was, a slight insinuation might have had all the effect that the best friend of Arthur could have desired.

The orderly met Arthur on the stairs. He was going to the colonel's room to ask if he had any orders for him.

"Oh, Mr. Wilton," said the sergeant, "the corporal told me to seek you."

"Thank you; I will go to him at once."

"Don't, Mr. Wilton. He says he don't want you any more, and that you are to go into the ranks and do your duty."

Arthur Wilton reeled back for a moment at this intelligence, as if some one had struck him, and then rapidly recovering his presence of mind, he said,—

"Certainly, I will. Although, for a time, I was, I hope, useful to the colonel in another capacity, I never forgot that I was a soldier."

"You are a gallant fellow," said the sergeant, "and you will be a credit to the regiment, Mr. Wilton. It is the drilling that will become irksome to you."

"Not at all, sergeant. I have paid so much attention to that part of my duty, under the instructions of Corporal Steady, that I think I am qualified to go into the ranks at once."

"If Steady says you are, why you are then," said the sergeant, "for there isn't a better soldier in the regiment than he is."

"Nor a better hearted man," said Walter. "I'm much obliged to you, sergeant, for all your kindness to me; and if the colonel should ask you how I took the announcement that he has done with me, and that I am out of his favour, you will be so good as to tell him that I took it like a man."

"I will."

Notwithstanding the manner in which Arthur managed to meet the change in his circumstances, he was deeply affected by it, not for its own sake, but because it showed that Captain Strachan had at last succeeded in ruining him with the colonel, which, of course, it was his great aim to do. Little did Arthur Wilton dream that Strachan really contemplated the frightful crime to which he had alluded, when he spoke to Walter of cutting the colonel's throat, and robbing him.

Before Arthur could get over the barrack-yard to speak to his friend, Corporal Steady, a mounted lancer, with a little red despatch box at his waist, rode through the gates, and attracted great attention.

"Despatch for the colonel," said the lancer, as he dismounted and shook his legs, which were cramped by a long ride.

The orderly sergeant advanced, and at once took charge of the lancer, and led him to the colonel's room, while conjectures were rife in the barrack-yard as regarded the contents of the despatch. Some would have it that the regiment was about to be sent abroad at once, and others that peace had been proclaimed; and in the midst of all the excitement, Corporal Steady touched Wilton on the arm.

"Mr. Wilton, what do you think of this affair of Captain Strachan's this morning?"

"I hardly know what to think, Steady; but the colonel has ordered me into the ranks."

"The devil he has!"

"Yes, I had the order from Sergeant Tucker this morning, and was seeking you. Oh, if I were only in any other company than Strachan's, all might be well enough; but to be specially under the command of that man is too much."

"It can't be helped, Mr. Wilton; and you must recollect, that if a soldier does his duty, it is rather difficult for an officer to oppress him now-a-days, without it being soon seen, and then the colonel, I'm certain, would interfere, and that would be all for your good, you know."

"You are right, Steady. It is of no use to anticipate evil. It is time enough to feel it when it comes, without grieving over it by anticipation! Hilloa! what's that?"

Cockles was in the middle of the barrack-yard with his drum, which he now began to belabour at such a rate, that it drowned all other noises.

"Ah," said the corporal, "we shall march. That is to get all ready and in marching order."

"Where to? Where shall we go?"

"That, probably, none of us will know till we get there."

March at noon was the order now passed from the officers to the sergeants; and in the course of about a quarter of an hour the whole barrack was one scene of commotion; and if any one had taken a peep into the colonel's room, they would have seen him again trying to pack up the impracticable boot-jack, for he never would let the orderly or his servants pack his things, having a fancy that he could do it much better himself.

In the midst of this bustle, Captain Strachan quite coolly and calmly walked into the barrack-yard, and looked about him, as though nothing at all had been in any way amiss with him.

"What's all this?" he said.

"We are on the route, sir," said the sergeant, to whom he addressed himself.

"Oh, indeed. Where to?"

"Don't know, sir."

"Very good. Oh, Captain Grant, where are we going to?"

"The colonel has not said," replied Grant, "and I have not the remotest idea, except that we are to be on the move by noon."

"By noon? Thank you."

"Are you better, Strachan?"

"Oh, yes, thank you, much better. I can't think what it was that upset me so; but a walk in the cool air of the morning has put me all to rights again. I fancy I must have been dreaming."

"No doubt of it."

Captain Grant bowed, and so did Strachan, and the latter at once proceeded to his room.

"So," he said, "we leave her, do we? Well, I can yet do you an ill-turn, Master Wilton, before we do so. They refused to let me have the letter at the post-office this morning, so I have done myself more harm than good by asking for it. But no matter; that most likely won't be thought of again. People have too many things to attend to, to sum up such little reminiscences. Oh, if I could but altogether persuade myself that imagination had played me a trick last night, how much easier I should feel! But I cannot, I cannot."

Captain Strachan opened a secret drawer of his desk, and took from it the letter that Arthur Wilton had written to Amelia, some time before, and which it will be recollected he had succeeded in getting from the girl at the post-office.

"This will aid me again," he said. "The little talent that I have of imitating handwritings stands me in good stead now. We will see, Mr. Wilton, if another missive may not be despatched in your name to the fair Amelia."

With this, Strachan, after carefully studying Arthur Wilton's letter, and making himself, by numerous trials, master of the handwriting, which happened not to be a difficult one to imitate, wrote the following most rascally epistle to Amelia.

"Exeter.

"MY OWN DEAR AMELIA,—I cannot help writing to you again, although I have so very recently done so. My situation is none the better. Pray excuse my apparent inconsistency between this note and my last, as I really don't know what I said in it, except that I love you as truly as ever. That I can never forget.

"Oh, my Amelia, the colonel has a small chest in which there is gold enough, they say, to make any one for life. If you and I only had it— Well, well, we will say no more about that. I am not familiar with even the thought of crime, and it makes me shudder to think of it.

"I hope your father is quite well. I hope, too, that all our friends in the happy little village are kind to you and to yours. As regards Captain Strachan, I feel that I owe him so much evil, that it would serve him well if I were to play him the worst trick that is possible, namely, make him suffer for the crime of another person. But I will say no more upon this head to you. You are too good and pure, after all, to enter into the conditions and the heart-burnings of crime; so farewell, and may Heaven hold you in its special keeping.

"I am yours,

"ARTHUR WILTON."

"I think this will do," said Strachan, as he carefully looked over the letter, "surely this will do. It is a bit of mis-

chief, and nothing more. She will not say anything, very probably, about it to him; and if she does, why he can't say 'twas I that wrote it, that is certain, and, therefore, it shall go."

Captain Strachan took good care that the letter should be sealed and directed in the same style that Arthur Wilton's were, and then he went himself and put it into the post so that it would arrive by the next post, after that which would carry to Amelia the letter Arthur had himself written over night.

While Strachan was thus occupied, the most active preparations were being made for the departure of the regiment from Exeter, and by half past eleven o'clock the whole were under arms, and ready with bag and baggage for the road.

The colonel's orderly was leading his horse to and fro in the barrack-yard, and the officers were discussing together upon the probabilities of their destination, and wondering why the colonel kept it so close a secret as he did.

CHAPTER XXI.

THE OLD HOUSE AT HOME IS ONCE MORE VISITED.

THE surprise of Captain Strachan when he came out to take the command of his company, and found Arthur Wilton in the ranks, was immense.

"Sergeant," he said, "how is this? I thought Wilton was to be at the service of the colonel as secretary, and all that sort of thing?"

"The colonel has turned him into the ranks, sir, this morning."

A flush of triumph came from beneath the arched eyebrows of Captain Strachan, and his features relaxed into a hideous smile; but he had presence of mind enough to subdue these appearances of satisfaction almost as soon as they could be at all observed.

"Indeed!" he said; "that will be a change for the young man; but how is it that he is able to take his place in the ranks, sergeant? I was not aware that he had gone through the necessary drilling."

"No, sir; but it appears that a corporal has taught him the usual exercise; and upon testing him about an hour ago, I found him as perfect and as able as any in the regiment."

"Indeed!—A corporal? What corporal was so kind as to spare us so much trouble?"

"Corporal Steady, sir."

"That will do."

The sergeant saluted his captain and left him.

"So," muttered Strachan, "Corporal Steady is the man, is he? Well, well, we shall see, Corporal Steady, how far your great friendship for my enemy will benefit you in this matter. We shall see—we shall see. Ah, the colonel!"

Colonel Percival at this moment made his appearance on the ground, and approached his horse. The officers slowly

congregated round him respectfully, and Strachan was among the number.

"Ah, Strachan," he said, as he settled himself in his saddle, "they told me you were very bad."

"I am better, thank you, colonel."

"Well, you know, there is no occasion for you or any one to do duty in the regiment in defiance of sickness."

"I thank you, colonel, but I am quite well enough; and I think that to go through the ordinary routine of my duty is more apt to do me good than harm. It was, after all, only an attack of indigestion."

"Oh, well I am glad you are better."

"Colonel," said the major, "shall I put the troops in motion?"

"Yes, Cuthbert. Get them all outside, and I will then join you."

It was very commonly the duty of the major to put the regiment into regular marching trim, and then the colonel would take the head of the column and give the order to march. As yet, the officers were in perfect ignorance as to where they were to go, and it was not etiquette to make the inquiry. Of course the major knew, and they thought they saw a lurking kind of a smile upon the face of the colonel, too, which seemed as though he was very much amused at the state of mystification they were all in."

"It's to London," whispered one to another.

"Oh, no, my dear fellow, you may depend it's to Dover."

"Dover? Why Dover?"

"Why, you see, Napoleon is making exertions to land on the coast, and so our regiment is sure to go upon active service."

"You are both wrong," said a third. "I will wage anything we are to go to Ireland."

"The devil!" said half-a-dozen of them in chorus. "Anything but that."

The roll of the drums now convinced them that they must take their places with their respective companies, and in a few moments more, with drums beating, and colours flying, the regiment marched out of the barrack gates. The old officer who was permanently at the barracks as Fort Major, saluted them as they passed out, and then he shook hands with the colonel, and the major, and the surgeon, and the gates were closed.

"Halt!" cried the colonel. "Right face! Take open order. March!"

Away they all went, and wonder as to their destination was still depicted upon every countenance except that of the major and the surgeon, who were both riding with the colonel.

"They are all mad to know where we are going," said the major.

"Then let them remain so," said the colonel.

"Precisely. It will be rather a surprise to them, I think."

"Well, but," said the surgeon, "I don't know."

"My dear Brown," said the colonel, "can't you guess?"

"Not I."

"Then I will tell you. The fact is, we were called away from our last quarters on account of a rumoured loss of a pitched battle in Spain, in which it was said that our forces, under Lord Wellesley had been dreadfully cut up, and so all the available forces in country cantonments were to be sent off to Lisbon forthwith ; but it turned out to be an unfounded rumour, as the French have been knocked to pieces by a force half their number."

"Of course," said the major.

"Well, I confess that to an English soldier it is of course, and now that the fight at the war office is over, we just quietly, my dear Brown, you see, go——"

"Back again," said Brown.

"Exactly so. We shall be in our old quarters in a very few hours, I hope, and as comfortable as we were before in the picturesque neighbourhood, where we made many friends, and where the regiment, too, enjoyed the very best health, as I took occasion to let General Brotherton know in a dispatch that I sent to him yesterday."

"I am quite delighted," said the surgeon, "and I do think there is not an officer or man in the regiment that will not be delighted, too."

"Yes," added the colonel, "I think I can say it with truth, as I do with pride and pleasure, that my officers always leave behind the greater regrets the longer they stay anywhere ; and they are always welcolmed back again; and that they are, without exception, gentlemen ; I cannot name one who is not."

"Captain Strachan," said the major.

"Eh?"

"I beg your pardon, colonel,"

"I beg yours, major. Did you wish to make an exception of Strachan?"

"Oh dear, no. I was only going to say that he looks horribly ill this morning, and that I think he is extremely ill, that is all. What do you think, Mr. Brown?"

"Bilious," said the doctor.

"Well," said the colonel, in a low tone, as though he were conversing with himself rather than speaking aloud. "If he complains it is then time for us to give him every care that he requires. Till then I can see nothing but a man doing his duty, and so long as he does it, I am not to suggest his imbecility."

This was an opinion neither the doctor nor the major were at all likely to run counter to, and the conversation dropped upon the subject of Strachan; but the major, when the surgeon rode back to look after some affairs of his own, connected with the baggage waggons, took occasion to say to the colonel—

"So I see you have placed Wilton in the ranks?"

"Yes, Cuthbert, I was uneasy about the fellow, and I am uneasy still."

"How so still?"

"Because I am afraid I am doing him a wrong."

"Nay, you can do him no wrong by placing him in the ranks. He enlisted, you know, and expected nothing else. All the favour that you showed him by engaging him as your secretary was something extra, that is all."

"Yes, but he knows that I have lost confidence in him; and I feel that, as yet, I do not know, and probably, never shall know who is the rogue and who the honest man, between him and Strachan."

"Rely upon it, you will know. Circumstances always, in the long run, develop themselves, so that that is settled beyond the shadow of a cavil. You have only to wait, colonel, and all will be well; and most of all you will be guided by the conduct of Strachan to Wilton."

"I will protect Wilton against him, by Heaven! So long as Wilton does his duty, I will stand his friend, although I cease to have any personal communication with him, and I sincerely hope that I am not acting hardly by him."

"You are not, indeed. He is in Strachan's company, but that can make no sort of difference to him, for, as the army is conducted, it is a very difficult thing for any officer who values his own character and connexions to go out of his way to oppress any soldier."

"It is, I hope, in my regiment, impossible."

"I think it is."

We will now pass over the incidents of the march until the officers began to have a suspicion that they were bound for their old quarters in the immediate vicinity of Riversdale, and when the colonel found that there was such a general information, he gave the major leave to let them know as much.

The information was received by them all with pleasurable feelings, with one exception. That exception was Captain Strachan. He thought that this sudden and, to him, most unexpected march to their old quarters in the immediate vicinity of Mr. Revis's farm might have the effect of rather confounding his tactics, and most of all did he lament that he had been so hasty in sending the letter to Amelia.

Nothing could be more natural, now, than for her to mention that letter in a particular manner as regarded its contents to Arthur Wilton, and then he, Wilton, would become aware of the fact that some one was sending, in an admirable imitation of his hand-writing, letters to Amelia, and would, of course, take means to counteract such a plot accordingly. Who, too, could he suspect but Captain Strachan?

The countenance of the villanous captain turned still more ghastly and pale as these disgusting thoughts passed through his mind, and he felt scarcely able to keep his place at the head of his company.

Muttering curses between his clenched teeth, he rather alarmed the sergeant whose place it was to be close to him.

Then, again, it was just possible that the regiment would arrive at their destination even before the letter; and what if Arthur Wilton should actually be with Amelia when it came? There would be an exposé.

"No, no!" muttered Captain Strachan, "I will take good care to provide against the latter contingency by keeping him on duty. Yes, I am his captain, and I can easily prevent that."

The reader may judge of the surprise of the inhabitants of Riversdale and its neighbourhood when they heard the sound of drums beating, and, after a time, saw a regiment of troops approaching, which, in the dust that they kicked up, could not be, for some time, recognised, but as they got nearer, were seen to be the very same who had so recently left the place.

The news spread like wildfire that the troops had come back again, and there was a grand turn-out of the inhabitants to welcome them, for the colonel had spoken no more than the truth when he said that wherever he and his officers had once been, they were welcome again.

Flummery, as an official personage, found that his services might be in a state of requisition, and he marched into the streets with his constable staff in his hand, and ordered everybody to move on in the king's name; but finding that the people only laughed, he thought he had better move to the farm, and let Revis and Amelia know that the troops had returned, and that Arthur might soon be expected.

Nothing could more show the kind of estimation in which old Wilton was held in, better than the fact, that no one thought proper to trouble themselves to come to him to tell him that the regiment in which his son was had arrived, or all but arrived, again in the old quarters.

Just as Flummery reached the garden

gate of the old farm of Riversdale, he met the postman leaving it.

"Hilloa!" cried Flummery, "have you heard the news?"

"What news?"

"Why, the regiment has come back again, and we shall all be as gay as larks once more."

"You don't say so? D—n it!"

"Why, what's the matter with you?"

The postman dealt his own hat a blow upon the top that sent it nearly down to the bridge of his nose.

"Don't ask me, Flummery," he said. "Don't ask me."

"Well, I won't then."

"I merely wish to remark, that I am a desperate postman, that is all, my dear fellow—Flummery, that is all."

"Lor! you don't say so?"

"Yes. I thought the regiment had gone for ever, and I was beginning to be just a little comfortable; but now my heart turns to pipe-clay again, and I shall do nothing but dream of drums, and guns, and fifes, and firelocks, and ramrods."

"You don't mean that? But, I say, what does it matter to you, you know? Lor! bless me, if twenty ragiments was to come, I shouldn't be put out of my way."

The postman snatched his hat off his head, and wiped his heated brow with the little bag.

"Flummery," he said. "Oh, Flummery?"

"Yes, here I is."

"I have a wife—yes, a wife; and in the regiment there is a Corporal Green. Oh, Flummery, that Corporal Green is always in our kitchen—always. Don't mention it again; but I am a desperate postman, and all along of Corporal Green."

CHAPTER XXII.

ARTHUR FINDS THAT HIS AMELIA'S HEART IS UNCHANGED.

THE letter that the villain Strachan had written to Amelia in the name of Arthur Wilton, had just been delivered by the desperate postman as he met Flummery, and Amelia read it with both surprise and concern.

Astonishment and grief increased in the heart of Amelia as she re-read this strange epistle; and she could only come to the conclusion that real mental suffering had driven poor Arthur Wilton a little mad.

The letter was something like the style and tone of the one which had arrived only a few hours before by the first post on that day; but yet that former one had not pointed so significantly to criminality as this did. Alas! poor — poor Amelia! The severest blow that could have fallen upon her heart, not to absolutely crush it, had fallen now.

She wept with the letter in her hand; and it was some time before she could understand that the shadow which fell through the French window looking into the garden by which she sate, was beckoning to her. Hastily rising, she opened the window, and there stood Flummery.

"Oh, Miss Amelia," he said, "I have come all the way without a bit of breath left, do you know, all for to go to come to tell you——"

"What, Flummery? Oh, what?"

"The big dog——"

"The big dog! What of him?"

"Excuse me, miss, but I don't come here often enough, and he don't know me as he ought to do; and as I was a getting over the little fence to get to this here part of the garden, to save going round by the poultry-yard, what do you think he did?"

"I don't know, Flummery; but you should come often enough for him to know you. You are well aware that you are always welcome to the place, and that we look upon you as a very particular friend."

"Why, yes, miss; but if you'll believe it, always saving your presence, Miss Amelia, the dog tried to take a piece out of my leg, miss—hem!"·

"I am sorry for it, Flummery."

"Well, but it ain't no matter. Listen! Do you hear that, Miss Amelia?"

The sound of the drums and fifes came clearly upon her ears.

"Good Heavens, what is the meaning of that? Such sounds as those are perfectly familiar. Alas! I dream of those sounds, and awake to weep."

"Yes, I know, miss. But, you see, there's a regiment a-coming here."

"Another regiment?"

"No, Miss Amelia—I hope I have broke the news nice and easy to you, and let you feel quite comfortable—but, you see, it's the same regiment, and Mr. Wilton will, of course, be with it, and at the old place as often as he likes."

Amelia burst into tears.

"There, now, I have done it," said Flummery. "I tell you what it is, Miss Amelia: that twenty *pun* isn't wasted. It's all right at home, miss, and who knows but now, as there's to be no fighting done, but the king and Colonel Percival might be glad to divide it atween 'em, and let Arthur Wilton go? Only think, it would pe a matter of ten *pun* a piece to 'em, you know, Miss Amelia. I'll just run and get the twenty *pun* at once, that I will."

"No—no, Flummery."

"Oh, but yes, Miss Amelia, I had better, and then you can have the twenty *pun* in your own hands, you know, and you will be sure of it."

"Mr. Flummery, I thought I had fully explained to you that my father is now in no want of means, and that the farm and all upon it were clearly his without the least incumbrance; so that, grateful as I am to you for your kind offer, we are not, indeed, in want of it; and if ten times the sum you mention were requisite for the freedom of Arthur Wilton, my father could in a moment command it."

"Ten times twenty *pun?* Oh, lor! Why, that comes to—Let me see: ten times twenty is—no it isn't—twenty times ten *pun* is—Stop. Ten times—that is, ten *pun* no, twenty *pun*—Dear me, I never was good at 'rithmeticals, no, never, Miss Amelia. But don't you hear the drums a-beating now?"

"I do—I do."

"Lor bless you, yes. They are going down the old road. Oh, lor, no—no they ain't. Oh—oh!"

"What is the matter, Flummery? You alarm me."

"Oh, nothing—nothing at all; only, you see, Miss Amelia, they ain't a coming down the old road, but by the lane, and right past the old chestnut tree at the corner of the five-acre field; and if you go and stand in the hedge—I mean sit on the holly fence—Oh dear, no, I don't mean that—but I mean scramble up the bank, and hold on to one of the low branches of the old chestnut, you will see them all go by."

"Yes—yes, oh, yes. I will go at once. Poor Arthur! He will see me, and it will be such a joy to him."

Amelia was in a half frantic state to get a bonnet and shawl on, so that she might go to the corner of the lane that had been mentioned by Flummery, and see the regiment pass; and in an incredibly short space of time she was making her way across the garden and then across the five-acre field in the direction of the old chestnut tree that Flummery had mentioned.

The sound of the drums and fifes came plainly now upon her ears, and each moment more and more distinct, so that there could be no mistake about the fact of the regiment having taken the short cut to its destination down the lane, instead of going the round by the high-road.

"Yes, I shall look upon him again." thought Amelia; "I shall see if he is altered by the sad situation in which he has been. Cold hearts have been about him, and he has missed the cheerful smiles of those who loved him. Alas! poor Arthur, I too, have suffered, but not as you have suffered."

"Stop a bit, Miss Amelia," cried Flummery. "Stop a bit."

"What for, Flummery?"

"'Cos, you see, I took a short cut across the kitchen garden, and that dog has been at me again, and got hold of the skirts of my coat, and here I is without it."

"Never mind, Flummery."

"Oh, it's all very well to say never mind, but that Master Prince has took a sort of objection to me lately, I don't know why. But, Miss Amelia, I say, Miss Amelia?"

"Yes, Flummery."

"Suppose I was to run home, and get the twenty *puns*, and then just as the colonel is passing the end of the lane, hold them up to him in the little bag I've got 'em in, and say, 'Now, colonel, here's the money. Here's twenty *puns* to let Mr. Wilton go. Now or never.' Don't you think, Miss Amelia, that the sight of the money would be rather too much for him?"

"Oh, Flummery, when shall I succeed in convincing you that we have no want of money? My father is well to do, I assure you, Flummery, and no sum at all in reason would be considered too much if it purchased the release of Mr. Wilton. My father feels that it is for my sake that he has placed himself in such a position, and therefore is it that he would do anything to release him."

"Oh, ah, I know—I understand all that; but, you know, twenty *puns* is twenty *puns*."

"Yes, Flummery, I know that. But here is the old tree. I will get up upon the bank, and watch the regiment pass."

"Yes, Miss Amelia, and I'll give you a leg up—Dear me, what is I a saying of? I mean, Miss Amelia, that I'll help you up. Lor!"

This exclamation of Flummery's arose from the fact, that Amelia, with the lightness and agility of a fawn, had sprung up the bank without any help at all, and caught by the branch of the old tree that was nearest to her, and was in perfect security, and elevated sufficiently to see well into the lane.

"Well, I never!" said Flummery. "If

I was to go for to try to get up the bank in that way, something strikes me forcibly I should be in the ditch."

"No, Flummery," said Amelia. "The rapidity of your ascent will save you. You saw we do it?"

"Yes, I did. But you *flewed* up, Miss Amelia."

"No—no. You may come in the same manner. Come, Mr. Flummery. You wish to see your old friend Arthur, I am sure."

"Well, so I does—so here goes. Lor bless us! if she can take a hop, skip, and a jump, and get to the top of the bank, surely I can. Here goes. Shut your eyes, and do it capital One, two, three —here I goes!"

Flummery made a rush at the bank, and got about half way up it, when the treacherous surface gave way with him, and, as he had predicted, he was, in another moment, lying flat upon his back in the ditch that drained the field.

"Well, I said so. That's satisfactory, at any rate. I said as much, and here I is."

"They come — they come!" said Amelia.

"Very likely, and here I lies in the ditch a soaking. Oh, lor!—oh, lor! Why did I try to get up a bank by making a kind of *flew* at it all of a lump? Oh, dear!—oh, dear!"

"Yes, I shall see him once again. They are all in the lane. I can see the tops of their caps; and how the bayonets glitter in the sun!"

"A large frog, about the size of a dust-shovel, and all his family, have just crawled over my face," groaned Flummery.

"Nay, I see Colonel Percival and his horse. Ah! they pause—No—no, they do but make a change in the line of march, owing to the narrowness of the lane, that is all. They advance again. They come—they come!"

"That frog was the oldest inhabitant, I'm certain, of this ditch. Oh, murder! there's something got hold of my toe."

"Yes, I shall see him once again. My Arthur!"

"And I feel him! A horse-leech! Oh, dear—oh, dear!"

By a violent scramble, Flummery succeeded in getting out of the ditch, and rolling on to *terra firma*. At that moment the head of the column of troops reached the part of the lane where stood Amelia, with her beautiful face flushed by excitement, and her hair dancing about her neck and shoulders in the fresh breeze of the morning—for the bonnet had fallen back

without her noticing that it had done so— and her bright eyes sparkling like diamonds.

Colonel Percival looked at her face for a moment, and then seemed to be thinking, and a rather puzzled air appeared upon his face. Amelia slightly bowed, and the colonel at once saluted her with his sword in a graceful manner.

"An angel!" said the major.

"Yes," said Colonel Percival, "I know her now."

"Lucky individual!"

"Pho! pho! She is the young girl who called upon me to solicit the discharge of Wilton, and who was so obliging as to stand upon my box and help me to lock it." The major cast up his eyes, but he said nothing, and now the attention of all the officers was directed to poor Amelia, who clung to the bough of the old tree, and felt as though she were ready to sink into the very earth with shame and terror. She had not contemplated how many eyes she would have upon her by getting to such an elevated position to view Arthur Wilton. She had thought only of him, and not at all of the fact that he was accompanied by a whole regiment.

Flummery said something, but his voice was completely drowned in the clamour of the drums and fifes, which in the lane made a prodigious clatter indeed. Gladly now would Amelia have descended from the post she occupied; but that was no easy matter, for the height was considerable, and she dreaded that in her agitation she might fall and so make her situation appear more ludicrous than it was. She had not seen Arthur, and there was yet, therefore, that great inducement to keep her where she was.

The officers took their cue from the colonel, as well as liking the joke themselves, and each one as he passed Amelia gravely saluted her, so that she found herself in the predicament of holding fast to the bough of an old tree, and being forced, in common politeness, to bow to a whole regiment.

And now a sight met her gaze that she would gladly have been spared. That sight was the hideous—to her—countenance of Captain Strachan. His company had reached the spot, and, as the other officers had done, he saluted Amelia; and as he did so he bent upon her such a glance of concentrated hatred that it chilled her to the very heart.

It was only for a moment, though, that Amelia allowed herself to be awed by the sight of the villain, Strachan. Mustering all her resolution and courage, she looked calmly at him, and did not return his salute.

"By Jove, she won't bow to Strachan," said the lieutenant of the company to the ensign.

"No, and that shows her taste, too," said the ensign. "See, she bows to us."

"She does."

Both the officers saluted Amelia respectfully, and then they saw her let go her hold of the branch of the tree, and standing unaided by any support on the bank, she clasped her hands together, and cried :

"Arthur ! Arthur !"

There was a slight commotion in the ranks, and Arthur Wilton was upon the point of darting towards the bank, when Corporal Steady laid a hand upon him, and held him firmly back by his belt.

"Mr. Wilton," he said, "would you ruin yourself? Be cautious. You are in the ranks. For her sake as well as for your own, stay where you are."

It wanted but a moment's reflection to let Arthur feel that the corporal was right, and that the sudden impulse which would have led him to forget his duty, and to fly to Amelia, would have been a destructive one. He shrunk back into his place again, just as Captain Strachan glanced around him, crying—

"What is that?"

"Nothing, sir," said the sergeant.

Arthur was marching on with a confused look, and so Amelia saw him apparently going past without a glance at her. But such was not the case. He raised his eyes, and in the one look that she got from him she saw how much he loved her, and how she was still his and only his, and how she had his whole heart, for his whole heart was centred in that one look.

Amelia had now eyes for nothing but Arthur, and she heeded not the salutes of the officers as she strained her gaze after him.

"Murder !—hilloa !—murder !" cried Flummery. "Here's Mr. Shooter."

CHAPTER XXIII.

ARTHUR AND THE CORPORAL RESCUE AMELIA FROM GREAT DANGER.

THE sudden and alarming cries from Flummery, require some explanation.

About a month previous to the occurrences which we have detailed, Farmer Revis had become possessed of a bull of great strength and size. A more ferocious animal could hardly have been found, and that very five-acre field had been, on account of its being well fenced, appropriated to the gentleman. Notwithstanding, however, the thick holly fence that surrounded the field, and the high bank that shielded it from the lane, the bull managed to make so many escapes, and create such consternation in the neighbourhood, that Revis had to get rid of him and get another, who turned out to be almost as bad as his predecessor.

Now, the first bull, on account of his size, was called Mr. Long facetiously by the village wits; and the second one, who was much the smaller animal of the two, was named Mr. Shorter.

Mr. Shorter, then, take him for all in all, was tolerably well behaved for a time His home was in a field adjoining the five-acre one, which was fenced in on purpose to keep him within its bounds ; but upon the occasion of the regiment passing down the lane, Mr. Shorter had gone nearly frantic. The drums and the fifes—the red coats—the flying colours—all had contributed to assure Mr. Shorter, that society at large was making a dead set at him, and he was not likely to stand that quietly. After various gambols, then, and certain dances—one of them might have been the polka for all we know—Mr. Shorter, finding nothing and nobody, as Mr. Flummery would say, to toss in his own field, began to make a vigorous assault upon a wooden fence that kept him from the five-acre meadow. At first Mr. Shorter tried his head, and then he tried his stern, and the latter succeeded in breaking down the fence, and in strutted Mr. Shorter to the five-acre field like a great conqueror.

The first movements of friend Shorter, were to paw up a quantity of earth, and to cut several eccentric gambols. He then met a mole hill, which he scattered in a moment ; and then he happened to cast his bull's-eye upon Mr. Flummery, who crawled out of the ditch just in time for Mr. Shorter's special amusement.

"Boo—boo !" roared Shorter.

"The devil !" said Flummery, and sitting up, he looked in the direction of the sounds, and saw Shorter tucking in his head, and lashing his tail about with the evident intention of having a game at pitch and toss with him, Flummery. No wonder, then, that the alarmed village beadle roared out murder in the way he did.

We think that most persons in the situation of Mr. Flummery would have been induced, likewise, to cry murder.

Amelia, hearing the cries, looked down

from her elevated position, and saw Mr. Shorter in the belligerent attitude we have described. She considered that the destruction of poor Flummery was certain, and she screamed aloud.

"Help—help!" she screamed. "Help! Oh, help!"

The bull made a rush at Flummery, but the latter rolled over into the ditch again, and disappeared from before his enemy, who reached the spot of the five-acre meadow upon which he, Flummery, had been sitting, and found, to his amazement, that there was nothing to toss.

"Boo—boo!" said Mr. Shorter again; and then he turned, and raced to the other end of the field, in order to survey the ground, and make another attack.

"For Heaven's sake don't tell him I'm in the ditch," said Flummery, "or he'll be down upon me! Oh, dear—oh, dear! I'd give my twenty *puns* to be safe at home, that I would."

"Help—help!" again cried Amelia.

The voice—that voice, every tone of which he knew so well—reached the ears of Arthur Wilton, and every other circumstance was in a moment forgotten, but that Amelia was in some danger, and called to him for help. In another moment, too, he heard her call upon him by name, and bounding from the ranks, he flew, rather than ran, towards the spot where he had seen Amelia last.

She was still clinging to the branch of the tree, but just as he reached the corner of the lane, he saw the branch break, and Amelia disappeared into the field. Ignorant of the amount, or the nature of the dangers that had threatened her, Arthur could do nothing but seek to ascertain it by rushing up the bank, and then it was that, about the middle of the five-acre field, he saw Mr. Shorter, looking very suspicious, and evidently preparing for another attack.

Amelia lay partially stunned by her sudden fall, just at the foot of the old tree to which she had been clinging, and which had failed her at such an inopportune juncture, for she would have been safe enough from Shorter if she could have retained her position upon the bank.

"I am here!" said Arthur. "I am here, my Amelia, I am with you."

There was one crash of the hedge, and despite all the obstacles that it presented, Arthur Wilton burst through it, and sprang down the bank into the field.

The bull prepared for another rush, and this time it was at Amelia that the furious animal directed his attack, but Arthur rushed forward some half dozen paces, and stood

with his arms extended, and so astonished the bull by that act, especially as he was in regimentals too, that Mr. Shorter drew up and looked a little staggered.

"Holloa!" said a voice from the hedge. "Holloa! What's the matter?"

It was the voice of Corporal Steady.

"The bull," said Arthur. "Don't you see him?"

"Oh, by Jove, yes, I do. Here's your musket. You dropped it, Mr. Wilton."

"Throw it to me."

"There you are."

The musket came with a dash to the ground, and Arthur seized it at once.

"Corporal," he said, "if I look round again, the bull will make his rush upon us. Get Amelia through the gap in the hedge into the house."

"All's right. Now, miss."

"Oh, no—no! Arthur—Arthur," said Amelia, "you will be killed."

Arthur merely waved his arm, and Corporal Steady took Amelia in his arms and carried her into the lane in a moment. Mr. Shorter, upon this, got desperate, and made a furious rush at Arthur Wilton, who just dashed aside in time to prevent it being fatal to him, and inflicted a wound upon Mr. Shorter's shoulder with his bayonet, that did not by any means improve that individual's temper, for, with a roar of rage, he turned as quickly as he could, and made another rush at Arthur, and the young soldier unfortunately fell upon the damp grass. Another moment, and he would have been upon him, but, to his astonishment, Shorter suddenly turned round with a louder roar than ever, and allowed him to escape.

"How do you like that?" said Corporal Steady, who had, after raising Amelia, made his way back into the field again, and just in time given Mr. Shorter such a touch of his bayonet in his rumpsteaks as made him think of nothing else for some minutes.

"Fly, now, Arthur," said the corporal.

"Not without you."

"Oh, don't mind me. You be off."

"No, Steady, my friend. We will go together."

"Come on, then. Let's keep him at bay, and effect as orderly a retreat as we can. This way, Mr. Wilton. All's right. The young lady is in the lane, sitting upon Cockle's drum."

"Thank Heaven she is saved!"

Arthur and the corporal now effected a very gallant retreat with their bayonets pointed at Mr. Shorter, who evidently had had quite enough of their points, and did not feel disposed to come into contact with the cold steel again; so he kept his distance, and amused himself by making as many hideous noises as he possibly could express of his disappointment that, after all, he had tossed nobody.

In this way Steady and Arthur reached the hedge, when, to their astonishment, up sprang Flummery out of the ditch, crying—

"Twenty *puns* to be safe at home! Twenty *puns* to anybody who will catch Mr. Shorter."

"What, my friend, Flummery?" said Arthur.

"Oh dear me, is it you, and the British

THE CONSTERNATION IN THE BARRACKS BY THE APPEARANCE OF CLINTON.

Army? Oh, oh, you can't think what a time of it I have had in the ditch, Mr. Wilton. Oh, my back! Where is Mr. Shorter?"

"There he is."

"Eh! Oh, the devil!"

Mr. Flummery, the moment he cast his eyes upon Shorter, made just such a dart at the bank and the hedge as he had been recommended to make by Amelia when he had fallen into the ditch, and he was in the lane in a moment. Arthur and Corporal Steady were soon with him, and then the battle with the bull might be said to be over, although Mr. Shorter kept up a great bellowing, as if he had got the victory, instead of having been, as it was quite clear he was, most signally defeated.

"All's right, now," said the corporal. "We have certainly left the field to the enemy, but I rather think we have brought off all our forces uninjured, and that's not what every general can succeed in doing."

"Twenty *puns*," said Flummery, "twenty *puns* to be safe at home !"

"Why, you are safe."

"Eh? Oh, where's the bull?"

"Over in the field, to be sure."

"What, Mr. Shorter? You don't say so?"

"My name ain't Shorter, I can tell you, my friend. My name is Steady—Corporal Steady, and I'm a friend of Mr. Wilton's."

"So am I," said Flummery.

"And so am I," said Cockles; "and so is my drum."

"Amelia, Amelia," cried Arthur, as he sprang towards her, and caught her in his arms ; "tell me, Amelia, that you are not hurt—tell me that you have escaped, and I shall then feel that all other misfortunes are light, indeed. You are pale, my Amelia, and you do not speak to me. Oh, God this is dreadful !"

"No, no, Arthur, I am not hurt—I am not in the least hurt; but I am terrified, Arthur, so terrified !"

She sunk upon his breast, and wept freely.

"Do her good," said Cockles, "a world of good. I say, Steady?"

"All's right, my boy."

"Don't you rather think, taking things on the average, and in the long run, Steady, that we are all in for it a bit, my dear fellow?"

"Yes, my boy."

"Ah, I know you would. Here we are, three babes in the wood—no, in the lane; but it comes to much the same thing—all as good as deserters. We have left our ranks when the regiment was in marching order, and staid behind on a kind of caper of our own all about a mad bull. Oh, my eye, there will be a nice row about it; and if Captain Strachan has got an evil eye on Wilton, now is the time for him to begin a winking of it, and letting him know what's what in the way of serving of him out."

"Cockles?"

"Yes, corporal?"

"Hold your tongue, will you? The worst can only come to the worst, and that's all; and the less you says about it afore the young lady, why, all the better, Cockles."

"Mum as a drum without no parchment," said Cockles.

"Did you happen," said Flummery "to see the tail of a coat in the five-acre field, gentlemen ?—'cos if so be as you did, it's my tail on the off-side."

Amelia still sobbed bitterly upon the breast of Arthur Wilton ; but they were blessed tears those, and as they gushed from her eyes, she felt her heart grow lighter; and in the course of a few minutes she was able to look up into the face of him whom she loved, and to listen to his softly murmured words of dear affection.

"And do you love me still, my Amelia? Do you love your soldier, who, but for you, would perhaps do some desperate deed to save himself from the cruel routine of this life? Oh, my dear, dear Amelia, only tell me that you love me still, and I shall feel, indeed, that I have a sweet reward for all the past, and much courage, too, to face all that may be in the yet dim and uncertain future."

"Arthur, do you doubt me?"

"No, oh, no, love! Could I doubt the goodness of Heaven?"

"Hush, Arthur—oh, hush. It is upon that goodness that you and I must most depend. We will not even in supposition doubt it."

"No, Amelia, I merely meant how impossible it was to doubt it, or you. Is your father well? Does all go on smilingly and smoothly at the old farm? And you too, my loved one—you are happy?"

"Oh, no—no! I think of you, Arthur, and how can I be happy? The thought, likewise, that you suffer so much for us, lies heavily upon my father's spirit. Oh, if we could but release you from your present condition!"

"Do not let that fret you, dear one," said Arthur. "It may not be. While there is war still raging, it may not be, and I have nearly schooled my mind to patience. The time will come, I hope, when all that I go through will appear but as a dream ; and when, by some happy and contented fireside of our own, we shall look back to this time as one so far gone past, and so completely done with, that we shall hardly credit that it had once such an existence as it has now. Surely it was Providence that brought me to this spot in time to save you, dear one."

"It was, Arthur; and, therefore, we will not doubt that Providence is kind and good to us, and watchful over us. But there is your friend to think of. He, too, was good and true, and helped you, Arthur."

"Without my kind friend, Steady," said Arthur, "I'm afraid I should have had but a poor chance with the furious bull. Steady?"

"Attention!" said the corporal.

"Do you see who is coming down the lane?"

"No; but I see what. It is a sergeant's guard, Mr. Wilton."

"Yes," said Cockles, "and I happen to know what they come for. It's all up now, I rather take it."

"What do you mean?" said Arthur Wilton. "What do you mean, Cockles?"

"Oh, you will soon find out. Here they come. Corporal Steady knows well enough what I mean, don't you, corporal?"

"Why, yes, rather," said the corporal, "I do!"

"Tell me, then," cried Arthur. "Why do you both make this mystery about it?"

"It ain't no mystery whatsomdever," said the corporal. "It's quite a ordinary sort of transaction, Mr. Wilton. The fact is, that sergeant's guard is coming to arrest us all three, that's all about it, my good friend."

CHAPTER XXIV.

CAPTAIN STRACHAN IS RATHER DISAPPOINTED.

ARTHUR WILTON looked about for a moment, and then a smile crossed his face as he looked at the party advancing. Amelia, however, had heard the word, arrest, and it was to her full of horror. She clasped Arthur by the arm as tightly as she could, and said in a whisper—

"Arthur, Arthur! What does he mean? Why do you smile, and yet look so pale? Speak to me now. What is the meaning of all this?"

"It is of little moment," replied Arthur. "Do not distress yourself; but promise me that you will do me a favour."

"Oh, yes, anything, Walter."

"Upon your sacred word, Amelia?"

"Upon my sacred word!"

"Then, go home as quickly as you can, and let Flummery go with you, to see you safe to your father's door."

"Oh, but Arthur, what is meant by this arrest?"

"Amelia, you promised to go home. Will you go?"

"I will—I will. Mr. Flummery, come with me."

"Won't I," said Flummery. "I begin

to suspect that Mr. Shorter did not toss me, after all, do you know."

Arthur saw the affliction that was in the face of Amelia He folded her in his arms for a moment, and then he said—

"My Amelia, fear nothing. The corporal, and I, and Cockles the drummer, you understand, left the ranks without leave, to come to your aid when you were in danger. That is a military offence quite irrespective of all circumstances connected with it, so we must be arrested for it; but when the colonel comes to know the truth, it will all amount to nothing."

"Are you sure, Arthur?"

"Quite sure, Amelia. There is surely justice in the land. Now go. I will come to your father's house as soon as my duties will permit me; but I beg of you to go at once!"

"I will—I will. Farewell, Arthur. You are sure that you are in no danger?"

"None in the least, dear one—none in the least. Farewell!"

Amelia immediately left the spot, after hastily bidding adieu to the corporal and to Cockles. As for Flummery, he was much too glad to get out of the way of the sergeant's guard that was rapidly approaching, and which, for all he know to the contrary, might try to mix him up in the transaction in some way, and take him into custody likewise.

The guard came on with deliberation; and when close at hand, the sergeant cried "Halt!" and advanced at once to Arthur and his friends.

"I am sorry for it," he said, in a low tone; "but Captain Strachan has ordered your arrest. You must fall in, and follow us."

"All's right," said the corporal.

"Row-de-dow-dow," said Cockles.

"You are only doing your duty, sergeant," said Arthur, "and we are obliged to you for doing it kindly."

"Oh, it can't come to anything; you know," said the sergeant, "for, after, all it is of no consequene; only some notice must be taken of these things, for the sake of discipline, you see."

"Certainly," said Walter. "I quite expected a step of this sort, and I only hope that the colonel will settle the matter himself."

"That he will be sure to do, for it is the duty of an officer who orders a man into arrest to report the same, with all convenient speed, to the colonel, and doing so within twelve hours, or he himself commits a breach of discipline. Fall in at once. I was in hopes not to find you."

"It don't matter," said the coporal. "Here we are."

"Now, march—take open order. Prisoners, take your places.—March!"

Arthur and the corporal and Cockles found themselves then in custody, with a couple of soldiers before them, and a couple behind them; and so they were marched towards the barracks, instead of marching with the rest of the regiment in all the panoply and glory of colours, and drums, and fifes, and amidst the admiring glances of the gaping rustics.

The moment they got within the barrack-yard, they met, as if it were quite by accident, Captain Strachan.

"Oh, are these prisoners?" he said.

"Yes, sir," replied the sergeant.

"Ah! I recollect—they tried to desert in the lane, yonder?"

"No, sir," said Corporal Steady.

"Silence, scoundrel! So these are the three men, sergeant, who thought they would give us the slip?"

"No, sir," said Cockles.

The captain directed a withering glance at Cockles, and then added,—

"This is no time to show leniency to men who desert their colours. We must show an example of strict discipline to the regiment. Where did you find them, sergeant?"

"In the lane, sir."

"Oh, hiding, of course?—Ah!"

"No, sir," cried Cockles and the corporal at once.

"Silence!" cried Strachan, stamping his foot with rage. "How dare you answer me, rascals? I say, you were trying to desert along with that scoundrel there —Wilton!"

"Captain Strachan," said Arthur, "you know——"

"Nothing!" said the corporal, as he placed his hand over Wilton's mouth. "Nothing at all! Hold your tongue, Mr. Wilton, will you? One stray word of yours may commit a trifling affair into a serious offence."

"I thank you, Steady," said Arthur, "for preventing me committing myself. I forgot at the moment."

"So — so!" said Strachan, giving a fendish-like sort of laugh. "Upon my word, this is good. A nice set you all are. Place them in separate cells, sergeant, in the black-hole! Do you hear?"

"Yes, sir."

"Highly proper, no doubt," said a voice. "Certainly, sergeant. Captain Strachan would not give such an order but upon proper grounds. Take them away at once, sergeant, and let them be strictly kept upon prisoner's allowance."

Captain Strachan turned as if some one had struck him, and close to him he saw Colonel Percival and Major Cuthbert.

"Oh, colonel," he stammered. "I—I —that is, these men—these prisoners——"

"Have committed some very grave offence, no doubt, which you would have reported to me at once, Captain Strachan?"

"Yes, sir, I was coming to report it to you."

"And in the meantime they will go to the black-hole, and serve them right. I have no doubt they deserve much worse than that."

"Why, colonel," added Strachan, biting his lips with vexation, for there was a terrible tone of quiet irony about the colonel, "they have, to my humble judgment, committed an /offence. They tried to desert, sir."

"Indeed?"

"Yes, colonel, that is the offence."

"This is serious, and shall be seen to at once. If I find that there is good reason to think so of them, I will send them under a guard to head-quarters at once, and not keep them here another hour. They are a disgrace to the regiment. Bring them to the officers' guard-room, and I will see to this affair at once. You will have the goodness to come with me, Captain Strachan."

Corporal Steady gave Cockles a nudge with his elbow; and Cockles, when nobody, as he thought, saw him, made an imitation roll of the drum with his fists. The few soldiers who were within hearing of the slight colloquy could hardly keep from laughing, for they knew well enough, by the colonel's manner, that he was only having his joke at the expense of Captain Strachan, and that the whole affair would end in nothing. Strachan, if he had been cool and collected, would, no doubt, have adopted a very different course; but his temper was most completely thrown off its equilibrium, in the first instance, by the thought that he had it in his power to punish the very three persons whom he most hated in the regiment, all at once; and then, by the manner in which Corporal Steady and Cockles had constantly kept on saying, "No, sir!" to his charge of a wish to desert.

The colonel, with the major, led the way to the officers' guard-room, as it was called, which was a handsome apartment where the officers specially on duty sat and whiled away the time in conversation, or in a game at cards, or in any other way that their fancies and the opportunities they there had permitted them. Upon the walls of the room there was a tolerable library; and about it, take it for all in all, there was much elegance as well as comfort.

The colonel took a seat and motioned Strachan to do the same, and the prisoners were brought in and placed at the end of the apartment next to the door.

"These fellows belong to your company, of course, Strachan?" said the colonel.

"Yes, sir, I am sorry to say they do."

"Why, so am I."

"And so am I," said the major.

Captain Strachan looked from one to the other, and was half in the mind to say, "Gentlemen, are you making sport of me?" but he controlled the impulse; and then the colonel said—

"Well, sergeant, how was it that these fellows deserted?"

"Don't know, sir."

"You don't know? Why, I thought you knew all about it, and were their accuser and captor?"

"Oh no, sir. Captain Strachan sent me with a guard to the lane, sir, to take them, that is all I know of it."

"Oh, then, you knew were they were, Strachan?"

"Yes, I thought—that is, I suspected—"

"That comes to the same thing," said the major, quietly.

"I—that is, colonel, they left the ranks in a shady lane, and tried to make their way across the fields, you understand; therefore, as early as possible, I sent a sergeant's guard after them."

"And very proper, too. Did they resist, sergeant, or try to get away?"

"Oh dear, no, sir. Quite the contrary."

"Well, corporal, what do you say to this?"

"Your honour," said Corporal Steady, "in the first place, God bless your honour, and may you live to long and happy old age, to be the soldier's best friend, and the gallantest officer and the noblest gentleman that ever wore a sword."

"Amen !" said Cockles.

"My heart echoes that sentiment," said Arthur Wilton.

"You see, your honour," added the corporal, "as we were all marching up the lane, and thinking just as much about deserting as of taking the moon by assault, or of undermining the Tower of London, we saw a young lady on the top of a bank, holding on by the arm of an old tree, your honour, and suddenly down she went, your honour, and then she screamed out for help, and then Wilton here forgot that he was in the ranks, and made a rush to her aid."

"Well ?"

"Why, then, your honour, I, who ought to have remained, went too; and we found that the young lady would have been gored to death by a furious bull if we had not got into the field and saved her; and as soon as we did so, we all came back into the lane again."

"But what has the drummer to say?"

"Your honour," said Cockles, in a high, cracked voice, "when I saw Mr. Wilton and Corporal Steady a-going it over the hedge like mad, I went too; besides, I heard the young woman, your honour, crying out for help; and I hopes as the day, or the night either, will never come in old England, when a woman or a gal cries out help, and there's a man as has any heart in his busom as won't go and help her, but stops to say—'I mustn't, 'cos I'm on duty!'"

"Let me tell you, Mr. Drummer," said the colonel, "that that doctrine of yours is quite wrong, and at variance with military discipline. But I can't take your own statements of this affair without some corroborative evidence. Have you any witnesses to all this?"

"Not that I know of, sir," said Arthur Wilton; "but it is true."

"It is all false, colonel," said Captain Strachan. "I am sorry to say that it is so, but the fact is, there was a regularly organised plan to desert upon the part of all the three of them; I heard the young female they speak of call to Wilton, and they all tried to get across the fields, no doubt to be secreted in some farmhouse close at hand."

"But the bull, Captain Strachan?" said the colonel.

"There might have been a bull or a cow, or something of the sort, colonel, which impeded their progress. and now comes in very handily to eke out their story."

"I hope it won't come in," said the colonel. "But allow me to say, Captain Strachan, that in your zeal for the service, I think you have just a little mistaken the facts of this case."

"Oh, no, colonel, I can make no mistake in the matter. The facts are too plain to make any mistake about."

"Well, to me they appeared a little different, captain."

"To you, sir?"

"Yes, to me, for the fact is, that at the end of the lane Major Cuthbert and I paused to let the regiment march past us, and hearing a cry, I, being mounted, had an opportunity of looking over the hedge, and saw the whole affair.

"So did I," said the major.

"And our impression was," added the colonel, "decidedly in favour of the story told by Corporal Steady."

"Precisely," said the major. "I may say for my own part that I have no doubt at all upon the matter."

"Nor have I," continued the colonel; "for I recollected the transaction with some anxiety, considering that the men were in danger from the mad fury of the bull."

CHAPTER XXV.

ARTHUR IS RESTORED TO THE CONFIDENCE OF THE COLONEL.

WHEN the colonel uttered these words, Captain Strachan absolutely reeled again, and had he not succeeded in grasping by the back of a chair, the probability is that he would have fallen, so overcome was he by this sudden and most unexpected testimony in favour of the prisoners. He had had every reason in the world to believe that the colonel and the major were far enough off at the time of the affair in the lane and the field; and now to find that the whole had taken place immediately under their observation was more than a defeat to him, inasmuch as it clearly showed the revenge he had against the whole three of the prisoners, and that his great object was to destroy them, if possible.

The silence that succeeded the last words of the colonel was very ominous and awful indeed. Captain Strachan felt that it was his part to break it, and he did so in a choking tone of voice that sufficiently betrayed the agony he was in.

"Colonel," he said, "if you saw the transaction, and consider it blameless, of course that suffices. I had not that advantage."

"Indeed? I understood you that you had, Captain Strachan, for how could you know that these three prisoners had been in the open field at all, unless you saw the affair?"

"I saw too little of it."

"Ah! so it seems. Well, of course, now you are satisfied. Nothing but zeal for the service, I am quite certain, can aminate any officer of my reigment. But now I hope you are convinced that you are mistaken, and that you will be good enough to order the men to their duty."

"Not in your presence, colonel. I, I, that

is, you judge this affair, and, of course, any order must emanate from you.'

"Very good. You can go to your duty, prisoners; but, mark me, it was an offence to quit your ranks; and it is only in consideration of the fact that you did so by an evident feeling of gallantry to go to the aid of a female, that I am inclined to overlook this matter, for which your captain very properly placed you under arrest."

The prisoners bowed, and made a speedy exit.

"Row-de-dow! Row-de-dow-dow-dow-dow!" cried Cockles. "Here's a nice affair. Oh, dear—oh, dear! How Strachan did look, to be sure."

"Eyes right," said the corporal. "Don't speak too loud. He will owe us all one for this."

"That I fear," said Arthur Wilton. "The colonel happened to be near enough to serve us this time; but Strachan will pant for his revenge."

"Never mind, my boy, never mind," added the corporal. "You do your duty, and Colonel Percival will stand by you, and you can't come to much harm. Why, the colonel would have despised any man in his reigment who would not have done as we all did, when the young lady called out for help. I know him well enough for that; and if he had not seen that we were quite capable of conquering the bull, I shouldn't have been a bit surprised at seeing him in the field himself, to take it by the horns."

"Ah!" said Cockles, "you did better than that, corporal."

"How do you mean?"

"You didn't meddle with horns, you know; but you took the enemy in his rear, and produced no end of confusion."

"When Colonel Percival was alone with the major and Captain Strachan, there was rather an awkward silence for some few moments; and then Strachan said—

"I hope, colonel, that the little transaction in which I have had the misfortune to be mistaken will not have the effect of lowering me in your opinion?"

"Captain Strachan," said the colonel, "I feel myself compelled to say to you what I never yet said to an officer, and that is, I wish you would leave my regiment."

"Sir?"

"I say, I wish that you would leave my regiment. It is quite optional upon your part to construe my words into a personal offence; and if you do, you know that

I shall not shield myself under any mask to avoid the consequences. I repeat it, sir, that although I do not intend to take any further public or private notice of this affair, I wish you would leave the regiment."

"Very well, sir."

"You will leave it?"

"I will consider, and suit my own convenience."

The colonel rose, and walked to the door of the room, and the major followed him.

"Major Cuthbert, a word with you, if you please," said Strachan.

"I decline it, sir," said the major, and in another moment Captain Strachan was alone.

For a few moments he remained in the same position that they had left him in, and then he uttered a sound that more nearly approached a yell of rage than anything else in the human vocabulary. All his wildest evil passions were, for a few minutes, in the ascendant, and he roared out—

"What! am I to be perpetually foiled by this smooth-faced, fawning, damnable Wilton? Each time that I try to hit him does the weapon I use revert upon myself! Curses—curses on them all! I will have revenge—Ay, deep and bloody revenge. Curses on everybody and everything! Leave the regiment?—Ha! Leave the regiment? He wishes that I would leave the regiment, does he? I won't leave it.—No, I'll stick to it like a leech. I'll let them all see who they have got in the regiment. All has been child's play up to now; but, from this time, I will not rest till I have had my revenge. Leave the regiment? No, by h—l, I will not leave the regiment; but there are others who shall leave it, and by a blood-stained path, too."

Captain Strachan caught sight of himself in a mirror that was in the room, and he was startled at the demoniac look of his own face.

"This will not do," he said. "I must smother up my passion until, by its sudden blaze, I can destroy those whom I hate. I must show a smiling face to them all, and seem to be all that I am not. There shall be a slumbering volcano in my heart, that one day shall hurl destruction upon them all. I will dissemble, though, till then. Yes, I will dissemble. I'm glad I have got back to this place; now I can consult with Hunks. Yes, that villain will do anything for gold—Hunks is my man."

With all his anxiety to go to Huncks, the village lawyer, Captain Strachan found it impossible to leave the barracks until the evening had closed in upon the face of the landscape around, and before the several little events had taken place with regard to the persons in whom we are interested.

"Major Cuthbert," said the colonel to that officer, as they sat over their wine after dinner that day. "Pray put down the name of Corporal Steady for promotion to the next sergeantry that is vacant."

"It will give me a great pleasure to do so," said the major.

"I hope," said Captain Grant, who was sitting with them, "that you will let me have him in my company?"

"That I cannot do," said the colonel. "I make it a rule to keep a man even after he is promoted among his old companions if possible, unless he himself wishes the contrary, which is sometimes the case."

"That is very right, and very kind, too," said the major. "Now this Corporal Steady is one of the best men in the regiment, and is greatly esteemed by his fellows. There is not one among them I believe, who would not go through fire and water to serve him. But about Cockles. What do you mean to do with him?"

"Cockles is an original," said the colonel, laughing, "and I don't know what I can do with him further, than letting him have leave whenever he asks for it, and taking care that he is not imposed upon by Strachan."

"And Wilton?" said Captain Grant. "What of him?"

The colonel looked perplexed. "I am very much afraid," he said, "that I have done Arthur Wilton an injustice, and I begin to think that it is just possible Strachan may have made the extraordinary speeches to him that he reported, and made them, too, with the precise object that Wilton himself imputed to them."

"To get him out of your favour, colonel?"

"Precisely so. In which he succeeded, I regret to say."

"But did Wilton not think that Captain Strachan was serious in what he proposed to him?"

"Certainly not. The opinion of Wilton was, that Captain Strachan said such things to him on purpose to carry to me, that he, Wilton, should appear to me like the bearer of extravagant tales, and so have his general credit with me shaken, for a liar, of course, loses credit for all other qualities. The moment Wilton saw that I cooled towards him, he hit upon the truth at once, or what

I suspect now more than ever to be the truth."

"But the experiment we tried," said the captain; "Strachan did not commit himself then."

"Captain Grant—all craft, I suspect."

"Well, then, what do you mean to do as regards Wilton?" said the major.

"Get his discharge as soon as I can. I shall write to General Brotherton about it, and if I can get it I will; and in the meantime, I think I cannot do better than take him out of the ranks again, and re-instate him as my secretary and clerk. I think of having him in at once, and saying as much to him; for although fate has made Arthur Wilton a private soldier, he is a gentleman."

"Exactly."

"Well, then, I will send for him."

The orderly in attendance was summoned, and told to get Wilton as speedily as possible. There was no great difficulty in finding him, as he was with his two friends, Corporal Steady and Cockles, in close consultation about the probabilities and possibilities of the future, and in considering, too, by what means he, Wilton, was to get leave to quit the barracks to call upon Farmer Revis, as the ordinary mode, namely, by asking leave of his captain, was shut out to him, owing to that captain being the villain Strachan.

It was just at this juncture, when neither Steady nor Cockles could think of how to do it, that the colonel's orderly made his appearance.

"Wilton is wanted," he said.

"By whom?" said Arthur.

"The colonel."

"It's all right, then," cried Corporal Steady. "Attention! Eyes right! Dress and care for nobody. It's all right again, Arthur, my boy."

Cockles made a fierce drumming upon the table, and Wilton, with a pale and agitated countenance, followed the orderly to the presence of Colonel Percival.

"Wilton, sir," announced the orderly.

"Send him in," was the order, and in another moment Arthur was in the presence of his kind-hearted, although somewhat eccentric, colonel. Arthur drew himself up with military promptitude, and saluted his officer.

"Wilton," said the colonel, "I am afraid I have done you an injustice."

At these words, Wilton nearly fell to the floor, so affected was he to find that his character was, in the colonel's mind, being cleared of the mist which suspicion had surrounded it with.

"Sit down, Wilton."

"Sir—sir, I—colonel——"

He was too much affected to go on, and the colonel added in a kind tone of voice—

"You must forgive me, Mr. Wilton, for acting upon ideas and opinions which ninety-nine men out of a hundred would have had likewise in my place. It did seem so very impossible that Strachan should say what he did; but, really, now I am staggered, and from my soul, Wilton, I believe you."

"You may," said Wilton, in a voice that shook from emotion. "Captain Strachan is my deadly enemy, and he will yet destroy me."

"Oh, no. Have no such fear."

"He will, Colonel Percival. He or I will fall. I know not but that already I may be in the toils of his deadly hatred. Oh, it is terrible to have such an enemy, and to have nothing to offer to him but honesty and truth. I cannot use his weapons. The assassin triumphs, sir, while the unsuspecting man, with his open front to the foe, and his naked sword in his hand, is helpless."

The officers looked at each other for a few moments in silence, and then the colonel said—

"Believe me, Mr. Wilton, I am more distracted at all this than I can express to you. You see, I have nothing very definite to act upon, and although I have told Strachan that I wish he would leave the regiment—of course, this is private—yet I feel that I am not yet authorised to take steps to force him to do so."

"No, sir, I feel all that. He is too crafty for you and for me. He will soon concoct some plan that will be more efficient for my destruction than the last."

The colonel rose and paced the room for a few moments in silence; then stopping opposite to Wilton, he said, emphatically—

"Wilton, do not take so gloomy a view of your position. I will do all I can to shelter you from Strachan. In the first place, I will procure your discharge as soon as it is possible to do so; and until then, you can be with me as you were before this little misunderstanding, and so you will be out of the way of Strachan, and most entirely free from his control."

"Oh, Colonel Percival, how can I thank you! If the devotion of my life could only show you how grateful I am to you, I might hope then to do so; but I have no words in which I can clothe my feelings. You have saved me, I do think and hope."

"Well, then, take a glass of wine, Mr. Wilton, and don't think no more of

Strachan than you can possib'y help. Come, sit down."

"Colonel, I—I am a soldier, and you are my colonel."

"Oh, stuff! Understand me, Wilton. There is no man more than myself who stands up for the discipline of the army; but you are in a peculiar situation, you know, and, while no one is looking on, we can afford very well to treat you, Mr. Wilton, in your private capacity as a gentleman. I hope and trust nothing will ever again

CAPTAIN STRACHAN AND HUNCKS MATURING THEIR VILLANOUS PLANS.

occur to create the smallest distrust between us."

"Colonel Percival, I need not say how with all my heart I echo that hope," replied Wilton. "It was by a voluntary act of my own that I placed myself in the situation I now occupy, and I had no thought of avoiding its duties or responsibilities; least of all had I a thought of meeting with such pure and disinterested kindness as I have met with from you."

"Come—come, say no more about that,

but take a glass of wine, Wilton, and sit down with us comfortably."

CHAPTER XXVI.

ARTHUR WILTON'S AFFAIRS WEAR A SMILING ASPECT.

IT was quite impossible, even if Arthur Wilton had felt inclined for any foolish punctilio of rank, to refuse the colonel's kind offer. A happy hour was spent in the society of his officers, and, finally, Wilton asked for leave to visit the farmhouse, where all he most loved on earth was to be found.

"Certainly, Mr. Wilton," said the colonel. "Mind, you have a general leave to go whenever you like. It is not often that I shall want you, and if you are absent when I happen to do so, my affairs will wait, I dare say, very well till you come back to the barracks again."

"But you are not going to remain at the barracks," said the major, "are you?"

"No. I forgot that. I happen to fancy that our sojourn here will be for a considerable time, and, therefore, I am about renting a villa that is in the neighbourhood, where I shall reside, and where our interviews can be much more free and mutual than in the barracks."

"I shall be happy to attend upon you there," said Arthur, and then he left the apartment, and hurried to the farm of Riversdale.

Upon that evening there were two interviews between old acquaintances. The one was between Arthur Wilton and Amelia. The other was between Lawyer Hunks and Captain Strachan. We rather prefer giving precedence to the former.

The reader may imagine with what bounding steps Arthur made his way to the farmhouse. The distance seemed, to him, great, and yet never had he traversed it at such speed as upon that occasion. When he reached a little wicket-gate leading to the flower garden, at which he had often met Amelia, his heart beat with such rapidity, that he was compelled to pause to recover a little.

While he stood holding by the gate something came against him with such a bound that he was nearly thrown down, and in another moment Prince, the favourite dog, that was such a guard and companion to Amelia, was upon his hind feet almost round the neck of Wilton, and whining, and barking, and in very dog-like fashion testifying his joy to see him again.

"Ah, Prince, my poor fellow," said Arthur, as he caressed the huge creature. "I am, in truth, glad to see you."

Prince was in raptures; but suddenly he left Arthur and was off along the little gravelled path close at hand at such a rate, that Wilton was lost in wonder to know what was the meaning of it. In a few moments, however, back came Prince, barking and frisking about, and looking so delighted, that it was quite evident he had something upon his mind of a very gratifying tendency, indeed.

"Now, my good Prince," said Arthur, "let me pass you, for the path is narrow, and you contrive to block it up tolerably well."

"Bow-wow-wow!" cried Prince.

"Arthur!" said a voice. "Oh, Arthur, is it, indeed, you?"

"Amelia!"

Making a rush past Prince, which, by-the-by, the large, four-footed individual took in very good part, Arthur in another moment had his Amelia in his arms, and she was sobbing upon his breast.

For the space of about five minutes, now, they neither of them spoke. What need had they for speech? Although silent, did not their hearts speak in eloquent, natural language to each other? Ah, yes, and there was more expressed by that silent rapture that they both felt, now that they were together again, than the most laboured love-speeches could possibly have given utterance to.

At length, Arthur Wilton, in a low tone of agitation, spoke—

"You are better from your alarm of to-day? You are quite well, dear one?"

"Oh, yes—yes. And you, Arthur—you are happier?"

"I am, indeed! Much has happened since I saw you, love, to make me so. I am now again reconciled to Colonel Percival, and high in his confidence and good opinion."

"Thank Heaven! And that man—that Strachan?"

"Is in disgrace. He and I, Amelia, take it by turns. When I am fortunate, and the heavens are smiling upon me, he is in disgrace. When I fall, he rises as it were upon my ruin. But yet, I think the colonel knows him too well now to listen to any of his villanies."

"He should know him, Arthur."

"Depend upon it, he does. Ah! Amelia, did you think it possible that I might be at the old spot here, by the little gate?"

"I did, Arthur; and so Prince and I both waited for you, and he gave me notice that you were here."

"He is a noble fellow, is Prince."

"Bow-wow!" cried Prince, and he began dancing round the young lovers in quite an ecstacy of real delight.

"But, Arthur," added Amelia, "when I left the lane after that perilous encounter with Mr. Shorter, as they call him, did I, or did I not see you taken away as a prisoner?"

"Ah! you broke the spirit of your word by looking back?"

"I did, indeed!"

"Well, then, I must tell you all about it, and it will serve to strengthen an argument that I have often heard you insist upon, namely, that out of evil springeth good."

"Oh, yes, that is so true, Arthur; but it is out of seeming evil only, you see—those kind of circumstances which we in our feeble wisdom mistake for evil, but which, in good truth, are not so. But tell me all."

Arthur then related to the attentive Amelia all that had taken place at the barracks, and how signally Captain Strachan had failed in punishing him, and the corporal and Cockles. He concluded by saying, "And now, Amelia, I cannot help thinking that a great blow and discouragement is given to Strachan by all this, and that I have achieved over him a signal victory."

"I tremble, Arthur."

"Nay, dear Amelia, what can he do?"

It will be seen that Arthur reasoned differently with Amelia regarding the power of mischief of Captain Strachan than he did with the colonel, but the fact was that he wished to give as much peace and security as possible to Amelia, while, with the colonel, he reasoned as one man would with another, just upon his emotions.

"Yes, Arthur," she said, "I do, indeed, tremble to think what that desperate and bad man may in his feelings of revenge think of doing. He is more dangerous now than ever to you."

"Oh, no—no. There is one thing that will always keep such a man as Captain Strachan within bounds."

"And what is that, Arthur?"

"Considerations for his own safety. Such a man is, and must, in the natural order of things, be a coward; therefore, he will always be restricted in what he does, by a dread of mischief to himself. I grant you, that if Strachan, with all the wish to injure me, had positive recklessness regarding the consequences to himself, he would indeed be most dangerous."

"Do you really think this?"

"Oh, yes, Amelia. Why should you doubt that I do? But, come— we will find some more pleasing topic of conversation than the villain Strachan."

For more than half an hour now they strolled to and fro in the little pathway, and Prince regularly marched behind them, looking as gratified as possible, and no doubt fancying that he was performing some very extraordinary duty upon the interesting occasion. Amelia informed Arthur that but little change had taken place in the farm and the village since he had left. She told him that she thought his, Arthur's, situation preyed very much upon the mind of her father, for that his temper was not nearly so agreeable as it had been; and then she begged him to come into the house and speak to her father.

"Yes," said Arthur, "I will do that with pleasure; and I hope that he will see cause from my appearance, as to feel himself more at his ease regarding me."

"It is kind and good of you to say that, Arthur, and to put on an air of content when you cannot but feel much depression."

"Do not fancy that, Amelia; the confidence that I have in your love, and the joyful hope of now seeing you often, since Colonel Percival has given me such an amount of liberty, really make me feel happy."

"Yes, Arthur, we will meet often; I feel that now I am bound to you for ever and ever; and it would be but a poor return for all that you have done for me and for my father, were I affectedly to conceal from you that my heart is wholly yours."

How could Arthur Wilton be otherwise than happy with such a being to love him as the fair Amelia! With her hand tenderly pressed in his, they walked towards the farm-house, followed by Prince, who, when they got near to the old porch, which in the summer-time was such a peaceful garland of fine flowers, he set up such a barking, that Mr. Revis came out to see what was the matter, and met his daughter and Arthur on the threshold.

"Arthur Wilton!" he exclaimed.

"Yes, Mr. Revis," said Arthur, holding out his hand. "Allow me to hope that you are quite well, and that everything thrives upon the old farm."

"Come in—come in, Arthur, come in."

It was evident that Mr. Revis was too deeply affected to say much just then, and Arthur followed him into the sitting-room that he knew so well. It was that sa room in which the money had been p that had saved the farm from the clutches of Strachan.

Then, making a great effort, Mr. Revis turned and took Arthur by the hand, as he said, in choking accents—

"Mr. Wilton, what can I say to you? What can you expect me to say to you, now, when I feel that—that——"

"Say no more, sir," interrupted Wilton. "I can well imagine all that you feel, and would express; but believe me, Mr. Revis, I do not feel unhappy. I will not say that I have not had some disagreeables to contend with; but let me again and again assure you that I do not regret the step I took when I enlisted."

"Oh, Wilton, do not say that."

"It is true, sir. I hope and believe that I saved your home by so doing."

"You did, indeed."

"Then I am quite satisfied. Colonel Percival tells me that he will try all he can do to get my discharge, and in the meantime he makes my situation more than tolerable; so let me beg of you, while you grant to me your fullest confidence and friendship, not to think of me as one who is suffering for your sake."

"It is noble and kind of you to speak in such a way, Arthur, to me; but Amelia gathered from the tone of your letters, particularly your last one, that your mind was most distressed."

"I know not what I wrote. Say no more of my letters. There was a time when everything around me seemed black and dreary, and then I wrote I knew not what. You will, I am sure, never say anything further to me of my letters, Amelia?"

"If you wish it, no."

"I do wish it, indeed, for I feel that they were written under such circumstances of depression, that they did not rightly convey my impressions and opinions."

"It is a relief, Arthur, to hear you say that."

After some further conversation, during which Arthur exhibited quite a cheerful mind, Mr. Revis looked wonderfully relieved, for, to tell the truth, he had pictured to his imagination the young man lamenting that he had sacrificed himself in the manner that he had to save his home; while he, Mr. Revis, although he would give half he possessed to place Arthur Wilton in the same situation that he had been before the day he enlisted, was utterly helpless in the matter.

Amelia looked at her father's altered demeanour with eyes of delight, and her grateful feelings towards Wilton were highly enhanced by his present conduct at the farm.

"And no changes have taken place in the village?" said Arthur.

"No. Everything remains as usual," replied the farmer. "I had a visit from Mr. Huncks, who came, as he said, to hold out the right hand of friendship and consolation to me."

"But surely, sir, you did not stoop to speak to such a man?"

"Well, I think I said something, and then I sent Prince to show him off the premises, for which he threatened me with an action; but I have heard nothing of him since."

"The villain," said Arthur. "There can be no doubt but that he is the base accomplice of Captain Strachan, and that they both were most intent upon wrenching your farm from you, by means of that extraordinary bond—that—that——"

"That must still, in all its particulars remain a secret," said the farmer.

"Pardon me, sir, for alluding to it. I spoke rapidly, and without thought."

"Say nothing of it, Arthur. It is a painful secret with which I do not wish to burthen either your mind or Amelia's. The time will come when you will both know all; but until that time, do not, I beg of you, ask me anything concerning it. Oh, Heaven, no! I cannot tell you. My heart is ready to break as I think of it. It haunts me night and day!"

Mr. Revis rose and paced the room in great agitation, and Arthur Wilton felt the greatest regret that he had named the deed, and so awakened such a train of acute feeling.

Amelia wept, and, for the life of him, Arthur Wilton did not know what to say. At length, however, Mr. Revis stopped short in his agitated pacing the room, and in a voice of much tenderness, he said—

"Amelia, do not weep, and you, Mr. Wilton, forgive this ebullition of feeling upon a subject I cannot help feeling strongly upon; I hope that for the future I shall be able to combat such feelings as these. We will say no more upon the subject."

"Not a word, sir," said Arthur.

For about a couple of hours now, Arthur Wilton enjoyed the society of her whom he loved; and but for the fact that he was in his regimentals, he might have imagined that all that had taken place in regard to his position in the army was but a dream, and that, as of old, he was seated by the fire-side of the farm, and looking into the sweet eyes of Amelia. Truly, that evening was the happiest one that had passed for

Arthur for many a day, and he looked at Amelia, as he repeated softly—

"The sun of a pure joy, dear one, is now shining upon us."

CHAPTER XXVII.

CAPTAIN STRACHAN CALLS UPON MR. HUNCKS, AND THEY BOTH HAVE AN ALARM.

WE feel a sensation of regret at turning from the fire-side of Farmer Revis, and where there were such pure hearts, in order to follow Captain Strachan in the tortuous path of his iniquities; but it is requisite that we should do so.

As soon as his regimental duty would permit him so to do, Captain Strachan muffled himself up in a cloak, and slouching his cap over his eyes as much as possible, he went towards the residence of Mr. Huncks.

It is not saying too much when we say, that that most unworthy lawyer had got about the best house in the place. It was his, too, although the way by which he had got possession of it was not exactly such as would come to any one of a right thinking frame of mind. It was the old story. The once owner of the house got into a little pecuniary difficulty; Mr. Huncks lent him a third of the value of the house; and then followed his residence in it—a long bill—discounts—and finally a settlement of the affair by Mr. Huncks agreeing to accept the house as a set-off against all other claims, and quietly and legally — oh, so legally!—having the freehold himself.

We believe that such is the ordinary way by which lawyers acquire house property now a-days, as well as in the days that have long gone past.

Probably the wily and unprincipled attorney had some idea that he might during the evening receive a visit from his friend, the captain, since the regiment had arrived again at its old quarters, a fact which was well known to Mr. Huncks, in common with the whole neighbourhood. Certain it is, that that highly legal character was by the garden-gate of his own house when Captain Strachan reached it, and they were face to face with each other in the gloom of the evening before either could say exactly who it was.

"Mr. Huncks, I think," said Strachan.

"Ah, yes," replied the lawyer. "I think I have the pleasure of seeing, although very dimly, my excellent friend, Captain Strachan."

"Yes, confound you."

"Ah, now, indeed, I know him, for he always has something civil to say. I thought, do you know, at first, in the dark, mind you, that it was some gentleman."

"Huncks, it is no use for fox to snarl at fox. If it comes to that, my best plan will be to throttle you at once."

"Or remain to blow up the secret of your rascalities, bargaining only for conditions, and pardon for myself."

"Pho!—bah! Why have we commenced these snarlings?"

"I don't know, captain."

"Then let there be an end to them. How are you, Huncks?"

"Pretty well, Captain Strachan; how are you? Walk in, if you please. I am glad to see you, to tell the honest truth."

"Did you ever do such a thing?"

"What thing?"

"Tell the honest truth, Huncks?"

"Why, yes, by accident, sometimes, and always when it answers my purpose better than a lie. I have found out, captain, with all due consideration for lying, though, that when you can tell the truth, with an equal regard for your own interest, it always pays better in the long run."

"Indeed?"

Captain Strachan, with a sneer upon his face that he did not take the trouble to suppress even after he had been shown into the lawyer's private room, entered the house. Huncks conducted him to the clients' room, which was rather a seedy kind of apartment, with three very old chairs in it—a library table, that looked as though it were the first rude experiment that was ever made to construct such an article of furniture; and nothing on the floor but a slip of exceedingly well-worn-out oil-cloth.

A miserable fire was faintly flickering in the grate of this room, and a tall fender kept everybody at a respectful distance from it.

"Now, captain," said Mr. Huncks, "sit down and make yourself comfortable."

"Comfortable, did you say?"

"I did, indeed, captain."

"How the devil do you expect that anybody is to make himself comfortable in a dog-kennel like this? Come, come, Huncks, you have decent, comfortable enough rooms in the house. Why do you bring me into this one?"

"This is the business room, captain,"

"Stuff! you know well that our business is not of the usual kind."

"Really, you surprise me, captain."

Captain Strachan rose and took two steps towards the door. Then he paused and turned, and looked the lawyer full in the face, as he said—

"I don't know what has come over you, Mr. Huncks, or what particular game you are now playing; but it is requisite that I should have a complete understanding with you. We have worked together in affairs before now, that were not exactly what a judge and jury would applaud. If you are inclined to cry off, and to let our connection together cease from this time, say so at once, and I shall know how to act."

"Why, Captain Strachan, as to that—"

"No equivocation, sir; answer me at once. You have already been well paid, and I know that you will be well paid for what you do, and if you aid me, you shall be so; but I will not have a man as an accomplice——"

"Accomplice, captain?"

"Yes, that is the word—I will not have a luke-warm accomplice. Answer me at once; are you willing to aid me as heretofore by your advice and assistance, or not?"

"I will—I will."

"Then what in the name of Lucifer do you mean by this ambiguous sort of reception of me? Are you mad, that you think it worth while to get up a feeling in my mind that we cannot work well together?"

"No— no; but, you see, captain, after all, what is to pay me in the time to come? There is no more money coming from my old quarters that I know of, now that Farmer Revis has paid his two thousand pounds on the bond, you understand; and I would just put it to you as a man of sense, to ask you what motive I could have for occupying myself with your little affairs without good profit coming from them?"

"Oh, that's it, is it, Hunks?"

"Well, that is about it."

"Be at your ease upon that score, and listen to me."

"Well?"

"As sure as you are now a living man, you shall yet be my agent, and have the care of the Riversdale property."

"You don't mean that?"

"I do. I tell you I do, and it shall be done. I stake my life upon it."

"But not mine?"

"Oh, no, no. I will run all the risk myself, I tell you. All I want of you is such advice and assistance in this matter as will enable me a little to carry out my designs; and, besides, I may want to lodge with you other property that nobody in all the world will think of coming here to look for."

"Oh, well, in that case, if there is no danger to me."

"Concerning that part of the business, you will be the best judge yourself, and no man is better able to decide such a question than you."

"Thank you for the compliment. Do you think that there is any chance of money if you should not succeed in your sanguine expectations regarding the Riversdale property?"

"There is a certainty of a large sum."

"Oh, that will do. Pray, Captain Strachan, follow me."

The attorney rose and led the way from the room. Captain Strachan followed him without a word, and they were soon in a handsomely furnished parlour, where there was every luxury and convenience that could be crammed into it. Hr. Huncks unlocked a chiffonniere, and took from it a couple of decanters of wine and some glasses, which he placed upon the table, and then pointing to an easy chair, he said to the captain.

"Be seated, my old and valued friend, and pray let me know what it is that I can do for you."

"Oh, much," said Strachan, "for you are a clever man, Mr. Huncks, and you know the law well."

"I flatter myself I do a little."

"In the first place, then, you have no business, for you happen to know, that if you had not retired to this rather obscure place, and so got out of the way of observation, you would, for certain little malpractices, have been struck off the rolls by the Lord Chancellor."

"Hem !"

"That you admit?"

"I never admit anything, Captain Strachan. It is a bad practice to admit anything. You should always put your enemies upon the proof, even if it should only relate to the time of day, or the state of the weather."

"Well, it don't matter; I say it, and you know it to be true, that you have no business, and that the two thousand that you have had of me is the largest sum you have seen for a long time past. Come, now, that is the fact."

"Captain Strachan, you will allow me to remark, that I am an independent man— that this house is my own, and a very pretty little property it is—that I likewise own property in this village, and likewise in London; therefore, business is not of that importance to me that it might otherwise be."

"Exactly; but you have no sort of objection to improve your property, Mr. Huncks, I know, and, therefore, let us work ogether, I to get revenge, and you to get money."

"Very good, sir. Take a glass of wine."

"Thank you. Here's success to roguery."

"Hush! Hush! You are much too candid, captain. I always drink to virtue, which I believe is its own reward. That is to say, I never heard of anybody getting anything by it in this world, from any other source."

"Nor I either. You are right, Huncks. And now tell me what has occurred here since I was last in the locality."

"Nothing."

"Well, that's shortness. But has no one been down to the— the marble quarry, eh?" Captain Strachan lowered his voice, and looked anxiously around him. "Has no awkward troublesome gossip-producing discovery, taken place, eh?"

"About what is down below there?"

"Yes—yes."

"None. All's right; and if the winter goes by" — here Mr. Huncks lowered his voice likewise, and looked uneasily about him— "if the winter that is coming goes by without any discovery, it will be all right enough, I take it. Decomposition, and the rain, and the snow, and the floods, and streams, will knock it to pieces."

"The body?"

"Yes—yes. Oh, you know what I mean."

The captain nodded; and then, as he drew his chair a little closer across the fireplace towards Mr. Huncks, he added, in a tone a little above a whisper—

"I have seen him since!"

Mr. Huncks gave a great start, and upset his glass of wine.

"Who? Who?"

"Clinton."

"No—no, you don't mean that, captain? You are only joking? Tell me at once that you are only joking, captain!"

"Do I look like it? Cast your eyes upon me, Huncks, and then ask yourself if I look like a man who is indulging in a joke."

"Why, no, I can't say you do."

"Then I tell you again, that I have seen him since, and one object of my coming to you to-night is, to ask your opinion as to what I am to think of the affair, with all its attendant circumstances, which I will now detail to you, and for which I beg to bespeak your earnest attention."

"Yes," gasped Mr. Huncks. "Oh, dear, yes."

"Then listen. I tell you, I saw him, and these were the circumstances." Captain

Strachan hereupon related to the lawyer the appearance of Clinton in his room at the barracks at Exeter, as it is already well known to the reader, and ended by sayng,— "Now, Mr. Huncks, that is the whole story. I do not like to give way to the idea that this was a supernatural appearance, for if once we let one's mind take that course, there is no end of the horrors that it may give rise to; and yet, if anything, I rather more dread to think that it was really Clinton."

The lawyer was silent.

"Why do you not speak? It is your firm and unprejudiced opinion that I seek in this affair, Mr. Huncks."

"Then I will give it to you. The appearance was not supernatural."

"Ah, you think not?"

"Certainly not; and it was not real."

"Not real, and yet not supernatural? You speak in riddles, Mr. Huncks. What is it you would have me believe to be your opinion of this most horribly sad and perplexing matter?"

"Just this, captain, that you owe the appearance entirely to your own imagination, and nothing else. That is my opinion of it."

Captain Strachan drew a long breath.

"Oh, if I could only come fairly and entirely to such a belief, Huncks!"

"I have."

"Yes, but you did not see those eyes glaring at you, as they glared at me—you did not see the wild looking face, with its long matted hair—you did not see the blood that was about the lips—no—no, you would go mad—quite mad if you had seen what I have."

"Hold your tongue, will you?"

"Wherefore?"

"Because I do not like at this time of night for anybody to go on speaking in that sort of way to me; I am alone in the house, with the exception of my housekeeper and the boy that runs the errands. Don't go on in that sort of way, Captain Strachan, don't."

"But it is all true. I tell you, I did see him, Huncks. It's of no use your telling me that it was a matter of imagination; I saw him as plainly as—as—Oh, God!— Help! Mercy! There he is now! Mercy!"

"Murder!" shouted Huncks, as he bounced off his chair, and looking in the direction of the window, he saw the dim outline of a face on the outside, flattened against a pane of glass.

CHAPTER XXVIII.

A FESTIVAL TAKES PLACE IN THE VILLAGE.

THE consternation of Captain Strachan at this most alarming appearance at the window of the room was immense. He made a rush to try to leave the apartment, but as Mr. Huncks was actuated by the same feeling, and tried to do the same thing, it was not very successful, and the two scoundrels only impeded each other in their efforts to escape.

"Let me go," said Huncks. "Let me go, captain."

"Go to the devil," cried Strachan, "so that I get out of this place."

"Stop, oh, stop," said Huncks, suddenly. "We are both mad."

"You are, if you like—I am not. This is some trick of yours, Huncks, I feel assured."

"Upon my soul, captain, it is not; but I say, we are both mad to allow ourselves to be scared in this manner. There is no good to be done by it, and there may be harm. Here we are both in the passage outside the room, to be sure, but, after all, we are by no means sure that we have not been frightened by a mere shadow."

"The shadow of the dead !"

"No, captain, I don't believe in ghosts, I never did, and I am not going to make the remainder of my life miserable by beginning now. I will go back. After all, it may only be some one attracted by curiosity to the window, and our fears—I may, perhaps, say our consciences—may give him the resemblance to Clinton."

"Hush! do not name him. I am faint !"

"You faint, and a soldier?"

"Silence ! I can face any mortal danger well enough. I am not a coward, Mr. Huncks; but I do not like, I own, to have anything to do with the dead."

"Captain Strachan, listen to me. It is necessary for our safety that we should know who this intruder is."

"No doubt—no doubt."

"The only way to do so is to resume our station in the room we have so recently left. It is possible that, be he whom he may, he will come again."

"Well ?"

"You have arms with you."

"How know you that ?"

"Because I am quite sure that your many fears, captain, never permit you to move without them. My advice, then, is, that we both go back to the room, and appear to be engaged in conversation as before; but that you keep an eye upon the window, and at the first appearance of any one there, I would have you fire one of your pistols."

"Yes, I have pistols."

"I knew it ; and I know, too, that you could not possibly make a better use of them."

"I will think. It may be so; and I agree with you most entirely, that if it be Clinton, and not his apparition, it is impossible that I could make a better use of my arms. Oh, Huncks, if he still live——"

"Well, if he still live, what then ? I do not, after all, see that there is such great danger to me or to you, even if he should still be in life."

Captain Strachan shuddered, and evading the question of the danger they might both be in provided Clinton were in life, he said, in a low, querulous tone of voice—

"And yet, Huncks, would you not have sworn to his destruction in the old marble quarry?"

"I would."

"And I too. I thought, and until very lately, you cannot think what a consolation the thought was to me, that there he lay festering and decaying in his blood. I thought each night that I went to rest, there will be another few hours added to the time which must elapse ere decomposition claims that body for its own ; and when I arose in the morning, I asked myself, 'How does it look now ?'"

"Ah, a pleasant question, truly."

"Yes ; but not so horrible, for I understand your taunt. I say, it was not so horrible a question as that which now proposes itself to me in the words—'Does he live ?'"

"Ah, well, I cannot help it."

"Who said you could ? But I have made, now, a thorough determination."

"What may that be?"

"To search the quarry to-night. Will you join me ?"

"The attorney shrugged up his shoulders, as he replied—

"I suppose I may confess that I don't like the job ?"

"Confess what you please, so that you come. Is it a bargain between us? Do we understand each other upon that point? Will you accompany me to the quarry ?"

"I will consider ; but in the meantime let me beg that you will accompany me into this room again, and it may be that something will happen that will render such a visit to the marble quarry of no importance to us."

"I am ready."

They both now returned to the room, and the first thing that Captain Strachan did was to fill himself a bumper glass of Mr. Huncks' wine, which he drank at a draught, and then he felt a little more courageous than he had been.

"Let him come," he said, "I am prepared for him, be he man or devil, I care not."

CORPORAL STEADY RUMINATING ON THE AFFAIRS OF ARTHUR WILTON.

"Allow me to advise," said the attorney, "that you do not keep too fixed a gaze upon the window. as, if you do, that may have the effect of defeating our intentions. Trust to me to keep the watch, will you?"

"Yes—yes. You will do it better than I."

"I think so. And now, captain, what were we talking of? Ah! There he is again."

Captain Strachan had his hand buried in the breast of his apparel, and upon Mr. Huncks saying this, he suddenly drew it out, with a pistol in his grasp, and fired at a dim object that looked like a human head at the window.

"Fiend !" he said, as he fired. "If you can die another death, you have it now. I do not miss my aim often."

"Ha ! ha !" laughed some one upon the outside, but the laugh had no mirth in it. It did not sound human, and the wild, sardonic tones made the heart even of Mr. Huncks turn cold in his bosom.

Captain Strachan had risen immediately upon firing his pistol, but when that dreadful laugh come upon his ears, he fell back into his chair again, as if he too had been shot.

"God ! What is that?" he gasped.

"Murder !" cried Huncks, as he made a sudden dash and hid himself under the table.

The concussion that the explosion of the pistol had given to the air of the rather small room had the natural enough effect of putting out the light, so that the two worthies, or we might rather call them unworthies, were in total darkness, and all that could be heard, now that the echo of the dreadful laugh had died away, was the rain pelting upon the window-frames.

"Where are you ?" cried Captain Strachan, after a few minutes of intense and painful silence. "Where are you ?"

"Nowhere," said Huncks.

"Yes, you are in the room. Speak again."

"Oh, don't."

"Don't what? What do you mean?"

"Don't kick so; I am under the table, my good friend. Is there any danger now? Oh—oh—oh !"

"So, you are under the table, are you?" said Strachan, plunging with his feet in that direction to the great affliction of the attorney. "Take that, then, for your cowardice, and come out. Get a light, will you? Are we to remain in the dark now, because you are a coward?"

"But that laugh—Was it a laugh?"

"Curses on you, get a light."

The attorney scrambled out of the room, and on the landing outside the door he found his household assembled in the shape of the old woman who attended upon him, and the boy who went his errands. They had both been naturally enough alarmed at the report of the pistol, and their impression was that Mr. Huncks had at last compounded with his conscience by committing suicide.

"What do you do here?" he cried.

"Oh, sir," said the old woman, "we thought——"

"Stuff! I don't care what you thought. Give me that light. Now go to the kitchen again, and never think, whatever you may hear above here."

"Very good, sir; but you see, Mr. Huncks, we thought——"

The attorney having possessed himself of a light, paid no further attention to the garrulity of the old woman, but at once entered the apartment again, where he and Strachan had been holding their guilty conference together.

Strachan looked more pale and haggard than the attorney. Probably he was a man of stronger passions, and, perhaps, considered that he had a greater stake in the proceedings that he meditated than Huncks had. He did not speak, however, but observed the motions of the attorney in silent wonder.

The first thing that Huncks did, was to draw the window curtain close, and then he took a hat and placed it on the back of a chair rather closely, so that, shining through the curtains, it should look like some one's head. Turning then to Strachan, he said—

"We will go round now, if you please, captain, by the garden and through my little greenhouse, and so reach to the outside of the window, and who knows but we may yet make some discovery?"

"Think you so?"

"I don't think one way or the other, but there is a chance, you know. You either killed the fellow or you did not. If you did, there he is—if you did not, captain, why, he is very likely to come again; and in that case I am quite sure you have another pistol ready for service."

Strachan nodded.

"Ah! I know it. Come on."

"I will follow you, Huncks, you have more courage in an emergency than I gave you credit for."

"And you"—— less, the attorney was going to say, but, as Mr. Flummery would say he thought that it was better not to be "aggrawating," so he did not say it, and the captain very prudently took no notice of the hiatus in his speech, but followed him from the room.

The intention of the attorney was to get into the garden without even allowing his servants to know that he was there ; so he trod lightly, and making his way into a little apartment, the window of which was a French one, and from which the garden could be easily reached, he opened it, and whispering to Strachan to tread with care, they were both in another moment in the open air.

"This way, captain," said the attorney in a low tone. "Keep to the right, and we shall get behind some thick currant bushes, and soon be in the part of the garden we wish."

Strachan, with more respect for the attorney's tact and courage than he had ever had before, followed him closely to the right; and they soon, although at the distance of the width of a little lawn, came into sight of the window of the room within which they had left the light burning.

The curtains were but of a flimsy material, and permitted the light to shine through them pretty strongly. The shadow of the hat was very plainly perceptible, and might very well, indeed, be mistaken for a head.

"There, you see," said Huncks, "all is right in the room."

"Confound the room," said Captain Strachan; "that is of no consequence. It is what takes place out of the room that I look to. Do you see anything on this bit of lawn that is before us, Huncks?"

"Nothing. Do you?"

"Not I; and, therefore, the enemy has escaped, if it were mortal at all. What do you advise now?"

"Why, they do say, that the advise of a lawyer and a doctor for which nothing is paid, is good for nothing; but as you, no doubt, will have no objection to my putting the affair down in your bill, I advise that we wait here for some little time behind this pear tree, and see if any one comes to the window again to try to peep in. If they do, why then, my dear sir, you can try the thickness of their skull with a pistol bullet."

"Then I will wait. Oh, that the regiment had never come back to this place! I was fool enough to rather rejoice at it at first; but now I would rather be anywhere than at this village."

"Well, that don't seem kind."

"Why not?"

"Because to-morrow there is to be a fete, or entertainment, or festival, call it which you will, given in the village, in honour of the regiment, and I expect there will be tubs of ale drank, and a few bonfires lighted in the evening, and the whole place in an uproar."

"To-morrow?"

"Yes But how oddly you speak. What can it concern you, I wonder?"

"No how. But I tell you, Huncks, that I am satisfied our watch here will be futile. I am more than ever anxious to visit the quarry."

"I will meet you, then, at midnight at its brink."

———

CHAPTER XXIX.

THE MIDNIGHT VISIT TO THE QUARRY IN SEARCH OF THE DEAD.

CAPTAIN STRACHAN now seemed as anxious to get out of the garden of the lawyer as if he felt certain that he would be charged something handsome for every minute that he remained within its precincts.

Perhaps, if he had such a supposition as that, he was not far wrong.

Mr. Huncks watched him as he retreated down the lane at the back of the house, and then, when he was quite sure that he was out of ear-shot, he said—

"I feel pretty confident that you will be hanged some of these days, Captain Strachan, but I hope to make something more out of you before that catastrophe takes place, rogue as you are. Well, well, what is a man to do in this world but make money? for is not the worship of wealth, after all, one of the first lessons that the world takes care to teach him? To be sure it is."

With this piece of practical philosophy, which it would be very difficult to gainsay, Mr. Huncks retreated to his house to make such preparations as might be needful for his midnight expedition with Strachan to the old quarry.

The attorney was quite as curious as Captain Strachan could possibly be to discover if Clinton were dead or alive; although, probably, he did not view the solution of that mystery with the same alarm that Strachan did, and, therefore, was it that he consented to accompany him upon the uncomfortable, if not perilous expedition to the old marble quarry.

That the captain had missed the person whom he had fired at at the window, Mr. Huncks fully believed, for he did not, after all, share in the superstitious feelings of Strachan, although it is a wonder that he did not, for superstition is generally one of the most prominent adjuncts of criminality.

"Yes," added Huncks, "I will meet him at the quarry, and I will satisfy myself of the fact of the life or the death of this fellow, Clinton, who, after all, may be a hinderance to the captain carrying on that little nice concern, which in its results will certainly have the effect of filling my pockets."

It was necessary that Captain Strachan should show himself at the barracks in the course of the evening, before he should leave for the purpose of meeting the attorney upon the brink of the quarry; so he went at once to the quarters of the troops.

Two or three of the soldiers whom he met on his road, took good care to salute him with the most careful preciseness, and the sentinel at the gate of the barracks did the same.

Just within the gate, Captain Strachan met Corporal Steady, and it was really quite a sight to see how Steady drew himself up to salute the man whom he held in such contempt.

Cockles was close at hand, and when the captain had passed, he said to Steady—

"I stood up in the dark of this doorway, Steady, for I felt as if I couldn't salute that vagabond."

"Then you are wrong, Cockles."

"Wrong? Why, you know as well as I do what a bad man he is."

"Yes, the man is, Cockles; but it was the captain I saluted, not the man."

"Eh?"

The distinction which the corporal was drawing between the individual and his rank, was rather too fine for Cockles, and he looked puzzled.

"Now let me explain to you what I mean," said Steady. "Of course you are a loyal subject, Cockles."

"In course."

"Well, you cry out 'God save the king!' and all that sort of thing, and I would just ask you what you mean by it?"

"What I mean by it?"

"Yes; what idea have you when you say 'God save the king?'"

"Why, that I mean the king to be saved."

"No you don't."

"Oh, don't I?"

"No, Cockles, you don't. It don't matter one straw to you whether the king is saved or——"

"Stop, that's flat treason."

"Well, I won't say it; but you know what I mean. It isn't the king, but the situation—the institution of royalty that you want saved, because it seems to work well with us Englishmen. The king, as an individual, is no more to you and to me, or to any one except himself, than Captain Strachan; but we find a captain to a company in a regiment a very good thing, so we salute the captain, not the man, just as we cry out 'God save the king,' meaning the king as a king, and not the individual who happens to hold the situation at the present time, you see."

"Oh, I begin to see."

"I thought you would."

"Row-de-dow-dow! I understand all about that, Steady, my boy; but still, a king, you know, is a king, and a queen is a queen, and not like a captain, whose son or daughter has no more to do with the regiment after he is dead than the man in the moon."

"Ah!"

"How do you get over that, Steady?"

"This-a-ways," said the corporal, assuming an oratorical attitude. "If the crown was not hereditary, there would be such a row at the death of one king to know who should be the next, that we should all be in hot water."

"Then, do you mean to tell me that the king's son or the king's daughter comes to the crown just for the sake of peace and quietness?"

"Just so."

"And not by the grace of God, as they say on the shillings, at all?"

"Certainly not, Cockles."

"Oh, well, I never! Row-de-dow-dow! I'm bothered if ever I thought of that before."

Whilst Cockles was thus taking a lesson in the philosophy of king-craft, Captain Strachan had taken his way to the officers guard-room, where there were some three or four officers of the regiment taking their ease upon the comfortable chairs there provided; but the moment he stepped into the room, up they all got, and off they went in a moment, as if he had the plague, and they were afraid of contagion if they only so much as remained in the same room with him.

The expression of the face of Captain Strachan when he thus found himself alone, was truly horrible. He felt that the words the colonel had spoken to him must have been freely reported to all the officers, and that, henceforth, he would be shunned like a moral pestilence, and be compelled to lead a lonely life.

"Well," he muttered, "be it so. The colonel all but hinted to me that he would fight me, if I were so inclined. I am much obliged — oh, very much obliged; but I know a better trick than that. Oh, a much better trick. Ha—ha!"

The captain now repaired to his own quarters, and, although he met several of the officers of the regi ment as he went, not one of them so much as looked at him, or paid the smallest attention to him. They saw him as though they saw him not.

This was truly anything but a delightful state of things for any man to endure in a regiment, and such as rendered his prolonged stay in it quite impossible. Probably, if Strachan had not had some ulterior designs, he would have that very night resigned his commission, or taken steps to sell out of the army; for an exchange into any other regiment, with the character he would take with him, would be completely out of the question.

His military career was ended, virtually, from the moment the colonel had spoken to him in the manner we have taken occasion to detail.

The colour, which was usually deep upon the face of Captain Strachan, now almost entirely left it, and it never returned again to the intensity that it had maintained. One would fancy that by this he felt keenly the disgrace that had fallen upon him, but such was hardly the true explanation of his state of mind. He was really ill from the wild passions that had because cankered in his breast, and from the impatience he felt to be fully and completely revenged upon those whom he chose to call his enemies, but who would never have been so but for his own conduct, and then they were the enemies of that conduct, and not the man.

"Revenge !" he said. "Yes, that is the only word now that to me sounds delightful. Revenge! and I will have it. Nothing but blood will satisfy, and it must flow in abundance. I will see it—feel it, scent it, and I must know that it is the blood of those whom I hate, and then I shall know some peace, but not till then."

It was rather too soon for him to repair to the quarry to keep his appointment with Mr. Huncks, but he put on a great coat which was a much more effectual concealment of his dress and figure than his military cloak, and sallied out of the barracks to give some ease to his mind, by the rapid exercise of walking, for the very air of the barracks was hateful to him.

Again as he passed through the exercising ground and out at the gate, he was ceremoniously saluted, and perhaps the same idea that Corporal Steady had managed to make Cockles understand, passed through the mind of the captain, namely, that it was his rank and not himself that they saluted.

If he thought so, he thought the exact truth, for we may venture to say that he was as thoroughly detested as any officer could possibly be.

Revolving such matters in his mind, and feeling in anything but a pleasant mood, Captain Strachan took his way to the brink of the quarry. We have before mentioned that the night was dark and rainy, and it had by no means improved during the last hour or so. The rain which had been only lightly falling had thickened to a regular fall of thick, dim moisture, which had every promise of continuing for the remainder of the night.

Cursing the weather—Huncks—the regiment, and, finally, himself, Captain Strachan reached the meadows contiguous to the quarry, and very shortly after stood within a few paces of the brink, trying to look through the misty right over in the direction of the deep excavation,

"I suppose," he said, "I must not expect that lawyer yet, confound him. Oh, if I could only do without him, what a pleasure it would be to cut his throat."

"Would it?" said Mr. Huncks, stepping up to the captain from the shadow of an old pine tree. "Would it, indeed?"

Strachan started at the moment, but he quickly recovered his ordinary composure, as he said,—

"A good scheme, wasn't it?"

"Excuse me, captain, I don't think so. You can hardly suppose a man to think it a good scheme to have his throat cut."

"Pho ! pho ! my friend Huncks, you don't understand me. I saw you hiding in the shadow of the tree, and I wanted you to come out; so, you see, I said what I did on purpose to produce you, that was all, and it has succeeded."

"Oh, that was it, was it?" said the lawyer. "Ah, well, there's no harm done, captain, for, after all, whether you want my throat cut or not, I know very well that you won't try to do it. So we will say no more about it, if you please, but set to work, as we are both a little before our time here at the old well known spot.

CHAPTER XXX.

MR. FLUMMERY QUITE INNOCENTLY FRIGHTENS THE CAPTAIN AND THE LAWYER.

CAPTAIN STRACHAN did not quite like the manner in which Mr. Huncks spoke to him, but as he was only too glad in any way to get rid of the rather awkward idea that he really did meditate some mischief against the man of law, he tried to laugh and to say that all was right.

Right, indeed ! When would all be right with such a man as Captain Strachan? If at one blow he could have compassed the death of all those whom his evil motives made him hate, would all have been right then with him? Oh, no. Short, indeed, would have been the space of time that would have elapsed before the restless spirit of villany would have begun to prey upon itself in him of another victim.

"Well," said Huncks, "I confess that if the night had only chanced to be a fine one, instead of the one it is, I should have liked this little appointment all the better."

"It don't matter," said Strachan.

"Oh, don't it, though. You may be waterproof, captain, but I can assure you that I am not."

"The night is favourable to us, Huncks, so for that we are much less likely to encounter any one. Business alone would bring any one out in this heavy, penetrating rain."

"Well, there is something in that; so now let us get the job over as quickly as we can. I must say that I am rather curious about the affair, for until to-night I could have taken my oath that a certain party lay as snugly at the bottom of the quarry as you and I could wish him; but you have, by your relation of what you saw at Exeter, staggered me."

"I am myself staggered. I cannot make it out. There is some awful mystery in the matter that we have yet to solve. Oh! Huncks, never forget that you and I now are fairly embarked in the same boat, and that it is useless for us to strive the one against the other. Recollect that, Huncks, in all you say and do."

"Oh, stuff! captain, stuff "

"You may disregard what I say, if you like; but it is true for all that."

"Well, well, we won't dispute about it. Come, will you commence the descent, or shall I? The rain has made it slippery enough, I will be bound."

"Not a doubt of that. I will go first."

"Very good, captain, and I will follow you, you may depend, most faithfully. It won't do to be too particular about what we lay hold of, so I provided myself with a pair of riding gloves, that neither thorns, nor briars, nor nettles will be able to get through. But don't you think it now an odd thing that in an old marble quarry there should be so much vegetation?"

"Not at all."

"How do you make that out?"

"The vegetation is all upon shelves and ledges of the stone, and into which the rain has washed soil from the surrounding meadows, and the wind in the summer time has carried dust, and then as the weeds decayed, the seeds of which sprung up in such places, they added to the mass, and as years after years have rolled by, the place has become what you see it now,

quite a little wood, although the base of all the vegetation is the stone that forms the principal feature of the neighbourhood."

"Ah! well, you seem to know all about it, captain."

"I do. Come on; it is not so slippery as I thought it was; and you can follow me very well, and easily, too, if you like."

Captain Strachan had commenced his descent of the excavation, very carefully and steadily, at a point where he knew there was ample convenience for descending, and the attorney followed pretty closely in his footsteps.

"Mind you don't slip, Huncks," said Strachan.

"Not if I can help it. How kind and considerate you are, captain."

"Not at all. If you were to slip, you would fall upon me. That is why I spoke of it."

"Oh, dear! Ah! I ought to have thought of that."

For some time, now, they neither of them spoke, for the perils of the descent materially increased, in consequence of the rain having caused some loose pieces of the rock to give way, and so altered the path so much, that Strachan was rather at a loss now and then as to how to proceed. At length, however, they both reached a ledge of rock that was not above twenty feet from the pool, that had collected at the lower part of the quarry, and in which they had all along hugged themselves with the idea was lying the murdered body of Clinton,

"There it is," said Strachan.

"What—the body?"

"No ; I see nothing of that sort, but there is the spot where it ought to be, and where I yet hope we shall find it ; for, after all, it is better to have to encounter such a man dead than alive. The spirit of Clinton is better than the man himself."

"Oh, don't talk about spirits here, captain. I dave some in a bottle, though, which is the only kind of spirit that I——"

Smash went something against a portion of the rock at this moment, and Strachan called out in an eager tone,—

"What's that? What's that?"

"The very bottle I was talking about," replied Huncks. "Somehow or another, the pocket in which it was took a kind of swing, and crack it went, and now it's running away—the spirit, I mean, is now running away ; and here we are forced to the cold water system, whether we like it or not."

"Never mind. We must not be here

for long, Huncks. There is a zig-zag path that leads from this plateau upon which we are, right down to the lower depth below us. Let us descend at once."

The aspect of the weather at the depth that they were, was really quite alarming and dispiriting.

Probably the rain above was no more than it had been, but in consequence of striking against many little ledges, and likewise against the whole of the upper part of one side of the quarry, it came down to the lower part of it in a thick mist that was of the most perplexing character.

Numerous little rivulets, too, which came coursing down the side of the quarry, made up an uproar, that for a little time, until the ears got accustomed to it, was almost deafening, and such as effectually to stop convesation.

Twice the lawyer asked Captain Strachan if he had a firm foothold, before the captain heard him speak at all; but then he replied to him that it was all right, and he had only to spring down to the lower level where he was, and he would find it was all right.

It was rather adverse to the usual caution of Mr. Huncks that he should so readily as he did take the words of the captain for granted, and make a spring in the dark, but he did do so. Now, the ledge to which Strachan awaited the lawyer was very narrow, indeed, and rather sloped outwards, which was just the wrong way for any one to jump to with an idea of keeping their foothold when they got there; so that Mr. Huncks, the moment he alighted, found his feet slip from under him as though they had been laid hold of by some one, and away he went right into he very pool at the bottom of the quarry which they had both come to examine with the hope of finding within it the dead body of Clinton.

"What is that?" cried Strachan. "What noise is that?"

"Murder!" gasped the attorney. "I'm a dead man."

"Where the devil are you? Speak again, will you, and let me know where you are?"

"Oh—oh—oh!"

"Confound you, who has caught you? Curses on this place, it is the source of nothing but disasters. Now, Mr. Huncks, if you want any help from me, you will be so good as to signify where you are."

"Here! Oh, dear! here, in the pool at the bottom of the quarry. Here I am, half drowned. Oh, what shall I do?"

"Get out."

"I am getting out as well as I can."

"Then you can't do anything better. Where is your light? I thought you said you would be sure to bring a lantern with you?"

"Yes. Oh, oh, it is here. I am all over bruises, and soaked to the skin besides, and I rather think that some of my bones are broken; but I don't feel quite sure about that. Oh, why did I come here at all, upon your business, too, captain—oh, why did I?"

"Hold your noise, will you?"

"Well, but——"

"If you don't be quiet, Mr. Huncks, I shall send a bullet after you. By that uproar that you make, you bring danger upon me as well as yourself. The latter would be of no consequence; but I am not disposed to be brought into mischief upon your account.

"Well, I am quiet, and here's a light. I wonder how far I have fallen? Here's a light. The only wonder is that the water has not got so to the candle that it won't light at all."

Mr. Huncks did succeed in lighting the wax candle that was in a small pocket lantern; and then he cast a ray of strongly reflected light around him, and for the first time seemed to be fully awake to the idea that he had been, and was now, upon the very brink of the pool into which both he and the captain believed that the dead body of Clinton had fallen upon the occasion of their former visit to the place.

It was with quite a cry of terror that Mr. Huncks made this most unwelcome discovery, and there he stood with the lantern in his hand, shivering and shaking like a man in an ague.

"Good gracious!" cried Strachan, "what is the matter with you, now? You are enough to drive any one mad.'

"I am mad I think. Why, I have been plump into the very pool where we thought *he* was. That's where I have been, and I didn't know it."

"All the better."

"The better, say you? That's a matter of taste. I have cold shins, and my teeth chatter, and—and I shall never be able to get out of the quarry again."

"Then stay, and be——excuse me, Huncks, I don't mean that; I will help you out of the quarry, provided you will, now that you are there, thoroughly ascertain if the sight we expected to see is to be seen or not."

"I will—I will."

"Then be quick about it, for I assure

you I have no liking to stay here one moment longer than may be necessary."

"Oh, yes, I will. As you say, now that I am here, I may as well look about me. I do not shrink from that."

One thing was quite evident, and that was, that the faculties of Mr. Hunks were not at all improved by the tumble he had had. It is rather a curious thing to notice what an effect any little derangement of the physical structure will have upon some minds, and the fall that the lawyer had had appeared as if it had given such a shake to his politic brain, that he was no longer, for the time being, able to think and to speak as he ordinarily did, and instead of being the clever, acute, and unscrupulous man of business that he usually appeared, he became an exceedingly common-place sort of personage.

"Are you looking?" said Strachan.

"Yes, oh, yes, for the—the——"

"The body."

"To be sure, captain, as you say, I am looking for the body, and all I have to say is, I don't see it by any manner of means."

"You don't see it?"

"No—no. There's nothing at all like it here. There is nothing but mud and rubbish in the pool of water here, captain. You may take my word for it, that there is nothing of the sort that we expected."

"Then, it is too true."

"What is too true?"

"My fears that Clinton escaped. Oh, fool that I was not to make quite sure at the time. Put out your light, and come away from this place, Mr. Huncks. We can do no further good here. Come away at once. We do but waste our time now."

"I know it," said Huncks, as he extinguished the lantern; "and now, captain, give me your hand, or, shaky as I am by the fall I have had, I shall never be able to raise myself up to the ledge where you are again."

The captain knelt, and took hold of the outstretched hand of Mr. Huncks, and helped him up to the ledge. He thought the lawyer might still be useful to him, or he would have left him there to rot without the least compunction of conscience upon the subject.

"Now," said Strachan, "let us leave this place as quickly as we can."

"With all my heart."

They both turned towards the face of the quarry, and just commenced the ascent, when they heard a voice from the brink say—

"There he goes now. The time was when I wouldn't have taken a matter of one *pun* ten for him, and this is the end of him. Well, good-by, Jacob."

"Good God! what's that?" said Huncks.

"Hush, idiot, hush!" whispered the captain. "Hold on to the weeds; by Heaven, somebody is coming down."

These words had hardly escaped the lips of the captain, when, crashing and dashing through the weeds and birch-wood that lined the sides of the quarry, there came a something evidently of size and weight more than any human being could possibly be. There was but one hope for the captain and the lawyer, and that was that the heavy body would bound over them; but that hope turned out to be fallacious, for it came right upon them both, knocking them away from the feeble hold they had of the weeds and bramble bushes; and in another moment they were in the pool, and half-smothered in the collected mud at the bottom of it, and overlaid by something that seemed as heavy as a house.

"Good-by," said the same voice from the brink of the quarry. "I'm sorry to have to say, 'Good-by' to you, Jacob, for it's the mortal truth that I wouldn't have took one *pun* ten for you only a week agone. Oh, dear me, this here is the way the world wags. We is always a-losing some old friend or another."

That this voice was that of our old acquaintance, Mr. Flummery, the reader will have no sort of difficulty in at once deciding.

CHAPTER XXXI.

THE COLONEL TAKES POSSESSION OF HIS NEW QUARTERS.

A VERY few words, indeed, will suffice to explain the strange occurrence with which we concluded our last chapter.

Mr. Flummery had been possessed for some years past of a donkey, to whom he gave the patriarchal name of Jacob, which donkey had stood very high in the estimation of Mr. Flummery, and of all the village. But donkeys are mortal, alas! and so it chanced that Mr. Jacob bade the world good-by, and went to that "bourne from whence no" donkeys "return."

The grief of Mr. Flummery was very great, and as it was rather an inconvenient thing to bury a donkey, on account of the space occupied by the legs, he thought that it would be just as well to topple him over the side of the quarry, and leave him there to resolve himself into these elements which alike make up the mortal frame of donkeys and men. By the aid of a hand-barrow, Mr. Flummery had brought the departed Jacob to the brink of the excavation, and never for one moment fancying any one could be there, he toppled Jacob over, accompanying the act by the lament that we have heard him utter respecting the value and the merits of the deceased.

Little did Mr. Flummery imagine that Jacob would wreak for him such a *post*

AMELIA REVIS WATCHING THE MARCHING TROOPS FROM THE HEDGE.

mortem venges upon the two men whom he, Flummery, held in least esteem. If he had but suspected the state of affairs at the bottom of the quarry, he would have thought even the death of Jacob a cheap calamity, since it had resulted as it had. But Mr. Flummery walked away with the manly tear of feeling in his eye, little imagining what had taken place, and upon whom the weight of Jacob's remains were even then reposing.

"Ah!" he said, "I would have given

two *puns* to have kep' him, that I would ; but we is all dust and ashes, and so we goes out like pieces of tinder, we does !"

With this reflection, which is almost as good as many others to the same purpose which are uttered by much more exalted individuals than Mr. Flummery, he walked home to repose upon his griefs.

Neither Mr. Huncks nor his friend the captain, in truth, remained above a few moments oppressed by the weight of Jacob at the bottom of the quarry ; but to them both, moments appeared, while they were in such a situation, to be hours. When they did extricate themselves, they were more like two drowned rats than anything human ; and even then it was some time before they could find out what it was that had came down upon them in such an awful manner, for the light that Huncks had with him was obstinate, and would not ignite.

At length, by the feeble flicker of one of the matches with which he was provided, they caught a sufficient sight of the departed Jacob to be aware of his station and quality ; and then it was that Huncks gasped out,—

"Somebody has thrown a dead donkey at us, captain, and that's what has done all the mischief. Oh, dear !"

"A dead donkey ?"

"Yes, a dead and heavy donkey. Oh, dear, oh, dear, I feel a sort of presentiment that this night will be the death of me, captain ; and if so, I beg that you won't leave my remains here, but will see that I am decently interred in the old churchyard. You will be so good, too, as to have a tombstone put over me, with on it the words—

" ' Just in life, and beautiful in death,
   He—' "

"Bah !" said the captain, "hold your nonsense. Come along now ; I am half smashed myself with the weight of the load upon me, and I am in such a condition from the water of the pool, that I must get to your house and change my clothes as quickly as possible. Follow me."

"What an odd tone you speak in, captain."

"Do I ? Hark you, Huncks: I will find out who it was that played us this trick, and if I don't make his head lie as low as the animal's yonder, my name is not what it is. It's some one in the village, no doubt. You heard the voice ? Did you not recognise it ?—I thought you knew every one about here."

"I was in such a fright that I could not recognise any voice or anybody. You

must recollect, captain, that I had one tumble before the donkey came."

"Oh, so you had. That's one comfort."

"A comfort did you say ?"

"Yes, to be sure it is. Come on, now. Oh, but I will have my revenge for all this, never you fear, Huncks."

With immense labour and difficulty, they did, in the course of about twenty minutes, succeed in getting out of the quarry. They looked cautiously around them, but not a vestige of any person was visible, and they made their way, then, across the meadows to Mr. Huncks' house, satisfied upon one thing, at all events, and that was, that the body of Clinton, if ever it had been in the quarry, was not there now.

We now leave this pair of rascals to take their own course, and to sit together until the dawn of morning, concocting their villanous schemes, while we proceed to a relation of what is occurring to others of our characters in this eventful history.

The villa which Colonel Percival had rented in the immediate neighbourhood, and whither he intended to move at once, was a very fine old fashioned residence indeed. It belonged to a family too changed in circumstances to enable them to live in it in the style they wished, and so they would not live in it at all from a foolish pride, which is to be found in all conditions of life, and which sways more human actions than any other feeling.

Since being deserted by its legitimate owners, it had been from time to time occupied by different persons, who, during the summer season, had rented it of the solicitor in London in whose hands the affairs of the reduced were, and from whose hands they were, of course, never fated to emerge.

It is a strange thing in England, that when a wealthy family meets with reverses, the residue of their property is generally made a present of to some solicitor.

This place, however, which was called, on account of some peculiarity in its architecture, The Abbey, had not been suffered to go to decay. A gardener and his wife had lodging and a small salary to keep it in good condition, so that when Colonel Percival, after a brief negotiation, rented it, he might go and take possession at once, without any further difficulty.

We are thus particular in describing the Abbey, because it will be the scene of some very important acts in our story, which will immediately present themselves to the notice of the reader.

It will be recollected, then, that several events were to take place on the day following the night upon which Captain Strachan and Mr. Huncks visited the quarry. In the first place, the fete or entertainment which was to be given in the village by the surrounding gentry to the regiment, was to come off. Then some time during the day Colonel Percival was to take possession of the Abbey, whither, of course, Arthur Wilton would repair, and take up his quarters temporarily.

The excessive rain of the night cleared all off by daybreak, and, as is very often the case in our fickle climate, the morning shone out after the night of storm and disagreeables with a lustre and a beauty that was truly enchanting.

The rain had freshened the vegetation, and imparted to every tree, and bush, and flower, an unusual beauty; and the little stream that usually in peaceful murmurings wound its way through the village, had all the appearance of quite a turbulent river, materially adding to the picturesque character of the place.

Light, flimsy clouds added rather than detracted from the deep serenity of the blue sky, and the sun had that warm, yellow tinge which is so promising of continued fine weather when it so shows itself to us in England.

The effect of the weather upon some constitutions is immense. It produces a hopefulness of feeling, that raises the imagination above the petty trials of life, and not unfrequently, too, enables the mind fairly to grapple with the more important evils. Thus, then, upon that fair and beautiful morning Arthur Wilton arose refreshed alike both in mind and body, and with such feelings of hopefulness as he had not had for many a long day.

"Surely," he said to himself, "all will be well now. I am once again reinstated in the favour of the colonel. He, too, promises to use all his influence to procure for me my discharge from the army ; Mr. Revis receives me with kindness as the acknowledged suitor of his daughter; and he who is chief, and, I may say, only enemy, the villain Strachan, is in well-merited disgrace with every one in the regiment, as well as out of it. Surely I have now much to be thankful for."

Truly, it did seem as if the clouds that had lowered about the fortune of Arthur Wilton were at length upon the point of clearing away, leaving nothing between him and the fair sunshine of prosperity and joy.

Alas! how little he expected that as yet evil fortune had been but playing with him, and that the worst stroke that destiny could give him was not yet delivered.

By an early hour the village was all life and animation, and the green—for it had one of the old fashioned greens, without which, in our opinion, an English village loses its chiefest characteristic and beauty—was occupied by busy parties fitting up tents, and erecting a huge pole like the mast of a ship, at the top of which was a garland of great size and beauty. Barrels of ale were rolled out upon the short, crisp grass, and supported upon trestles, preparatory to being drained of their contents. An ox was to be roasted whole, and the smith with a couple of sooty-looking assistants, were fixing in the ground a temporary grate for the purpose of doing justice to such a roast.

All was life, hilarity and bustle, and when the drums beat for the regiment to turn out, it was seen to be in its best array, and was greeted by shouts of approval.

The band took up a prominent position upon the green, and played favourite old English melodies and the dances. The officers, in their best uniforms, appeared upon the scene, all with the exception of Captain Strachan; and then a number of carriages brought the surrounding inhabitants of the villas and mansions; and the colonel opened the ball at three o'clock in the afternoon with a young lady who was the daughter of a baronet, and a magistrate of the neighbourhood.

"There," said Colonel Percival, as the dance was finished, and he led the young lady back to her friends. "That is not what I have ventured upon doing for these twelve years past."

"Twelve years, colonel? Oh, but why?"

"Because, my dear, my dancing days are over."

The young creature laughed at the colonel for saying this, for she could not conceive how dancing days could possibly fly away, and only be thought of among past blessings with a sigh. Youth, even, thinks itself immortal.

The ball upon the green being thus formally opened, the dancers seemed as if they would never tire ; and to do the villagers, as well as the soldiers, ample justice, there was not not one solitary instance of inebriety during the whole proceedings ! which shows that even Englishmen, although the fact has been so much doubted, may be, if they like to be so, merry and wise at the same time.

It is a great pity that such fete's and re-unions of all classes are not more common in this country. We are quite convinced, that far from having the effect of diminishing the respect which the poor and the lowly are expected to have for the rich and the mighty, they would have the effect of very materially raising it, because the respect would be based upon affection rather than upon dread

At present, in this country, a poor man is respectful to a rich man, because he is afraid of the consequences of being otherwise, and not from any sense of benefits conferred, or to be conferred upon him or his; but let there be a more frequent communion of feeling between all classes, and then respect would deepen into gratitude.

Colonel Percival set the example always in his regiment of a fusion of ranks at times. Thus, upon the present occasion, the officers mingled quite freely in the dance, although their *vis-a-vis* might be a corporal or even a drummer, and, in fact, Cockles, who had succeeded in ingratiating himself into the good graces of a very pretty country girl, indeed, found himself opposite to Major Cuthbert in a country dance, and the major called out in quite a friendly tone—

"Now, Cockles, down the middle and up again."

"Yes, sir," said Cockles, and down the middle and up again de went with a spirit that lent quite a glow to his cheeks.

Arthur Wilton, too, was in this same dance as the partner of Amelia, and a handsomer couple than they were could not be found. The villagers, too, soon saw the kind of estimation in which Arthur was held by the officers, and Amelia's heart throbbed with joy to hear the colonel speak to him in the way he did, which was more that of an equal than a commanding officer to a soldier.

And while all this was going on, while fine jollity and harmless mirth was the order of the day upon the village green, Captain Strachan sat in his solitary room at the barracks, with his arms crossed upon his breast, and gave himself up to gloomy thought.

With that gloomy thought was mingled evil thoughts, for the villain even then had the shadow of the darkest crime he had ever yet committed, or thought of committing, upon his soul.

"It shall be done!" he muttered. "Yes, it shall be done. I am at last resolved. I thought I was resolved before, but I begin to think I was not, and that not till now did the full determination to do a dreadful deed come upon my soul."

He rose and paced the room with rapid and urgent strides, and then as he passed by the window, he could hear the swell of the military music from the green, and occasionally the loud joyous laughter of those who were so happy.

"Ay," he said, "laugh on. It will go hard with me if I do not change some of that laughing to wailing. I will make that music play yet a different measure ere many days are past—Days, do I say? I will count the time by hours. So, you would have me leave this regiment, would you, Colonel Percival? Indeed. Ha! ha! I will make you leave the regiment yet, before I do."

CHAPTER XXXII.

CAPTAIN STRACHAN MAKES SOME PREPARATIONS.

THE fete at the village was fair and beautiful to look upon, while the bright sun shone, and lent the resplendence of its beams to the soft eyes of beauty; but when the twilight came, and some thirty huge torches, hoisted upon poles, so as to elevate them some twelve feet above the heads of the dancers, sent a ruddy glow over the scene, the effect was really in its beauty quite magical.

Vauxhall upon a gala night, with the twenty thousand extra lamps, could not look more resplendent than did the village green.

But, then, there was the light shining upon the leaves of tall old trees in the immediate vicinity, and giving to the green that strange unearthly hue that all sorts of artificial light gives to vegitation; and the uniforms of the officers, and the gay dresses of the ladies, and the hearty laughter of all, and the good humour that lit up every face, and sparkled in every eye, were worth any number of extra lamps you like to mention, and quite did away with all idea of night.

We are really afraid to hazard even a guess how many young couples agreed, from that evening forth, to "keep company" together—and how many who had been keeping company actually settled the time and place of their intended wedding, and were as happy as happy could be in the prospect before them, although it might be one of toil and uncertainty.

Well, all these things occurred to the great gratification of Colonel Percival, who fully intended that they should occur, for it they had not, he would hardly have thought the village fete such a success as it really and truly was. One circumstance, too, gave to Arthur Wilton and Amelia the most unfeigned delight.

Just at the termination of a dance, and when Arthur had led Amelia to one of the tents, in which there were plenty of seats, some one suddenly clasped her round the waist, and kissed her, to her intense astonishment and dismay. She uttered a faint shriek, and called upon Arthur to protect her.

The young lover, the moment he heard the voice of the loved one in tones of alarm, darted forward to the intruder, but his uplifted arm was stayed upon the instant as he saw who it was.

Old Mr. Wilton, the stern father, who has been already slightly introduced to the reader, stood before his son.

"Arthur!" said the old man, and his voice betrayed the agitation with which he spoke—"Arthur, my son—my boy!"

"Father!" said Arthur Wilton, as he sprang forward and caught the old man in his arms—"dear father, how kind and good this is of you."

"Can you indeed say that, Arthur—from your heart, my son?"

"I can indeed, father. Oh, why should I not say as much to you?"

For a few moments more, now, old Mr. Wilton could not speak, and then it was only in a faint and faltering voice that he could manage to say, as he held the hands of his son between both his own, and looked at him with tearful eyes—

"I have been harsh and cruel to you, Arthur, but all that has passed away; new and better thoughts have come over me, and I feel that I am still a father."

Poor Amelia could not restrain her tears upon witnessing this scene, and she wept aloud. Arthur himself, too, was very deeply affected, but he looked with joy through his tears into the face of his father, as he said—

"Let the past be no more remembered between us, father; it is for the future that we will live, and I can only say, that you have made me very happy indeed this night, and Amelia likewise—she, I know, shares with me the pure delight of this most happy reconciliation."

"Indeed and in truth I do, sir," said Amelia.

"And I, likewise," said a voice, and in another moment Mr. Revis, who had been an unsuspected spectator of the scene, made his appearance from a portion of the tent which was shaded by a number of evergreens—"and I, likewise; and I hope there is no one here who will deny me the privilege of deeply and truly enjoying this scene."

"Ah, Mr. Revis, I am not that one," said old Mr. Wilton, with a smile, as he held out his hand to the father of Amelia. "Can you, too, forgive me?"

"With all my heart, if there be anything to forgive, which there is not; so now we are all friends."

"To death we are," said Arthur.

"And beyond death," said Amelia.

"Yes, my dear girl," said Mr. Wilton, "and beyond death, as you say—for we will all hope to meet in that land beyond the stars, where there is no sorrow. But come now, I feel that I am but casting a cloud over the sunshine of your joy; I will go home, and let me have the hope of seeing you both, and you too, Mr. Revis, if you can come to me early in the morning, for I have much to say to you all, and particularly to the young couple, who will, I hope and trust and believe, be so very happy."

"We will attend you, Mr. Wilton," said Farmer Revis.

"But you will stay here, father," said Arthur, "and enjoy with us these harmless sports?"

"No, my boy—no. I am much disturbed in my mind; I—I have had a dream."

"A dream, father?"

"Yes, my son, I have had a dream, concerning you, which has troubled me much—but I will not relate it to you now, for it might perchance have the effect of marring some of the happiness of this evening; you shall hear it all tomorrow."

Now Arthur knew very well that there was nothing that affected his father more than a dream, so he did not think so much of his words as he otherwise might; and when Amelia put on a look of sympathetic alarm with old Mr. Wilton upon his fears, and then saw a quiet smile upon the face of Arthur, she hardly knew what to say.

"Farewell, then, for the present, all of you," added Mr. Wilton, "and God bless you."

With these words, the old man left the tent, no doubt much happier than he had been for a very long time, and went homewards alone.

"What a strange thing," said Amelia, "that a dream should so much have distracted the mind of Mr. Wilton—is it not so, Arthur?"

"Yes, Amelia," replied Arthur, "it is strange; and I may say that it is the only weakness of my father. Some dream that accidently, I suppose, came true in his early life, has made a deep impression upon him."

"This dream he speaks of, though," said Mr. Revis, "can be no bad one, since it has induced him to the course of action he has pursued to-night."

"True, sir, and so let my father to-morrow say of his dream what he may, I will still contend that it is a happy vision."

While this little interlude, as it were, was going on in the tent, the sports on the green had suffered no sort of intermission ; but rather, if that were possible, increased in gaiety and freedom ; although the admirable love of good manners that pervaded the whole assemblage, effectually prevented that freedom from going in the slightest degree to any licentious or blameable excess.

We have noticed how delightful a night it was for such an entertainment ; but we shall soon see that, after all, nothing in all the world can be so thoroughly treacherous as a serene-looking sky in England.

It was about half-past nine o'clock in the evening when several of the dancers paused in the mazes of the figure they were performing, and asked each other if the sullen, heavy drops of moisture that fell among them could really be rain. The officers, too, began quickly to remark that there was an excessive sullenness in the air in comparison to its condition but a short time before.

"Are we going to have a storm," said Major Cuthbert ; "or what does this portend ?"

The words were scarcely out of his mouth, when there came such a bewildering flash of lightning over the scene, that not a person present was able for some moments to convince himself or herself that they were not blinded, so powerful an effect upon the eye had the particularly vivid light produced.

There was, at the same moment, a loud crashing noise, and a tall old chestnut tree, that had withstood the storms and the frosts of eighty years, was rent from its topmost bough to the roots, and fell in wild disorder, occupying a space upon the ground of enormous width and length.

Mingling with the crash of the falling tree, now came the thunder-clap, and a most awfully majestic sound it was. Some had taken the precaution to hold their hands over their ears in expectation of it, but even to them the sound was truly prodigious ; while to those who had taken no precautions at all to deaden the effect, it was truly appalling.

The scene of confusion that now ensued baffles all powers of description. The affrighted villagers were scampering hither and thither in dismay, some fancying that the end of the world had surely come, and others again madly supposing that the village was the place specially marked out for destruction, and that it was to be swept from the face of the earth.

In the midst of this turmoil, Colonel Percival now raised his voice and tried to reassure the terrified people by the cheerfulness of his tones.

"What's the matter with you all?" he said. "It's only a thunder-storm, at the worst, of which you must have seen many, I suppose. If you wish to fly in all directions upon its account, do so rationally, but don't make so much noise about it."

These words had the effect of making some few rather ashamed of their terrors ; and they paused. No other flash of lightning had come, and the thunder had quite died away in distant echoes ; so that there could be no very fair excuse now that there was anything particularly to fear in what was going on. The colonel saw the effect he had produced, so he spoke again.

"Our little entertainment had better here conclude, at all events," he said. "It is about time that it would have done so, I suppose, under the most ordinary circumstances ; but we soldiers, with our accoutrements, are particularly obnoxious to a ducking, and as there is very likely to be a good chance of one, as the rain is already falling, we will bid you all good night, and good spirits for the next merry-meeting."

With military promptitude and decision, the soldiers formed in columns, and it was astonishing to see how quickly the village-green, which had been so lately the scene of so much hilarity, was completely deserted by every one. It was like the rapid change of some scene in a play, which, at the prompter's whistle, disappears in an instant, and is beheld no more that night.

Colonel Percival would not leave the barracks to go to the abbey, as the weather was so very unpromising, but he told Arthur Wilton that he, Arthur, might consider his time at his own disposal until ten on the following morning ; and so they parted for the night.

Arthur, after seeing Amelia and her father home to the farm, and being half-smothered by the caresses of Prince, who had been chained up at home, to prevent him from being in the way of all the dances on the green, which assuredly would have been the case had he been loose, thought that the best and the most gracious thing he could possibly do was to go to his father.

When Arthur arrived, he found the old gentleman waiting for him, and the moment he appeared, old Mr. Wilton said—

"I knew it. Oh, yes, I knew it."

"Knew what, father?" said Arthur.

"That you would come here to-night, my son. My dream told me so."

"I hope, father, that you really will not allow any foolish dream to disturb your peace of mind. You know that dreams, after all, are but mental phenomena, that have no connexion with anything but foregone facts, which they present again to the mind in confused fancies."

"No—no. I don't know any such thing, Arthur. But come now, sit down in your old seat by the chimney-corner, and in a very few words I will tell you what I did dream."

"Very well, father, I will listen to you. But, after all, now, father, is not Amelia a most beautiful girl?"

"Yes; but, as I was saying, I thought that I heard a loud clap of thunder in my dream, and that an old tree——"

"And she is as good as she is lovely," said Arthur, whose thoughts were all upon his Amelia, instead of upon the dream that his father was relating to him.

"And then," added old Wilton, "I thought that you came towards me, holding out your hands, which were covered with blood, and that you said to me— 'This looks like murder, father, but I am innocent!'"

"Did you really dream that, father?"

"Yes, my son, I did. Is it not truly dreadful?"

"It is so; but yet I cannot bring my mind to think anything of it. Was that the whole of the vision?"

"No. I fancied then that a throng of people came to lay hold of you, calling out in loud accents, 'Death—death to the murderer!' and that they would have dragged you away, had not an angel stepped forward, and with its long silken hair dried the blood from your hands; and then when you held them up they were as white and as pure as could be; and the same people, who but a moment before would have dragged you away to death, kept calling out 'He is innocent! He is innocent!' and with those cries ringing in my ears, I awoke."

"It was a strange dream that, to say the least of it, father."

"More than strange, Arthur, and you will see what will come of it. It means that you will pass through some great danger, and that then you will be saved by some pure heart from it consequences."

Arthur felt disheartened, in spite of himself, at this dream of his father's. He was very far from being superstitious, and yet there was a coherence and consistency about the dream, that seemed to come upon his mind with a conviction that it really meant something more than such visions could usually portend to.

"Father," he said, "I will not deny but that it is a strange dream, and coupling it with the fact well known to me that I have an implacable foe in the regiment, it leaves a warning to me to be most careful how I expose myself to the villany of his machinations."

"Do be careful, oh, do be careful, Arthur, for recollect that I have no son but you, and that you are dearer to me than all the world besides."

CHAPTER XXXIII.

CAPTAIN STRACHAN FANCIES THAT HE HAS HIS VICTIM IN THE TOILS.

BY half-past nine Arthur was at the barracks, and writing the orders of the colonel. The orderly upon duty, who had, in common with all who came in contact with Wilton, a friendly feeling towards him, said, almost immediately—

"Well, Mr. Wilton, I fancy that we shall get rid of Strachan."

"Ah, indeed!"

"Yes, he is very ill, confined to his own room. The surgeon has been to see him, and says he cannot make out what is the matter with him; but he is evidently very ill, indeed."

"Well, I would rather he left the regiment than died in it."

"So would I, Mr. Wilton; but there is the colonel calling. I must attend to him."

The orderly soon brought back word that it was Wilton who was wanted, and when Wilton appeared before the colonel, the latter said—

"Good morning, Arthur. Your old enemy, Strachan, is very bad, I believe. I am as vexed as possible that he should take ill while with the regiment, for after what I have said to him, leave it he must, you know. But that is not what I sent for you for, of course. I intend to move to the Abbey to day, although I find by my letters that Mrs. Percival will not be able to be with me till to-morrow. I want you to assist me, Arthur, and there is your old friend, the box, with the brass clasps, that I wish you to take particular care of."

Arthur looked at the box, which had more the appearance of a very large desk than a box, and he said—

"I wish—that is——"

"Well, Wilton, what do you wish?"

"I was going to say, colonel, that I wish you would send that box to some place of greater safety."

"So I would if I knew one; but it contains all I am worth in the world in the shape of cash and jewels. It is the second hoard I have been able to make in my life. Once I had a sum of money which went more than half way towards procuring for me a gentlemanly independence. By way of taking care of it, I lodged it with a banker in Lodon. In three months afterwards the man was in the gazette, and I got twopence-half-penny in the pound upon all my savings."

"That was unfortunate, sir"

"It was, and from that time forth I made up my mind to be the custodian of my own money, so I take it about with me, for upon my word I am afraid to trust anybody. I am not afraid of robbery. That is a very different thing indeed; but what I am afraid of are those legal robberies, by which bankers and attorneys, and those sort of people appropriate your money, and then gratify you and themselves by the sight of a balance sheet, which they seem to think is to settle the whole affair."

Arthur Wilton was not a very business-like person, but yet he could not help feeling that the colonel was prejudiced against whole classes of people, on account of the delinquencies of a few, and that he ran much more risk with his savings by carrying them about with him, than he could ever run by properly investing them; but it was no business of his to tender advice, so he said no more upon the subject, and the colonel added—

"I wish, of course, to get comfortably settled at the Abbey before night, and then I have several letters that I wish you to be good enough to attend to for me, and perhaps it will not be inconvenient for you to stay at the Abbey all night?"

"Not at all, sir."

"Very well, then, Wilton, we will consider that as settled; and now I am going to pack up."

The packing up of Colonel Percival the reader has already had some idea of; but upon this occasion, as Arthur helped him, and as, to tell the truth, only a box or two had been opened, the principal difficulties vanished, and the goods of the colonel were soon in a fit state for removal to the Abbey, under Arthur's superintendence, and accompanied by a sergeant's guard likewise, as was the custom.

Wilton was no stranger to the Abbey and its beauties; often and often had he, when a boy, wandered about its old garden,

so that the place had quite a familia charm to him; and yet he could not shake off the feeling of depression that was upon him when he entered the building. He felt quite faint and sick, and more than once, while the soldiers were placing the colonel's goods in his rooms, he said—

"What can this mean? The very air of this place seems to weigh me down."

Despite all the efforts that he made to fight out against this feeling of depression, he could not shake it off. It did not grow upon him, for if it had really got much worse, he would not have been at all able to go through with the most ordinary duties of the day; but there it remained, like a black shadow upon his mind, which nothing could enable him by any means to get rid of.

More than once he thought of mentioning it to the colonel, and asking leave to go home; but then it did seem so weak and foolish to make such an excuse for neglecting the few duties that the colonel required of him, to say that he felt uncomfortable, that no wonder Arthur Wilton hesitated to say as much.

The brass-bound box, which, after what the colonel had said about it, had become really a horror to poor Arthur, was safely deposited in a small closet that opened from the colonel's bed-room, and from which there was, as Arthur took care thoroughly to ascertain, no other mode of egress. In fact, it had not even a window, so that, although it was as large as a room of ordinary dimensions in more modern houses, yet it was there entitled to no other name than that of a cupboard.

"There, at least, it will be safe," said Arthur as he looked at the box, and a shudder came over him as though in some way his own fate were mixed up in it.

Colonel Percival was very well pleased with all the arrangements that had been made for him; and after going over a portion of the building, he pitched upon a pretty enough little room that opened to the garden, and said,—

"This, Wilton, you can call your own room, if you please, while you are with me. Now, don't fancy that I am going to forget my promise to you of trying what I can with General Brotherton to get your discharge from the army; but it is very difficult just now, and I may be some time before I succeed, so you must just be content in the interim."

"How can I be otherwise, colonel, when I have your great kindness to stand between me and all subjects of discontent?"

"Well—well, never mind that, Wilton; I only hope you have got rid of that nervous feeling you had regarding Strachan, and his capability and will to do you some harm."

"I do not deceive you, colonel. I have not gotten rid of that feeling."

"Then you ought, Wilton. What on earth can he do?"

"It is that uncertainty of his wicked power that makes him appear to me so formidable. When once you are con-

STRACHAN'S HORROR ON BEHOLDING THE SUPPOSED APPARITION OF CLINTON.

vinced you have an enemy who is unscrupulous enough to do anything, you may give imagination the rein and fancy any horror that can possibly happen."

"Pho—pho, Wilton, you are too fanciful by far. I tell you that there is one grand limit to all that such a man as Strachan can do, and that limit is defined by his own fears. He may wish to injure you—he may even wish to destroy you; but he won't attempt it, you may depend. I look upon him as harmless, and that you are quite as safe from him as I am."

What a strange shudder came over Wilton as the colonel said these words!

Not to let the colonel see that he was the prey of some unknown fear, he now bustled about, and tried to engage his mind upon various matters; but still the dread of something that might happen clung to him like a giant that he could not shake off.

The little room, opening upon the garden, which the colonel had ceded to him, he took personal possession of, and tried to please himself with the idea that Mr. Revis, and his daughter, the fair Amelia, would there visit him, and walk in the sweet shadow of the tall trees in the Abbey garden, and that his own father, too, would come, and they would pass many a happy hour in that old place.

"Mr. Wilton," said the orderly, looking into the room, "did the colonel mention to you anything about a guard?"

"No—no."

"Well, I suppose he will have a sergeant's guard always here, at all events. It's a great old rambling house, and there ought to be as much as that about, at all events."

"You had better go to the colonel at once, and ask him," said Wilton, "for the night will soon be here now."

"Yes, Mr. Wilton, it will. I shall see to the guard at once."

The orderly returned to say that the colonel had ordered one sentinel at the gate on the outer side of the lawn, and another by the garden wall outside, and that the ground kitchen was to be made as comfortable as possible as a temporary guard-room.

"That will do," said Wilton. "Who is on duty here now?"

"Sergeant Brown."

"Oh, I don't know him."

"No, sir; he belongs to Captain Ausbuther's company. They say, sir, that Steady is to have the first sergeantcy that is vacant. Is that a fact, sir?"

"I am glad to be able to confirm it."

"We are all glad to hear it, sir, for there isn't a man in the regiment who is better liked than he is."

"Nor a man who more deserves to be well liked," added Arthur. "He is a thorough good fellow."

"He is, sir, indeed. If there's anything that we can do for you to make you comfortable here, sir, I'm sure you have only to mention it, and it is as good as done."

"Thank you, no. Nothing just now. My bedroom is over the first floor, I believe?"

"Yes, sir, only two doors off the colonel's, and on the same landing."

Arthur was alone again, and the shadows of the evening were gathering over the old garden. The colonel had given him some half a dozen letters of no importance, with a request that he would reply to them in his name, in the spirit of a little memorandum of the nature of the reply which was written upon the back of each, and it was a great relief to Wilton to have even that much to do. The letters were very soon finished, and a soldier was sent off with them to the village post house, and then Arthur felt very lonely again, and listened with the hope that the colonel would send for him, but no summons of the sort come, and still the evening grew darker and darker, until, in the strongly excited imagination of Arthur Wilton, he began to fancy that strange shapes of unearthly things were flitting past the casement of the little room.

Rousing himself from this lethargy, he sprang to his feet.

"This will drive me out of my mind," said Arthur. "What can be the meaning of it? I never before felt so terribly depressed. I will not give way to it, or it would go so far that I shall be unable to contend against it at all. I will walk in the garden."

With this intention, he opened the window, and stepped out into the old garden. The cool breeze upon his brow had a good effect, and he felt much calmer as he strolled down a long avenue of flowering shrubs towards the orchard.

As he neared the wall, which was covered with climbing trees of fruit and flowers, he heard the monotonous march to and fro of the sentinel, who was placed in that direction; and then as the clock of the not very distant church struck ten, he heard the guard coming to relieve the sentinel, and the latter drew up and shouldered his musket.

These sounds were a relief to the oppressed spirits of Arthur Wilton, and after the brief ceremony of changing the guard was over, he turned to walk again towards the house. At one of the windows he saw a light. It was the window of the colonel's bed-room, and he could see the shadow of Colonel Percival passing to and fro.

"All is well," said Wilton, to himself. "I must be ill to encourage these odd fancies that have possessed me all the evening. No one else has them, and why should I?"

He now made a vigorous effort to shake off the feelings that had made him so unhappy, and recollecting that there was some books in a room upon the ground floor, close to the little apartment which he called his own, he entered the house again, and taking the light in his hand, he opened the door of his room, and crossed the hall in search of the small apartment, the walls of which he had observed were lined with volumes.

"To rest," he said, "it is useless for me to attempt to go. If I return to bed I shall only get more imaginative, so I will sit up and try to read myself into something like composure of spirits, or into such weariness that I shall be sure to sleep."

CHAPTER XXXIV.

TAKES A REVIEW OF CAPTAIN STRACHAN'S PROCEEDINGS FOR A NIGHT.

CAPTAIN STRACHAN—we regret to return to him—passed a rather busy night upon the occasion of the village fete.

It will be no doubt recollected by our readers, that we took a passing glance at him in his solitary room at the barracks, when he found himself prohibited virtually, if not by express mandate, from mixing in that society into which it should have been his greatest pride to have got, and his greatest care to keep.

But certainly, in this respect, Captain Strachan was, to use a common expression, one of those who don't know when they are well off. His passions and his evil thoughts ever waged war with his well doing. He wanted revenge as well as success in this world, and although he was old enough to do so, he had not reached that height of philosophy which teaches content, and which raises serenity above all earthly blessings that can appertain to humanity.

It will be recollected that he had made rather a vehement speech to himself, in which he had threatened all whom he considered to be opposed to him, in interest or in passion, with all the pains and penalties which angry and vindictive men think they can inflict upon whomsoever they please, but which, in ninety-nine cases out of a hundred, recoil assuredly upon their own heads.

After a time, Strachan began to arrange the closest particulars of his hellish design. That design need be no secret to the reader, and so we give it in the muttered words of Captain Strachan him-self, as he stood with his arms folded, looking at the rapidly darkening night, as it sent its huge shadows over the barrack-yard.

"I have to be revenged on Arthur Wilton," he said, "first and foremost, because he baulked me in the plans I had for the ruin of Farmer Revis; and secondly for the present condition in which I am placed in the regiment, solely upon his account."

Captain Strachan seemed quite to forget that if he had only been so good as to leave Arthur Wilton at home, he need have been in no such position.

"Then," he added, "I have to be revenged upon Amelia Revis, for has she not repulsed me with all the scorn and contempt she could put into a repulse, and all on account of this very Wilton? Curses light upon his head!"

Again Captain Strachan was wrong, for it did not follow at all that Amelia, if she had been quite indifferent to Arthur, or if no such a person had existed, would have chosen Captain Strachan for an admirer or a lover.

"Then," again added the scoundrel, "have I not a deep debt of vengeance to settle with Colonel Percival, for has he not attacked me in the most deliberate manner, before others, too, and made it, as he fully intended he should, impossible for me to remain in the regiment? And if I leave it, what am I do? To be sure, there is the price of my commission, which I could receive; but a few hundreds will soon fly if I chance to have a run of ill-luck at the gaming-table, and that is the only species of excitement that I feel any degree of pleasure in now. Otherwise I am penniless. To be sure, there was a large sum got from Farmer Revis; but what with the share of it that that rascal Huncks would have, and what with a little ill-luck I had at play while the regiment was quartered at Winchester last year, that is all gone."

At this stage in his cogitations, Captain Strachan paused, for the purpose of uttering a number of oaths, with which we need not encumber our pages, however illustrative they might be of the character of the arch-villain of whose proceedings we are writing now.

After this explosion of rage was over, he resumed, with tolerable coolness, the review of his affairs.

"Well," he said, "what if I avail myself of the gracious privilege Colonel Percival vaunted he would accord me, and I fight him? What if I do that? I might kill him, and if I did, I should be hunted to death for it—while, if he killed me, which would be just as probable, everybody would look quite delighted, and I should go out of the world thoroughly baulked of all my revenges. No, I will not fight the colonel."

Perhaps a little cowardice had as much to do with this resolution as any other feeling of the exemplary captain's.

"No," he added, "fight I will not; I will give no one the chance of killing me, but I will kill those whom I may wish dead, because they are as vipers in my path."

The darkness was momentarily increasing now—and the extra guard for the night was placed at the barrack-gate. All this Captain Strachan could hear very well from his room in silence, while the tramp of the soldiers echoed in his ear as though they could have heard the guilty meditations of his demon spirit.

All was still again.

"Yes," he added, "I will live for revenge, and for the acquisition of money. I must have money, and I must have revenge: both are dear things to me—and for what else do I live for? Nothing—nothing. And now for the means of murdering—yes, I must not flinch at the word—of *murdering Colonel Percival, and involving Arthur Wilton in the consequences of the crime!*"

Yes, that was the crime the guilty imagination of Captain Strachan had been brooding over for so long, and which he now declared to himself in the most inequivocal language.

Now that he had got over all doubt as regards his intentions—now that he had made up his mind to the step in crime that he intended to take, there was nothing further requisite than to consider the means —the means of doing the deed, and the mode of fixing the guilt upon another— upon the innocent head of the noble-minded, just, fearless, candid, and honest Arthur Wilton.

There was no time to loose.

That was the first position that Strachan laid down. There was no time to lose: his position in the regiment was such that he could not but feel he ought at once to do something. The very soldiers looked askance at him now, and the punctilious manner in which they saluted him was sufficient to show that they hated him and feared him.

Like Macbeth, when he had declared upon a deed of blood, he could have said—

"'Twere well done, if 'twere done quickly."

We shall now rather record the acts of Captain Strachan, than the course of reasoning, by which he arrived at the conclusion of the necessity of those acts.

He fully intended that the deed should be executed at the Abbey were the colonel was going to reside; but, as yet, he had not information enough concerning that place to enable him to act. Could there be a better opportunity of getting that information than when the colonel, and the whole of the officers and soldiers, with the exception of those who were to guard the barracks, were occupied at the fete? Certainly not.

Captain Strachan folded his cloak about him, and sallied out at the barrack-gate.

At first he took the route to the village, in order to deceive anyone who might have an eye upon his movements, and the sentinel at the gate, after the captain had got far enough off to be out of earshot, said to a comrade, who was close at hand—

"I suppose the captain, after all, means to go and have a dance with the rest of them on the green?"

"I don't know that," said the other. "If Strachan goes north, the likelihood is that he means south."

The sentinel laughed, and resumed his walk by the side of the gate.

Now, the soldier had made a shrewd guess as to the peculiarities of Captain Strachan, for it was south that he intended to go, although he had gone north; and as soon as he had got about a quarter of a mile from the barracks, he crossed a stile, and made his way in the direction of the Abbey.

The grand object of Strachan was to see what mode of entrance to the place there was without taking the legitimate one, by the gate; and for that purpose he approached the wall which skirted the garden. The night was, as we have before said, very fine and light. Indeed, when Captain Strachan was examining the wall of the Abbey garden, it was just about one hour before the storm took place that so effectually and so quickly dispersed the village fete.

Strachan was not long in finding that at one angle of the wall the bricks were very rotten and loose, so much so, that he was able to displace several of them with his hands. This was quite enough for him, and in the course of half an hour he had worked for himself up that angle of the wall quite a set of steps.

The bricks that he removed he took care to carry to some little distance and to cast into a pond, so that they should not, by their presence about the spot, betray what had taken place.

He would have then made his way into the garden, for the descent by the aid of the old wall-trees that grew there in abundance was about as easy a thing to a man of any astivity as you could very well encounter, but he heard some one in the garden, and he paused to listen.

He soon found that it was the gardener talking to his wife about the fete in the village and other matters.

"The colonel seems a main good sort of a man," said the gardener, "for he told me when I waited upon him, that we were not to put ourselves out of the way at all on account of his coming, and that the only difference he hoped it would make to us was doubling what we got for taking care of the old place."

"Ah, that's gentleman-like," said the wife. "I told you, Daniel, when you felt all of a heap-like at the idea of soldiers coming here, that it wouldn't do us any harm at all."

"So you did, wife—so you did; and all you have got to do is to take care and make the colonel and his wife as comfortable as you can."

"That I will, Daniel. What do you say to sending for our niece, Peggy Slim, out o' place now, you know?"

"That's a good idea; now, I didn't think of that."

"How should you, Daniel? You know if there's anything to be thought of it's me as does it."

"That's true."

"Very well, Daniel, then I'll send for her; only she can't come to-morrow, you know, for it's a long way to Devonport."

"So it is, wife, so it is; but suppose, now, she comes as soon as she can—eh?"

"What an idea, Daniel! Why, you are getting quite wise, old man, that you are. After all, she'll be here soon enough, for didn't the colonel tell you that he didn't expect the lady coloneless would be here till the day after to-morrow?"

"'Deed did he."

"Very well then; come in and have your supper, Daniel, for the night air is getting a bit chilly, I think."

"Ay—ay, so it be."

The old couple left the garden, and Captain Strachan heard them chatting together in their odd way until the sound of their voices died completely away in the distance.

"Good," he said; "the colonel don't expect his wife till the day after to-morrow, and then there will be the niece of these infernal people as well. Two more wo-men in the house won't increase the facilities of what I propose doing. The deed, if done at all, shall be done to-morrow night."

Captain Strachan now considered that he ran no risk at all by descending the wall into the garden, and he accordingly did so; and, as well as he could, by the night light, made himself acquainted with that side of the house and the approaches to it through the garden. Every piece of information he could get of the locality, for all he knew, might be of the greatest service to him.

After about twenty minutes or so spent in examining the house, and trying some of the old casements on the ground-floor, which he thought there would be no sort of difficulty in forcing open, he found that the night was getting so dark that he could do no more good by remaining in the garden, and he left it.

It was on his route back to the barracks that the storm which dispersed the dancers on the green took place, and Captain Strachan arrived at the barrack-gate in a state of terror, for the flash of lightning had appeared to him as if it had passed within very close proximity to his person, indeed, and the roar of the thunder had sounded in his ears like a foretaste of the vengeance of the Almighty, for the awful crime he even then meditated.

Breathless and alarmed, the villain sought and gained his own room, and locked it upon the inside before the colonel and the officers returned to the barracks. But it was not for long that the place was in solitude. He soon heard the laughter of the officers as they sought their different quarters, and kept calling to each other about what happened at the fete, and the probability of there yet being a more formidable storm before the night was fairly over.

No one asked for Captain Strachan. It seemed as if by general consent his very existence were ignored by the officers of the regiment.

Clinching his fists and shaking them violently in the air, he muttered—

"Oh, but the time shall soon come when, if you do not speak of me, you shall speak of my acts, and I hope that the next colonel you have may be a man who will lead you a very different life to what this easy-going Percival has done. By all that's terrible, I will make a change in the regiment."

"Hilloa, Wilton," cried some voice upon the stairs. "Is that you, Wilton?"

"No, sir," said a voice. "Mr. Wilton

has gone home. The colonel gave him leave, sir."

"Oh, very well; all right."

"Indeed! So they ask for Wilton, do they ?" muttered Strachan. "That was Major Cuthbert's voice. So, they could not go to supper without Wilton; and Corporal Steady, for that was his voice that replied to them, must needs call him Mr. Wilton. Ha! Well, Mr. Wilton, we shall see—we shall see. I must be ill now—too ill to leave the brarracks for some time. That is easily managed."

After some search among his effects, Strachan produced a little medicine-chest, from which he procured a drug, that, while it would eventually do him no harm, would produce real sickness and a most cadaverous expression of countenance. He took rather a full dose of it.

"This will make me suffer for some hours," he said, "but it will have the effect of establishing the fact of my being ill; and as the illness will be mysterious, I can feign to-morrow as many symptoms as I please. I think I am a match for a regimental surgeon."

CHAPTER XXXV.

CAPTAIN STRACHAN DECEIVES THE SURGEON OF THE REGIMENT.

IT gave Strachan some satisfaction to be as troublesome as possible, so he waited until half an hour past midnight, and then, opening his window, he called out in the barrack yard—

"Sentry—sentry !"

"Yes, sir," replied the soldier on duty by the officers' quarter.

"Pass the word to the guard-house that Captain Strachan is very ill, and requires the surgeon in his own room, at once."

"Yes, sir."

This was a piece of duty which the sentry could not refuse to execute, so he passed the message to the next man on duty, and he to the next, until the officer of the guard was made aware of it, and with a shrug of his shoulders he said to the sergeant—

"You must just go and knock up Dr. Smith, sergeant, and tell him. The fellow must not have any complaint against us. Go to the doctor, sergeant."

"Yes, sir."

The doctor of the regiment, who was in a very delightful first sleep, was duly roused with the information that an officer was ill, and he sprang out of bed with professional alacrity, and hurried on his clothes, and was in the barrack-yard in a very few moments.

"Who is it, sergeant? Not the colonel, I hope?"

"Oh, no, sir; it's Captain Strachan."

"The devil it is ?"

"Yes, sir, just so."

The surgeon bit his lip, for he felt that it was wrong to say anything before the sergeant ; but he was so provoked at having to get out of bed for such a man as Strachan, that it was really quite a triumph of temper to him to hold his peace.

By all this we may see how Strachan was universally detested in the regiment, and how freely the officers had spoken of him and his actions.

"Well, Captain Strachan, you are ill, it is reported," said the surgeon to his patient, when they were together. "What is it, sir?"

"I don't know. Look at me."

The surgeon took up the candle listlessly, and by its aid examined the pallid countenance of the captain. The drug had done its work, and he looked really dreadfully ill.

"Humph! what do you feel?"

"Dying."

"You don't say so?"

"Yes. I have controlled this illness for hours, as I did not wish to disturb you, doctor ; but as I thought it would not sound well that I should be found dead in my room, I thought I would send for you."

"Oh, you are very good. Are you sick?"

"Yes."

"In pain ?"

"Awful !"

"And what has occasioned all this? Can you give me any idea yourself upon the subject, Captain Strachan?"

"I have but one supposition, and that, perhaps, only grows out of the mysterious nature of my malady."

"Pray what is that ?"

"Poison."

The doctor rather shuddered.

"Do you mean to say that you have taken poison on your own account, Captain Strachan, or that it has been administered to you by some one ?"

"I assure you, doctor, that I am not at all tired of existence, and have several things to do yet before I die ; therefore, I am not likely, knowingly, to take anything that I do not think perfectly wholesome. I may be wrong altogether in my surmise; but if I am right, some enemy has managed to give me a dose."

The surgeon was rather alarmed.

"I will send you an active emetic, captain," he said, "and if you should get worse, pray send for me again."

"I am much obliged."

Captain Strachan spoke in a low, enfeebled tone of voice, and then affected to fall back in the chair he was sitting in, as though the exertion of talking to the doctor had nearly extinguished the little remnant of life that was left in him.

A professional feeling now overcame all others in the mind of the surgeon, and he prepared to do his duty by the detested Captain Strachan as cleverly, and to the utmost of his ability, as he would have done it to any other officer of the regiment.

The emetic was brought, and Strachan had the courage to take it, and it certainly did him good. He declared himself better —a tonic was left him—and the surgeon went to his own quarters again, much marvelling in his own mind at the mysterious illness of Captain Strachan, and really thinking that he was much worse than the rascal knew himself to be.

Thus it was that the news spread all over the regiment on the following morning, that Captain Strachan was not long for this world, and that he was not at all likely to leave his room alive.

This was just what he wished should be the impression upon the minds of every one in the regiment, and there he lay upon a couch in his own room, fully relieved from all duty, and at perfect leisure to think over his nefarious plans for the time that was to come.

During that day he wrote, in so capital an imitation of the hand-writing of Arthur Wilton, that any one would be deceived by it, a letter to the following import.

"Barracks, Riversdale, Devon.

"To the Manager at the General Steam Packet Company Office.

"SIR—Can you be so good as to inform me, provided I arrive in London any morning by an early hour, by what route I can most expeditiously make a Dutch port? Is Hamburgh open to English visitors? Please to address as above.

"I am, sir,
"Yours faithfully,
"ARTHUR WILTON."

This letter Captain Strachan carefully sealed and addressed to the office in London.

After that he wrote various memoranda upon the leaves of a perfectly new pocketbook, such as the following:—

"Best route to America.—Go to Hamburgh, or Amsterdam. Stay there a week, under assumed name, and then embark in American trading vessel for any port in United States."

"If any jewels in box, get rid of them in Holland.—Query: Any Jews in Holland?"

"Send for A. in short time, and persuade her—it won't require much after what has passed—to leave old R. When a girl has bidden adieu to her virtue, she don't want much asking to follow the man of her choice."

"Memorandum. Try to think on what would be most likely to fix the affair on S. That would be glorious."

Upon different pages, thus Captain Strachan made entries upon these most common-place subjects, and wrote down little sums in figures, as though the pocket book had been made a receptacle of accounts, as well as many other descriptions of memoranda. It took him some hours to prepare this horrible book, upon the blank leaf at the beginning of which he wrote "A. Wilton," in a straggling, careless manner, as a man would in an idle moment write his name in his own pocketbook.

"That will do," said Strachan. "Ah! how cheerfully the drums and fifes strike upon the air."

He crept to the window of his room, and he saw that the whole regiment was going out for a morning march, for the sake of exercise. A footstep without reminded him that some one was approaching, and he had just time to fling himself upon the couch again, when the doctor appeared.

"Well, sir, how are you this morning?"

"Better—but, oh! so weak."

"Well, that will go off. You had better not attempt to leave your room."

"I could not if my life depended upon it."

"Continue the tonic that I ordered you —I see you have plenty of it. I will see you again at mid-day."

"Good day, doctor."

The doctor slightly inclined his head, and retired.

The smile that lighted up the features of Captain Strachan as he listened to the retiring footsteps of the doctor, was truly diabolical. He then crept to the window again, but he took care not to show himself, and he saw the doctor go up to Colonel Percival, and say something, and then they both glanced up towards his, Strachan's, room; and in a few moments more, the regiment had marched out, with the exception of a few who were on barrack duty for the day.

"This is as it should be," said Strachan, as he rose. "They will now be absent for some time, and I will see if I cannot, by some means, stow this pocket-book in a safe place."

The officers' quarters, he knew perfectly well, would not be visited by anyone for some time, so that he considered he might, with perfect security, leave his room. He did so, and sought the officers' retiring-room, as it was called, where they were in the habit of leaving their caps, cloaks, and swords, when they came into their own apartments.

That room was a wide, dark, straggling-looking apartment, with tables in it, and upon the walls a number of pegs for hanging the caps and cloaks on. What would Strachan not have given to have found some garment of Wilton's there! But such a piece of good luck to his atrocious plans was not to be, and he gazed around him like some famished tiger, as he looked for a place in which to put the pocket-book that he had prepared with its damning memoranda, and which he intended should be found after the murder of the colonel.

In one room lay a heap of old newspapers and periodicals. He knew that room was only cleared out once a week, and that the day before, no doubt, it had undergone that process.

"In six days there will be another clearance here," he muttered, "and then anything concealed will be sure to turn up. Go thou there, then, mute but excellent evidence."

As he spoke, he thrust the pocket-book right below the heap of waste paper, and then he hastily left the room. There was a brown great-coat hanging upon a nail on the outer side of the door, and Strachan recognised it in a moment to be the doctor's. After a pause, he took it in his hand, and muttered—

"If I could only find, now, one of his cocked hats—"

Rushing hastily to the room, he soon found what he sought—which was, a cocked hat, such as is worn by the surgeons of infantry regiments, and which makes them tolerably conspicuous when amongst the officers, or holding a place to the right of the regiment.

Captain Strachan might or might not have had a very clear idea of what he meant to do with the doctor's coat and hat, but he took both to his own room, and carefully examined them.

"Now," he said, "I most wish for night. Let me see how far I have this

Wilton in the toils. There are the lette to Amelia, which she will be compelled produce. There is the memorandum boo and there will be the letter to the shippi agency office in London; and then it w go hard with me but I find a means placing in his possession a somethi which shall be easily proved to have con from the captain's chamber. And no for my tools."

The tools that Strachan spoke of co sisted of as complete a set of hous breaking implements as it was possible procure. Heaven only knows what kin of career that bold bad man had go through previous to his joining the arm but from the manner in which he handl the tools that he produced, it was qui clear that he knew the use of them pe fectly well.

"I must risk something," he sai "as all must who engage in such enterprise as this that I am going upon but I do not think I risk much. Oh, what value now would a real accompli whom I could trust be to me; but have none such. No. There is no on whom I dare trust in this affair—n even Huncks; although I will make hi useful, and force him to be my accompli to a certain extent, whether he like it not."

The idea of Captain Strachan was t make Huncks the depositary of the stole property from the colonel's brass-boun chest, and if he, Huncks, made the leas diffidence about it afterwards, he intende to threaten to accuse him, in case he Strachan, should be himself accused, o a complete complotment with him in th murder.

Such a threat he knew well would frighten Huncks out of his life almost, and at all events secure his most complete silence, and force him to do al in the affair that he, Strachan, require him.

CHAPTER XXXVI.

THE NIGHT OF HORROR COMMENCE AT THE BARRACKS AND ENDS AT TH ABBEY.

ALL that day, then, Captain Stracha kept his room at the barracks. The surgeon looked in upon him at twelv o'clock, and he found his patient decidedl no better. Of course the surgeon, i such a case, having no suspicion that the illness was in every way feigned, was compelled to take for granted what hi patient told him.

THE POST-MAN'S JEALOUSIES AROUSED ON THE RETURN OF THE REGIMENT.

"I can't sleep," said Stratchan.

"Oh, well, we must procure you sleep, then, by a different remedy. You, probably, have no objection to an opiate?"

"None in the least."

"Very well, I will send you one."

"I shall not take it until night," said Captain Strachan, "however, for sleep in the day time always disturbs my faculties. I presume I may count upon being quite undisturbed during the night if I do take a sleeping draught?"

"Of course. I will give orders that no one is to awaken you by any means."

"Sir, I thank you for your kind attention."

The surgeon was in good mind to say that it was no kind attention at all, for that in professionally attending Strachan, he was only complying with the strict letter of his duty; but, after all, he did not think it worth while to provoke anything in the shape of a discussion upon that point, and he left the designing villain to further plot

No. 15.

and plan the horrors with which his mind was full.

The sleeping draught was brought to Strachan in due course, and he took it into his room with quite a sad and hypocritical look, which impressed the soldier who brought it exceedingly with the seeming fact of the protracting illness under which he, Strachan, was then suffering so acutely.

"I don't think that the captain will be long in this world," said the soldier to a companion. "He looks as if he had his route."

"And a good job too," said the other. "You may depend upon it he will have a warm billet in the other world."

"Ah, like enough, that."

Strachan's first act when he was alone was to throw away the sleeping draught.

"I require to be wide awake to-night," he said, "so you are of no use to me. And now for my arms."

The weapons that he had provided himself with consisted of a pair of very small pocket pistols, and a dagger or Malay knife, the blade of which was sharp upon each edge, and measured about eight inches in length. It had a handle that afforded a capital hold, and was in every way a most fearful and murderous weapon.

Upon the stock of one of the pistols he scratched the letters A. W., and he did the same upon the handle of the dagger, so that if by any accident he should be compelled to leave them behind him, or thought proper as circumstances might turn out to do so, they would seem to belong to Arthur Wilton.

It will be seen how this arch-traitor neglected no little means by which he could entangle his victim.

And now the night fairly crept on, and all was dull and dreary in the barrack-yard. It was a gloomy pleasure to Strachan to hear that the wind was rising, and howling and screaming round the barrack roof and chimney tops. That the weather would be extremely squally all night long there was but little doubt. The storm that had so recently happened appeared to be the precursor of a very unsettled state of the atmosphere.

"Ay, blow on, winds," said Captain Strachan; "let the stormy gusts make their weak voice heard. There will be, I hope, a storm to-morrow of a diffent sort. Men will look at each other in dismay, and for many nights to come their dreams will be of blood."

In order to husband his strength as much as possible for what he had to do, he now lay down to rest, but not to sleep; and until it was eleven o'clock, and the barrack-gates had been shut two hours, he did not rise.

Of course, notwithstanding the gates might be shut, there was free ingress and egress for all officers.

The thought now struck Strachan that it was just possible something might occur to induce a visit to be paid to his rooms before he returned to them, and in that case his absence would undo much that he had been doing. To provide against the possible consequences of such a contingency, he now set about rather a cunning scheme.

Captain Strachan folded up some of his more bulky clothing, and placed them in his bed in such a way that it had very much the appearance as though some one were sleeping there, and then he stuffed out a night-cap to the shape of a head, and placed it, partially covered by the clothes, upon the pillow, as though some one there slept. He took care to close the shutters of the room, so as to darken it as much as possible, and then drawing a table to the bed-side, he placed upon it the bottle that had held the opiate he had flung away as useless.

"That will do," he said. "If they come into the room they will, at a glance, think they see me lying there, and surely there will not appear to be any sufficient reason to awaken me."

After this he put on the coat and the cocked hat of the surgeon, which articles, it will be remembered, he had possessed himself of. The surgeon was not so tall as Strachan by a few inches, but after a little practice in his rooms, he found it was easy enough to stoop, so as to reduce his height without it being observable that he was doing so at night.

And now that all his preparations were complete, all he had to do was to arrange to quit the barracks as quietly and unobserved as possible, and to induce the sentry at the gate to think that he was the surgeon, who was going forth on some business.

The whole barracks seemed to be amazingly quiet. Not the slightest sound met the listening ear of Captain Strachan, and he began to think that now was his time to descend from his room and cross the yard. If any one were to meet him, and speak to him, of course his risk would be great, but still that was a chance there was no avoiding, except by giving up the enterprise, and that was not what Strachan was at all now likely to do.

Standing, however, at the door of his

room, he listened for the space of about five minutes, to assure himself that no one was really at hand, and then closing the door, he rapidly and lightly descended to the barrack-yard. Of course, attired as he was, none but an officer would speak to him; and, perhaps, his greatest danger lay in the chance of meeting with the surgeon himself; but that was, after all, but a very remote chance.

One sergeant crossed Strachan in the barrack-yard, and saluted him as he passed, and Strachan, in the manner that he had frequently noticed the surgeon, returned the salute. That man had a peculiarity, as, indeed, all men have if it be watched for, in their simplest actions.

In another minute the gate was gained, and Strachan opened the wicket and passed out. The sentinel took a look to see who it was, and then drew himself up and saluted, as he supposed, the surgeon of the regiment.

Again Strachan imitated the manner of the surgeon in replying to the salute, and then he passed on.

"That is done," he muttered to himself. "All that danger is passed; and now for the Abbey."

Captain Strachan reckoned without his host, for he had not gone far ere he was met by a corporal returning to the barracks, who had been out till twelve o'clock upon leave. The moment the corporal saw, as he supposed, the surgeon, he stopped, and after saluting him respectfully, he said—

"If you please, sir, I am no better."

This was rather a puzzler to Strachan, for it evidently related to some former circumstance of which he could have no knowledge.

"Indeed!" he said, in as good an imitation of the surgeon's voice as he could improvise at the moment.

"No, sir, not a bit. Shall I take any more of the medicine?"

"Yes, oh, yes."

"Very good, sir. Perhaps you will see me before roll call, sir?"

"Certainly. Good night."

"Good night, sir."

Strachan passed on, and he was conscious that after going a little way towards the barrack, the corporal had stopped to look back after him, and the terror that he might be suspected, if not absolutely recognised, came so strongly over Strachan that he was half in the mind to go back and take the corporal's life. Strachan would have cared little for the sacrifice of half-a-dozen lives if they stood between him and his purpose; but then he was so

close to the barracks that it might be a very dangerous thing to attempt, and he walked on. The awful maledictions, though, that in a muttered voice he heaped upon the head of the man who had given him this alarm and hindrance, were truly diabolical.

It was not until he had got quite away from the barrack wall, that Strachan ventured to look round. The corporal was gone, and now he began to please himself with the idea that after all the man had never paused, and that it was a delusion of his own to suppose that he had done so; and, therefore, the murderer breathed again a little more freely than he had done.

Buttoning the coat closely up to his throat, and pulling the cocked hat down over his eyes, Strachan now, with rapid steps, went upon the road to the Abbey.

Oh, what a thing is guilt! How often upon that route did Strachan start at his own shadow, or fancy that he saw faces glaring at him in the hedges as he passed. Once, too, he thought he heard a pattering step close behind him, and he turned with a cry of fear, but he saw nothing to create any alarm.

On—on, he went, until he got within sight of the Abbey, and then as he emerged into a little bit of the road that lay higher and more exposed than that which he had been traversing, he fully descried what a rough and boisterous night it was, for he could hardly keep the surgeon's hat upon his head, and the sharp, cold, pouring rain came with such a dashing force into his face, that he was glad to turn his back upon it.

Struggling on, Strachan passed some tall trees that were on each side of the road, and the mad riot that the wind made among them, was something hideous to listen to.

"It is all the better," muttered Strachan. "The rougher the night, the less liability is there of my meeting with any one. Ah, that sound again."

He heard the pattering footsteps behind him, and his really craven heart shook with fear, as he shaded his eyes with his hand, and tried to pierce the obscurity of the night.

He saw nothing.

"This must be imagination," he said, "and nothing but imagination. I am letting my senses play the fool with me. Curses on it, cannot I go upon a little affair like this without suffering all these terrors?

The pattering of footsteps came again, and this time Strachan, with a feeling of desperation, turned and rushed in the direction of the sound with a pistol in his hand, and he fell right over a young calf which had strayed from some neighbouring pasture into the high road.

If the animal had not recovered its feet first, and made off at full speed in good time, there is very little doubt but that Strachan in his anger would have killed it; but as it was, he had discretion enough, even in his anger, not to desist in his intentions by following the animal.

A few hasty oaths settled the matter, and, rather shaken by his fall, the captain resumed his journey to the Abbey. That there would be a sentinel somewhere about the outer wall, he well knew, and now he approached with the most extreme caution in order not to be observed by him. The hour was rather unfavourable, for, in all probability, the sentinel was a fresh one only a little time before, as it had gone twelve o'clock while he, Strachan, was speaking to the corporal near the barracks; but still, as the night was so intensely dark, he thought it would be no difficult matter to get over the wall without the sentinel noticing anything of him.

The wind each moment now seemed to gather strength, and the rain, without being at all continuous, came now and then in such dashing gusts, that it was perfectly perplexing—the sky was perfectly black —not a star could peep out from amid such a mass of clouds ; and as Strachan cowered down in an angle of the wall, the wind among the trees in the old garden came plainly upon his attentive ear.

CHAPTER XXXVII.

TAKES A GLANCE AT THE STATE OF AFFAIRS AT THE ABBEY.

SITTING in his little room that had been ceded to him by the colonel, in the Abbey, was Arthur Wilton. Twice he had opened his window and gone out into the old garden to look at the weather, for the wind at times made such an uproar, that he could not help thinking the elements were in a greater state of commotion than was really the fact.

The dashing rain had forced him to retreat again to the room, and the last time he made such a voluntary excursion into the night air, something prompted him, he knew not what, to bolt the window in the inside.

The colonel had retired to rest, and the guard was by the fire in one of the old kitchens gossiping upon such subjects as chanced to come uppermost, while the sergeant was laid at full length upon an old dresser, and quietly dozing.

Arthur Wilton had some eight or ten books with him that he had got from the library which has been alluded to; but do all he could, he found it impossible to settle his mind to reading, and an extraordinary wakefulness, to which he was by no means subject, took possession of him.

It seemed to him as if by some strange means all his senses were preternaturally acute, and more than once imagination deceived him into the idea that there were strange noises in the garden mingling with the roar of the wind.

This was, to say the least of it, a very painful state of the nervous system to get into; and once more casting aside the book he in vain tried to read, Arthur Wilton unfastened his window and stepped out into the garden.

The free open air, so fresh and full of keen moisture, had the immediate effect of restoring him to a more healthful peace of mind, and he smiled at the strange sensations that had come over him within doors ; and yet he was young and healthy, and tolerably happy and full of hope for the future, which all seemed to be spread out smilingly before him; and, therefore, it was something more than strange that he should feel so mentally distracted.

"What can it mean?" he said, as he strolled along beneath the tall trees in the garden. "What can it mean? Is there any truth in the idea that great events and great changes in one's life and prospects send before them such strange feelings, in some manner to prepare the brain for the shock of the real and unmistakable reality?"

This was a question which had puzzled deeper casuists, and more elaborate thinkers than Arthur Wilton, and no doubt it is one which at some time or another presents itself to the minds of all persons.

"Well," he said, after a time ; "the more I think, the more I get lost in the mazes of such intricate inquiries, so I will think no more about them. The daylight will dissipate all such fears, and, indeed, if we think of such things at all, they should bring a healthy mid-day intellect to bear upon them, and not one clouded by night's shadows and excited by that mystery which to a certain extent always accompanies the absence of the sunlight.

Arthur Wilton had reached the wall now, and he heard the regular tramp of the sentinel without. He thought it quite a relief to be able to speak to somebody, and he called out—

"Hilloa! sentry, is all quiet upon your post?"

"Yes, sir," replied the soldier, from the other side of the wall. "I think you are Mr. Wilton, sir?"

"Yes; don't you know my voice?"

"I do now, sir. All's right."

"When is your relief?"

"At two o'clock, Mr. Wilton."

"Oh, very well. Good night. Be vigilant."

"Yes, sir. Good night."

The soldier resumed his march along the shadow of the wall, and Wilton turned towards the house again, quite satisfied in his mind at having said something to a human being and had a reply. To be sure, there was nothing in the world to hinder him from going to the guard room, but he was the colonel's sentry, and he rather shrank from an association with those whom he had come into social contact with, from an accident that no doubt would soon be undone, as the colonel had promised to get him his discharge as early as possible.

Arthur returned to his little room again, and lay upon one of the benches and tried to read himself weary, so as to feel an inclination to retire to his rest.; but still he felt wide awake as before, although the strange fears that had possessed him had in a great measure vanished.

There was in one of the turrets of the Abbey an old crazy clock, and during the day, a soldier of the guard, who had been in the business of a clock-maker before joining the army, had paid great attention to the ancient time register, and had boasted that he had made it strike. That boast was no idle one, for now at a quarter past twelve the old clock began to strike, and to his great surprise Arthur Wilton counted no less than twenty-four sounds.

It was not until it occurred to him that he had heard the soldier say something about the old clock that he was able to move, from the surprise that the unexpected sounds awakened in him; and then he laughed at the idea of the evident consternation that any one who had no means of explaining the phenomenon, and who might be of a superstitious turn of mind, would probably feel at hearing so insane a clock.

That clock, with its twenty-four strokes, did shake even the nerves of Captain Strachan a little, for he, to whom we must now return, heard it as he crouched down close to the old wall.

It was in vain that he strove to explain the phenomenon. He had no evidence upon the subject, and he tried to think that it might mean something that it would be well for him to profit by. The rapid approach of the soldier, though, as he took his march upon the limits of his post, warned him that there was no time to be lost if he would reach the garden.

By creeping along stealthily he soon reached the corner portion of the wall where it will be recollected he had, while quite free from all interruption, arranged an easy mode of climbing over the obstruction. There he waited until the sentry had gone to the limit of his march, and had turned again. The back of the soldier was now to Strachan, and, therefore, then was the time when the ascent to the top of the wall was to be made.

Rather nervously, upon his hands and knees, Strachan ascended, and got on the top of the wall. In a few minutes then his head was below it, and he was comparatively safe. He clung to the wall-fruit with a desperate clutch, and had just got about one third of the distance down the inner face of the wall, when his foot slipped, and his whole weight depending upon rather a slender branch that he had hold of, it come away, and down fell Strachan into the garden-bed below.

The distance that he fell was inconsiderable, but it was the fright and the uncertainty of where he was going that completely for a time prostrated all the energies of Strachan, and made him lie like one dead beneath the wall; and yet he was only a little shaken. Those shakes, however, tend to unnerve a man much more than a positive wound would, and Strachan, when he did recover sufficiently to rise, felt that another such misadventure would go far towards totally incapacitating him for the work he had come upon.

"Nothing but accidents," he muttered. "Surely everything is bent upon thwarting me in my plans; but if all hell were to rise up against me, I would persevere."

He walked to and fro for a little time in the garden, now, until he had in a great measure recovered his usual condition.

Certainly, so far as he had gone, Captain Strachan might consider himself to be tolerably successful, for he had not only avoided the sentinel at the back of the garden, but he had achieved an entrance into the premises without creating any alarm, or very materially disturbing his economy, notwithstanding the little malapropos fall that he had had from the wall.

It may at first sight look very much like a want of vigilance upon the part of the soldier on duty at the outer side of the garden wall, that he should have permitted Strachan to ascend it as he did; but if we come to consider that there could not possibly be upon the mind of the soldier the least idea of any danger, we shall hardly be surprised that he should consider the duty he was on more as a form than a utility.

Who could have fancied for one moment that in England Colonel Percival needed any protection? To be sure, as the colonel of the regiment, it was in accordance with military usage that a sentinel should keep a nominal kind of watch over his abode; but that was done without the most distant thought that there was any real exigency in the case to require it.

Hence was it, then, that Captain Strachan had managed with so much apparent ease to get into the garden of the old mansion.

The pattering of the rain upon the trees now was the only marked sound that came upon the ears of the midnight assassin; and after a few minutes more, to assure himself that he was all right for the dastardly enterprise he came upon, Strachan proceeded to move towards the house.

"Now," he said, "what is to stop me in the course that I have marked out for myself? What is to stop me in the commission of the deed I come here to commit? And oh, above all delightful thoughts, what is to stop me from placing the consequences of that deed upon the head of Arthur Wilton?"

This feeling of diabolical revenge against poor Arthur was apparently stronger in the mind of Strachan than his wish to commit the murder, by which he hoped to profit so much, for he was resolved to take possession of the small chest which contained the colonel's principal cash and jewels.

By walking through the flower beds in the garden, instead of taking a route by the paths, Captain Strachan considered that he accomplished two important objects.

In the first place he had not the least risk of meeting with any one, for it was not likely that any but himself would set about perpetrating so much wanton destruction by taking such a course, and in the next place, his footsteps upon the soft mould were completely silent.

In this manner, then, he, in the course of some five or six minutes, happened to emerge just opposite the window of the room that was occupied by Arthur Wilton.

It was, under ordinary circumstances, certainly, a thing of not the smallest importance whether Wilton chose to fall asleep in a chair in his room, or go to the chamber that was prepared for him; but upon the present occasion it was a most important matter, and one that, happening as it did by pure accident, was pregnant with the most important results.

There sat Arthur, then, sleeping in a chair, with his head resting upon his hands, and an open book before him, and a candle just down in the socket of the candlestick, and flickering unsteadily, threatening each moment to go out.

Captain Strachan, after gazing at the window for some moments, felt quite certain that through the blind which Wilton for a wonder had drawn down he saw the reflection of a light.

"Curses on whoever is up at this hour!" he muttered.

For a few moments, it seemed to Strachan as if his whole project were knocked upon the head, by the untoward event of some one being up in that part of the old villa.

To be sure, he knew well that the guard in the kitchen would be up, but then he likewise knew that it would be merely upon a point of duty that they were so, and he hoped that he should get the deed he meditated done before they could take any alarm. But now to find that in a room remote from that which had been made into the guard-room some one was apparently sitting with a light, was a contingency he had not looked for.

"Is it the colonel?" he said to himself.

He feared that he should be obliged to answer that question in the affirmative, and if such were the case, he felt that he would not have the courage to attack him.

To be sure, a pistol would, no doubt, securely do the deed, but the report of fire-arms, of all other sounds, would be the first thing to give an alarm to the guard, and then his escape would be next thing to an impossibility.

We cannot stain our pages with the record of the dreadful expressions that fell from the lips of Captain Strachan when he found this obstacle in the way of his murderous proceeding. Suffice it to say, that for some moments he did nothing but give utterance to the most frightful imprecations; and still the light continued to shine with a flickering and a sickly radiance through the window.

Time, now, was speeding fast away, however, and Strachan felt that if that night he was to accomplish anything, it must be done quickly, or he would have the grey light of morning upon him before he could get back to the barracks and take possession of his own room again.

He was much surprised that all remained so still in the room from whence the light proceeded, for he had not, of course, the least idea that the occupant of that room was sleeping; but this stillness engendered another idea in his mind, which was, that probably there was no one there at all, but that a light had been left in the apartment by accident.

"I must ascertain that," he said.

There was a tolerable breadth of pathway in front of the window; but still, by treading very cautiously, Strachan thought he might approach it without any noise, and he, at all events, made the attempt so to do, and succeeded.

Applying his eyes close to a corner of the window where the blind did not exactly cover the glass, he peeped into the room.

The light was very nearly expiring; but still, as it sent up a fitful flame for a moment, it was sufficient to enable him to recognise Arthur Wilton.

———

CHAPTER XXXVIII.

CORPORAL STEADY FINDS HIMSELF RATHER BENIGHTED WITH COCKLES.

WHILE, with feelings which it would be in vain to attempt to classify or analyse, Captain Strachan is gazing upon the slumbering Arthur Wilton, we must, in order that our narrative of this fearful night's proceedings should be complete in all its points, leave him for a few moments to repair to the guard-room, as it was now temporarily called, of the villa.

It was in this large kitchen, being upon the ground-floor, for there were no excavated apartments to the villa, that the guard sat by a large fire they had managed to kindle of wood that they found in some of the yards of the old place.

It was but a small guard, and the soldiers felt that there was no particular duty to do, but that all that was required of them was just the routine work that they were accustomed to in their ordinary quarters. But two men were pacing the night air as sentinels—that is to say the one who had been so successfully evaded by Captain Strachan, and the one who was holding his watch at the front entrance of the villa, where there was a portico that he got under to protect himself from the rain.

We must state, too, that the guard was simply commanded by a sergeant, as the colonel had given the officers, who, by right, ought to have been with it, leave of absence; in fact, the whole affair was conducted as a mere form and ceremony, for which there was no necessity.

Any one who might have had the opportunity of peeping into a guard-room in the middle of the night, will have observed that the soldiers who were not off duty take things pretty easily, and endeavour to assimulate as much comfort with their duties as they possibly can.

One will be stretched before the fire upon his great coat; another will have availed himself of one of the benches as a sleeping-place; some two or three more will be sitting nodding and winking at the glaring fire; and there will always be some one who, in an under tone to a half-asleep neighbour, will be wondering why they are not permitted to have a pipe in the guard-room.

On the present occasion, the guard at the colonel's house were occupied very much in the fashion we have stated. The sergeant had found four chairs and laid himself upon them, and was snoring most unmusically. The men were disposed according to their own notions of comfort as best they could.

"It's a very hard thing, indeed," whispered one, jogging the elbow of a slumbering comrade—"it's a very hard thing."

"Damned hard," said the other; "but what can you expect from a wooden bench?"

"I didn't mean that."

"What the deuce did you mean, then?"

"Why, that it was a very hard thing to have a regimental order against smoking while a man's on duty."

"Oh! I thought you meant the bench."

"No, I didn't. When I 'listed, I said to the sergeant—'Sergeant,' says I, 'is smoking allowed? 'cos if it isn't, I don't think the army will suit me.'"

"And what did he say?" laughed the other.

"Why, he looked at me, and cried out —'Allowed? To be sure it is—only the colonel will keep presenting you with his choice cigars, and as it don't look friendly, and would hurt his feelings if you did not smoke them, it is only when he don't know it that you will be able to take a pipe to yourself.'"

"Ha! ha!"

"D—n it, who's that making a noise?" grunted the corporal, from the dresser.

All was still again in a moment, but the soldiers continued, after a little time, to converse in an under tone.

"It wants a good hour and a half,"

said one of them, "to the changing of the guard, and the corporal wants a bit of rest."

"Small blame to him either," said the other; "but do you mean to tell me that you were actually gammoned in that sort of way about the cigars?"

"Well, I was—but I was precious green then."

"So I should say. Well, I'll try to get a bit of sleep again, hard as this infernal bench I got out of the hall is."

"Well, but, I say, ain't it a hard thing?"

"Don't bother."

The grumbler about his pipe was silent; and resting his head upon his hand, only looked in the fire and sighed for his pipe. Perhaps he was an imaginative soldier, that, and out of the embers could shape strange forms of happy looking pigmies, enjoying their pipes, and grinning and nodding to him, as much as to say—"Ah, old fellow, you can't come this sort of thing."

After a time, however, that soldier, too, forgot his wrongs, and his eyes gradually closed, and he seemed more than once to be on the point of tumbling headlong into the fire; but at the moment, when you would suppose him gone past all redemption, he would right himself again with a lurch backward, and look about him for a minute, and then muttering something about its being very hard, he would resign himself to sleep again.

The rain happened to set that way, and now it beat against the old casement of the kitchen with vehemence, and once or twice the wind came with such a sharp gust, that the whole frame-work of the window shook again.

The effect would then be as if a hand had laid hold of it, and rattled it to and fro as a warning to the guard that the life they all valued was in danger.

They knew it was the wind, though; and the sergeant, after saying "Hilloa!" and being told all was right, would resign himself to sleep again, while the dreaming corporal would mutter in his sleep:—"Eyes right!—Attention!—Left shoulders forward!"

It was just at this time, when every one in the guard-room appeared to be sleeping, that there came from without in the front of the house the sharp, sudden ring of a musket, as it was brought to the charge, and the sentinel's voice was plainly heard, as he called out in clear, sharp accents—

"Who goes there?"

The sergeant jumped up off his four chairs—the corporal rolled off the dresser with a loud crash—the slumbering soldiers sprang to their feet, and seized their arms, that were piled up in a corner by the fire-place.

They heard a conversation going on without, and the musket of the sentinel grounded again upon the stone pavement underneath the balcony.

"Pass on," they heard him say.

"Who the deuce is this?" said the corporal.

The door of the guard-room opened, and two figures, soaked with rain, presented themselves before the astonished eyes of the guard.

"Who comes here?" cried the sergeant.

"Lord bless you, Sergeant White, don't you know me?" said a voice. "Am I so like a drowned rat that you don't know Corporal Steady?"

"Sergeant Steady," said a voice behind him. "Didn't you get a promise of the next sergeancy that was to be had, and don't we always call a man sergeant from that there time, and no mistake?"

"Why, bless me," said the sergeant of the guard, "that is Cockles."

"Cockles it was. and Cockles it is," said the drummer. "Row-de-dow-dow!"

"Yes, here we both are. Come to surrender," said the corporal.

"Yes. Row-de-dow-dow! Prisoners of war."

"Why, what does all this mean?"

"Exp*licate to Sergeant White what it's all about. Steady, my boy, while I get to the fire. Lord bless me, I smoke like a laundry with a month's wash a-going on in it. Dear me, what a smother!"

"The fact is," said Corporal Steady, as he dashed the rain water from his cap, "the colonel gave us leave to be out till ten, so as we had danced with two rather pretty girls on the green yonder, you know, and they had told us they lived close at hand at a place called the Watermill, we thought we would pay them a visit."

"Right it is, and right he's a-telling of it," said Cockles, "and no mistake at all, right and tight as a drum. Row-de-dow!"

"Well, then, close at hand turned out to be nearer eight miles than seven, and when we got there, of course, we couldn't say right-about-face in a minute, for the people would make us taste their old ale."

"True as gospel," said Cockles, "and down as twenty hammers."

"Hold your tongue, will you?"

"Yes, I—that is—row-de-dow! I'm a-holding of it, as fast as I can; but when you mentioned the old ale, somehow, a strange sensation came over me."

"A strange sensation. How do you mean?"

"Why, some of the old ale seemed to be trickling down my throat, and then I heard a voice say, 'Cockles, ain't it good?'"

"You will excuse me, I am sure, Cockles," said the sergeant, "but some-

THE KIND RECEPTION OF ARTHUR BY OLD WILTON.

thing strikes me that you have had a drop too much of the old ale."

"Oh dear, no, not a drain—not a row-de-dow—a drain, I mean; but here we are, Steady and me, and we gives ourselves up to the guard as prisoners. We mean to speak to the colonel about it, and not to go to the regiment till he says it's all right, for the colonel is a trump, and no mistake. Row-de-dow-dow!"

"You had better sit down by the fire, and dry your things, both of you," said the sergeant.

———

CHAPTER XXXIX.

CAPTAIN STRACHAN STILL PURSUES HIS
MURDEROUS INTENTIONS.

WE left Strachan peeping through the windown from the garden at the slumbering form of Arthur Wilton in his room.

The sensations of the villain Strachan were of a mixed character as he so gazed upon the man whom he fully intended to destroy. If it had not been that he considered the death of Wilton, in an ignominious manner, for the supposed horrible crime of murdering the colonel, all but certain, in consequence of the measures he had taken, there is very little doubt but that there and then he would have assassinated the young soldier, for situated as he was, nothing could have been easier.

"Now I could have him as he sleeps," muttered Strachan, "but, after all, what a miserable and poor revenge would that be. Death! Why, it is but one pang and then is over, and no more is heard or known of it. It is the torture of the mind that I want to make him suffer, and which I will make him suffer, or perish myself in the attempt. Curses on him!"

The very serenity with which Arthur Wilton now appeared to be sleeping, was a crime in the eyes of Captain Strachan, for he knew that he never slept in such a manner, with his scared conscience to remind him of his iniquities.

"Oh, if I dared but kill you," muttered Strachan—"if I could but convince myself that such a revenge would satisfy me —But no—no. It would not, I know it would not. Death, sudden and unexpected, is nothing but a passing pang, and then the spirit suffers no more. It is the living who suffer, not the dead. No, I will not kill you, Arthur Wilton, though I could easily do so now—I will not do you that favour. It would be one, for I am determined that you shall suffer much more than death alone could make you suffer. I will not kill you."

The villain now shrunk back, for fear that by any chance Arthur Wilton should look up and see that awful face, full of wild, vindictive passions, glaring at him through the window.

"Now, I must find some mode of entrance to the house," thought Strachan. "I had, too, at the moment, forgotten that there was the gold of the colonel to be obtained, with some of which I must still contrive to silence that devil in human shape, Huncks, or he will yet play me some trick."

The revengeful feelings of Strachan must have been great, indeed, when, even for one passing moment, he could have forgotten that there was treasure to be had by the death of the colonel, provided he could manage that death with silence and skill, and get quite clear of the old villa after the deed were done.

Beyond a general notion of the interior of the place, the knowledge that he, Strachan, had of the house was not much; but he thought that by one of the windows he might manage to effect an entrance.

Making his way, then, to a part of the house distant sufficiently far from the guard-room, and from Arthur Wilton, to diminish to an imperceptible amount any chance of being overheard by them, the murderer crept close to the lower windows and tried then.

"Fastened," he ejaculated. "Fastened, by all that's disappointing. Do they suspect anything amiss, or is it but the ordinary precaution of a man who sleeps in a strange house? Surely it is nothing more?"

It was quite in vain that Strachan strove to shake one of the windows. The shutters upon the inside were strongly barred, and although by a little force and perseverance he might truly enough have succeeded in bursting them open at one of the windows, the doubt as to the room he might be making his way into being empty, and the possibility that in the effort he should make noise enough at that still hour of the night to be heard, affected him.

"Curses on them all, must I fail now," he muttered, "after all that I have hitherto done in safety and so well? No—no! What is this? A tree of great thickness nailed to the wall. What hinders me to climb it, and so reach the upper windows, which are not at all likely to be made fast? Ha! this is what your pious people now, if they were going upon any venture of their own, would call quite providential. Ha! ha!"

With such awful ribaldry upon his lips, Strachan carefully commenced the ascent of the tree, than which, with a firm hand and anything like care, nothing could be more easy, for the branches were all thick, and there were numerous strong stems standing out from the wall which would have sustained ten times the weight of Captain Strachan.

In the course of two minutes the villain had reached the balcony of a window that opened on to a staircase. That window was not fastened, and it yielded to a touch, so that after listening for a few moments and hearing no sound, he stepped at once into the villa.

Strachan left the window open to facilitate his escape in case he might have to make it hurriedly, and then he crouched down upon the staircase, and after again listening and finding all remained still as before, he commenced his search for the chamber of the unfortunate Colonel Percival.

After prowling along the landing-place for some little time, Strachan encountered something over which he nearly fell, and upon feeling it he found it was a portmanteau that no doubt formed part of the baggage of the colonel. There were several other articles likewise lying about, so that the progress of the murderer was necessarily slow and anxious; but those objects convinced him that he was close to the chamber of Colonel Percival.

With the most extreme caution he placed his hand upon the lock of a door, and taking a full minute to turn it, he found that the door yielded. He was terrified at the idea that the hinges might creak, but they did not, and in a crouching attitude Strachan glided into the room.

Then, like some wild and half-famished animal listening for his prey, crouched Strachan, with the hope of hearing the breathing of the colonel; but the stillness in the place soon convinced him that the room was empty.

This apartment into which he had made, was in reality the sleeping chamber of Arthur Wilton, which it was a world of pities he was not occupying, for he would have been safe from the assassin, and possibly he might have heard something of what was going on, for the slightest alarm would have been sufficient to make the dastardly murderer fly in terror from the place.

The window-blind was not down in this room, and the faint night-light came into the room, by which Strachan could see that it was a sleeping chamber he had got into; and now, being pretty well assured that it was vacant, he crept to the bed and felt it.

"No one has slept here as yet, to-night," he said. "Ah, it is Wilton's. Here is a coat, and here some boots. Yes, it is Wilton's room. I will yet make some use of this discovery."

Creeping out of the room, then, he made his way along the corridor to the next door and laid his hand upon that lock with a kind of conviction that it was that of the colonel's chamber.

"Is this it?" he murmured. "Am I so near to him at last? Is this it?"

He shook now so much, that he found it impossible to open the door, until he had recovered a little of his usual villanous equanimity; but that was not long in coming back to him.

"All is well yet," he muttered; "I shall do it yet. I shall be enriched, and Wilton will die!"

These words inspired him with fresh determination, and he slowly turned the handle of the door. It yielded, but the hinges began to give an ominous kind of long-drawn groan.

Strachan stopped the progress of opening the door in a moment, and the perspiration, induced by intense fear, broke out upon his brow.

If that were really the colonel's room, and he should chance to awaken and make a rush out on to the landing with his customary precipitancy of action, Strachan felt that for him there would be no chance. The mere dread of such a circumstance, now that he had got so far, all but convulsed him with fear.

It was some five or six minutes before this agony of apprehension that the villain suffered from subsided, and he was able to convince himself that if the colonel really did sleep there, he slept securely.

By applying his ear to the narrow opening of the door now, he heard the deep regular breathing of some one. It could be no one but Colonel Percival, since Arthur Wilton was below ; and, therefore, he, Strachan, had gained the room he was in search of. That opening of the door, though, that had been absolutely achieved at the risk of the sound of the hinges on their rusty centres awakening the colonel, was too narrow to allow him to pass through, and he felt that now he must either abandon his criminal enterprise with all its, to him, promising results, or run the risk of getting the door wider open in spite of all obstacles.

Captain Strachan, though in the pursuit of his villanies, brought to bear an amount of ingenuity, which would have gone far to have advanced his fortunes in some honest and honourable course, and he now tried an experiment which was crowned with success. That experiment was to dash open the door with sudden swiftness, so as to overcome in an instant all resistance of the hinges. He knew that frequently the creaking sound was completely obliterated by following such a course.

He shook again at the risk he was about to run, for it was just possible that the hinges of the door, instead of being silenced by such a course, might give a loud scream, and if they did, there was nothing left for him, but to try to escape with all speed.

Laying hold of the door, then, with both

hands, Strachan swung it suddenly open. The faintest possible sound, only, was produced, and then all was still again.

"Succeeded!" he gasped, in a faint whisper, and he stepped at once into the room of Colonel Percival.

Oh, how little did that pure and generous-spirited man, when, with a smile and a blessing upon those dear to him, he laid himself down to rest upon that night, think that in this world, with all its cares and joys, he would never rise again!

How little did she, the wife of his bosom, who on the morrow thought of the joy of being with him once again, dream that she was never more in this mortal state to look upon him but in the cold apathy of death!

The murderer was now hovering around the couch of his victim.

Crouching quite close down to the very floor—creeping along like a serpent to his prey—scarcely daring to draw breath, lest some pitying angel should waft it to the ears of the sleeper—Strachan moved his way to the bed-side of Colonel Percival, and each moment his eyes got more and more accustomed to the dim light of the room, and began to see the outlines of the different objects.

There was the tall old-fashioned bedstead with its sombre hangings—there was an old wardrobe, enriched with grand carvings, the top of which reached nearly to the ceiling, and upon a chair close by the bed-side lay the colonel's clothes. His sword was upon the table, where besides was an open book.

Captain Strachan did not see these minute objects just then, but he saw the outline, shadowy and indistinct, of the larger ones, and then he paused close to the head of the bed and listened, as though he were listening to the regular breathings of the colonel, as he lay there upon the brink of that eternity, which, however he might reach it through pain and blood, could have no terrors for such a spirit.

And, now, as he shook with apprehension—a dire apprehension that yet a something might occur to baulk him and stop the perpetration of the dreadful deed he had so long meditated—Captain Strachan slowly rose up from the side of the bed, where he had been crouching, and strove to bend a steady gaze upon his victim. His hand was deep in the bosom of his apparel, and there he grasped the double-edged poniard, with which, on account of its noiseless operation, he meant to do the deed.

The colonel moved slightly.

Flat upon the floor sunk Strachan, upon the instant, for he feared that the colonel was about to awaken; but it was only the slight movement of sleep, and yet it would appear that some dream was disturbing the soul of that man who stood on the very threshold of eternity, for he said, faintly—

"Well, then, I say it—God bless you."

The villain Strachan shook so as he heard these words, that he had to clutch his hands as tightly as he could to try to still their intense agitation. In a few more moments, though, all was still again, and the colonel was breathing deeply and regularly.

"Only a dream, after all," muttered Strachan, as he rose up again—"only a dream. Now—now is my time."

He opened his eyes in order to get as accurate a view as possible of the sleeping figure, so as to know where, with a great certainty of inflicting immediate death, to strike, for there was nothing now he dreaded so much as only wounding the colonel, and so inducing a struggle, with all its concomitant uproar. If he were to strike at all, he felt that he must strike home at once.

It was no very easy matter, though, upon that dark night to see exactly how the colonel was lying, and yet he, Strachan, thought he saw enough to enable him to plunge the knife-like poniard into his heart by one blow. To be sure, the bed-clothes were rather in the way, and might, by a possibility, turn aside the point of the dagger; and the only way to guard against that contingency, was to strike so heavily that nothing could resist the weapon, and that was what he determined to do.

How tranquilly the colonel slept!

A spattering dash of rain came against the windows of the room, and Strachan thought that the noise ought to have been sufficient to awaken the colonel, but it did not do so, and the fact that it did not, gave rise to another thought in the mind of the murderer.

"I may as well," he thought, "be very sure of the blow. It is but a movement of my other hand, and then I remove the bed-clothes from his heart. If that is done, I am certain of the fact that, one stroke of this glittering steel will finish the job: otherwise, in the dark, even with all the force I can use, I may only wound him."

That the colonel would, in all probability, awaken at the effort to move the bed-clothes from his heart, Strachan believed; but he intended the death-blow should follow so rapidly, that his victim should not have time even to utter an exclamation.

Dash came the rain again against the window-panes, and with a dull roaring sound the night wind came down the chimney.

It seemed as if the elements were doing their best to shout "Murder!" in the unconscious ears of the sleeper.

"I must be quick," thought Strachan, "now. Ah! he moves."

The colonel muttered something that was not articulated sufficiently clearly to be understood by Strachan, except the last word, and that was, "Charge!"

It was evident that the noise of the wind and the rain had mingled with his slumbers, and induced the idea that he was on the battle field in command of his regiment. He tossed one arm over the coverlet of the bed, and again repeated the word "Charge!" and then he was still as the grave again.

"Ay," shudderingly muttered Strachan, "the red glare of battle will never shine upon your eyes again. You are doomed. I—I will now do it."

He raised his hand, but even then a dreadful fear crept over his heart, and it seemed to him as though some voice had shouted in his ear, "Forbear!" It was only by a great effort that he stopped himself from uttering a shout of terror, but he did succeed in suppressing the sound ; and, then, as he forced his clammy hand on his brow, he whispered—

"I'm the fool of my own fears. If I linger longer over this deed, I shall go mad—stark staring mad. Better to go so after it is done than now."

Once again he was raising his arm to drag the clothing from the chest of the colonel, when there came a piece of old mortar from the chimney-top, rolling down into the grate, and Colonel Percival started up in bed, as he said—

"What's that ?"

Strachan had sunk right down to the ground in a moment, and if the colonel had got out of bed he must have trodden upon him as he there lay.

"What was that ?" repeated the colonel.

Another loosened piece of mortar fell into the grate, and bounded out into the room with a sound that at once proclaimed what it was.

"Oh, it's the rain and wind only in the old chimney," said Colonel Percival. "It is of no consequence, after all."

He at once laid down again and composed himself to sleep, little dreaming of who was breathing in the same room with him.

"A rough night this," he said. "How the wind howls to be sure, and how the rain splashes against the windows. Well, I have slept on a battle field in a louder storm than this ;—storm ! did I call it ?—pho ! this is no storm."

With these words, the colonel closed his eyes again, but it was many minutes before Captain Strachan could persuade himself that he had gone to sleep. It was not until the loud yet regular and deep-drawn respirations had continued for some time, that he could come to the positive conclusion that affairs were now as they had been before the pieces of loosened mortar fell from the chimney ; but at last it was no longer possible to doubt the fact, and he again rose, and was now regarding his victim as steadily as he could do so.

"Now," he said—"now I will do it."

With his left hand he took a cautious clutch at the bed-clothes, and in the other, that was his right hand, he held the poniard. With sudden force he pulled the clothes from off the breast of the colonel.

"God ! Help !"

These were the last words of Colonel Percival, for before they had well left his lips, the poniard of the murderer had sunk deeply into his breast. There was one spasmodic gasp, and then all was over.

CHAPTER XL.

TAKES A GLANCE AT AMELIA, AND SHOWS HOW SHE MET WITH AN ALARM.

WHILE this dreadful deed was being executed at the colonel's villa by the villain Strachan, we have shown how the guard dozed in the old kitchen, little suspecting what horrors were taking place beneath that roof. We have shown how Arthur Wilton slept in the room upon the ground floor, dreaming not of the awful crime that was being perpetrated so close to him, nor of the meshes of that fearful net of iniquity which his enemy was gradually drawing round him.

We will now proceed to the old farm house, were fate, foreknowledge, or Providence, call it what you will, seemed to be slightly shadowing to the beautiful and innocent Amelia something of the deed of blood that was being committed upon that awful night.

Amelia Revis, then, had retired to rest, feeling rather unwell. There was an unwonted weight upon her spirits that she could not account for ; for never since the moment Arthur Wilton had, to save her father from destruction as regarded his home, enlisted in the army, had affairs seemed to wear so pleasant and prosperous a guise as they otherwise then did.

She knew that Arthur had been restored to the full and entire confidence of the colonel. She knew that such an exposure of his enemy, Captain Strachan, had taken place, that there was nothing he could do or say now that could weaken the esteem in which the colonel held Wilton. Nay, she fully expected that soon Arthur would get his discharge from the army, and that then he would make her his wife, with the full and free consent both of his father and her own.

So far, then, everything looked smilingly and well, and yet Amelia retired to rest, as we have said, with a feeling upon her mind as though she were upon the eve of some terrible calamity.

That feeling was not likely to leave her even after sleep had shut out from her perception the external world.

Imagination exercised all its magic powers in her brain, and she thought that Arthur Wilton came up to her, and holding out his hands, from which blood was dripping, cried out—"Amelia, Amelia, oh, come and save me ! Here is blood, but it is not of my shedding. Amelia, come now, and save me !"

The vision so terrified her, that she sprang from her bed with a cry of dismay, and the relief upon finding that it was but a dream, was amazingly great. She knelt and said her simple prayer, and then crept tremblingly into her bed again, and was soon asleep.

It seemed to her, that scarcely had she closed her eyes, when the same wild and startling vision came before her alarmed senses, and again she saw Arthur Wilton with the blood dripping from his hands, and again she heard his voice crying, in imploring accents,—

"Amelia, Amelia, come and save me. Here is blood, but it is not of my shedding. Oh, Amelia, Amelia, come and save me !"

The terror of the second vision, for a time, completely unnerved the young girl, and in a paroxysm of fear and apprehension, she lay awake, but unable to move. The idea then grew upon her each moment that the vision was sent for some special purpose—that it was not a mere dream, but that it had its object, and was a warning to her, which it would be cruel upon her part to turn a deaf ear to, or in any way to neglect.

This was a notion that, when once it took possession of her imagination, was not at all likely to leave it again quickly; on the contrary, it was just one of those ideas which, the longer they are brooded over, only gather the greater strength and confirmation from the morbid condition of the excited imagination. We must not, therefore, feel surprised that Amelia, after about half an hour passed in restless thought, rose from her bed with something like a vague idea of obeying the injunction of the words she had heard in the dream that had so distracted her.

"Amelia — Amelia, come and save me !"

Yes, these were the words that appeared to ring in her ears, and to be repeated over and over again amid the air of her chamber.

"I will—I will, Arthur," she cried. "Oh, who shall say but that Heaven has sent this vision to me for your special good? I will—I will seek you."

She trembled so, that it was with difficulty she could dress herself, but at last she succeeded in so doing ; and then she heard the rain pattering on the windows, and still it appeared to her as if the voice of Arthur kept crying—

"Amelia, come and save me !"

She felt certain that if she were to attempt to sleep again, and the same vision should come to her, that it would drive her to madness, and then she would be incapable of the action that was required of her.

"I will seek him," she said. "Oh, yes, I will seek him. But where shall I do so? The old villa, of course. Yes, he is there; and yet alone — Oh, God, direct me. What shall I do? What ought I to do?"

She sunk upon her knees, and wept and prayed, but the excitement of her spirits did not give way in the least, and springing to her feet again, she thought of rousing her father.

"The dream will satisfy him, surely," she said. "He will rise and come with me. Oh, yes ; and yet—no—no. What will he think? He cannot feel the truth of this warning vision as I feel it. No one to whom it has not come can by any possibility understand it. It is intended to act upon my mind, and mine alone, and how can I hope to render it tangible in its effects to the feelings of another? Oh, no—no. I must go alone—alone !"

If the imagination of Amelia had not been in the excited state that it was, such a step as this would have appeared to her to be little short of insanity ; but she did not think as she usually thought. She was half-maddened with the idea that possibly Arthur was about to encounter some great danger, from which she might rescue him. That was her dominant idea;

and so, heedless of the state of the weather, or of the distance she had to go, she hurriedly covered herself up in a cloak, the hood of which she drew over her head, and then crept down the stairs of the old farmhouse.

Familiar as that homestead was to Amelia, she could have no sort of difficulty either by night or day in traversing every part of it; so, without making any noice sufficient to disturb any one, she let herself out into the front garden in a few moments.

A growling sound came to her ears.

"Ah," she said. "It is Prince. Thank Heaven, I shall not now be without a friend and protector. I will take him with me."

The faithful dog heard her voice, and began whining with delight, and when she approached his kennel, where he was chained up, he did not know how sufficiently to express his gratification.

Amelia released him, and Prince then began such gambols that she was compelled to hush him down, and then he seemed to understand that the expedition they were going upon was to be a secret one, and he was quiet and submissive as a young lamb.

Amelia let herself out of the garden by a little wicket gate, the key of which was always hidden amid the thick foliage of a pear tree that was close at hand, and where she knew how to place her hand upon it in a moment; and then closing the gate after her, she ran along by the side of the orchard-wall, followed closely by Prince.

Perhaps it was the cold night air that had an effect upon her brain, which first made Amelia, after she had got some couple of hundred yards or so from her home, pause to wonder what the world would say of her, if it should ever come out that she had risen at midnight for the purpose of seeking her lover. She did not in the least apprehend that Wilton could, by any possibility, put a construction upon her acts different to that which they ought really to have; but then, he was not alone at the villa.

Amelia paused and covered her face with her hands, and wept. The dread of going on and the dread of going back appeared equally to oppress her, and she knew not what to do. Prince whined, and stood upon his hind-feet, and strove all he could to convince her that he was there, and ready to protect her; but poor Amelia could not attend to him in the agony of spirit that she was now enduring. She was torn and distracted by conflicting emotions, and whether to go or not to go, was, indeed, with her, a fearful question.

In the midst of this perplexity, Prince uttered a short bark of defiance, and Amelia saw then that some one was approaching with a lantern. Her first idea was to get out of the way, but upon Prince barking again, she heard a voice that she knew well say—

"Hilloa, Prince my boy, is it you or yer ghosteses?"

The voice was that of Mr. Flummery, and the moment she heard it, Amelia made a determination that she soon put into practice.

"Dear Prince," she said, "do you not know friend from foe?"

Prince, the moment he heard the voice of Flummery, who was an especial favourite of his, knew him well enough, and made a rush at him that nearly knocked him down, and endangered the safety of the lantern.

"Don't," said Flummery, "don't, I tell you. Bless us, Mr. P., haven't I been a helping Farmer Wilkins to catch slugs in his orchard, and now you want to upset a fellow on his blessed road home. Don't now, Mr. P. Here's a pretty mess I shall be in with your dirty paws on such a night as this. Oh, dear—oh, dear, Prince, when I sees you, I thinks on the poor departed Jacob, I does, and I feels lonely now."

"Bow-wow," said Prince.

"Now, Mr. P., if so be that you feel you must stand on your hind feet and place your two for'ard paws on me, just keep so, and don't be plumping down every minute and getting up a couple of shovelfuls more mud to put on me, there's a good dog; but if so be that you will keep down altogether, why, it's all the better for me, and I daresay the same to you, old fellow."

"Mr. Flummery," said Amelia.

"Oh, lor! who's that? Somebody said Mr. Flummery. There's the only eighteen-pence half-penny I have got in the world, and cut my throat at once, do."

"Mr. Flummery, do you not know me?"

Amelia stepped up close to him, and then Flummery, holding up the lantern, looked in her face, as he said—

"Bless us, and save us, if it's not Miss Amelia!"

"Yes, Mr. Flummery, and I am so glad to see you."

"Oh, lor! what a time o' night."

"Prince, you see, was with me."

"Yes. I ought to have know'd as some o' the family was nigh at hand, by Prince being out at such a time, and a nice mess he has made me in. Can't you get down, Mr. Prince, do? What would you say if I were to dabble my hands in the mud and then plaster it all over your coat, eh? How should you like it? Be off, now, with you, like a chicken."

Prince danced round Flummery with mad delight, till Amelia spoke to him in a severe tone, and then he became as grave as a judge, and stood stock still, staring at them both, and only during the next few minutes made one attempt to take the lantern from Flummery.

"Mr. Flummery," said Amelia, "I wish you to do me a favour."

"A favour, Miss Amelia?"

"Yes, a very great favour."

"Hurrah! hurrah! It's the twenty puns she wants. I'll go and get 'em at once. I know it's the twenty puns. Lor! Miss Amelia, you is as welcome to 'em as primroses in March, you is. I'll go and get the twenty puns."

"You mistake me, Mr. Flummery. Indeed, you do."

"Oh, lor! do I?"

"Yes. All I want of you is, to have the great kindness to come with me to the villa where Colonel Percival is lodging. You know it, no doubt. Do not say no to this request, Mr. Flummery, or I shall have to go alone, and that I am sure, as an esteemed friend, you will not permit me to do."

"Me permit? No, indeed! Miss Amelia, if you will go there, I'll go with you with all the pleasure in life, though I did hope that it was the twenty puns that you wanted; perhaps, though, you will take the twenty puns as well?"

"No, indeed, Mr. Flummery, I do not want them, I assure you. But if you will come on at once to the villa, and by the nearest way too, you will much oblige me."

"You mean the Abbey?"

"Oh, yes, it is called the Abbey. I am much obliged to you for consenting to come with me; you can't think what a relief it is to my mind. I have something to say to Mr. Wilton, and I did not like to go alone, although Prince, of course, would be with me; yet—yet——"

"Don't say another word about it," said Flummery. "I understands all about it. You have something to go about and like all young girls, you are rather afraid of what the old maids in the village might say; so you want a respectable parishioner with you like me, a man as can lay down his twenty puns any day to put a stopper on the woice o' scandal. Isn't that it, Miss Amelia?"

"A little of that, Mr. Flummery."

"Lor, bless you, I knowed it quite well. Come along. I'm going to see that all's right. Only you follow me, Miss Amelia, and I'll take you by a near way to the old Abbey. Will you be quiet?"

"Prince, how dare you be so troublesome," said Amelia.

"He has an eye to the lantern," said Flummery. "I don't mean to say but what he'd carry it just like a christian, if I was to go for to give it to him, except that it would be in his mouth; but I'd better keep it, as I know the nearest way and he don't."

"Thank you, Mr. Flummery, I will follow you. Come along, Prince."

"Ah, Miss Amelia, you don't know my misfortune, I suppose?"

"Misfortune? No, Mr. Flummery. What is it?"

"One o' my family, miss, is gone dead."

"I am truly sorry."

"Yes. Oh, dear! oh, dear! I shall never see another donkey like Jacob!" he cried.

CHAPTER XLI.

PRINCE SECURES MORE EVIDENCE THAN HE KNOWS WHAT TO DO WITH.

THE grief of Mr. Flummery for the loss of Jacob was so great, that he quite declined conversation now for several minutes, and Amelia, although, with her kind heart, she was sorry enough that Flummery should have even such a simple cause of grief as that, was not sorry to have a little time for her own reflections.

Perhaps if Amelia had been asked what precise object she had in view in taking her course towards the Abbey, she would hardly have been able to tell, since she might have shrunk a little from saying that it was just to recount to Arthur Wilton a dream that had twice disturbed her rest.

There are very many kind and good people, though, in this world who feel much more acutely than they reflect, and whose actions much more frequently result from that feeling than from anything in the shape of a regular train of thought, and probably we shall not be far away if we class Amelia among that number.

There was one thing, too, she knew quite well, and that was, however any one indifferent to her joys or her sorrows might laugh at the idea of her going some distance in the middle of the night on account of a dream, she had nothing of that sort to dread from Arthur Wilton. Well

CORPORAL STEADY.

she knew how glad he would be to see her, and any excuse would seem to him an excellent and valid reason that procured for him the pleasure of her company, even if it were at so strange an hour.

While this reflection brought some calmness to the mind of Amelia, Mr. Flummery was recovering the tenor of his feelings, which had been so cruelly racked by the loss of the illustrious Jacob. As for Prince, he seemed to be quite delighted with the whole affair, and trudged along apparently with a conviction that he was engaged upon a matter of unusual importance.

"Mr. Flummery," said Amelia, "I have no doubt but that my father will see that you want no assistance that Jacob, as you call him, used to give you. Any of the farm horses will be at your service at any time."

"Oh, thank you. That's all very well, in course, but a horse isn't a Jacob. Howsomdever, Miss Amelia, I shall have to throw myself back on my twenty puns, you see, and buy a new Jacob."

" You can do that, certainly, Mr. Flummery."

" Oh, yes, miss, I can do that ; but—oh, dear ! oh, dear !

> ' My heart is like a piece of brick,
>   I always shall feel sorry,
> For the Jacob I shall see no more
>   As lies in yonder quarry.' "

" Why, Flummery, you are quite a poet."

" Is I ?"

" To be sure you are. Did you make that really elegant verse yourself ?"

" Yes, Miss Amelia, I did. It's a bit of an elegy, they calls it, I think, on the death of Jacob ; and I fancy, Miss Amelia, as it smoothens down one's feelings to make a little poetry about the dear departed."

" Nothing is more probable, Mr. Flummery."

" Well, I'm glad you think so, Miss Amelia, 'cos that settles it in my mind. But, lor ! aint you getting very wet ?"

" Oh, no, Mr. Flummery, I shall do very well. I am only anxious to get to the Abbey as soon as possible, that is all, and I certainly do feel rather vexed at having brought you so far ; but you are so kind, that you must expect, you know, on that account, to be imposed upon a little."

" Imposed upon ? Oh, don't you mention that, Miss Amelia ; I'm only glad to go with you ; and I do hope as the time won't be far away when we shall all on us hear the blessed bells a-ringing on account of you being married to Mr. Wilton, who, I will say it, is a gentleman as never was. Yes, I will say it. He never laughed at me when I was deputy beadle, and the cocked hat wouldn't fit me, but kept a coming over my eyes, and the very parson laughed.—No, he didn't laugh, but he says, ' Mr. Flummery,' says he, ' put something in the crown of it, and keep it up,' says he."

" I do not think," said Amelia, " that Arthur Wilton would laugh at any one if he thought it would hurt their feelings at all."

" No, Miss, he would not. Oh, but you should have seed him about a year ago, when those fellows tried to rob poor old lame farmer Heathcote in the lane. Well, Mr. Arthur was coming along *permiscuious —*"

" Coming what ?"

" Well, perhaps that ain't the proper judgmatical way of saying it, but I means as he was coming along without thinking of nothing of that sort, you know."

" Oh, I think I understand."

" To be sure you do. Well, Miss, he huts himself into this here attitude, and he lays hold of one of the fellows in this ere way — Oh, lor !—don't—don't—oh, dear me !"

" What is the matter, Mr. Flummery ?"

" Oh !—oh !"

" Bow-wow !"

It appeared that in his anxiety to show Amelia, in the most graphic manner, how Arthur Wilton had laid hold of the thieves, Mr. Flummery had turned suddenly and laid hold of Amelia's arm, which Prince not approving of, had as suddenly laid hold of Mr. Flummery's leg, and hence the exclamations that had ensued upon all sides.

" Prince, Prince," said Amelia, " down, sir—bad dog—down, sir !"

Prince looked rather surprised at this reproof, for he had been labouring under the idea that he had done good service. However, he slunk away from Mr. Flummery, who shook his head at him, as he said,—

" He ought to have know'd me better, considering the many odds and ends, and nice little bits o' insides o' pigs, and such like things, as I have gived to him ; but that shows you what gratitude is in this here world, Miss Amelia. Oh, dear, you ought not never to go for to expect it."

" Don't blame poor Prince," said Amelia. " He made a mistake, that was all. You could hardly expect, Mr. Flummery, that upon the spur of the moment he should be able to distinguish between reality and mere illustration."

" Well, Miss Amelia, I only wish he hadn't illustrated the hinder part of my —oh, dear me, what is I a saying of ? Nothing at all, Miss Amelia. What a fool I am."

" Why, where are we going now, Mr. Flummery ? This stile leads into a farm-yard, by all appearance."

" Yes, it does ; its farmer Bridges's place, but it cuts off half a mile of the road, you see, and he won't mind me. All we have to do is just to go across to the stile at the other side, and then we are close to the road again."

" I understand ; I will follow you, Mr. Flummery."

Amelia was no town-bred young lady, who would have been a quarter of an hour getting over a stile, but accustomed as she was to taking long rambles by herself, she vaulted over it in a moment, and Prince made a flying leap over it after her.

" I hope there is no dog loose here ?" said Amelia.

The words were scarcely out of her

mouth, when a little terrier ran yelping towards her, apparently in the greatest rage that his little brows could possibly give currency to; but Prince just met him face to face, and made a short remark in the way of a growl, when off he went without another sound, and disappeared in his kennel.

"Hilloa!" cried a voice from the window of the homestead—"hilloa! who is there in the yard, eh?"

"It's only me, Bridges," said Flummery, "it's only me; I am going to the Abbey, and took this as a near cut."

"Oh, Mr. Flummery, ain't it?"

"Yes, that's about it."

"All's right.—Good night. You are quite welcome, Flummery; but, you see, I heard little Swager a barking at something, and I thought it might be a fox after the chickens, that's all. Good night."

"Good night," said Flummery. "Thank you."

The window was closed, and they proceeded on their way, which soon brought them to the corner of a little shady lane, at right angles to that which was immediately behind the walls of the Abbey garden.

"Now here we are, all but," said Mr. Flummery. "Which way do you think of going, Miss Amelia? 'Cos if you go to the front entrance of the old house, we must take the path to the right, now."

"Anywhere, Mr. Flummery," said Amelia, "so that we find some one who can call Mr. Wilton."

"Very good, then I say come to the front at once. You see, there's some of the soldiers on guard, as they call it, and one of them will soon tell us where to find Mr. Wilton. This way, Miss Amelia, this way."

"Hush! oh, hush!"

"Lor, what is it? Oh, Miss Amelia, what do you hear? I hear it now myself. It's a somebody coming along like mad. Oh, let's hide."

"As you please, Mr. Flummery, as you please; but I will remain here. Prince!"

Prince made a slight snarl in reply, and then uttered a low growl of dissatisfaction, for he, too, heard the sound of footsteps upon the ground approaching them as hard as they could come. It was quite evident that some one was coming from the direction of the Abbey in a tremendous hurry.

"Which way," said Amelia—"which way, Mr. Flummery, do those footsteps come? I seem to be confused by an echo here."

"There is an echo here," said Mr.

Flummery; "but if I might have an opinion, they are coming from the lane at the back of the old place."

The last word that Flummery uttered was drowned in the ringing report of a musket, as it was fired from somewhere about the direction that the footsteps appeared to be hurrying from.

Something went with a crash into a tree close at hand to where Amelia was standing; and Mr. Flummery, immediately that he heard it, fell flat on the ground, for he made sure that his last hour had come, and that he would soon follow poor Jacob to the grave. Amelia was, naturally enough, full of alarm and astonishment as to what it could all mean; but, before she had time to reflect or to move again, a dark figure dashed past her at full speed.

Amid the intense darkness of the night, it was quite impossible that Amelia, getting as she did so very trivial a glance at the figure, should be able to come to any judgment or conclusion with regard to its identity. All she could possibly take upon herself to say was, that it was something human, but it was gone before she could take a second glance at it.

With one bound, that cleared at once half the distance that was between them, Prince at once set off in pursuit.

Amelia now heard a cry from the fugitive, and fearing that Prince would do him some injury, and not at all knowing whether he might not be entitled more to her sympathy than her depreciation, she called to Prince as loudly as she could to come back. The faithful creature obeyed the call, and came bounding with long leaps to the side of Amelia, having in one of his leaps come right upon poor Flummery, and confirmed him in the idea that there was some rather fearful affair going on that was full of danger to him.

Amelia did not notice that Prince had something in his mouth, but as she held by a low branch of the tree close to where she was, she said—

"Oh, Heaven! has this actual occurrence and the fearful dream that I have suffered from, any connexion?"

This was to her a fearful question at such a moment, and one that laid hold of her imagination to such an excess, that for some few minutes she was quite incapable of making any effort to leave the place Mr. Flummery, however, when he heard that all was quiet, began to wince a little, and sitting up, he managed to say—

"The Lord have mercy upon us all. Amen!"

"Is that you, Mr. Flummery?"

"Yes, Miss Amelia, it's me or my ghost, I don't know very well which. Are you sure you are you?"

"Oh, yes; but can you tell me who it was that passed us with such speed, even now?"

"To be sure I can."

"Who was it, then?"

"The devil himself, I believe. I know one thing, and that is, that he had four feet and no end of claws, for I felt him jump on top of me with a force that nearly drove all the breath out of my body."

"Oh, that was Prince."

"Prince, was it? Oh, dear, no; Prince is not quite so big as an elephant, nor so heavy as a house, Miss Amelia. Oh, dear, no, it wasn't Prince, was it old fellow, eh? Was it now?"

Prince made a comical noise, as if he intended a bark, but couldn't do it satisfactorily, and Mr. Flummery, by looking closely at him, saw that he had something in his mouth which he was not willing to let go, and, therefore, could only bark in an odd, muffled kind of way, very different from the free, open defiance of his ordinary tones.

"He's got something, Miss Amelia."

"What is it? Give it to me, Prince—good Prince."

Prince was very affectionate, but he did not seem at all inclined to part with what he had got possession of; so Amelia gave it up as a bad job, and when Mr. Flummery tried it, Prince appeared disposed to have a battle with him, so he prudently let him alone.

"Oh, Miss Amelia, you don't wish to go to the Abbey now, do you?"

"Yes, Mr. Flummery, I do, indeed, and more urgently than ever. I am quite convinced that something is taking place which Arthur Wilton should be warned of. I do not ask you to come with me, but—but—"

"Don't say another word about it. I swear, by the memory of the departed Jacob, that when you like to go, I'll go, Miss Amelia—so come along, and let's make the old bell that hangs by the lodge at the front of the house ring; I dare say it will make some sort of sound if I give it a good pull."

"No, no, Mr. Flummery; the colonel might be awakened."

Alas! Colonel Percival slept that long sleep which knows no waking in this world. What a mercy it would have been if a bell could have awakened him!

CHAPTER XLII.

SHOWS HOW THE MURDERER RIFLED THE BOX, AND THEN ESCAPED.

WE now again return to the Abbey, and to that room in which the awful deed, which the wealth of words could not undo, was done by the villain Strachan.

It will be recollected that we left him in the chamber of his victim at that dread moment when he had taken the life he could never again restore—when he had extinguished that light which, in this world, was never again to be illumined—when the deed that was for ever and ever to press upon his soul was done—and when the good and the just had been hurried in blood to the throne of that Almighty who will not suffer the meanest thing that he has given the breath of life to, to fall without exacting an account of him who quenches the divine spark.

Yes, the murder was done, and the murderer was alone with his victim.

Did no shuddering sense of horror at that moment creep across the soul of Strachan? Did he not feel even then, while he stood by the still warm body of the man whom he had, by such a ruffian's blow, hurried to eternity, no pang of conscience? Alas! it would seem not.

Fear! Yes, fear was the only feeling that now found a home in the breast of Strachan. A dread of discovery, now the deed was done, and their was no such thing as gainsaying it, crept over him, and so completely, for a few moments, prostrated him, that he was unable to take any advantage of the fact that he had been so successful in what it would have been such a mercy both to him and to others that he had failed in.

The knees of the murderer smote each other, and then cold drops of prespiration rolled from his brow—his tongue seemed as though it would cleave to the roof of his mouth, and then hot blood would boil through his veins.

"No, no," he gasped, "I—I did not do it."

He dropped upon his knees to the floor, and then, as he clutched the counterpane of the bed, he thought he heard a noise in the front of the house.

There was the steady tramp of armed men for a few paces, and then he heard a voice say,—

"Halt!"

A pause ensued, and then he heard the ring of the muskets as the soldiers brought them to their shoulders. The tramp of feet again come upon his ears, and then all was still.

"They have been changing the guard," he gasped out, in an agitated whisper; "that is all. They have only been changing the sentinels. I—am better now."

Dashing with his right hand the blood from his face, for some had spirted on it from the body, although he did not know it, he rose to his feet.

At that moment something dashed against the window, and he fell to the floor again in mortal terror, crying out,—

"No, not I—I did not do it, Wilton is the murderer—Arthur Wilton did the deed, not I."

It was but a poor benighted bat that had struck its leathern wings against one of the panes of glass of the window, and then, as it fluttered hastily away upon the damp cold night air, all was still again.

"I am surely going mad!" said Strachan, "since every trifling natural sound appals me. I did not think to suffer thus, or perhaps I had not been here on such an errand."

He had had faith in his own nerves, which it appeared by the result he ought not to have had; but now he had proceeded so far in crime, that to

"Go back were worse than to move on;"

and so he tried all in his power to rouse himself to sufficient strength and courage at all events to avail himself of the consequences of the dreadful act he had committed, so far as those consequences might be made conducive to his own interests, in which he connected his revenges.

All was still in the bed. The dreadful fear that from the first had most possessed him was, that the blow he might give the colonel should be something short of mortal, in which case the struggle that would ensue with the victim would be a dreadful one.

If such a struggle had ensued, there can be very little doubt but that it would have been fatal to Captain Strachan.

The colonel was a much stronger man, in the first place, than Strachan, and if he had not been so, a man fighting for life against a ruffian, animated by fear, would soon overcome him; but that dread had passed away.

The dagger had reached at once that brave and noble heart, and the emancipated soul had sped to its creator with scarce a passing pang to mark its departure from the body.

And now that Strachan had become slowly satisfied that no alarm had been given—that the guard was changed without the soldiery at all suspecting that anything was amiss — that the noise

against the window was but the beating of a bat's wings against it, and that Colonel Percival was with the dead, he gathered courage—that kind of spurious courage which enables a villain to carry out his villany; and rising to his feet again, he strove to calm himself.

"All is well," he said. "Yes, it is done, and all is well. It is done, and quite successfully, too. Oh, so very successfully! There is nothing now in the world to baulk me in the progress of this enterprise."

He stole softly to the door of the chamber, and stepping out upon the landing, he bent his head to listen. The most perfect stillness reigned in the house.

"I am safe—safe," he said.

Stepping, then, back to the chamber, he closed the door, and fastened it by a touch at the small bolt that was at the under part of the lock. By so doing he guarded against any surprise during the progress of what he had still to do.

The next object of the murderer was to provide himself with a light. He had matches with him, and of course he concluded that there would be a candle in the room, which the colonel had had to light him to his rest.

Carefully igniting a phosphorus match, then he held it up till the wood had caught, and then, upon the dining table he saw the candle, with its extinguisher upon it, and he immediately lighted it, and glanced around him.

It was with reluctance that he cast his eyes towards the bed, where lay his victim, but he shudderingly withdrew them again, and then his gaze was carried round the room, till, upon the top of a large travelling trunk, he saw the brass-bound box that he expected would contain the rich booty, for the which he had so far perilled his soul.

Placing the candle upon the top of that box, he now rapidly looked to the fastenings of it. He thought that if it were locked he would surely find the keys somewhere in the room.

It was locked.

Upon the dressing table lay a number of articles. The colonel's watch—a small pair of highly finished pocket pistols—a purse—some letters—and, lastly, a bunch of keys, upon which Strachan at once eagerly seized, never doubting but that the one he so much wanted would be found amongst them. Nor was he wrong. It was there, and he soon had the brass-bound box open.

A pang of disappointment shot across the heart of Strachan, for he saw nothing but paper in the box. To dash his hand among them was the work of a moment, but nothing in the shape of valuables met his gaze, save an old seal and a few silver spoons.

"Curses on him, where is his money?" gasped Strachan. "Ah, what is this?"

There was a piece of paper, with some writing upon it, pasted on the inner side of the lid of the box. Hastily catching up the light, he held it in such a position as to throw its full rays upon the writing, and while his brain seemingly was about to burst with rage and vexation, he read as follows:—

"Whoever you are, my good friend, who shall come to the sight of these words without leave of him who wrote them, I beg to inform you that you will find nothing in this box to gratify your cupidity. Upon the advice of a dear friend, I have placed all my cash and valuables in the hands of a banker; so be so good as to shut the box again, if you please, and don't spoil the lock."

The candle dropped from the hands of Strachan, and he staggered to a seat as he cried out—

"Foiled at last—foiled at last, and after murder, too ! Oh, God!—Oh—no—no—not that ! That name must never now pass my lips. I belong to—" He shuddered as the name of the antagonistic demon arose to him; and there he sat in the dark, for the candle had gone out, ruminating upon his bitter disappointment.

About a quarter of an hour might have elapsed during this state of inaction, and then it began to strike Strachan in what a perilous position he stood, and he sprang to his feet.

"Escape—escape !" he said. "Yes, that is the thing now."

Groping his way past the bed, after treading upon the candle and nearly falling, he got to the door of the room, and then he paused, for he began to recollect that, although he might not succeed in enriching himself by the fearful murder which he had committed, he might in procuring revenge. Besides, the surest way for himself to avoid the consequences of his dreadful crime, was to put it upon the shoulders of another, so that justice would seem to be satisfied; and that other, upon whom he hoped to heap all the accumulated horror of guilt, was Arthur Wilton.

With a feeling of the most desperate rage at being so far frustrated in his intention to rob the colonel, Strachan now sat about his proceedings for the purpose of securing himself from his crime, and involving Wilson in it.

Approaching the table upon which the various articles belonging to the colonel lay, he took the purse from among the others, and once more crept to the door with it.

"Oh, if I could but find the route to the room occupied by Wilton," he murmured to himself, "surely I could make such a disposition of the purse and other things, that I should live to see him writhing on the gallows for this night's work."

Clasping both his hands over his face for a few minutes now, the villain gave himself up to diabolical thought; and then in a low voice, he added—

"Yes, I will try it. It will be a bold thing, but I will try it yet. It shall be done."

With the view, now, of carrying out the design that he had formed, he approached the side of the bed, for, in order to carry it out, it was necessary that he should possess himself of the dagger which, still was buried in the breast of the colonel.

It was with dreadful fear and trembling now that he moved his hand over the body to find the handle of the weapon, but at last he did touch it, and then averting his face, he collected all his strength to pluck it forth.

The dagger came slowly from the colonel's breast, and a sigh from the body followed it.

It was but the passage of some pent-up air struggling with blood through the wound, for the colonel was quite dead; but it alarmed Strachan to a fearful extent, and holding the reeking dagger in a posture of defence, he staggered from the room, expecting each moment that Colonel Percival would rise from the bed and follow him. He got some distance down the stairs before he got rid of that dreadful idea that had taken possession of him.

And now we may say that the plan of Strachan, as regarded Arthur Wilton, was about the boldest thing he had thought of yet, if it was, at the same time, the most infamous. It was to find the room in which Wilton was sleeping—to enter it—and to leave the dagger with him, and then escape by the window into the garden again, and so leave the premises over the corner of the wall, by the same way he had entered them.

The only risk of this manœuvre, of course, was, that Arthur Wilton might awaken as he, Strachan, was making his passage through the room, and if he did so awaken, Strachan intended to strike him down by a blow upon the head before he should be sufficiently aroused to make any movement to lay hands upon him and detain him.

We shall soon see how far the murderer succeeded in these villanous objects of his, after he left the chamber of his still bleeding victim.

CHAPTER XLIII.

SHOWS HOW AN ALARM WAS GIVEN, AND HOW STRACHAN ESCAPED.

THE reader, no doubt, has a full recollection of how poor Arthur Wilton was occupied upon the night in question. Overcome by fatigue and many harrowing thoughts, he had fallen asleep in that little room to which Strachan had looked from the garden.

Little suspecting what was taking place overhead, he still slept, and busy imagination was painting to him many scenes, probable and improbable, as the colonel was breathing his last breath beneath that same roof that covered so many who would have hazarded most freely their lives in his defence.

Strachan, from the outside of the old house, knew the position of that room very well, and that was all the knowledge he had to go upon regarding its position relatively to the interior of the mansion; but still he considered that there could not be much difficulty in finding it after all, as he knew that it was upon the ground floor, and there could not be so many rooms but what he might soon visit them all.

With this intent, then, Strachan crept down the old staircase, holding the dagger in his hand, which, as he went, made many a bloody memorandum of his progress, and of the awful purpose it had so recently consummated.

Arrived in the hall, the first care of Strachan, now, was to ascertain where the guard was ; and the murmured conversation of some of the soldiers with Cockles and Steady, soon put him quite at ease upon that point, and prevented him from making the capital error of opening the door of the guard-room.

Turning, then, away from the immediate proximity of that room, Strachan tried the doors opening from the hall, as they came to his hand, by feeling carefully along the wall. They were none of them fast, and he could just see sufficient of them as he looked cautiously in, to be sure that he had not yet lit upon that which contained Arthur Wilton.

At length the ruffian hand of the murderer touched the door of the room he was in search of. A something seemed to tell him that he was right at last, and he re-doubled his caution as he gently opened the door.

Yes, there was Wilton, still sleeping, and far down in the socket of a candlestick flickered faintly the wick of a nearly expiring candle.

Strachan now must have been nerved by the hatred which he bore to Wilton to do what he did, for at heart he was a coward; but strong passions will lend those whom they attack a power of action, which, in their absence, they would not be able to command. The danger of some loved one will lend courage to the most timid. The spirit of dire revenge will make the cowardly murderer and the assassin do things that otherwise he would shrink from in mortal terror.

It was thus with Strachan. The strong conviction that if he could pass through that room without arousing Wilton, and leave the frightful witness of the deed of blood in his progress, the fate of the innocent young man would be all but certain, gave him a kind of spurious courage to attempt doing so.

The window was opposite to the door as nearly as possible, and it was evidently intended to be used as a thoroughfare to the garden, as it opened like long panelled doors, so that there could be but little difficulty connected with it.

" If he should sleep three short minutes longer," thought Strachan, "it is done; and why should he not ?"

There seemed, in truth, no reason why he should not. The slumber of Wilton was profound enough to all appearance, and Strachan found no difficulty in hearing the regular breathing of that innocent one for whom he designed in the depths of his wicked heart a much worse fate than he had inflicted upon poor Colonel Percival, who lay so still and calm now above.

Strachan entered the room : he did not care to close the door behind him. His sole object was to leave the dagger and then to escape.

There was a carpet upon the floor, and just beneath one of its corners Strachan slipped the dagger, and then with half-a-dozen long strides he reached the window. Wilton still slept, but he moved uneasily, as if some alteration, as no doubt there was, in the air of the room, had taken place, that had slightly disturbed the serenity of his slumbers.

Strachan reached the window, and saw, by the dim flashing light of the dying candle, that there was but an ordinary lever fastening to it, which, by a touch, he undid, and then slipping back the blind, he slowly pushed one half of the window open.

It was at this moment that the wick, far down in the candlestick, went out, and Arthur Wilton awakened.

Strachan heard him move in the chair, which creaked beneath his weight, and he dared not step out into the garden for fear his footsteps upon the gravel might betray him.

With all his cunning, though, and with all his forethought and caution, there was one thing that Strachan had not thought of. As he stood just outside the blind, and on the window-sill, and as the light in the room went out, the darkness in the room was considerably greater than the darkness outside, so that when Wilton cast his eyes towards the window, to his surprise, he saw the full-length shadow of a human figure upon it.

For a few seconds this seemed so strange a phenomenon to Arthur, that he could only gaze at it in surprise, without being at all able to comprehend it; and when he did feel convinced that it was a human figure, he only rubbed his eyes, and said, in a low tone,—

"I am, surely, dreaming still."

About half a minute had now elapsed, and the agony that Strachan was in to get away was so great, that he could stand it no longer, but drew back from the window. This movement served at once to assure Wilton that it was no cheat of the senses, but really a figure at his window, trying, as he thought, to effect an entrance to the room, and he sprang forward, crying—

"Who goes there?"

This was enough for Strachan. Nothing now but instant, headlong flight could save him, so he at once darted along the garden towards the wall. He could not take upon himself to say that he should be able, in the darkness, to fly direct to that spot where he could manage to climb over so easily, but he made for the wall in a staight line, darting over the flower-beds, and heedless how he went, so that he did reach it, and then he intended climbing it by the aid of the wall-trees, and jumping down into the lane.

Arthur Wilton, when he got convinced that there was some intruder in the garden, dashed the blind aside, and followed him, so that Strachan soon found that a potent runner was upon his track.

But what runner can outrun him who flies for his life? Strachan overcame obstacles that, under any other circumstances, could not have been by him performed at all. He reached the wall,

and, in quite a wonderful manner, succeeded in climbing to the top of it, when there was scarcely a foot-hold to be found, and when, if he had not gone at the speed he did, he must have fallen into the arms of Arthur Wilton, who was close upon his track.

"Hold!" cried Wilton. "Be you whom you may, I command you to pause."

With a tremendous jump, Strachan reached the lane, and then Wilton called out in a loud voice—

"Sentinel, fire!"

The soldier who was then on duty had been leaning upon the end of his musket, and, no doubt, thinking of some home that he had left far away, for he was evidently in a reverie that was far from being favourable to a strict performance of his duty. Starting from the position he had assumed, and with an indistinct idea that something was amiss, and that some voice of apparent authority had ordered him to fire, he called out—"Who goes there?" and at once discharged his musket at random.

A shot from the hunter's rifle amid a herd of startled deer could not have produced a greater effect upon the guard than the ringing discharge of the sentinel's musket. Everyone was upon his feet in a minute, and the sergeant called out—

"Form—shoulder arms—march!" and the men dashed out of the guard-room to the scene of action.

Upon the mind, too, of Strachan, all this had a most alarming effect. With the speed of a hunted hare, although in reality at that time no one was pursuing him, Strachan set off, and it was then that he passed Mr. Flummery and Amelia, and it was then that Prince made an unavailing effort to check the headlong speed of the fugitive, as we have already recorded.

Strachan continued his flight in as direct a route for the barracks as he could take, and it was not until he got tolerably near to the wall of that building that he could at all believe that he was not hotly pursued, and that he ventured to pause for a moment to take breath after his exciting race.

"Saved—saved!" he gasped. "It is done! It is complete, and I have escaped —as yet—yes, only as yet, though. I must be in my bed before I can say that I am quite safe. Ah, what is that? Good Heavens! what is that?"

It might have been imagination, but at that moment from the deep shadow in a corner by the barrack-wall, Strachan thought he heard a strange, wild laugh. His hair almost stood up with his mortal terror, and he felt as though the blood

MR. FLUMMERY SEEKS THE OLD PIT TO BURY THE REMAINS OF JACOB.

were congealing around his heart. I took the villain several minutes ere he recovered himself sufficiently to reason himself out of his fears.

"Stretching out his hands, then, he slowly and with staggering footsteps approached the wall, with the expectation, if there were any one there, of speedily ascertaining that fact; but he only touched the wet bricks, and then he whispered—

"No—no, it was nothing. The night wind, or some bird or insect. Oh, it was nothing. I am too excited—I am too full of all sorts of strange fears, and may at such a time as this imagine anything. I feel and know that it was nothing."

The grand object now was to calm himself sufficiently to enable him to pass the sentry at the gate of the barracks, still assuming the character of the surgeon of the regiment, as he had done before going out on that eventful night. It took him about five minutes more to succeed in soothing his nervous system sufficiently to make it at all safe to proceed.

Had it been daytime, or had there been

ever so little artificial light at hand, it would have been quite impossible for Strachan to play the part he was now assuming; but everything happened to be just then in the villain's favour. It was pitch dark, and a hazy kind of rain was still falling.

The sentinel at the barrack gate was in his box, with his greatcoat buttoned close up to his chin, when Captain Strachan treading as freely and firmly as he could, so as to take away the idea that any concealment of his footsteps was meditated, made his way up towards the gate.

"Who goes there?" said the sentinel, stepping out from his box.

"A friend," said Strachan, imitating the voice of the surgeon, as well as his agitation would let him. "Don't you know me?"

The dim outline of the cocked hat at once was sufficient for the sentinel, and he drew back, after bringing his musket to the attention and saying the words—

"Pass, friend."

Strachan entered the barracks.

At the guard-house door a sergeant was conversing with some one, and they both touched their caps so Strachan, who, with a slight raise of his hand, crossed the square.

There was nothing now to be particularly dreaded but the meeting in the barrack-yard with some officer whose duty called him to be up, and who, fancying he saw the surgeon, would naturally enough stop him to ask what took him out at such an hour. This was such a dread upon the mind of Strachan, that he thought he should have fainted before reaching the quarters where he lodged, and at the door of which another sentry kept guard.

There was an oil lamp just within the door-way, so that the sentry, if he had chosen to look keenly, might, perhaps, have seen that it was not the surgeon who passed him; but he took it for granted, and drew himself up in salute, and Strachan passed on, unscatched and unsuspected.

Another minute and he reached the room where hung the coats and hats. No one was there, and he hung up the surgeon's hat and the coat again, and then he flew rather than walked to his own rooms. He heard the sound of approaching footsteps, and a voice say—

"Who did you say crossed the yard?"

Fear nearly deprived him of the power of entering his own rooms, but he did contrive to do so, and then locking the door on the inside, he fell quite exhausted to the floor, and there he lay for more than an hour.

But Strachan felt that he had still something to do. Nothing with him was, he so told himself, to be left to chance, and rising, he lit a candle and proceeded with the greatest possible diligence to clean from his boots every trace of the wet road that he had been over. He then sat down and tried to think over his position.

The question that he proposed to himself was—'What have I now specially to guard against, that might in any way harm me?'

"Yes," he said, "that is it. That is what I have to think of, and it is a most admirable beginning when I feel that I have some trouble in answering it. That shows me that nothing has happened so much amiss as to press upon my mind as a great danger."

He did not for a moment think that he had been recognised by Arthur Wilton. The darkness and the confusion of the pursuit would surely, he considered, be quite sufficient to prevent that person, whom he now more and more hated, from recognising him.

"Oh, curses on him!" he muttered. "If I had but slipped ever so little in climbing the garden-wall, I must have been involved in a personal contest with him; but surely, now, I have him fairly enough in the toils. Surely, now, his doom is fixed: how can he possibly escape the accumulation of circumstances that I have built up around him, as presumptive of his guilt?"

The more Strachan resolved the matter over in his own mind the more he felt convinced that Wilton was thoroughly entangled in the meshes of that plot that he had laid for his destruction; and, finally, he flung himself upon his bed, with a conviction upon his mind, that, although he had not bettered his fortune to the value of a farthing by the murder, he had achieved all his revenge.

CHAPTER XLIV.

AMELIA AND MR. FLUMMERY UNEXPEC-
TEDLY MEET WITH ARTHUR.

HAVING thus far disposed of Strachan upon that dreadfully eventful night, we now again take up our place by the side of Mr. Flummery and Amelia on their route to the Abbey.

The alarm and the flight of the demoniacal-looking figure who had made good an escape past them, so confounded poor Flummery, that he did not know which way to turn; and it was not until

Amelia spoke to him twice, that he was able to pay any attention to, or understand what she said to him.

"Mr. Flummery, come with me—oh, I pray you come with me to the Abbey at once. Something dreadful has happened, I feel convinced," she cried. "It is Providence that has brought you and me here to-night."

"Oh, lor, has it?"

"Yes, Mr. Flummery. Oh, come on—come on. I had a doubt of the propriety of seeking Arthur Wilton, but I have none now."

"But we shall be killed. Murder! Oh, lor, somebody is a-coming now, I declare; don't you see a light, with a soger in his hand?"

"A what, Flummery?"

"Oh, dear me, here he comes, as large as life, Miss Amelia, and we shall all be killed. Murder! There's more of 'em a-coming, now. Oh, lor! oh, lor!"

Amelia saw through the gloom that people were approaching with lights, and then she heard a voice say—

"Whoever it was, sir, they are off safe enough now, you may depend upon it."

"So it seems," said another voice; "and yet I am certain there was some one in the garden."

This latter voice belonged to Arthur Wilton, and the moment Amelia heard it, she knew the well-remembered tones, and called out, in a loud tone,—

"Arthur—Arthur!"

Not more exact in recollection to the ear of Amelia was every tone of Arthur's voice, than hers to him, and when he heard his name pronounced in those dear accents, at such an hour, and in such a place, he could not, for the moment, believe in the reality of the circumstance.

"Surely, I must be dreaming," he said. "This is impossible."

"What, sir?" said the sergeant.

"I heard a voice."

"And so did I."

"What did it say?"

There was no occasion for the sergeant to repeat what the voice had said, for on the moment it came again, and Amelia called still upon Arthur, having approached now considerably nearer to him.

"That's it, sir," said the sergeant.

"It is—it is Amelia," cried Arthur, and springing towards her, he, in another moment, held her in his arms, and in the joy of that moment forgot that it must be something unusual that had brought her there at such an hour.

"Oh, Arthur," she said, "you are safe and well?"

"Quite so—I never was more so, I presume. Why, Amelia—why these tears. What has happened? Your father——"

"Is well, Arthur. But it is for your sake I came here."

"And alone?"

"No," said Flummery, who was close at hand, and heard the question. "Here am I, Mr. Wilton. I protected her, and it's all right. If poor Jacob had only been in this here world instead of the t'other, she should have come on his blessed back; but, you see, Mr. Arthur Wilton, that a dead donkey is not of much use, after all."

"Thank you, Mr. Flummery—thank you; but, Amelia, there is some reason for your presence here?"

"Oh, Arthur, you will not know when you hear me tell you the reason, whether to laugh at me, or to be angry with me Indeed, you will not."

"Yes, dear one. I do know that I shall do neither. Come, now, let me implore you to tell me at once."

"It was—it was——"

"Well?"

"A dream."

"A dream?"

"Yes, Arthur. I knew how you would start at that, but, in good truth, it laid hold of my imagination, so that I could not rest till I had seen you; and so here, you see, Arthur—here I am."

"Blessings on you, my own Amelia. I care not to what accident I owe the joy of seeing you, so that I do see you. Besides, we have had an alarm at the Abbey. You see, some one has been in the garden."

"Oh, yes—yes, I know; some one fled past us."

"Indeed. Which way?"

"I can tell you," said Flummery. "He went either straight on, or else he turned to the left or the right, or he got over the hedge and went back again. I'll swear he did one or the other, though."

"Thank you, Flummery," said Arthur. "We shall be sure to find him, after that luminous description of the course he took. Are you there, Sergeant White?"

"Yes, sir."

"Well, it don't seem at all likely now that we shall catch this fellow, be he whom he may."

"No, sir."

"Not a smell of a chance of it, Mr. Wilton," said Steady, stepping forward.

"What, Steady, are you here?"

"Yes, sir; and so is Cockles."

"Cockles it is, and Cockles it were," said that individual stepping forward. "Row-de-dow! Mr. Wilton, we want you to be so good as to say a good word for us to the colonel in the morning, as we have been out of quarters without leave, you see. You can tell him that we were babes in the wood."

"How so, Cockles?"

"Why, we lost our way among the trees, sir, that's all, and I dare say if we had died, that the dickey-birds would have gone into mourning, and covered us over with leaves, don't you think so, Steady?"

"Very likely," said Steady.

"Are you staying at the Abbey?"

"Yes, we is; for, somehow, we fancy if we go to barracks without seeing the colonel, that things won't be pleasant."

"Ah, I see. Well, we had better all go back again, for the man who was in the garden has fairly escaped. Amelia, you will go home?"

"Oh, yes, Arthur. I am ashamed of being here at all."

"Nay, say not so. As early in the morning as possible, dear Amelia, I will be with you. Steady?"

"Yes, sir. Attention!"

"Will you be so good as to see Miss Revis safely home to her father's farm?"

"Of course I will. Cockles?"

"Cockles it is, and Cockles it were. Row-de-dow-dow."

"You had better come too."

"Oh, lor!" cried Mr. Flummery, throwing himself into an extraordinary attitude, "can't I look arter her?—can't I do the thing as is right in seeing her home, when I brought her here? To be sure I can. Look at me, I'm as big as any soger. Do you think I'm a going to eat her as we goes back, Mr. Wilton, that I'm not to be trusted with her? Oh, oh! Does anybody want twenty puns?"

"My kind and good friend," said Arthur Wilton, "it is quite impossible that anybody should esteem your goodness more than I do; but I thought that Corporal Steady would be company for you on the road, that is all."

"Oh, well, if that's it——"

"It is, indeed, Flummery."

"Very well; then, I'm sure I shall be glad of Steady's company, for now that poor Jacob is gone, I don't know any one who I would rather speak to in an ordinary kind of way than Corporal Steady."

"Thank you," said Steady. "Who was Jacob?"

"Oh, don't ask. Oh!"

"Your brother?"

"No, no."

"Your father?"

"Oh, gracious, no; Jacob was a donkey."

The soldiers could not keep their countenances at this, and they at once burst into a roar of laughter at Corporal Steady's expense, who, however, took the joke against him in very good part.

"Never mind, Mr. Flummery," he said; "I will do all I can to supply the place of Jacob to you as we go to the farm. You had better stay with Mr. Wilton, Cockles."

"Very good," said Cockles.

Corporal Steady took Wilton aside for a moment, and whispered to him—"Mr. Wilton, I think that there is very likely to be more in this affair of to-night than meets the eye, and it will be just as well for you to be most particularly upon you guard against any secret attempt upon the part of a stranger to get into the Abbey. We don't know, sir, what rascals may be about the place."

"That is true, Steady. I will keep Cockles by me, then, if you please. And now, Amelia, good night."

Amid the throng of soldiers, Amelia and Arthur only shook hands; but Amelia said—

"Arthur, I came to save you, and I hope you are warned."

They all heard those words, and, slight as they were, it will be seen of what significance they afterwards became to Arthur.

"Farewell," he said, "there is no danger now."

Amelia left the spot, accompanied by Mr. Flummery and Corporal Steady, and Arthur returned to the Abbey with the soldiers.

"I hope the colonel has not been awakened by all this," said the sergeant who was on duty.

"It is almost impossible but that he should be," said Arthur; "the discharge of the sentinel's musket ought to be sufficient to do that; and I only wonder that we have seen nothing of him as yet upon the road."

"He would not leave the Abbey, sir."

"Well, perhaps not; but we shall see him, no doubt, as soon as we arrive."

"Very likely, sir."

"Perhaps, after all," said Cockles, "it was only some one after the fruit in the garden, or the cabbages, for, to be sure, there isn't much fruit to take just now. Are you sure you saw a fellow in the garden, Mr. Wilton?"

"Quite—he was at my window."

"At your window! Oh, lor! What up stairs?"

"No, Cockles; I had not gone to bed, I had dropped asleep just in my chair, in a lower room, that has a French window opening to the garden, and it was at that I saw him, and, without waiting, I flew towards him."

"Oh, I understand now. Well, you had better go to bed at once, now, Mr. Arthur, when you get to the Abbey, and, in the morning, if you will speak to the colonel about Steady and me, I shall be obliged to you. Row-de-dow-dow—dow-dow! Here we are in quarters again."

The guards left at the Abbey reported that they had heard nothing of the colonel.

"Is not that rather singular, Mr. Wilton?" said the sergeant.

"Well, perhaps it is; but you may depend upon it he sleeps soundly, and perhaps a cannon discharged at his ear would not awaken him just now."

"Well, it would me, and with a pretty start, too; but, however, as he isn't stirring, I suppose—but you know best about that, Mr. Wilton—I suppose it isn't proper to go and awaken him?"

"Certainly not; for, after all, what have we to tell him that will not keep till the morning quite well?"

"The morning won't be long in coming now," said Cockles, "for I fancy it's getting light already."

"I shall not go to bed to-night," said Wilton. "I think I will sit up and read a little. I shall be in my room, sergeant, if you should want me for anything."

With these words, Arthur Wilton took a light from the guard-room and stepped across the hall till he came to his own apartment, into which he entered and closed the door. The window was still open, as it had been left by him when he darted into the garden after Strachan, and a puff of cold air in a minute put out the light.

Arthur did not close the window now, but he stepped just outside of it, and stood in the garden and listened if he could detect any sound at all indicative of the presence of other intruders in that place; but all was profoundly still. After a time he could faintly hear the tread of the sentinel on the other side of the wall, and then, feeling satisfied that whatever danger there had been was over for the night, he closed the window and sat down in the dark.

An uneasy feeling was upon the mind of Arthur, which he had been trying to contend against for some time past; and now that he was alone, it come upon him with redoubled force. The statement of Amelia that she had been induced by a dream to come to him, probably had been the main cause of that uneasy feeling. He knew that she was very far from being superstitious, and it must have been a something beyond a common vision of the imagination which had so fearfully acted upon her.

After sitting for about half an hour, he muttered to himself, as a drowsy feeling came over him,—

"Now, if I were full of superstitious fears and strange fancies, I should say that something was about to happen with regard to me that involved my future fate in this world; but, after all, what can the strange feeling be, but one of those foolish excitements of the imagination which vanish with daylight? I will sleep."

Arthur Wilton fell asleep in much the position in which Strachan had found him upon opening the door of his room, and while he so slept, it is not to be wondered at that he dreamt in a wild and disordered manner.

CHAPTER XLV.

THE MORNING AT THE ABBEY DISCLOSES THE MURDER.

"Good morning, Mr. Wilton, good morning, sir. Oh, it's only me, sir. How you did start."

"What has happened?" cried Arthur Wilton, springing from his chair, as he was aroused thus by the friendly and well known voice of Corporal Steady.

The morning had come with great freshness and beauty—the early sunshine was shining in at the window—the birds were fluttering past upon joyous pinions, and making the air ring with melody, and the rain drops were glittering like gems upon the trees, as the sunshine, with the magic of its beauty, shone upon them.

"Why, it's only me, sir," added the Corporal.

"Oh, Steady?"

"The same, Mr. Wilton. You see, sir, I knocked at the door several times, but you did not answer, so I made so bold as to open it, and then I found that you were still fast asleep in the chair."

"You are quite right, Steady. I have passed but a sadly disturbed night, and I suppose I had dropped into a deep sleep. What is the time?"

"Seven, sir."

"Oh, well, that is not so bad, after all, though. Is the colonel stirring yet?"

"No, sir, not yet, and it's rather a wonder, for he is so early, as a usual thing;

but still, he may oversleep himself like any one else at times."

"Surely he may. It will be just as well not to disturb him, Steady, I think."

"Certainly not, sir; but Cockles and I want to speak to him as soon as we can about being out of barracks all night, for we don't want now to come into contact with Captain Strachan, you see, Mr. Wilton, though they do say he has fretted himself into a kind of fever, and may not get up again in a hurry. The colonel will listen to reason and excuse us, but he wouldn't."

"Row-de-dow-dow!" cried a voice in the garden, and Wilton upon glancing through the window, saw Cockles enjoying the fresh morning air.

"Well," said Wilton, "I do wonder that the colonel is not on the stir by this time. Perhaps the sergeant of the guard had better be told of it. He can awaken him or not, as he likes, as he has his report to make."

"True, sir; but don't you hear that?"

"Yes, the tramp of a horse."

"It's one of the officers from the barracks, I'll be bound, sir, and he will go up to the colonel's room, no doubt."

Wilton and Steady went to the front of the villa just as Major Cuthbert got off his horse at the entrance of it, and throwing the reins to a soldier, he called out,—

"Ah, Wilton, good morning to you. Which room does the colonel call his breakfast apartment? But I suppose he has long since done that meal, has he not?"

"No, major, he is not up."

"Not up?"

"No, sir."

"You don't mean that? Why, it's past eight o'clock."

"I thought it was only seven," said Corporal Steady, producing a watch that had run down at that hour in consequence of the corporal's perturbation of mind making him forget to wind it overnight.

The major looked at Wilton, and Wilton looked at the major, and now they were joined by the sergeant of the guard, who had turned out his men.

"Well, sergeant, how is this?" said Cuthbert; "the colonel not stirring yet?"

"No, sir."

"All quiet, I suppose, in the night?"

"Not quite, sir. There was some fellow in the gardens, I rather think, sir; but though Mr. Wilton and some of the men went after him, he got off, sir."

"And the colonel not up?"

"Shall I let him know that you are here, major?" said Wilton.

"Yes, thank you. No—stay. Show me his room, and I will go myself at once to him. I hope he is not ill."

"I trust to Heaven he is not," said Wilton. "I did not think of that, or I should certainly have awakened him before this. Pray go to him at once, major. This way;—I will show you his room door now, if you please, at once."

"Lead on, Wilton."

The major followed Arthur Wilton rapidly up stairs to the door of the colonel's room. It was closed, and they concluded locked, although such was not the fact. The major tapped at it with his knuckles.

No answer.

"Colonel Percival!" he called aloud. "Colonel, awake!"

Oh, would that that brave and gentle spirit could have been awakened by the voice that called to it! But no; it slept that sleep which, in this world, knows no waking, and the silence of death was in the chamber which they hoped soon to hear echo to the cheerful voice of the living. They began to be uneasy.

"I don't like this at all, Wilton," said the major.

"Nor I, sir. Heaven send nothing has happened to him in the night, for I have been oppressed all the night long with the idea of some great calamity."

"Have you? I only wish, then, you had called the colonel. But I can't stand this any longer."

With the promptitude and decision of his character, the major placed his hand upon the lock and found that the door at once yielded before him.

"Oh," he said, "the door is not fast. Come in, Wilton. Hilloa, colonel, we have come to take you by storm for lying so long in the morning."

"He does not speak," said Wilton, as he stumbled slightly over a chair, and placed his hand, to save himself, on the side of the bed.

"It's dark as night," said the major. "Stop, I have got hold of the shutter now. There it is. The morning has found its way in. Now, colonel."

"Help!" shrieked Wilton. "Oh, God!"

The major hearing these exclamations from Wilton, made but two strides from the window to the bed, and there, stretched in death, and lying in a mass of coagulated blood, he saw the colonel. It was a sight, that, to shake the stoutest nerves; and that man who had faced death upon the battle-field, and seen it in some of its most awful shapes, staggered back, until he was stopped by the wall, and gazed in silence for some few moments upon the dreadful spectacle.

Arthur Wilton was by the bed-side, in the same attitude of surprise and horror which he had assumed at the moment of making the dreadful discovery of the colonel's condition, and so they both remained for the space of about half a minute, completely horrified by the scene that was before them.

It was Major Cuthbert who first recovered from this state of inaction, and in a voice that rang through the room, he cried out—

"Why, how is this, Mr. Wilton? Colonel Percival is murdered!"

"Murdered!" echoed Wilton.

"Ay, in cold blood, too—brutally murdered."

He flew to the landing outside the door, and in a voice that was like the blast of a trumpet, he called out,—

"Guard! guard! The colonel is murdered! Guard! Help! Murder has been done here!"

The words reached those below, and in a moment came the dash and clatter of arms. The sergeant rushed up the staircase with his drawn sword in his hand, and horror in his looks; Corporal Steady and Cockles followed him, and the guard with their muskets thronged up after them again.

"Forward! This way," shouted Major Cuthbert. "The colonel is murdered here in his bed, in cold blood. Here, in his house—in his own chamber, with his own troops about him. Murdered! murdered!"

Overcome by the intensity of his feelings, the major staggered back before the advancing throng of persons, and sinking into a chair, he could only keep repeating the word "Murdered! murdered! murdered!"

It would be in vain to attempt to describe the scene of confusion that occurred. The chamber was thronged by the soldiers, and they all looked with tears and lamentations upon the sad sight that the bed presented to them. Arthur Wilton had dropped into a seat that was near to the head of it, and there he sat, with his hands clasped and his mouth rigidly shut, looking more like a spectre than a living man. No one seemed capable of giving any orders, and, at length, the sergeant stood before the major, and saluting him, said,—

"Orders, sir, orders!"

The major sprang to his feet.

"Yes! Send to the barracks for the surgeon, and for all the officers who are on duty. Let a captain's guard, too, be brought to this house, and let no one presume to quit it but the messenger."

"Who shall I send, major?"

"I will go," said Corporal Steady, stepping forward.

"How came you here?"

"Lost my way, sir, and gave myself up to the guard in the middle of the night along with Cockles. Staid here, sir, with the hope of seeing the colonel, and getting excused; but little thought that—that—"

The tears started to the eyes of Steady, and he could say no more.

"I excuse you," said the major.

"And Cockles, sir?"

"Yes, yes. You go to the barracks, Steady, with my message; you will find my horse at the door of the ill-fated house. Mount it, and ride as fast as you can—the animal is quite fresh, and will want no spur. Can you ride?"

"Yes, sir."

Corporal Steady was down stairs, and mounted in a minute, and then off he went at a gallop.

Arthur Wilton fainted now, and fell from the chair he had been sitting upon to the floor of the room.

"Look to Mr. Wilton," said the major. "Clear the room, my men, I will stay here. Yet no—you, sergeant, stay with me. We will examine it together."

It was Cockles who, assisted by one of the soldiers, led Wilton down stairs, and took him out into the garden; and then, when he seemed sufficiently able to speak, he gasped out,—

"Oh, that I rather had died this night than that such a deed had been done as this. Where will the horrors connected with it end now?"

"God knows," said Cockles.

"Yes. God only knows," said Wilton. "But something seems to tell me that the greatest suffering from this dreadful act will come. Did none of you hear any noise in the house in the night?"

"No sir. Did not you?"

"Alas! no. The alarm of a man being in the garden was all that I heard, and I am so utterly confounded, that I can hardly take upon myself now to say, whether that was or was not a delusion of the fancy. Leave me, oh, leave me, and let me think."

They left him to himself upon a bench in the garden, and then, with his head resting upon his hands, poor Arthur Wilton thought that he should surely go mad with the intensity of his feelings upon the fearful catastrophe that had taken place.

As yet he had not the dread that was so soon to come upon him, that he could by any possibility be suspected even of a complicity in the death of the colonel.

His conscious innocence kept such a feeling as that from off his mind.

That horror was to come in its own time.

In the meantime, and while poor Arthur Wilton was thus occupied in the garden of the Abbey, the major, assisted by the sergeant, made a search of the room in which the colonel had slept and died. They found abundant proofs of the presence of some one there about the apartment with bloody fingers, and they found the brass-bound box, which had attracted the cupidity, no doubt, of the murderer, open.

They repeatedly passed the bed, but neither of them liked to give more than a mere passing glance at the mournful-looking occupant of it.

The sergeant only once ventured to say—

"He is quite dead, sir ?"

" Quite dead," cried the major, starting round, and pointing to the face. " Look!"

"Oh, yes, sir."

" Do you doubt it, sergeant ?"

"No, sir—no, sir; I see now. The calm of death is there. Oh, yes, sir, he is dead. God bless him!"

" Amen !"

" A better man—a better officer or kinder friend to the soldier—a braver, nobler heart, never—never——"

The sergeant was too overcome to proceed, and he stood by the window, trying to look out through the mist of tears that obscured his eyes.

" You cannot say too much, sergeant," said the major, "in praise of him that is gone. He was all that you have said, and much more to those who knew him well. His very eccentricities were amiable ones ; but he is gone now."

" Yes, sir. But he has a wife."

"God, yes, I forgot her. There is yet more suffering to come. That is a horrible thought. Well, it can't be helped ; but I would not break this intelligence to Mrs. Percival for the certainty of the command of a brigade as my recompense."

" No more would I, sir."

"Well, sergeant, we have done all we can do till the arrival of those whom I have sent for from the barracks. You may go, if you like. My duty is here."

"Let me stay with you, sir ; or shall I mount guard outside the door while you go down stairs? Sir, this is but a sorry sight to have before your eyes, perhaps for an hour, major."

" Never mind, we will stay here together, sergeant. We both knew him, and loved him, and we will not desert him now."

CHAPTER XLVI.

ARTHUR WILTON FINDS HIMSELF SUS-
PECTED OF THE MURDER.

IT wanted just twenty minutes to ten o'clock, when Corporal Steady reached the barracks with the major's horse in a foam, and dashed into the open yard.

The appearance of the corporal in such a state, and with the steed of Major Cuthbert, at once induced the opinion that something had happened to that officer, and there was a rush of soldiers and non-commissioned officers round Steady to get the news.

"What is it, Steady?—Where's the major?—What has happened?—Where have you been all night yourself?—Where is Cockles?

Such were a few of the questions that Corporal Steady found pouring in upon him on all sides.

Throwing himself off his horse, he raised his voice, and in one stunning sentence replied to all—

" The colonel is murdered!"

The throng fell back at once, and Corporal Steady made his way towards the officers' quarters. He was met at the door by several of them, who from the windows had seen him arrive in such haste upon Major Cuthbert's horse, and they were to the full as eager for the news that Steady had brought as the men had been.

" Well, corporal," said one. " What's the meaning of all this?"

Corporal Steady drew himself up and saluted the officers respectfully, and then in a voice that he tried to render firm, but which was strange and cracked by emotion, he spoke—

" The colonel lies murdered at the Abbey, and the major desires that every officer off barrack-duty should come to him with the surgeon."

" Murdered?"

" In cold blood."

" Murdered? The colonel?"

Corporal Steady said not another word, and after a moment's gazing in each other's faces, as if they would hope to gather doubt about the possibility of such an act, the officers made a rush to their rooms to get their caps and swords.

The surgeon was called for loudly, and soon appeared; and in the course of ten minutes he and every officer off duty had left the barracks, along with a company of the regiment, for the Abbey.

It was then, when the tumult in the barrack-yard had ceased, that Captain

CAPTAIN STRACHAN SHOOTS AT THE GHOST-LIKE FACE AT HUNCKS' WINDOW.

Strachan, crouching down before the window of his room, ventured to peep out.

The face of the murderer was pale and haggard. His eyes were blood-shot, and the hot breath that came from between his parched lips showed what a night of fever he had passed.

"They know it now," he muttered. "Oh, yes, they know it now, and in twenty-four hours all England will know it. Oh, yes, it will soon—too soon become the talk of all men; and I did it—I did it. No—no—what's that?"

There had come a tap at the door of the room.

"Come in," said Strachan.

The sick-orderly, as he was called, was there, and a soldier carried in the sick officer's breakfast under the orderly's direction. Neither of the men spoke to Strachan to ask him whether he were better or worse, for they did not care, so they would not trouble themselves to pretend they did. He felt that neglect, for he knew how different it would be with any other sick officer, and with what officious and yet respectful zeal and interest he would be attended to.

And now Strachan wished, and yet dreaded, to ask what had happened that had produced so much confusion in the barrack-yard; for, although he knew so well that it was the news of the colonel's murder, yet he longed to hear what sort of complexion was put upon the deed by the men. His curiosity was terrible upon that point, and yet how much he feared lest by asking anything he should betray too suspicious an interest in the affair.

The tray with the breakfast was laid down in profound silence, and the soldier was about to retire, when, unable any longer to control his intense desire to know what was thought of the murder, he said—

"I heard the galloping of a horse in the barrack-yard, and much confusion. What was the matter?"

"Corporal Steady, sir, from the Abbey," said the soldier. "The colonel is murdered!"

Captain Strachan put on an incredulous look.

"It ill becomes you to jest with me," he said.

"It's no jest, sir; it's true, so they say.'

"But how—where—when?"

"At his quarters, they say. I don't know anything further about it, sir, if you please."

"I am amazed and afflicted. Oh, it cannot be. So kind and good a man, too. Impossible."

"Can I do anything more for you, sir?"

"No—no. But it seems too absurd this idea of the colonel being murdered. Who did the deed?"

"Don't know, sir."

"I sincerely hope you will know soon. Mind that you come to me at once and let me know as soon as it is ascertained who the miscreant really is."

"Yes, sir."

"You can go now."

The soldier saluted Strachan as his officer, and left the apartment, not at all sorry to escape from the questioning of a man whom he, in common with all the regiment, now despised and detested.

Captain Strachan was alone again.

"I must now think on all the past," he said. "I must thoroughly know my position. Let me consider, now, if there is any circumstance, however trivial, that can bring suspicion to my door."

With his head resting upon his hands and his eyes closed, so as to shut out all surrounding objects, Strachan gave himself up to thought.

"No," he said, "there is nothing to hurt me. Let me turn the matter over in my mind how I will, there is positively nothing to hurt me. I am quite safe, quite—quite; and everything points to Wilton as the murderer. What abundant evidence there will be of the fact of my illness here in the barracks. Why, it will appear to be so true, that they will all but swear they saw me at the very hour the murder was committed. Yes, I am safe—I am quite safe."

With this comfortable conviction, we may now leave Strachan to himself, while we proceed again to the Abbey in advance of the party from the barracks that was making its way in that direction.

After a few minutes' more thought, the major had all at once recollected that a Mr. Bevan, a magistrate, resided not a quarter of a mile from the spot; and as the murder of the colonel was a case with which the civil authorities would have to deal, there could be no doubt of the propriety of sending to that gentleman at once.

One of the soldiers was despatched with a note, and the magistrate was at the house in something less than half an hour, for the soldier had just happily met him on horseback at his own door.

Mr. Bevan ordered his clerk to follow him as soon as he could, and then, when he reached the Abbey, he was shown at once up stairs to Major Cuthbert, who met him at the door of the room.

The magistrate knew all the officers of the regiment quite well, as they had been, by invitation, to his house several times, and he had more than once dined with the mess.

"What is this I hear, major?" he said. "There must be some mistake."

"None at all, sir. Here is the proof."

The sight of the dead body upon the bed was proof positive, indeed, and the magistrate at once felt that he was at the commencement of an affair of magnitude and, no doubt, complexity and difficulty.

"Who did this?" he said.

The major shook his head.

"Suicide?"

"Oh, no, no. Nothing like it. Colonel Percival was the very last man in the world to dream of such a thing, my good sir. Dismiss such an idea from your mind."

"What surgeon has seen the body?"

"No one yet, but our regimental one will be here now very shortly, I take it. Ah! there they come. I hear the tramp of the company."

From the window of the colonel's room

could now be seen the advancing troops. A halt was called upon the lawn in front of the house, and the officers and surgeon at once made their way up stairs.

"There," said the major, as he pointed to the bed. "There is our colonel."

The officers were truly grieved, and a death-like silence sat upon the hearts of all.

"Permit me, gentlemen," said the magistrate, "to request that you will be so good as not to alter, in any way, the aspect of this room, or the position of any article within it, if you please. It will be my duty to lock it up until the inquest takes place. The surgeon will be so good as to examine the body."

The regimental surgeon now stepped forward, and, although he was a man who possessed a large share of that professional *sang froid* which is rather desirable than otherwise in such a pursuit, even he could not help being affected at the sight of one whom he so sincerely respected, and with whom he had passed so many happy hours, lying so cold and still, and dabbled in gore, as was the poor colonel.

"Quite dead," said the surgeon, after he had laid his ear on the region of the heart, and listened for a moment or two. "Quite dead."

"For long ?" said the magistrate.

"Yes, some hours. Look here. A punctured wound in the chest, and I should say, from its direction, it has pierced the heart. No doubt, death was all but instantaneous."

"There, gentlemen," said the magistrate, "permit me to lock the room now. I shall feel obliged, too, if you will place a sentinel at the door of it."

"That shall be done," said the major. "I must write to head-quarters at once likewise."

The room was locked, and the magistrate took the key. A sentinel was placed at the door, with orders to let no person whatever to have access to the apartment on any pretence until further orders; and the magistrate, with the officers, went to the room below, where the clerk was in waiting, and a couple of constables he had brought with him.

The magistrate took a seat, and said solemnly—

"Now, here I am, in my magisterial capacity, ready to take the depositions of any one who has anything to say upon this subject. My clerk, here, will take down any statement at once."

Major Cuthbert at once stated then, how he and Wilton had gone up to the room to awaken the colonel, and how they had found him dead.

"Where is Mr. Wilton?" said the magistrate.

"In the garden, sir," said one of the guard. It was the corporal of the guard who spoke. "He is in the garden, sir."

"Fetch him at once, then."

"Why, sir, I—that is, I don't know, sir."

"You don't know what?"

"Whether I ought to wait till Mr. Wilton does come, or say now what I know. I am quite sure it will come to nothing, for he is innocent of crime."

There was an exclamation of surprise and interest in the room upon this; but the magistrate said, gravely,—

"Silence, gentlemen, silence. We will hear, corporal, what you have to say now at once, upon oath."

The corporal was sworn, and with considerable agitation he deposed to the following facts, which were all of them strictly true, although the conclusion that they would appear to point at was about as erroneous as any conclusion could possibly be.

"There's the mark of blood, sir, on the balustrade of the staircase from the colonel's room, and it goes on till it gets to the back of the room door where Mr. Wilton sat up all night. I looked about that room, and I saw that one corner of the carpet had been hastily ripped up, for the nails were sticking in it, and just underneath I found this."

The corporal held up the poniard with which Captain Strachan had done the fearful deed.

There was a look of surprise and horror upon every face.

"Keep the door fast, gentlemen," said the magistrate.

"That is so, sir," said the major.

"Do you mean to say, corporal, that Mr. Wilton was up all night?"

"Yes, sir."

"Wherefore was he so?"

"Don't know, sir. But about the middle of the night he said somebody was in the garden, and the guard was hurried out, but nobody was taken."

"Mr. Smith, be so good as to look at this dagger, if you please."

The surgeon did so.

"Speaking, now, from the little information you already possess of the wound that killed Colonel Percival, do you think that is a likely weapon to have inflicted it?'

"The very thing. Why, there is wet blood upon it now."

There was a silence of some few moments' duration, and then the magistrate said, quickly—

"This is found in the room of a person who was up all night, and marks of blood were traced to his door. Gentlemen, do any of you know anything further that may bear upon the matter in respect to Mr. Wilton?"

"There were some absurd statements," said Major Cuthbert, "made to the colonel regarding Wilton's expressed intention to rob him and murder him; but nobody believed them."

"It is my duty," said the magistrate, "to order Arthur Wilton into immediate custody. God forbid that I should prejudge anybody, but my duty is quite clearly before me, and you will oblige me, Major Cuthbert, by aiding the officers in this matter."

CHAPTER XLVII.

SHOWS HOW THE INNOCENT ARTHUR WAS ARRESTED FOR THE MURDER.

ARTHUR WILTON is in custody, and formally accused of the murder of his colonel—that man, who, of all others in the world, he most esteemed and respected—that man, before whom he would, at any moment, have stepped, if he saw danger coming to him—that man, whose noble and chivalric character had, ever since he had known him, served to him a model for imitation.

It was, indeed, a terrible blow to poor Arthur.

Did he sink under it?

There can be no doubt but that many natures would have at once sunk under such a calamity, but Arthur Wilton's was not one of those natures. To be sure, for the moment, it staggered him, and he felt almost inclined impiously to doubt the justice and the wisdom of that Creator who could allow the most innocent of his creatures thus to be confounded with the most guilty.

Better and nobler thoughts, however, soon came to the aid of Arthur Wilton, and gradually his spirit rose to the occasion, and he looked proudly in the face of the disastrous circumstances which surrounded him.

In a moment, as if by a stroke of lightning, the whole frightful plot by which he was implicated as a principal in the murder of the colonel was unfolded to him. There was but one thing that baffled him, and that was comprised in the question that he put to himself of—

"Who really did the deed?"

That was a question which Arthur Wilton found himself utterly unable to answer.

Of course, his suspicions at once would have gone to the name of Captain Strachan, had he not known, or he thought he knew, that that individual was confined to the barracks by severe illness.

Who, then, was he to suspect and, in his own mind, accuse? No one. There was not another living soul with whom Arthur Wilton had ever come into contact whom he thought at all capable of even dreaming of such a deed.

Amazed—confounded—horror-stricken at the murder as an accomplished fact, and at his own arrest for it so falsely, he found himself hurried before the magistrate with an officer on each side of him, and an astonished corporal's guard behind him.

The soldiers who were off duty crowded into the room. The officers from the barracks looked pale and anxious; Major Cuthbert wore the aspect of a man who could never smile again; and the magistrate was much agitated, and probably not a little perplexed to know what to do.

Arthur Wilton, to tell the truth, was recovering much more rapidly from the shock that the extraordinary turn things had taken had given him, than any one else.

Casting his eyes round the room from face to face, he at last fixed them upon the magistrate, and said—

"Is it by your orders, sir, that I am a prisoner?"

"It is so."

"For what, sir?"

"Murder. The murder of Colonel Percival."

"Is it possible?"

"Prisoner," said the magistrate, "it is my duty, after ordering a man into custody, at once to inform him why I do so, and then, in accordance with the liberal and humane spirit of the English criminal law, it is my duty to warn him that whatever he may say will be carefully noted, and used for or against him, as the case may turn out. After that warning, it is open to you to make any remark you please, or to adopt the wiser course of being quiet."

"Stop, sir. That may be a wise course to a criminal, but it cannot matter to an innocent man what he says, unless he should be so lost to reason as falsely to accuse himself. Oh, how weak and insufficient the words, I am innocent, appear to me to express my entire freedom from this imputed guilt, and my horror of the crime !"

"Very well. I will now take sufficient evidence to warrant me in remanding you."

"Evidence, sir?"

"Yes, evidence. I cannot remand you without some fair and reasonable ground for so doing."

"But this is absurd. Evidence against me? Why, sir, there is none. There can be none. It is an impossibility."

"You will see."

"Who is the perjured villain who will stand forth as my accuser?"

"No one stands forth as your accuser," said the magistrate. "It is not necessary that they should. All we require is, that there should be certain facts deposed to which should seem to imply the probability of your guilt, and then the affair proceeds regularly in legal order of inquiry. I don't say you are guilty, God forbid that I should. Nor do I think there is one person here present who will take upon him to say so."

"Not one," said Arthur, as his eyes ranged round the circle of faces.

There was a pause of a few moments' duration, and then the magistrate had the man sworn who had found the knife or dagger in Arthur's room; and the weapon, still crusted with the blood of the colonel, was produced.

Arthur looked bewildered.

"Have you any questions to put to this witness?" said the magistrate.

"Oh, no—no—not one. The man would not swear to what he did not feel was the truth. After hearing him say that he found the weapon in my room, I have no more doubt about it than that I am standing here."

"I assure you, prisoner, that what you say is being taken down."

"Sir, I did not say that I placed the weapon where it was found. Do not so mistake me, for by all my hope of eternal life, I declare I never cast eyes upon it until this moment."

"Very well. We will proceed."

The marks of blood all the way down the stairs to the room of Arthur was deposed to, and he listened with the wild kind of wonder to the evidence that a man gives when he is dreaming, and yet is sufficiently awake to suspect as much.

"Is it real?" he said.

No one answered him.

Then it was deposed that he was up all the night, and he said at once, in a clear voice—

"That is true—I was; but I can hardly say why or wherefore, except that I fell asleep in an attempt to read a book, and that then that sort of indolence that comes over a man who is in a state of half repose, prompted me not to go to bed at all. I can explain it in no other way."

"Then you have nothing to ask of the witnesses, prisoner?"

"Oh, nothing. I believe every word that they say. I do not from my soul think that there is a man in the regiment who would tell an untruth about me, excepting my declared enemy, Captain Strachan."

"Captain Strachan is very ill, indeed, and confined to his bed in the barracks," said the surgeon.

"Yes. I believe that is just so," said Arthur Wilton.

He passed his hands in a strange, confused manner across his brow, and they all thought that he was overcome by the discovery of his frightful guilt.

"Unhappy young man," said the magistrate, "for the third time I warn you to be careful of your words, as you are here without a legal adviser; but it is my duty to say to you now in a formal way, what have you to say to this charge?"

"Stop, I remember. Yes, my full recollection is coming back to me now. Hear me, sir, and you all, gentlemen of my regiment, and you, my brother soldiers, for I will now tell you what happened last night. It is all quite clear before me. Oh, so clear—so very clear."

The magistrate shook his head.

"Listen to me," added Arthur. "I came here to remain with the colonel as his secretary, and I took possession of the little room below opening into the garden. I sat there reading, as I tell you, and I fell asleep. Once during the evening I went to the library to get a book, but I fell asleep with it upon the table before me; I awoke by a noise that some person made who was looking in at the window of my room from the garden. I made an immediate alarm, and gave pursuit; the soldiers joined in the pursuit, but the person eluded them all and escaped."

The magistrate shook his head again.

"That person, be he whom he may, is the murderer," said Arthur Wilton.

The magistrate turned to the guard, and said—

"Did any one here see a stranger in the garden? When the alarm was given by Arthur Wilton, did any of you see a fugitive?"

"I did sir," said one soldier.

"And I did," said Cockles.

Arthur breathed more freely.

"I think I have other witnesses to that

fact, too," he said; "but I cannot call them at this moment. Oh, sir—and you, Major Cuthbert, is it possible that I can be seriously suspected of this crime?"

"I am too amazed and afflicted, Wilton," said the major, "to know what to think."

"Well, gentlemen, I have said all I have to say."

"It is my duty, then," said the magistrate, "without any prejudice to your case, and, of course, without the remotest expression of an opinion upon it one way or the other, to commit you to prison for one week on remand."

"As you please, sir."

"During that remand you will have time to collect all the facts bearing upon your case, and during that week the inquest upon the body of the colonel will be held. If you be as innocent of the deed as you say, I pray to Heaven that you will be speedily delivered from all suspicion."

CHAPTER XLVIII.

ARTHUR WILTON IS CAST INTO PRISON AT EXETER.

THE plain, natural good sense of Arthur let him see in a moment that the magistrate was doing nothing more than his mere duty, and that it was quite out of the question he could do otherwise than as he did.

"Sir," he said, I thank you for the courteous manner in which you feel yourself compelled to send an innocent man to jail upon a charge of murder."

The constables now whispered to the magistrate, and then he, turning to Major Cuthbert, said—

"The constables seem rather timid of taking a man charged with so very onerous a crime to Exeter alone. Will you spare a corporal's guard?"

"Certainly, sir. Let a corporal and two more accompany the police with the prisoner. I, of course, sir, give up completely this soldier, Wilton, to the civil authorities, and as his officer, I have nothing further to say to him or to do with him."

Arthur bowed; but he thought that the major might at that early stage of the proceedings have spared him the latter part of his speech.

A great bustle now ensued in the villa, and after a little consultation, the officers decided upon handcuffing their prisoner and starting with him at once. It was a relief to Arthur that the corporal sent

with him was not his friend Steady, and, oh! what a relief it was to Steady.

Arthur would fain have said something more to Major Cuthbert, to try to erase from his mind any idea that he could really be guilty; but the kind major was too shocked at the bare suspicion to come near him.

As the officers, one on each side of him, led him out into the garden. Steady and Cockles walked up to him.

"Mr. Wilton, we don't believe it," said Steady,

"No," said Cockles, "it's not the fact. I'll eat my drum if you did it, Mr. Wilton."

At these words, for the first time since the accusation, poor Arthur felt that he was nearly giving way to the emotion which was gathering at his heart; but by a great effort he succeeded in controlling his feelings, although he was deadly pale.

"God bless you both, and thank you," he said.

"Come, come," said one of the officers, "we can't allow any conversation with the prisoner."

Cockles, however, would shake the manacled hand of poor Arthur, but Steady was pushed aside by the officers, and, indeed, if they had knocked him down the poor fellow was too deeply affected, and too much overcome by his feelings to have resisted them.

Another moment, and Arthur was on the high-road to Exeter, a felon in appearance, although as innocent in fact as any of God's creatures can possibly be. Poor, poor Arthur. He gave but one backward ook at the Abbey, and his eyes rested for a moment on the closed blind of the colonel's room. With a slight shudder he turned them away, as he thought of the frightful spectacle that was there, and then he said—

"I am quite ready to go, as quickly as you please."

"Oh, don't you be afraid of that," said one of the officers; "we will go quick enough for you."

"Yes," said the other, "and time enough too; the Assizes will be on in about a fortnight, and then they will polish you off pretty quick, I rather think. Ha! ha!"

Finding that they were inclined to assume, as the police functionaries of the lower class are but too apt to do, that because he was in custody he must necessarily be guilty of what was laid to his charge, Arthur did not make another remark to them, and the whole distance was performed in silence.

This silence had one good effect, though,

and that was, that it enabled Arthur Wilton to compose his thoughts, and to decide upon some course of action. It so happened, too, with him, as it is with many persons of active intellects, that he could think best while actually walking, so that by the time he reached Exeter, he had resolved upon what he was to do in this new and terrible exigency.

His resolve was to send for his father and Mr. Revis directly, as the two friends upon whom he knew he could at once rely, and who would believe, as a preliminary to all that was to follow, his simple and clear assertion that he had nothing whatever to do with the crime laid to his charge.

This was a prudent enough resolve—but, oh, how the proud and innocent heart of Arthur Wilton bled to think of the effect which the tidings of his arrest would have upon Amelia! Yet let it not be supposed that, for one moment, he doubted of the views she would take of the matter; but still it was a pang for all that.

The jail at Exeter is not a very inviting abode, and it was with a shudder that Arthur Wilton crossed its threshold.

A little knot of official personages soon collected to have a look at the murderer, as they called him; and the governor paid his usual attention, and sent at once a note to the sheriff of the county to let him know what had occurred.

There was very little need of notes, though, to proclaim the facts, and all the exaggerations of facts, of what had taken place at the Abbey. Rumour, with her thousand tongues, spread the news in all directions, and before the day had far advanced, there was scarcely a soul in Devonshire that did not know a great deal more than all about it, and that had not made his or her comment upon the extraordinary affair.

And all this time there lay Captain Strachan trembling in his bed at the barracks.

Through sheer agony and fear, the wretch got really ill in the course of a few hours, so that when the surgeon returned from the Abbey, he found him in such a state of fever as rather surprised him, considering the remedies he had already, as he thought, had, and the quiet he had, as he thought, enjoyed in his own rooms at the barracks.

"Fever!" said the surgeon, abruptly, after looking at his patient.

Oh, how Strachan longed to ask him what had occurred at the Abbey. But until some one should tell him there had been a murder committed, how dared he know of it?

"You think me worse?" he said.

"Oh, yes."

"And—and if the fever should progress—it is a real fever, I suppose, is it not?"

"I never yet heard of a sham one. You will need to be careful, or it will lay hold of you worse than it has now."

"Oh, God! tell me—is there any chance of my becoming at all—delirious?"

"Likely enough."

"No—no, don't say that. Anything but that! Doctor, give me some medicine to prevent that. Let me keep my senses, and I care for nothing."

The surgeon looked at Strachan as if he had something beyond a suspicion that the state of things he, Strachan, so much dreaded had actually come to pass, and that already he was wandering a little in his intellects.

"You had better keep yourself quiet," he said.

"Oh, yes. I will strive to do that."

The surgeon's dislike to Strachan was so great, that, although the death, tragical and dreadful in all its details, of the colonel was the subject uppermost in his mind, he would not say one word about it to his patient, lest it might serve to provoke anything in the shape of a conversation.

With a very slight bow he left the room, and when the door was closed, Strachan breathed hard as though he were nearly choking, as he said in a low muttering voice—

"What does this mean, now? Why will he not speak to me of the colonel's murder? Is there any suspicion? Oh, no—no. That is quite impossible. There can be none—there can be none!"

The murderer then thought that if he could get a newspaper, it would let him know everything that was thought or said about the dreadful deed, concerning which, no one seemed inclined to talk to him.

Of course, though, no morning paper could possibly contain any intelligence of a fact which was not a piece of current intelligence until so late an hour; but he thought that the Exeter paper would publish, probably, a second edition rather than disappoint its readers of such a tale of blood.

With the determination, then, to wait awhile before he made any movement, and with the dread sitting brooding at his heart, that the fever which blackened his lips and appeared to be running riot through his veins might terminate in delirium, during which he would in all probability give utterance to the fearful secret of his guilt, the truly wretched Strachan passed many—many hours of the day.

How much happier, after all, was Arthur Wilton, even in a cell in prison, than Captain Strachan, free and unsuspected, as yet, of the awful crime that he had committed!

We do not mean to say that the consciousness of innocence is enough to carry a man with serenity through all the aggravations incidental to a false accusation, for in any case we can easily imagine that the sensation of being treated with such injustice would have the effect of almost maddening the temper; but certainly that consciousness opens so wide a door to hope, that he who is falsely accused never can suffer so much as he who is really guilty, and who is trembling lest some one should point to him, saying—

"Thou art the man!"

There was another person, too, whom we have rather neglected, but who, as soon as he heard of the murder, felt deeply interested in the possible results.

That other person was, Mr. Huncks the lawyer; he felt that he would have no difficulty in pointing to the author of the deed.

CHAPTER XLIX.

OLD MR. WILTON SENDS FOR ADVICE TO THE METROPOLIS.

THE first act of Arthur Wilton, when he recovered from the alarming effect which the whole affair might be said to have had upon him, and when he found himself placed in a cell in the prison, was to request leave to write some letters to his friends.

It is no part of the policy of the English law to oppress even a presumed guilty man; and the governor of the prison being sent for, replied to the request by saying—

"Yes, you can write to whom you please, only remember that no letter leaves this place or comes to it without being looked into by the authorities."

"That does not matter," said Arthur. "Being falsely accused, or rather, I should say, mistakingly accused, or suspected of a great crime, of which I am so innocent as even not to be able to suggest an explanation, I naturally write to summon my friends about me."

"Very well, you can do so."

Arthur wrote two letters, as briefly as possible, letting his father and Mr. Revis

know what, in all probability, by that time, had reached them by the voice of popular report—namely, that by some combination of circumstances, which were beyond his control, but scarcely explainable truthfully, he was accused of the murder of the colonel.

Arthur did not ask them to come to him. He knew that that would be quite superfluous.

Before he could fold his letters, he heard the sound of footsteps in the passage leading to his cell, and the turnkey who was on duty in that part of the prison, as he flung the door open, merely uttered the one word—

"Visitors."

In another moment, Arthur was in the arms of his father.

"Why, my dear boy, what is the meaning of all this? I could scarcely, till this moment that I actually see you here, believe it possible that such a mistake as this had happened."

Arthur smiled.

"A mistake, indeed, father! They say I murdered Colonel Percival."

"Pshaw! It is too absurd."

"That's just what I say," said Mr. Revis, stepping forward; "it is too absurd, and we must take immediate steps to release you from all connection with such a ridiculous charge."

"This is cheering," said Arthur. "You both seem in good spirits. You think nothing of this?"

"Indeed, but I do," said Mr. Wilton. "Is it nothing for one innocent man, even for a day or two, to be shut up in a place like this? What can the police be about that they do not find the real criminal, Arthur? That you should be suspected is perfectly inexplicable."

"It is, indeed," said Mr. Revis; "but I suppose it is some blunder of the magistrates."

"No," said Arthur, "I don't blame the magistrates—I don't blame the witnesses. I don't take it to be a blunder of any one's. It is to me a strange and inexplicable state of things, which, as yet, I cannot even to myself satisfactorily explain. But you have heard the evidence, I suppose?"

"Evidence?" they both exclaimed. "What evidence? There can be no evidence."

"Oh, but there is though, father."

"We know nothing, my boy, but the mere fact that you are here in prison, and remanded for a week. What evidence can there be?"

"Quite enough, although the inference

STRACHAN'S RAGE ON DISCOVERING WILTON UP ON THE NIGHT OF THE MURDER.

from it is all false, to justify the remand, as you will admit when I tell you."

Arthur then calmly and clearly related to his father and to Mr. Revis the events of the evening, and he concluded by saying,—

"You now see that it was impossible that the magistrate, in the absence of any one else to whom strong suspicion should attach, to do otherwise than have me arrested, and placed in my present position."

" I am confounded," said Mr. Wilton.

"And I," said Farmer Revis; " but Arthur—the dagger—the blood—how came all that ?"

Arthur shook his head, sadly.

"That is just what I want to know. Of course my own ideas can point but to one supposition, and that exists in the fact that a villain did the deed, who must while I was sleeping, have forced his way into my room, and there purposely left the witness of the crime, and whoever that was, it was the man whom I saw at the window, and whom I pursued."

"My poor boy," sighed Mr. Wilton. "This is more serious than I thought."

"It is no case of accidental suspicion," said Mr. Revis. "This is a plot."

"That idea," said Arthur, "has crossed my own mind more than once, but I dread to entertain it, for if it be such, you may depend that it is not yet wholly and fully developed, and I have more to dread than we are at all aware of as yet. If it were not for one circumstance, I should think, indeed, I was in the meshes of some terrible plot.

"What circumstance is that?" said Farmer Revis.

"Captain Strachan is very ill, indeed, and confined to his rooms at the barracks."

"Then he can have nothing to do with this affair."

"Not personally," said Mr. Wilton.

"And who will commit a murder for another?" said Mr. Revis. "You will scarcely find an associate who will go that length for an associate in crime. It does not seem to me, under the circumstances, possible that Captain Strachan could have had anything to do with this affair."

"That is my own impression," said Arthur. "I would not accuse even my bitterest foe unjustly. If Strachan had been well and about as usual, I would have begged of you to make every possible exertion to ascertain his minutest actions yesterday and last night; but as it is, all that is useless. His presence in the barracks can be proved, no doubt, in a moment with ease."

Mr. Wilton paced the cell in agitation.

"Arthur," he said, "this affair wears, to me, a much more serious aspect than it did. It is necessary that those who are from habit and professional practice accustomed to unravel these mysteries, should take this affair in hand."

"I think so likewise, father."

"Very good, my son. I will write to London at once. You recollect young Mr. North who was down here about a year ago on the circuit. He is the son of an old friend of mine, and I have the highest opinion of his talents. I will write to him at once, and ask him to come, if he can, professionally."

"Do so, father. I long to speak to some one who can possibly suggest to me some probable path out of the complexity of events that surround me. Here I am, as innocent as a babe of this dreadful deed, and yet I justify the magistrate in committing me."

"I will lose no time, Arthur. Of course we need not be under a moment's uneasiness regarding what the end of this affair will be. You will be as fully and completely exonerated from all shadow of suspicion as I am; but the provoking thing is, that for the time being you should be deprived of your liberty, and your name at all associated with such an affair in the ears of the public."

"It is most provoking," said Mr. Revis.

"I will try and bear it with what patience I may," said Arthur.

"Do so—do so."

"And, Mr. Revis——"

"Yes, Arthur. What would you say?"

"Does Amelia know of this?"

"She does, and I am sorry to say that the first shock of the circumstance made her faint, and she is now anything but well. I do not think that even my authority would have prevented her from accompanying us if she had been able."

"My poor Amelia!"

"Nay, now, you will make yourself as bad as she is," said Mr. Wilton, "if you begin to talk in that way. Of course, all will be well in a few days. Let me, Arthur, be able to tell her that you are in good health and spirits."

"Do so, oh, do so. Tell her that there should be no grief where there is no guilt."

"We will."

"Now, gentlemen," said the turnkey, "time's up, if you please. We don't like visitors here. Lawyers, in course, come and go, cos we can't help 'em; but what anybody can want a coming talking here, I don't know."

"Silence, fellow," said Mr. Wilton. "How dare you speak to us in such a manner?"

"Ha! go on, old gentleman, go on. Time's up, I tell you. Lor, if we was to let people come to these here murderers, we should be all day lounging about the door of the cell to see as they didn't smuggle them off in their pockets. I hopes now as you haven't brought in any 'bacca."

"Never mind what the man says, father," said Arthur. "It is his ignorance, and a certain amount of brutality connected with his profession, that makes him what he is. We should never quarrel with any animal for making the noise peculiar to it, you know, father. A bear cannot help growling."

"Oh, I'm a bear, am I, and a hanimal?" said the turnkey. "Well, it's one comfort that you'll be made to dance upon nothink for this here murder, I take it—Ha—ha! I may be a bear, but I shan't be made to dance that-a-ways, no—no. Ha!"

Arthur was alone again. Alone in a felon's cell.

And yet with what a firm and manful spirit had Arthur Wilton as yet held up against the circumstances that pressed him to the earth. How many there are who would completely have sunk beneath the accumulated weight of such most dreadful events! But he did not do so.

"No," he said, when he flung himself upon the rude couch in his cell, "no. How can I expect anybody to be true to me if I am not true to myself? No man is ever utterly lost until he gives himself up to that despair for which there is no redemption."

CHAPTER L.

THE EVIDENCE AGAINST ARTHUR ACCUMULATES, INSTEAD OF DECREASING.

IT is quite clear that during the week that is to pass before Arthur again is brought up before the magistrates, many important events for and against the supposition of his guilt—for, after all, he being really innocent, it could but be a supposition—must come to light.

Those various means by which the arch villain, Captain Strachan, had striven to strengthen the appearances against poor Arthur were to develop themselves. The inquest upon the dead body of Colonel Percival was to take place, and the friends of Arthur—those friends who knew him to be innocent from his own assertion, and who, from their knowledge of his character, would merely have thought him mad, even if he had told them he was guilty—were to place the whole affair into such order that everything that skill and judgment could dictate would be done for him.

During that week, too, Captain Strachan was to make up his mind as to the precise course that he intended to pursue, and he did so make up his mind, as we shall perceive.

While poor Arthur, then, is in the prison at Exeter, and while all those who love him and love truth were doing their utmost to save him from the consequences of the awful and sinister plot in which he was involved, we will peep into the camp of the enemy, and see what Strachan is about.

In the course of the day he heard quite enough to convince him that everything had gone on just as he intended it. In fact, the only untoward circumstance that had taken place in the whole transaction, as far as he was concerned, consisted in the fact of his having been seen by Wilton before he could leave the premises upon which the murder was committed.

But, even regarding that, he did not feel at all anxious, after some hours had elapsed, for those hours of peace and quietness, to him, were abundant proof that Wilton, although he had seen a form in the garden, had not identified it as his, Captain Strachan's.

So far, then, the villain felt himself to be safe.

Towards evening he got a paper that was published in Exeter, and from which he perused the whole particulars of the arrest of Arthur Wilton, combined with many statements which he knew must be exaggerations; for, as none knew better than he, Strachan, the innocence of Arthur Wilton, he felt how impossible it was that he could do or say the things which the newspaper scribe had reported of him, for the purpose of making out a good story.

It was strange to see, though, how, through the whole report of the case, the guilt of Wilton seemed at once to be an admitted fact; and if he had actually stepped forward, and said—"I am the man who did the deed," it would have been impossible to have agreed with a more perfect conviction of the fact.

This was pleasant news for Strachan.

As the villain threw down the paper, he burst into a laugh, exclaiming—

"He is in the toils fairly now! He is caught, Ha! ha! He is now environed by circumstances that the cunning of a world will not break through."

Strachan felt wonderfully better now. All his apprehensions had vanished, and as he rubbed his hands together, and pacced his room to and fro, he said—

"Who is to find, now, that I did this deed? What danger am I in? None. Who is to say that Strachan is guilty? Why none but Strachan himself, and he must first go mad ere he does so."

The feeling of exultation lent quite a glow to his cheeks.

"I have failed," he said, "enevitably failed, it is true, in making anything by the murder, in a pecuniary sense, but I have fully accomplished my other object, which consisted in revenge against Arthur Wilton; yes, and it is some revenge, too, against the colonel, to have cut him off in such a way, in the very prime of life. Surely that is something, and how very safe I am."

Strachan sat down and looked about him with perfect satisfaction in his looks, and as he spoke, there was a fulness of content in his tones.

"Yes," he added, "I have arranged this thing well. In the first place, it is done well because I had no accomplice. So far, I am safe from the treachery or the vileness of another. Then, again, I have, by this mock illness, established the fact, by very creditable witnesses, that I never left the barracks for a good eight and forty hours before this crime could possibly have been committed ; and, finally, although I ran some risk at the Abbey, I did escape without being in the smallest degree recognised, for if I had been by Wilton, he, upon his own account, would have been the first to cry out that it was I who did it. Yes, all is well and safe."

After thus satisfactorily settling, as he thought, the fact in his own mind, that he had done the deed, and effectually screened himself from even the remotest suspicion upon the subject, he set about deciding as to his future conduct in the affair.

"I must now," he said, "get gradually well. Not so fast as to provoke any suspicion that my convalescence is too rapid, but just fast enough to do credit to the skill of the doctor, and to put him into good humour with himself. After that, I must show great concern for the murder of the colonel, and give my evidence, as Arthur Wilton's officer, of his humanity, his integrity, and his generally blameless conduct, all of which, I must say, induces me to believe that it is quite impossible he could commit the murder. Oh, yes, I must play the friendly part to Arthur, and it will be quite as well if I call upon old Revis at the farm. Ha ! ha ! What will be my reception by the fair Amelia ? Ha ! ha !"

Captain Strachan was specially delighted at the whole aspect of affairs, and he was rubbing his hands together and smiling, when a tap came at his room door.

In a moment composing his features to a decent gravity, he said, in a low voice—

"Come in."

It was the doctor, paying his evening visit, and, with the scant ceremony that he displayed to Strachan, he entered the room, saying—

"Well, sir, how are you now ?"

"Better," said Strachan. "That last medicine has done me much good, doctor ; I feel quite a different man."

The last medicine, to tell the truth, had been cast under the fire-grate.

"Ah, indeed," said the surgeon, "that was a peculiar recipe of my own, and I had the greatest expectations from it."

"Well, doctor, I can assure that the effect is little short of magical. I am as strong again as I was. You have rare skill, doctor."

Alas! the doctor was a human being, and so open to flattery, and he smiled as Strachan spoke, so that the wily villain knew in a moment that he had discovered the weak side of that son of Esculapius.

"It is rather a pity, doctor," he said, "that such rare abilities as yours should be used up in a regiment. It is in the metropolis, with the private practice you would be sure to get at court, and among the highest of the nobility, that you ought to make your name."

"Well, Captain Strachan, there is certainly something in what you say. But that is not the question now. Allow me to feel your pulse. Ah, excitement and fever still."

"Yes," said Strachan, "since that dreadful news of the murder of the colonel I have been fevered. Can it be really true?"

"True enough. I saw the body."

"But it cannot be possible that Arthur Wilton did the deed. It is, unfortunately, well known that he and I, in consequence of some foolish rivalry about a village girl whom I ought never to have thought of, were anything but friends; and yet I am not blind to the fact that he was anything but the sort of person who would be guilty of such offences."

"Well, he is accused, at all events."

"I shall do all in my power, if I continue to recover as rapidly as I have done for the last twelve hours, to aid him. I feel certain that he is innocent, however appearances may be against him. But, I suppose, he will easily clear himself?"

"Not so easy, I think," said the surgeon, as he rose to go. "I will send you some more of the medicine which has done you so much good; and if, as you say, you go on as you have for the last twelve hours, you will, in a day or two, I daresay, be quite convalescent."

"But, sir, is no one else but poor Wilton suspected of this dreadful deed?"

"Not that I am aware of. Good afternoon, sir."

The dislike of the surgeon to Strachan was growing up again. It had only been partially hidden in the glare of the gross flattery with which Strachan had plied him, and now he felt angry with himself for giving way to the feeling, and he hurried from the room rather precipitately.

Strachan smiled.

"Ah, my worthy doctor," he said, "I have you now. I can prescribe for you, and make you take a much more potent dose than, in all your skill, you can present to me. I will dose your mind with the strong mixture of deference and flattery, and when I walk out into the barrack-yard to-morrow, as I shall do, I will present myself as a living specimen of your skill, and you shall be a living, smiling, well-tickled specimen of me in the art of flattery. Well—well, I have but to be true to myself and what can harm me?"

How strange it was that the very sentiment with which Strachan pleased himself was the one that kept up the courage of Arthur Wilton!

CHAPTER LI.

MR. HUNCKS FEELS DISSATISFIED THAT HE PARTICIPATES IN NOTHING.

WHILE Strachan was thus felicitating himself upon the prospect before him, and thinking that his revenge, at all events, was quite certain as against Arthur Wilton and Amelia there was an individual crossing the barrack-yard, upon an errand to him.

That individual was our old acquaintance, Mr. Huncks.

The wily lawyer had heard of the murder, and at once made up his mind that it was the handy work of Captain Strachan, although he had heard that that individual was confined to the barracks by serious indisposition. It was to seek an interview, then, with his worthy client that Huncks now made his way to the barracks, and with great politeness asked the sentinel at the gate the way to the officers' quarters, and was duly directed.

Up to a certain hour at night any one might walk into the barracks, and that hour had not yet come, so there was no objection made to Mr. Huncks availing himself of the privilege of entering the place.

It was Mr. Huncks's first appearance at the barracks, and as his evil fortune would have it, the first person he met in the yard was Cockles, who, after looking at him for a few moments and walking round him twice, to his great discomfiture, cried out—

"The lawyer it is, and the lawyer it was. Row-de-dow-dow! Don't you remember me, sir?"

"No, my good man, no. Dear me no. But I hope you are quite well and charming, and all that sort of thing?" said Huncks.

"Quite the other way," said Cockles.

"The—other way—what other way?" said Huncks, looking round him rather puzzled.

"Come, now," added Cockles, "are you tired of your life? Row-de-dow-dow!"

"God bless me, no!"

"Then look at me."

Mr. Huncks did look at him, as hard as though the sight of Cockles were the charm that was to preserve him in existence.

"Now you remember me," said Cockles. "Don't you know you were at the old farm, when the captain and you tried to turn the old man out of doors; and when poor Mr. Wilton, as is now in prison for doing what he never had a thought of doing, was obliged to take the king's bounty to save the old man and his daughter from being turned adrift into the road? Don't you know me now? Cockles I is, and Cockles I were."

"My dear young friend——"

"Stop a bit. Don't say that—I don't like it."

"But my good sir, allow me just to remark that I was then only in my professional capacity, and that my heart bled for the distresses of that noble and virtuous family at Riversdale Farm. Indeed, it did."

"You don't say so?"

"Yes, I do, and I may, quite in confidence to you, my worthy and exemplary friend——"

"No—no."

"Well, I won't call you that. I may say, my slight but esteemed acquaintance, if Mr. Wilton had not been so precipitate as he was in the matter, I was just going to pay the money myself to the captain to make up the amount, and so save the old man and his farm, and then I should have gone home with the tears of sensibility burning in my eyes. That is the real fact."

"Oh, lor!" said Cockles, "what we is forced to hear."

"My dear sir——"

"Row-de-dow-dow! Don't speak to me any more. What do you want here?"

"Well, if I must declare the fact, I came to see how my old chit and friend Captain Strachan was."

"Well, if I didn't think so. Birds of a feather flock together; but two of a breed, they say, won't agree. Good-by, Mr. Lawyer, I am very glad to see you. That's the captain's quarters, and don't hang yourself on any account, I beg of you."

"Thank you, Mr. Cockroach, thank you, I——"

"Cockles is my name, and not Cockroach. What do you mean by calling a fellow Cockroach?"

"A thousand pardons, my dear friend. Good evening—good evening. Curse you, I only wish I could serve you out in any way, and I almost begin to think that it would have been just as well for me not to come to this place; but, after all, the liberty of the subject is too sacred to be meddled with, and if they venture to assault me, I will take good care they smart for it, the wretches. Oh, no, they will not venture upon that. It would be too hazardous. Assault an attorney, of all people in the world! Oh, dear, no."

Perhaps Mr. Huncks was just a little too sanguine in his ideas regarding his security from assaults; but we shall soon see whether that was the case or not.

Cockles had pointed out the quarters of Captain Strachan correctly enough, and in a few minutes that worthy heard the tap at his door, that announced the arrival of a visitor.

Thinking it might be the surgeon again or an orderly with some more of the wonderful specific, Strachan called out, in his blandest tones—

"Come in."

Huncks opened the door, and appeared before the not very well pleased eyes of of his quondam friend and client.

"How are you, captain?"

"The devil!"

"Ha, ha, ha! not quite yet—all in good time, captain; you surely did not expect that gentleman quite so soon or unceremoniously as this, did you?"

"Bah! I am ill."

"So I heard."

"Well, sir, and believe it, of course?"

Huncks blinked his little eyes, as he said,

"I did, but I don't now. By these words you have convinced me of the contrary. Come, captain, you and I pretty well comprehend each other. Disguise is only a little loss of time between us."

"What do you mean?"

"Just what I say, captain, and nothing more or nothing less. Come, now, we row in the same boat. Why do you at times make yourself so very disagreeable a fellow-passenger?"

"I must confess, Mr. Huncks, that when you begin to be so very poetical as to speak to me in that manner, I am quite at a loss for your meaning."

"Indeed?"

"Yes, indeed, and in truth. Now, sir, I presume that accident has not brought you from your home here, so what do you want with me, Mr. Huncks?"

"This is good. I will very soon tell you what I want with you, Captain Strachan. I want my share."

"Your what?"

"My share of the plunder. Do you understand me now? I come for my share of——" Here Mr. Huncks dropped his voice, and glanced around him for a moment ere he proceeded. "I come for my share of the proceeds of the murder of Colonel Percival."

Hardened as he was in vice, and determined as he was to carry the affair with a high hand, Captain Strachan could not help blanching a little before this cool statement upon the part of Mr. Huncks.

"Is that all you have to say?" he replied.

"Enough, is it not?"

"No."

"Well, perhaps you will have the kindness to suggest something further upon the subject."

"Oh, yes, with pleasure. You have first to prove that I did the deed."

"Do you want me to set about it?"

Captain Strachan was silent, and Mr. Huncks laughed.

"Come, come, captain," he said, "you are tolerably safe, but not quite so safe as you think you are; but you may rely upon me in this affair, only I must and will have my share."

"Explain to me," said Strachan, "why I am not so safe—that is to say, explain to me what makes you think that I have done this deed, Mr. Huncks, and you will not find me unreasonable."

"Nonsense, captain; who did do it if you did not?"

"That I am not bound to say, or to think about."

"Well, as you please; I came to you in friendship to talk the affair over, but if you take high ground, and think you can carry the whole matter through without me, do so. It is quite a matter of immateriality, I assure you. Of course, I expect, being the only resident practitioner upon the spot, to be employed in the affair, and if I am employed for the prosecution of vengeance, or for the defence of Arthur Wilton, you can hardly suppose but that I shall do my best for those who pay me my fee?"

"Stop, Mr. Hunks.'

"Very good."

"You are not yet retained by those who are my foes in this transaction?"

"Not yet."

"Well consider yourself as retained by

me. When I come to think of it, nothing is more likely than this Wilton and his friends may try to cast some slur upon my character in the transaction; and in that case I ought to have an adviser."

"Very likely, indeed. Now you speak reasonably, Captain Strachan; and at a word, what did you get."

Strachan made a gesture of impatience, and then he said—

"When all is settled—when Wilton is no more—when Farmer Revis, in despair, sits down by his vacant hearth—and when Amelia is too depressed even to dart a glance of scorn at me—then, Mr. Huncks, name your fee, and it will be forthcoming. You need not doubt it."

"Humph!"

"I swear to you that I will keep my word."

"Don't. I would just as soon take your simple promise as your oath, Captain Strachan. The one is about as important as the other, I take it. But I don't feel disposed to wait till all this you mention shall happen."

"What can I do?"

"Divide the proceeds now. I will not quarrel with you on the idea that you may not be quite confidential regarding the full amount of which I ask a moiety; but let me have something in reason, and I am—throughout this affair, which has only just now begun, and the issue of which no man can tell—your fast friend and firm ally. In fine, if any difficulty should arise, I will pull you through it; and when I say that, you know I am to be depended upon."

Strachan was silent.

"Well, what say you?"

"Listen to me. You know that—that——"

"Go on."

Strachan rose, and opening the door carefully looked out, to be quite certain there were no eaves-droppers, and then returning to the lawyer, he added—

"You know that the colonel is dead?"

"Well?"

"We had a little dispute—he and I—and it was fatal to him, that was all;—you understand?"

"Oh, indeed! In plain language, you murdered the man to rob him, and to put the deed upon the shoulders of Wilton. Why mince the matter with me, captain? We lose so much time by beating about the bush, you know."

"Well, well, in the colonel's strong box there were jewels to a vast amount, which I secured."

"Ah!"

"Yes, and hid. As soon as the whole affair is settled, you and I will dig them up, and go halves in them. Does that satisfy you?"

"Well, hardly."

"The amount must be about thirty or forty thousand pounds. I tell you, that I buried that treasure, and that you shall share it with me. But take your own course, if you will not, for that is my ultimatum!"

CHAPTER LII.

MR. HUNCKS ACCEPTS THE CAPTAIN'S TERMS CONDITIONALLY.

MR. HUNCKS did not look over-well pleased at this proposition of Strachan's, and yet, to tell the truth, with all his cunning, he found it difficult to reply to.

"Humph!" he said. "My good sir—that is to say, my dear friend—allow me to state that, in my humble judgment, I think you have acted indiscreetly in this business."

"Indeed!—how so?"

"Why, after committing the—the—"

"Go on, Huncks—oh, go on. Since you are so obliging as to call upon me with so kind an offer of your services, I am not at all particular to a word or two. Pray say what you were going to say."

"Well, then, I think that if immediately after the murder you had only called upon me with the little proceeds, you would have done well, don't you see; but as it is not so, really I am afraid you have pursued a rather dangerous course."

"I don't see that."

"Well, now, only consider. You say you have hidden the property that you got from the colonel's bed-room?"

"Well, I do say so. The fact is, there was so much gold in ingots."

"Ingots!"

"Yes, and such a quantity of jewels. Between you and me, when the colonel was in India, he must have made a grand booty somehow, and kept it all to himself, and that was no doubt the reason he took it always about with him till he might find some opportunity of disposing of it without suspicion."

"You don't say so?"

"I do. The probability is, that he was waiting for the death of some of the old Indian officers, who might, if he had attempted to sell the jewels, have exploded the whole transaction."

"Perhaps so. Ingots!"

"Ay, and handfuls of rubies and emeralds!"

"Oh, gracious! my dear friend—my exemplary old acquaintance, and you really buried all these?"

"I have; I found that they encumbered my flight; I was not far off being at one time captured by that infernal Wilton, and then I ran against a dog, who all but laid hold of me—indeed, I think he did so. I was glad to get rid of my booty."

"Under a tree?"

"Why, you may say under a tree."

"But—but—dear me, you know what a dreadful thing it would be if, by some accident, any one were to find it out; it would be enough to drive you distracted, captain."

"And you too, Huncks; for, as truly as I speak it, you shall have half if all this affair goes on as I wish and expect. Now, bear that in mind."

"But the ingots! Oh, gracious!—the rubies—the emeralds! only think, if they were to be found. I am in a cold perspiration at the very idea. And now, my dear Strachan, if you will allow me to call you such."

"Oh, certainly; anything you like."

"Well, I tell you what I will do."

"Go on; I shall be delighted to hear a man of such consummate judgment as my dear and excellent friend Huncks."

"Well, then, you will describe to me exactly the place in which you have hidden the gold and the jewels, and I will take an opportunity of digging it up, and conveying it in safety to my house, where I will bury it in the garden; so that both our minds will be at ease about it."

"Thank you; but my mind is quite at ease, as it is."

"Oh!"

"Yes; I have hidden it so securely that I feel quite certain it is safe; and I like to leave well alone."

"But, my dear sir—"

"Nay, I have quite made up my mind that there the gold and the jewels shall remain. I daresay the value of them is nearer to one hundred thousand pounds than thirty or forty, though, when I come to think of the size and beauty of the emeralds—I never saw anything like them."

"Good gracious. But, Captain Strachan, allow me to say that you are not going the right way to—to——"

"To what, sir?"

"To conciliate—to procure—to—enable me, in fact, by every means to ward off from you any possible consequences of this little affair; for, despite all your fancied security, you don't know but that some little untoward accident, which slips your calculations altogether, may light up as a small spark will a giant conflagration—a flame of suspicion against you, that when once it begins to burn may not be so readily and easily quenched again."

This was touching Captain Strachan's fears closely. He, too, thought that some such little malapropos accident was just possible, and he said to Huncks with great gravity—

"Huncks, you speak wisely—I know well that some such accident may happen, and if it should I, of course, should be very much delighted to rely upon your talents to assist me in my extrication. If you think that the accession, after this affair is over, of one half of the colonel's effects a sufficient fee to retain you, it shall be so. If you do not, you have but to say so, and I will do the best I can without you. But recollect that in that case it is out of the question that you can get anything, for if I am to be suspected—if I am to be put upon my trial—if I am to be convicted, I would die without a breath of the secret of where I have hidden the gold and jewels."

Huncks groaned.

"You see, then, that your obvious policy is to save me, and then to stick to me like a leech till I pay you off."

Huncks did see that such was his obvious policy, and with another groan, as he could do no better, he acquiesced in it.

"Well—well," he said, "consider me as your friend; and if the worst comes to the worst, you know, now, that you have me to rely upon; and even if you should be put upon your trial, I will save you, if perjury can do it."

"Now, Huncks, I know you once again, and it will be just as well for you not to come here any more. I shall be well tomorrow or the next day, and if I find an opportunity, I will call and see you."

"Very good. I suppose you have no cash to spare?"

"Not a shilling. I was going to ask you for the loan of twenty pounds."

"Good morning—good morning."

Huncks bustled out of the room, and was gone before Captain Strachan could repeat the request.

"Curses go with you," said Strachan; "and yet you are a clever, ingenious, and most unscrupulous rogue; and if anything should go wrong with me in this affair, which, by-the-by, is quite impossible, I would not desire to be in better hands than yours. It is a glorious plan that of the mock buried treasure to make Huncks my humble servant. How that rascal's cupidity now gets the better of his judg-

THE CONFERENCE BETWEEN THE OLD GARDENER AND HIS WIFE.

ment! But that his imagination is dazzled by the idea of the ingots of gold and the emeralds and the cornelias, he would have seen through the flimsy device in a moment; but as it is, the mere suspicion that it may be true will keep him faithful. And now to play the part of the convalescent."

It was not at all difficult for Captain Strachan to get as rapidly well as he chose, inasmuch as it was impossible that the surgeon could take upon himself to say that there had been any disease. In fact,

the illness altogether was so mysterious, that the recovery might come at any time ; and as Strachan had the tact to persuade the surgeon that it was the result of his medicines, everything went on as capitally as possible.

Strachan was in the hope, too, now that Colonel Percival was no more, that he might be able to retain his place in the regiment, and that the little affair between him and the officers would blow over. He had a sanguine hope of that sort, too, contingent upon the accusation against Wilton, for if he should be convicted of the murder of the colonel, it would place his, Strachan's, conduct, as an opponent and an enemy of his, in a better light.

"All I have to do," thought Strachan, "is to say that I never believed the man, when he spoke of murdering the colonel; and then I must play the candid part, and hope that after all my feelings against him were but prejudices, that to this day I cannot account for and suggest how unlikely it is that such a man, so loaded with benefits and obligations by the colonel, could commit so horrible a crime."

How the villain chuckled now over his plans, those plans which were so well arranged, and which were known only to himself and to Heaven. Ah, he could not have thought of Heaven sincerely with the conviction that there was a Heaven, or he never could have done the deed he had.

At four o'clock upon that day an inquest was held upon the body of Colonel Percival.

The jury was composed of the principal resident gentry of the neighbourhood, and the proceedings lasted until half-past eight in the evening, although little was added to the evidence upon the matter, beyond what had already justified the magistrates in remanding Arthur Wilton. That evidence, however, was so very suspicious, that, as the coroner said—

"Gentlemen, you remember we are not judging this man, Wilton. We are only deciding upon the cause of death of the colonel, and, therefore, if there be sufficient grounds for the further solemn inquiry of a trial, we are bound to send Wilton before a jury of his country to abide that trial."

A magistrate who was upon the jury clinched the question, too, by saying—

"It is quite clear that he will be committed for trial by the magistrates, independent of what the coroner's jury may say; therefore, a verdict goes for nothing in reality, except as a matter of opinion."

After this, the verdict was pronounced, and it was wilful murder against Arthur Wilton.

Under the circumstances, it was easy to perceive that the coroner's inquest must so end, for nobody else was ever suggested as the murderer but Wilton, and the question arose in every mind along with the doubts of his guilt—"If he did it not, who did?"

We do not mean to say that the coroner's jury, as men of education and intelligence, would have committed Arthur Wilton upon this *non sequiter* kind of reasoning; but as they were only sending him for trial, it answered very well, and they acted upon it.

The news of the termination of the inquest was brought to the barracks by the officers, who in a body had atttended it, and it was now spread among the soldiers. Strachan heard the corporal talking in the yard, and he strove to catch the sounds in an articulate form, but could not. He would have opened his window, but that would not look well for a sick man to do, so he had nothing for it but to wait for the visit of the surgeon again.

At about nine that personage came, and Strachan announced himself as being wonderfully better.

"Well," said the surgeon, "if you go on in this way, you will be able to get out of your room to-morrow. I came to tell you, though, that you must be very cautious—very cautious indeed. A rapid change of temperature might produce a relapse."

Strachan smiled as he said—

"I seem as if I could defy sickness, while I have your skill and service to depend upon."

"Hem!" coughed the surgeon, "of course, we do the best we can. Good evening."

"Good evening. Oh, by the bye, pardon me for detaining you, but has the inquest taken place upon our poor friend, Percival?"

"Yes, it's over."

"And the verdict?"

"Wilful murder against that rascal, Wilton—the smooth-faced hypocrite. Good evening, captain."

"Good evening, and my thanks, doctor."

Captain Strachan was alone again, and when the last sound of the surgeon's retiring footsteps had died away, he burst into a fierce unnatural laugh.

"Ha! ha! Wilful murder against Arthur Wilton! and they begin to think him here, where he was once so popular, a smooth-faced hypocrite. Oh, that is good!—admirable!—most admirable! What, now, will the dear Cockles and the defiant Steady say of their great acquaintance? Ha! ha! Wilful murder! Good—good! Twelve men have been found to think and say that much, have they? Why, the next twelve that think and say it, will send him to the gallows! Consign him to the hangman! Ha! ha! A smooth-faced hypocrite they begin to call him already—such is popularity; and he will die with the detestation of society, while I—But no matter. What music there is in those words—Wilful murder against Arthur Wilton !"

CHAPTER LIII.

AMELIA CALLS UPON MRS. PERCIVAL.—A CONSULTATION.

THERE is, now, one person connected intimately with all the proceedings that have taken place, since those proceedings have ended in murder, concerning whom we have as yet only casually spoken, but who, for the noble part she took in the ulterior proceedings, contingent upon the frightful tragedy at the Abbey, deserves notice and attention.

That person is Mrs. Percival, the wife of the murdered colonel of that name.

A very few words will suffice to place before the reader the precise situation which this young and accomplished lady held in the world.

While Colonel Percival was in India, battling with those hardy native chiefs, who have given such a world of trouble to the British soldiers, an old comrade of the camp and battle-field died, and left him, Colonel Percival, sole executor and trustee of all his property, for the benefit of his orphan daughter, whom he, the decease officer, had, some years previously, sent to England for the benefit of her health, and the advantages of an European education.

This officer, whose name was Hammond, was a major-general in the service, and he had transmitted to, as he thought, a trusty agent in England, the whole of his estate, in the same manner that many other of the Indian officers were in the habit of doing.

In his dying moments, he thus addressed his old and much-valued friend, Percival :—

"I know, Percival, that I am going, and I go with all the less pain and anxiety, that I leave my only child, Mary, to your care. You are an old friend, and a gallant soldier. She is rich, for I have from time to time transmitted to England large sums to be invested for her. Among my papers you will find all particulars. Do you accept the task ?"

"I do."

"Then I die calm and happy."

In less than an hour after this conversation, General Hammond was no more.

The death of this old and valued friend preyed very much upon the spirits of Percival, and induced him to exchange into a home regiment shortly afterwards. He was a single man, and had not a soul in the world that he knew of to whom he could claim even kindred, so that he arrived in London with the one object of looking after the trust that had been reposed in him by his deceased friend.

The first and most prudent act of Colonel Percival had been to go to the solicitor who had, with integrity and skill, conducted his own affairs for him, and in his hands he placed the whole of the papers of the late General Hammond, together with the testamentary document that gave him, the colonel, power of action as trustee of the property, and guardian of Mary Hammond.

"Call to-morrow, colonel," said the solicitor, "and I shall have taken the first step in the affair."

Colonel Percival never had a thought of anything wrong in the transaction, or of anything going amiss, so he was rather surprised at the gloomy countenance of the attorney when he called upon him on the morrow, according to appointment.

"What is the matter, my old friend ?" said Colonel Percival.

"Everything, colonel—I have bad news for you."

"Poor Mary Hammond is dead, then ?"

"No. Not that I know of."

"Then what on earth is it that you have to tell me ?"

"I wish I had it not to tell you, but you shall hear all. The person who was intrusted by General Hammond with the conduct of all his affairs in this country was named Renshaw."

"Yes, Mr. Renshaw, solicitor."

"Exactly. Well, he is dead."

"That is awkward."

"Very awkward, indeed. Before he died he had made away with every penny piece of his own property, and likewise all that General Hammond had intrusted to him."

"What ?"

"You hear what I say. The mad spirit of speculation possessed that man, and he did not stop at his own ruin, but involved all others who trusted him in destruction."

"Good heavens !"

"One of his dupes proceeded criminally against him, and he committed suicide upon the night of the day when he was committed to prison. He was found dead in his cell in the morning."

"And Mary Hammond ? What of her ?"

"Alas ! alas !"

"Oh, tell me. Speak, my good sir. I am one who can hear bad news at once much better than as if I were what people call prepared for it."

"Then, sir, she was left utterly destitute by the villany of Renshaw. He had taken all."

"But where is she?"

The attorney shook his head.

"No one knows, Colonel Percival. After selling every little trinket she possessed, and even all her wearing apparel with the exception of a few common necessaries, she disappeared."

"Disappeared?"

"Yes, that is the story told to me. That is all I can learn of the affair in reply to my most diligent inquiries upon the subject."

Colonel Percival drew a long breath, and sat looking at the attorney for some moments in silence, and then he said,—

"Is this all, then?"

"It is, sir."

"You can do no more?"

"I fear not."

"Then I will."

"But what can you do, colonel? If you can think of any course, I will be glad to assist you might and main in it."

"I tell you what I will do," added the colonel. "I have now a good six weeks further leave of absence from the regiment to which I am attached, and I will employ them in one ceaseless search for Mary Hammond"

"But, my dear sir—"

"Her father was my oldest and dearest friend, and I will find her."

"But she is absolutely penniless, my good sir. What will you do when you find her?"

"What will I do? Why, keep her, to be sure."

The attorney smiled at the possible construction that might be put upon the carelessly uttered words of the colonel, and then he said,—

"You will find it a very troublesome and invidious thing, as you are a single man, to make any settlement upon a young girl of twenty."

"Twenty, is she?"

"Yes, that is about her age."

"Well, I don't care about her age, as I am forty, and so old enough to disarm scandal ; and find her I will, and she shall share what I possess. Thank God my means are quite sufficient for the support in comfort, if not in affluence and luxury, of a young girl as well as myself. I say, I will find her, sir, if she is above ground."

The attorney shrugged up his shoulders, and muttered something about the propensity of officers, and the troublesomeness of seeking out people who had nothing; and so the colonel left him, rather in a huff at his cold, calculating conduct.

Now, Colonel Percival was an eminently practical man, and when he had once fairly resolved upon any course of conduct, he was just the sort of person to carry it out by the shortest and most direct possible means.

Within two hours of the time when he had learnt the sad story of Mary Hammond's evil fortune, he drew up an advertisement, which he sent at once to all the London papers, to the following effect :—

"Mary Hammond.—If Miss Hammond, daughter of the late General Hammond, will call or write to the subjoined address, she will hear particulars concering her father, from an old friend of his, which will interest her."

To the advertisement the colonel appended the address of the hotel in London where he took up his abode.

In three days from the time when this advertisement appeared, the colonel received the following note, addressed to him at the hotel, and which he read with great pleasure.

"If the gentleman advertising for Mary Hammond will call at No. 32, Duchess Street, Portland Place, that lady will be happy to receive him."

In half an hour the colonel was rapping at the door of No. 32, Duchess Street. It was opened by a footman, who, as the colonel was on foot, did not think proper to be over courteous.

"Is Miss Hammond within?" said the colonel.

This inquiry appeared to receive the contempt which the footman had for the visitor, and he replied,—

"Oh, you want to see our governess?"

"Indeed! Is Miss Hammond our governess?"

"Ah! yes. Ah !"

"Well, you have much need of a few lessons in civility; and if you do not behave yourself with more respect, I shall have to give you one with this cane that you will remember."

"Murder!"

"Oh, you will have it, then?" said the colonel, as he commenced belabouring the supercilious footman with a cane he carried till he jumped and roared again.

This riot in the hall of the house brought out of the dining-room a remarkably fine lady, as far as silks and satins went, and in a voice which no doubt she thought exceedingly dignified, she cried,—

"Samuel, what is all this about?"

"Oh, if you please, my lady, it's—it's that low person, a follower, my lady, of Hammond."

"Of Hammond?" said the lady.

"Yes, my lady."

"Upon my word, this is too bad, and I particularly told Hammond when she came into my service that no followers were allowed."

"Yes, my lady, so you did," said Samuel, writhing from the pain of the cuts upon his back. "The cook, too, my lady, and both the housemaids, is forbid followers."

"Certainly," said my lady. "I will not allow it."

"And pray, who are you, madam?" said the colonel.

"Oh, oh!" said the footman, "to speak to her ladyship in that way! Shall I see for a constable, my lady?"

"Yes, Samuel."

"Perhaps he won't let me pass, my lady. I'll go by the area steps."

"Do, Samuel. And now, sir, I desire that you leave this house this moment, and I shall feel myself to be under the necessity of discharging Hammond at once, and without a character, too."

"Pray, madam," said the colonel, "is this Hammond you speak of a stable boy, or what is he or she?"

"A constable, sir, will soon convince you of who he is," said the lady, with a toss of her head.

"Madam, I have no wish in the world to behave with discourtesy to any human being in the shape of a woman, let her conduct be as disgusting as it may; so, calmly and quietly, I ask to see Miss Hammond."

"Then you won't see her."

"Then I will. Oh, here is a bell."

There was a bell in the hall, which connected with the upper part of the house, and which the colonel now rang with such violence, that every one who was up stairs come rushing down, thinking that something very awful must be the matter, and among the rest a young lady attired in plain black silk, and looking very pale and ill.

"I want to see Miss Hammond," roared the colonel.

"I am Miss Hammond," said the young lady in black silk.

"Then, how do you do, my dear? I am delighted to see you."

The colonel shook hands with her heartily; and then Mary, with tears in her eyes said—

"You knew my poor father, sir?"

"He breathed his last in my arms," said the colonel.

CHAPTER LIV.

MRS. REVIS MAKES A STRANGE REVELATION TO AMELIA.

WHEN Mary Hammond heard those words, she burst into a passion of tears, and was compelled to lean upon the colonel's arm for support, and my lady was so shocked that she cried out to two little girls who had come down stairs—

"Go up to your school-room again, my dears; I don't want your infant minds demoralised by the shocking immorality of your late governess."

"Immorality be d——d, madam!" cried the colonel, now thoroughly in a passion. "What do you mean?"

"Oh, gracious! I discharge you, Hammond, at once, without a character. Go away at once."

"Why, my dear," said the colonel, "are you a housemaid here?"

"Oh, no—no—I am not treated near so well as one."

"Then, what are you?"

"Only the governess," said my lady.

"Oh, really; and what are you supposed to do, Mary?"

"I have to teach English, French, Italian, music, geography, the circle of the sciences, plain and fancy needlework, and to make myself generally useful beside."

"Why, then, you get five hundred pounds a-year?"

"No—twenty pounds."

"And I won't pay her the last quarter," cried her ladyship, "for she has broken her agreement, and admitted a follower. Where can Samuel be with the constable, I should like to know? Oh, what a thing it is to be subjected to annoyance from low people!"

"D—n it, madam, I don't know anything worse," said the colonel.

"The constable, my lady," cried Samuel, "the constable."

"Now, what's all this?" said a man, who had been summoned from his shop, and who was a police constable. "Come, come—what's all this?"

"Take that low man into custody," said her ladyship, pointing to the colonel in a very grand way.

"What's the charge, ma'am?"

"The what?"

"The charge against him?"

"What is that to you, fellow? Surely, I, the wife of a City baronet, who was made so for going up to the Court with an address on the birth of a royal infant, may give a low man into custody?"

"Not without a charge, my lady."

"But I give them both into custody---that wretched young woman and her follower."

"And I give him in charge," said Samuel, "for caning of me."

"Ah!" said the constable, "I'm afraid, my lady, I can do nothing here. Now, sir, who are you?"

"There is my card."

"Oh, heavens! Colonel Percival!"

"Colonel?" said her ladyship.

"Colonel?" gasped Samuel.

"Oh, it's some mistake," said the constable. "This is a gentleman. We have all heard of Colonel Percival. Why, he is the officer who won all the battles in India, and that the king made all sorts of things of."

"Oh, colonel," said Lady Todgers, for that was the name of her ladyship; "oh, colonel, this is quite a—a little mistake. Pray walk in—and Miss Hammond, too; of course, I shall be happy to continue her in her place as governess, and to raise her wages five pounds annually."

"I begs yer pardon," said Samuel.

"Call a coach!" roared the colonel.

Samuel and the constable both wished to execute the order, and fell sprawling in the kennel together, and the constable was so enraged at that event, that he took Samuel into custody at once, and marched him off, and charged him with an assault.

The colonel hailed a coach that happened to be passing, and taking Mary under his arm, he said—

"Now, my dear, come along."

"Oh, sir, but—I—that is—ought I—"

"Your father said you were to trust to me."

"Then I will go with you, sir."

"That's right, my dear. This is the last time you shall cross the threshold of this house."

Lady Todgers, when she found the colonel was inexorable, relieved her mind for the whole of the next day by telling everybody of the scandalous way in which Mary Hammond had gone to "live" with Colonel Percival; but on the day after, she looked rather foolish, when the "Morning Post" had the following paragraph:

"Married yesterday, by special license, Mary Hammond, only daughter of the late General Hammond, K.C.B., to George Augustus Percival, colonel of the Bombay army, and K.G.B. After the ceremony, the happy pair, who were surrounded by all the rank and fashion in the metropolis, partook of a *dejeuner* with the Bishop of London, and departed for Paris."

Lady Todgers fainted away.

This, then, was the whole story of the courtship and marriage of Colonel Percival, and a more gentle, amiable, and affectionate wife, than Mary Hammond was to him, never existed.

It may well be surmised, then, what effect his murder was likely to have upon such a being.

Well might Major Cuthbert say that he would not be the man to have to communicate the tidings to Mrs. Percival.

We now proceed with the main current of our narrative.

* * * * *

It will doubtless be in the recollection of our readers, that Mrs. Percival was expected at the Abbey on the day following that upon which the colonel took up his abode there. In fact, the principal reason why Colonel Percival rented the Abbey at all, was, that his wife might have a home free from the disturbances of a barrack.

It was about three o'clock upon that eventful day, then, that succeeded the dreadful murder, that a post-chaise reached the gate of the Abbey, and the sweet smiling face of Mrs. Percival looked from it as she said to a lady who was with her—

"Oh, what a charming old place this is! How happy I shall be here! Look, what trees, what flowers, and a dear old mysterious-looking house."

"It is, indeed, quite romantic," said the lady.

"I quite love it. But who is this coming along the lane?"

"A gentleman, in black, I think."

"Yes, mourning. How solemn he looks, to be sure."

This was the magistrate, who had staid on purpose to try if he could not lessen the shock which must come upon the spirit of the young wife, when the dreadful truth became known to her. It was no enviable task that, but this gentleman, seeing that every one else shrank from it, undertook it as a duty.

Mrs. Percival was very well known to the regiment as being one of the kindest and best of women; and when she was with the colonel in barracks, or elsewhere, it was quite a certainty that any little breach of discipline would be excused if a petition were sent to her to use her good offices with the colonel.

No wonder, then, that she was beloved by all

No wonder, too, that those who knew her great kindness, and her gentle nature, should shrink from telling her of the frightful bereavement she had suffered.

It was to this lady, then, that, with a look that plainly said he had something sad to communicate, the magistrate advanced slowly and solemnly.

"Why, what can this mean?" said Mrs. Percival.

"I don't know, really," said the lady who was with her, "but I am afraid——"

"Of what?"

"I was going to say that I was afraid to think."

"Oh, surely, you do not think for a moment that anything can have happened to *him?*"

That it was the colonel whom she alluded to, the lady who was with her well knew, and the look of terror that accompanied the words induced her to say—

"Oh, no—no, Mrs. Percival, that is hardly possible; surely, all must be well. But this gentleman will tell us."

"Ladies," said the magistrate, "I am told that one of you bears the name of Percival."

"Yes—yes," said the lady.

The magistrate bowed, and began to address her, fancying she was the colonel's wife, as, in fact, in age she seemed so much more likely to be than the young and beautiful girl who sat by her side.

"You mistake," said the lady, pointing to Mary. "This is Mrs. Percival, sir."

"I beg pardon for my inadvertency."

"Oh, sir," said Mary, "before you say another word, ease my heart of a pang which doubt brings to it, and tell me if the colonel is well—tell me that, sir, at once."

"Madam, I——"

Mary turned deadly pale, and leant back in the coach.

"Go on," she said, faintly, "you cannot tell me that."

"Madam, I cannot."

"Oh, God, something has happened."

"Let me pray you to calm yourself, madam. We are all in the hands of that God who judges better than we can judge what is best for the happiness of those who, specially by the virtue of their acts, and the even and serene tenor of their lives, belong to him."

"He is dead!"

"Madam, the colonel is no more."

Mary shuddered for a moment or two, and then lapsed into a state of complete insensibility.

"Oh, sir," said the lady, "you have been very abrupt in this dreadful communication."

CHAPTER LV.

TAKES A GLANCE AT ANOTHER MOURNER.

WHEN the lady who had accompanied Mrs. Percival on a visit to the home that the colonel had provided, and in which so many happy hours would have been passed, spoke as she did to the magistrate, she was little aware of the great injustice she had done him.

She little thought that in saying what he had said to Mary, although he had stunned her by the fact that Colonel Percival was no more, he had, by keeping back the distressing fact of the manner of his death, spared her the more terrible pang.

"Sir—sir," she said, "you have killed her."

"If so, then, madam, it is the will of Heaven," he replied. "You do not suppose that the fact of her husband's death could be kept from her?"

"Oh, no—no."

"Then I hope and trust that you will believe that I communicated it as tenderly as I possibly could."

"Pardon me, sir, but she might have been better prepared."

"I have prepared her for the more dreadful fact, I hope, that will have to follow the communication she has just heard."

"More dreadful fact, sir?"

"Yes; the colonel has been most foully murdered."

"Murdered!"

"Even so, madam, and I will leave it to your tact to let Mrs. Percival upon her recovery know of that dreadful murder, by which her unhappy husband has departed this life."

"Oh, I cannot—I cannot."

The magistrate was just a little piqued at the manner in which the lady had reproved him for telling Mrs. Percival, as she thought, too abruptly of the death of her husband, he was determined to leave her the worse task of stating the particulars of the fearful deed which had produced such a catastrophe.

"Madam," he said, "I have performed this painful duty that I did not like to shrink from, because everybody else did shrink from it; and, therefore, I now bid you farewell, convinced that this unhappy lady is in very good hands with you. Farewell, madam."

"But, sir——"

The magistrate only bowed, and walked away.

It was not for some time that Mrs. Percival recovered from the swoon into which she had fallen, upon receipt of the dreadful intelligence of the death of her husband.

When the unhappy widow did recover sense sufficient to comprehend her sad bereavement, her most frantic wish and demand, for it amounted to such, was to see the body of the colonel.

It was then that it became necessary to tell her how it was he had come by his death, and the intelligence prostrated her again, so that it was quite noon on the following day before she began gradually to recover from the shock that her feelings had sustained.

If the seemly nervous and excited state into which she had been then had lasted, she would soon have joined her husband in the embrace of death; but Mrs. Percival was young, and there was that blessed and natural buoyancy of feeling, which is a sure and beneficial provision of nature for lifting the saddened soul out of a sea of troubles.

It does not lie within the scheme of an all-bounteous providence that profound grief should last very long; if it did so, the whole world would be weeping and wailing.

Somewhat reconciled, then, to the new and dreadful situation in which she was placed, Mrs. Percival sent for Major Cuthbert.

Now, the good-hearted major would rather have faced a battery than Mrs. Percival at that time; but as she did send for him, he never thought for a moment of disputing the order.

"Good gracious!" he said. "What shall I say to her? I wonder what she will say to me, too? Well, it can't be helped—go I will."

The major mounted his horse, and trotted to the Abbey.

There was something awful and affecting in the deserted room into which he was shown. There sat Mrs. Percival, looking so pale, so wan, and so much older than she had looked only a short day before, that it was enough to melt the stoutest heart to see her.

"Major Cuthbert, madam," said a servant.

"Ask him to—to—come in," sighed Mrs. Percival, and the major entered the apartment at once.

The mourner made a faint attempt to rise and welcome him, but her limbs failed her, and all she could do was, by a great effort, to restrain her tears.

"I hope," said the major, who felt that he ought to say something, "I hope that —that is, I hope and trust that—you are better, Mrs. Percival."

"I thank you, Major Cuthbert. He was much attached to you.

"Heavens!" said the major. "I—that is—oh, yes."

"I have sent for you, because—because——"

A flood of tears prevented the further utterance of what Mrs. Percival would have said, and while her friend tried to console her, the major walked about the room, wishing himself devoutly anywhere but where he was, upon the occasion.

"Confound it," he said, "why did she send for me?"

The poor major himself, to tell the truth, had taken the death of the colonel very much to heart, and, far from being able to comfort any one upon the subject, he was much in need of some one to say something to him which should tend to reassure him and restore him to something of his former state of composure.

"She is better now," said the lady.

"Oh!—ah!" said the major.

"Yes," said Mrs. Percival, "it is very kind of you to come."

"Oh, I couldn't help it."

"Eh?"

"No, you sent for me, and so here I am. But you see, Mrs. Percival, what's done can't be undone, and it isn't a wise thing to look too closely to the fact. We have all a future before us—and—and, you see, when—that is—Hang it, I don't know what to say."

"My dear sir, I know well what you feel," said the widow, "without your saying it."

"That's a mercy, then."

"You were the dearest friend that the colonel had, and I will tell you at once why I have sent for you."

"Ah, do—do. Come, now you speak more like yourself."

"I have sent for you because I wish to know the real truth concerning the—the dreadful deed that has been done here. I wish you to tell me all, from first to last, omitting no particle, for no one here will tell me, either from dread of exciting my grief too much, or from incapacity to do so, in consequence of a want of accurate knowledge of the particulars."

"Humph!"

"You will, then, tell me all?"

"If you wish it, yes; but——"

"Do not try to evade this request,

AMELIA'S ALARM IN THE LANE ON THE NIGHT OF THE MURDER.

major. I have stilled my heart to listen to everything, and I beg and pray of you to keep nothing from me."

"Very well, I will tell you all I know of the affair, Mrs. Percival, from first to last."

Upon this, then, the major gave to the afflicted lady all the particulars that he had gathered regarding the affair. It took him nearly half an hour to tell her, and she did not interrupt him once.

When he had concluded, she held her hands over her face for a few moments and then said, in an agitated voice—

"I thank you, sir—I thank you; will you call upon me again to-morrow?"

CHAPTER LVI.

ARTHUR WILTON IS COMMITTED BY THE MAGISTRATES FOR TRIAL.

LET us now take a glance at another poor, but great and good spirit, that has been prostrated by that dreadful murder to as great an extent as Mrs. Percival.

We allude to Amelia Revis.

It is true that Amelia had not a husband to mourn, but she had given her young and innocent heart wholly and solely to Arthur Wilton, and, therefore, the agony of her soul at the condition in which she was placed was no less than that of the bereaved wife.

Both of these women, though, found consolation.

The colonel's wife found it in the assurance that she felt that so good and blameless a spirit as her husband's could know nothing but bliss in that world to which he had been hurried.

Amelia found it in the deep conviction, which nothing could shake, that she had of the innocence of Arthur Wilton of the crime laid to his charge.

But still poor Amelia suffered acutely. It was not in the nature of things that she should not.

For a long time after the first intelligence of the arrest of Arthur Wilton for the murder, Amelia remained in a sort of stupor, from which her recovery was slow and painful. Even then she could not bring herself to believe that the intelligence was true.

As the tears coursed each other down her cheeks, she would look at her father and at old Mr. Wilton, who now passed the greater part of his time at the farm, and say—

"You must all tell me again, so as to assure me that I am not changing my imagination into a belief in something which has no foundation in truth. Oh, tell me again."

They would then again inform her of the terrible fact, and for a time the news seemed to prostrate her as before.

But this was a state of things that with such a disposition as Amelia's could not possibly last. Suddenly looking up, she said—

"Why do we weep? Why do we give ourselves up to grief, as if some real calamity had occurred, when, after all, it is but an imaginary one?"

"Oh, my child," said Mr. Revis, "what do you mean? What would you say to us. Imaginary, do you call our grief?"

"Alas," said old Mr. Wilton, "would it were; but it is too real."

"It is not real at all."

The old men looked at each other in fresh dismay, for they began to suspect that grief had unsettled the brain of poor Amelia.

They were soon convinced of the contrary. Amelia rose and dashed the tears from her eyes.

"Understand me," she said, with a sweet smile; "we ought to weep no more. I do not mean to say that I shall be able to stay my tears, but I will not again forget what it is that I really weep for. It is for grief and shame that so much injustice is done to Arthur to couple his fair name even with such a charge as this is that is made against him, for we know that he is innocent."

"He is—he is !" cried old Mr. Wilton.

"Of that, we, who know him," said Mr. Revis, "can have no doubt."

"Why, then, we will not weep," added Amelia, "but we will set about, as cheerfully as may be, to save him."

It was at this moment, while the two old men were looking with admiration at the radiant brow of Amelia, where truth and goodness had set their seals, that some one was heard approaching the farmhouse by the gravel path that led through the flower-garden. Whoever it was, he received a vociferous welcome from Prince, who rushed out of his large wooden house and barked furiously, and gambolled about the person in a great state of glee.

"Who can this be?" said Mr. Revis.

"I will retire, and call upon you again, my dear friend," said Mr. Wilton. "It is, perhaps, some one to see you, who may wish to speak to you alone."

"No, no, do not go. Ah, there are two people, and the one looks like an officer in poor Arthur's regiment. The other I can't see."

"It is Mr. Flummery," said Amelia, who caught a glimpse of that personage through the casement.

"What can they want? Admit them, my child. We are bound to think, now, that whoever comes to us, comes on some errand of mercy. Admit them at once. They may have something to say to us of poor Arthur."

Amelia moved quietly from the little parlour and opened the door of the house. Mr. Flummery hung back, rather, and Major Cuthbert, for it was he, bowed to Amelia, as he said—

"I hope, Miss Revis, you will not consider this as an intrusion?"

"Oh, no, sir. But you know my name?"

"Yes. I had the pleasure of seeing you upon the occasion of the alarm in the meadows, as the regiment marched to its quarters."

"Mr. Shorter, you know, Miss Amelia," cried Flummery ; "you recollect when Mr. Shorter wanted to give his mind to tossing. This is Major Cuthbert, one of the real officers of the regiment, and a real gent, and not like a wagabone of a Strachan; and he met me in the lane, and he says says he—'My good man,' says he——"

"I asked him the shortest route to the farm of Mr. Revis," said the major.

"Yes, he did. 'My good man,' says he——"

"Yes, Mr. Flummery, that will do," said Amelia. "Pray walk in."

The major entered the house; but Mr. Flummery cried out "Murder!" suddenly; and when they looked back to see what was the matter with him, they found that Prince had got hold of the skirt of his coat.

"Oh, lor!" said Mr. Flummery, "was there ever known such a dog as you is, Mr. P.? It's always the way you serves me, ever since I brought you a piece of liver in this 'dentical pocket, you serves me in this a-ways, you does. Now, do leave go, I begs."

"Bow—wow!" cried Prince; but Mr. Flummery then dexterously caught up the tails of his coat, and darted into the house after the major and Amelia, and so Prince lost him.

"I know he'll wait for me as I come out," said Mr. Flummery, "and I feel that nothing will satisfy him but the skirt of this here coat, and I shall have to give it to him some day. I hopes as you is pretty well, Miss Amelia, to day?"

"Yes, thank you, Mr. Flummery."

"And I hopes as you haven't gived your mind to any more bad dreams, Miss Amelia, eh?"

"No, thank you, Mr. Flummery. We have too many sad realities now to occupy us to indulge in freaks of the imagination."

"Oh," muttered Mr. Flummery to himself, 'I don't quite understand that; but I suppose it's some of the new fangled manures that old Revis has been putting on his turnip fields."

It was but two or three steps from the outer door to the parlour, and Major Cuthbert bowed with as much respect to Mr. Revis and Mr. Wilton as though he had been entering the presence of the commander-in-chief.

"I hope that this visit will be pardoned," he said, "upon the score that I am the bearer of a message to Miss Revis."

"This is Major Cuthbert, father," said Amelia.

"And most welcome is he," said Mr. Revis. "It is an honour, sir, to see so gallant a gentleman beneath this roof."

"You were always spoken of by my poor boy, sir," said Mr. Wilton, "as one of the noblest and the best of men. God bless you, sir, for your great kindness to him."

Major Cuthbert little expected such a chorus of compliments, and he looked as any modest man would look, as confused as possible.

"Really, I beg," he said, "that you will be so good as to allow all that to pass, and just to let me tell you that I sincerely sympathise with you in what has taken place, and that I am the bearer of a message to Miss Revis."

"From Arthur?" said Amelia.

"No, from a lady."

"A lady, sir? Who, I pray you?"

"Mrs. Percival."

There was a silence now for a few moments' duration, and every one looked in the face of his neighbour in some surprise. It was Amelia who broke that silence by exclaiming—

"Poor, poor Mrs. Percival!"

"Yes," said the major, "she is indeed to be pitied."

"Alas! alas! what can I say to her?"

"I do not pretend to guess what it is that she has to say to you," added the major; "but she sent me a note to the barracks to say that if I would take the trouble to see you and ask you to call upon her at the Abbey, she would esteem it as a great favour. I may, however, inform you, that it is not to ask of you any painful questions, for she knows all."

"Thank Heaven for that; and yet if she did not, what could I tell, her poor lady, I who know so little, but the grief of the deplorable events? It is I who want information."

"Then," said the major, "I have performed my errand."

"Stop, sir," said Mr. Wilton, and the tears flooded his eyes as he spoke; "you do not, sir—you, as a gentleman, a man of sense, a steadfast, and brave, and honest soldier—you do not think my boy guilty?"

"Sir, I can have no opinion."

The old man sunk back into a chair.

"Do not misunderstand me," added the major. "I only mean to say, that I, like all others to whom the truth must be hidden in consequence of the worst of information, must rest upon such facts as time alone can develop to us. But if you fancy that I prejudge Arthur Wilton, I beg to disabuse you of such an idea, and to assure you that I do not do so; and likewise I may add, that from all that I hear of him, I find nothing that can reconcile me to an idea of his guilt."

" Heaven bless you, sir, for that much."

" Poor Arthur !" said Amelia.

" Yes, poor Arthur indeed," said Mr. Revis.

" Cheer up," said the major; "this affair is at present involved in the most complete and terrible mystery. Who knows but it may yet be made clear?"

" Yes," said Flummery, " and if a small matter of twenty puns would do any good, and anybody would be kind enough to take 'em, I think I might say, that here they is."

" No—no," said Amelia, " your friendship is of more value than your money, and I will now ask of you again to escort me to the Abbey, for I will lose no time in obeying the commands of this afflicted lady. Ah, father, and you Mr. Wilton, and you Major Cuthbert, only think how light our griefs ought to be compared to hers."

" Light, indeed."

" She has met with a loss that no circumstances in this world can make up to her, while we, by the force of innocence, that sooner or later is sure to triumph, may have Arthur restored to us."

" I was about to say," added the major, " that I should be happy to see you safely to the Abbey myself."

" Sir, I thank you; but my old freind Mr Flummery, he will feel hurt if I do not make use of his services upon this occasion."

" I certainly admit Mr. Flummery's superior claim," said the major. " I, therefore, now take my leave, bidding you all be of good cheer."

The major's visit had had a good effect upon the little party at the farm, for the great confidence of his manner, and the message that he had brought to Amelia from Mrs. Percival, seemed to say as plainly as could be that there was nothing to dread in that quarter from any prejudice against poor Arthur.

Amelia felt very much agitated though at the thoughts of an interview with Mrs. Percival, although she did not know very well why she should be so, seeming that she so fully believed in the innocence of Arthur.

In the course of ten minutes she was ready for the walk to the Abbey, and Mr. Flummery felt quite proud that his escort had been preferred to that of Major Cuthbert on the occasion.

" Mr. Revis," he whispered. " Sir."

" Yes, Mr. Flummery?"

" Do take the twenty pun."

" No, my dear friend. Indeed, not I do want it."

" What a pity ! Mr. Wilton, sir."

" Yes, Mr. Flummery ?"

" Don't you think twenty puns would go a long way among those rogues of lawyer fellows, that will have to go on talking never so long about Mr. Arthur? Here they are in a little bag; twenty puns go into a small space, you see, Mr. Wilton."

" No, thanks—I assure you I do not want money."

" Well," said Mr. Flummery, this is provoking. Here I go about, with twenty puns, and nobody will have 'em. Was ever a man in such a fix to get rid of his twenty puns? What shall I do with 'em? I'll try Arthur when I see him."

CHAPTER LVII.

AMELIA AND MRS. PERCIVAL HAVE AN INTERESTING MEETING.

IT was with painful feelings now that Amelia traversed that very same route to the Abbey that she had taken along with Mr. Flummery a short time before, when she little suspected so fearful a catastrophe as that which had occurred had been at all likely to take place.

Every tree and every meadow served to remind her forcibly of that night, when, under the influence of the terrible dream, she had risen to go and warn Arthur Wilton of impending danger, or to assure herself that he was safe.

Even Mr. Flummery's ordinary loquacity was rather put a stop to, by the tenor of ideas which this walk conjured up.

" Ah, Miss Amelia," he said. " We is here to-day and gone to-morrow."

" Yes, Mr. Flummery, indeed we are."

" We is nothing but grass, is we."

" I fear not, Mr. Flummery."

" To be sure we is, and ashes and dust, too, we is, as the parson says. Now you see, Miss Amelia, here is the very spot where somebody passed us that night at tip-top speed, don't you recollect?"

" I do, indeed. Oh, Mr. Flummery, if you or I, or better still, if we both had caught but a sufficient sight of that person to be able to say who it was, we might be able to save Arthur, and be able to point to the real criminal."

Mr. Flummery shook his head.

" I don't like to say it, Miss Amelia," he said, " but—but—"

" But what? Oh, speak."

" I did think that by the eyes—I saw his eyes."

" Yes—yes."

" I did think that they was about as

like the eyes of that horrid Strachan as any two eyes could be like any other two. I wouldn't say it to anybody but you for ever so much, 'cos, you see, folks would think I was a donkey. Ah, that puts me in mind of the poor dear departed!"

"Who, Mr. Flummery? Who?"

"Jacob!"

"Oh, to be sure, yes. But do you really think—oh, Mr. Flummery! this is not, I hope, an after thought, arising from the wish merely to find some one who did this deed in preference to Arthur?"

"Oh, lor, no."

"Then you really think that—that it was Strachan?"

"No, I don't."

"Alas! I thought you said you did?"

"No, you didn't hear me all out, you see, Miss Amelia. I say, that I did catch a sight of the individual as he was racing along at such a rate, and I thought it was Captain Strachan; but I went to the barracks, and I spoke to fifty of the soldiers."

"That surely was imprudent."

"Oh, no, I only wanted to find out if he had been out about that time, but would you believe it? he hasn't been out of his own room for two or three days, and has got some sort of fever or another, and they say that its about as impossible for him to have left the barracks without them knowing of it, as it would be for the French to walk in with drums a beating and colours a flying, and they never to see 'em."

Amelia shuddered.

"How inexplicable the mystery is," she said, "in which this affair is enveloped. We must wait the good time of Heaven to enlighten us regarding it, Mr. Flummery. Surely that time will come?"

"Well, I hope so, but I did expect better things of Prince."

"Yes, he might have detained the man."

"Why, he had a hold of him, Miss Amelia."

"So I thought, too."

"And then away he bolts, and the fellow escapes, after all. Well, well, it can't be helped. But, here we are, and I say, Miss Amelia, you can just, you know, in a off-handed kind of manner, while you is a speaking to Mrs. Percival, say that you know of a twenty puns as she may have if she wants 'em. Now, don't forget that part of the matter, Miss Amelia, for who knows but such a sum as twenty puns would be very handy? You'd better take the bag."

"Oh, no—no."

"Well, there you go again. Nobody will have twenty puns! It's very hard, that it is. The more I offer people twenty puns, the more they won't have 'em."

By this time they had reached the front entrance of the Abbey, where a sentinel was posted, but upon stating that she was visiting Mrs. Percival, Amelia was allowed to pass, and Mr. Flummery said he would there wait for her.

Amelia, with a feeling of agitation that she could not repress, walked up to the house. The shutters were all closed, save one in a lower room, and in that room sat the young widow.

Corporal Steady was at the Abbey, and seeing Amelia, came out to speak to her, and show her the way to Mrs. Percival's room.

"All's right, Miss Amelia," he said; "the young woman who waits upon Mrs. Percival told me you were coming, and I'll go and let her know you are here."

"Thank you, Steady. Is Mrs. Percival very deeply affected?"

The corporal shook his head.

"Poor thing," he said. "She looks— she looks—I can't tell you how she looks, cos I never did see a ghost; but I should fancy that the ghost of some young and pretty creature would look just as she does now."

"Alas! what is my grief to hers!"

The corporal let the servant of Mrs. Percival know that Amelia was there, and in a few moments she was hushered into the apartment occupied by that poor bereaved one.

Amelia was too much affected to speak, but Mrs. Percival, in a faint sickly voice, which was more like the tone of some one slowly recovering from a long illness than anything else, addressed her,—

"It is very kind of you to come," she said. "I could not, you know, come to you."

"It is more kind of you to send for me," said Amelia.

"Oh, no—no. Come, now, and sit by me. I have heard all that every one can tell me, except what you can supply, and I wish to converse with you as a friend."

Amelia burst into tears.

"There now," said Mrs. Percival. "I —I—" she wept bitterly herself.

It was many minutes before they could either of them recover sufficiently to speak, and then it was Amelia who said,—

"Ah, madam, we are both mourners, but yours is a positive grief—mine may be but a trivial one, for justice may yet triumph, and the innocent go free."

"That is what I want to talk to you about," said Mrs. Percival. "Cuthbert and several other officers in the regiment have spoken to me of Mr. Wilton, and the general impression seems to be that it was impossible that he could have done this dreadful deed of which he is accused."

"It is impossible, madam."

"Well, you know that he is very much oppressed, being innocent, by this charge against him, or he is worse than tongue can tell being guilty. You know him, or ought to know him—Oh, Miss Revis, I have but one wish, but one hope, and that is, that innocent blood may not be shed for the frightful deed that has been done. Can you in any way account to me how and why it is that the man whom all conspire to load with eulogia, and who all consider to be incapable of the deed, should, by the force of circumstances, be the only one suspected?"

"Oh, God! what shall I say?"

"Will you answer me what I shall ask of you?"

"As I would to Heaven."

"And you will not think the questions impertinent or insulting?"

"Oh, no, no."

"Then did you ever notice any symptoms of strangeness or wandering of mind in Mr. Wilton?"

"No—that is—I—"

The singular letter she had received came across the recollection of Amelia, and she felt sick and faint.

"Be calm," said Mrs. Percival; "do not let me hurry you. But, before we go any further, Amelia, let me tell you one thing, and that is, that as one of your own sex—as one but few years older than yourself—I feel that, if your confidence in this idol of your heart, Arthur Wilton, is misplaced, it will be doing you a service to displace him; and, therefore, what may pass now between us, I will not promise shall be confidential—I dare not promise as much."

"Madam," said Amelia, "having nothing to conceal—having no thought, for a moment, but that the more is known of Arthur, the more must his innocence appear, I wish that all the world might know every word I utter to you concerning him; and so, in answer to your question, I say, that I have received strange letters from him at a time that he was suffering much from the cruel practices of Captain Strachan."

"Strange letters?"

"Yes, very strange letters; but a man may write a strange letter, and yet shrink from an evil act, surely, madam."

"Certainly; but you have not destroyed those letters, and will not?"

"I have not, and I will not."

"I see that I distress you very much, Amelia. However, forgive me, if my sense of duty, both to you and to myself, compels me to do so; but, now, will you tell me if any pecuniary difficulties prevented your union with Mr. Wilton?"

"Oh, no, no. My father has got through the only pecuniary difficulty he ever had. It was a mysterious one, of which I know little, except from its apparent effects; but it is past, and Mr. Wilton, senior, is well to do, and all were quite agreed and happy. The colonel, too, had promised to purchase the discharge of Arthur Wilton from the army from General Brotherton, and there could be no conceivable wish for his committing the dreadful act."

"It is very strange."

"It is, indeed."

"Well, listen to me, Amelia. I hope and trust that our interests may be by you, upon reflection, considered to be in a great measure identical—perhaps I ought to say, in feelings. If Arthur Wilton is guilty, it is as important to you that he should be declared so, as it can be to the society he has outraged by his crime. If innocent, it is important to all of us not to sacrifice one such in so dreadful a manner. Do you understand me?"

"I think I do, madam."

"Well, I am convinced that both you and I ought to do all we can for the truth, you comprehend, Amelia, without regard to persons."

"Yes—oh, yes,—that is right. But, indeed and indeed he is innocent, madam; it is impossible that he could commit such a deed."

"I hope so, Amelia. But, now, let it be understood, that you and I are friends in this matter, and that we do not act in hostility to each other. Let us both feel that we are afflicted, and that we are both actuated by but one desire, and that is, to learn the truth."

"Yes—oh, yes—that is it."

After this, although Amelia felt that her anxieties were very much increased by her interview with Mrs. Percival, it could not be said that she had any doubt regarding the innocence of Arthur Wilton. The only circumstance that preyed upon her mind with force, was the singular fact, that he, Arthur, had written to her in a strain so totally at variance with all his ordinary conduct, and all his ordinary modes of thought.

Amelia was exceedingly anxious, now, to get home, and look at those letters again.

"I see that your mind is away from this place," said Mrs. Percival, "and I will not detain you. But will you promise to come to me again?"

"Oh, yes; to-morrow."

"To-morrow be it, then. And, now, farewell, my friend, Amelia, if you will permit me to call you such."

"Yes, dear madam, if you will take to your friendship one so sad as I am."

"Say nothing of sadness—that is upon my side. I will expect you to-morrow."

"Yes," said Amelia, "and I will bring with me the letters."

"I did not venture to ask you to do so," said Mrs. Percival, "but I will not say that I had not a hope you would."

Amelia felt sick at heart now as she proceeded homewards, and she could hardly reply to the kind inquiries of Mr. Flummery, or afford the faintest smile at his quaint comments.

The moment she reached the farm she flew to her own little chamber, and unlocking a little cabinet in which she kept the few articles that were the most precious to her, from recollections or their intrinsic value, she eagerly laid her hand upon the packet of letters she had received from Arthur Wilton, and not one of which she had ever had the heart to destroy.

The particular one she wanted to read again, with an earnestness that amounted to positive pain, she soon found, and those lines which the villain Strachan had penned in the name of the innocent Arthur certainly at that time inflicted an amount of agony upon the heart of Amelia that would have rejoiced his guilty spirit to see.

He meant them for deep mischief, and they were, indeed, beginning to work their unholy errand.

"Oh, God!" cried Amelia, as she let the letter fall to the floor. "What am I to think? Is it possible, notwithstanding all my faith in him, and all the antecedents of his life, that he could do this dreadful deed? Oh, no—no. Pardon me the thought. It is high treason against nature —against virtue—against Heaven to believe it possible. He could not do it."

Poor Amelia! How pitiable is thy condition, now that the demon, Doubt, has once found its way to the portals of thy breast.

CHAPTER LVIII.

AMELIA ASKS A QUESTION OF HER FATHER AND IS FULLY ANSWERED.

WHEN Amelia had reached the farm after her visit to Mrs. Percival at the Abbey, she had found that her father was not in the house, so that she had been enabled to retire at once to her own chamber, and seek for those ill-omened letters.

As she sat with her hands over her face after the utterance of the words we have recorded, she heard her father's voice in the room below.

The agonised girl started to her feet, and hastily picking up the letters she replaced them among the others and locked them up in the cabinet.

"Heaven have mercy upon me," she said, "and preserve my reason. How strange it is that during the course of my young life so much should have happened that I have no clue to the comprehension of."

She paced her little chamber to and fro.

"I have no mother," she said, "or surely she would tell me all. How strange —how very strange it is that that bold and bad man, Strachan, should for so long a time have held such a power over my father. How very strange that, even now, at the mention of his name my father should shudder, as though he yet dreaded him! Oh, there is some mystery in all this, which I ought to know, and which it is possible might yet speak loudly for Arthur Wilton!"

"Amelia!" cried Mr. Revis, from below.

"Yes, father. I come—I come."

She paused at the top of the staircase for a moment, and during that moment Amelia made a resolution.

We shall soon see what it was.

Upon descending, Amelia found her father in the room below.

"Well, my child," he said, "you have seen poor Mrs. Percival?"

"Yes, father, and I will tell you all that passed."

Amelia then related to him as nearly as she could, word for word, what had transpired between her and Mrs. Percival, and when she had concluded, Mr. Revis sighed sadly as he said—

"Alas, my child, they do say that fresh evidence against poor Arthur has come to light."

"Oh, no—no."

"Yes—yes. They assured me of it, although I know not what it is. Oh, Amelia, I am staggered and confounded to that extent by all this affair, that I cannot see my way through it. I know not what to think. Everything appears to me a maze of mysteries."

"Yes, father."

"For the love of Heaven, Amelia, if you can give me any clue to escape from them, do so."

"I cannot yet, but I may do so when you, father, give me a clue to escape from other mysteries that hang over me, and which obscure my mental vision."

"I, girl?"

"Yes, father. I have made a resolution to ask of your love certain questions. I am no longer a child. Circumstances have thrown me into active life; I feel that I ought to know all."

Mr. Revis shook and turned pale.

"Oh, father, I beg of you to leave me no longer to vague conjecture, but tell me how and why it was that this Captain Strachan achieved a power over you, which I saw the effects of, but was never permitted to know the cause. Do not make me tremble with the thought that connected with those nearest and dearest to me there is guilt."

"Guilt?"

"Yes, father, guilt that I dread to think of. Oh, forgive me, but when the fancy is thrown upon its own resources, strange things will rise up and familiarise themselves to the mental vision. I implore you to dissipate them all, and to tell me the truth. I beg of you to trust me, father."

Mr. Revis was silent for a few moments, and then he said—

"My child, you have opened my eyes to a truth that I ought long ago to have perceived. I ought to have trusted you from the first."

"Oh, no, father, not if in your judgment you thought otherwise."

"My judgment?" cried Mr. Revis, "I ought never to have thrown you upon your imagination and upon conjecture for the explanation of phenomena that were taking place around you. I feel my error now."

"Dear father, perhaps it is I who even now commit an error by asking for your confidence."

"No, my child, you shall know all."

"All, father?"

"Yes, the time has come when nothing should be hidden from you. Those matters which have appeared to be inscrutable mysteries shall be so no longer; you shall know how and why it was that I dreaded this Captain Strachan so much, and how he acquired the power over me that he did."

"Yes, father."

"My child, it was through my tenderest affections that he hoped to wound me. It was at my heart that he aimed the deadly blow that was armed with all the venom of his dastardly and cruel nature. My child, that man is a villain of far blacker dye than you can imagine; for not having the knowledge of great crimes, you cannot fancy them as they really exist in this wretched world."

Mr. Revis was very much excited.

"Father," said Amelia, "I will not attempt to disguise from you that I am fearfully anxious to know that which you have to tell me; but I do not wish to know it at the price of so much disquietude to you."

"My dear child!"

"Keep the knowledge yet for awhile, father, and at some better opportunity, when your feelings are calm, you can tell me."

"No—no, I will tell you now. I shall never have the courage again to approach the theme. My dear child, you must know all now, or never. Listen to me."

"I do—I will, father."

Mr. Revis was silent for some few minutes as if he hardly knew how to begin his statement, and Amelia was still more distressed at the sufferings she saw depicted in his countenance.

"No—no, father," she said, "you shall not tell me now."

"Hush! hush! my child; listen to me. It is surely appointed by Heaven that I should now tell you, so I will. What if death should suddenly strike me and I had not informed you of all that you ought to know?"

"Oh, that is a terrible supposition, and it is one that I have invoked by my ill-timed curiosity."

"Not at all—no, no. Come, dry those tears, and listen to me attentively. You are now, Amelia, only nineteen years of age, and during that time you have not always resided here."

"No, I have a faint recollection of another home in a city."

"Yes, we once lived in London. But let me rapidly sketch to you how we came hither. Your mother was my second wife; by my first, I had a son. You have seen him, but it was long ago that you did so, when you were both children; for when you were born, he was but nine years of age, and his ungovernable character soon compelled me to send him from home; but do not mistake me—it was no fault of your mother's that he left my roof."

"It is kind and good of you to say that, father."

"It is the truth, my dear, and, therefore, I ought to say it. Well, when you were about four or five years of age, Job, for that was the name of my son, left us, partly of his own free will, and partly with my wish that he should do so; but he went well provided with every essential to succeed as an emigrant at the Cape of Good Hope, and was in the care of a worthy family proceeding to that region."

"And where is he now?"

"Stop, my dear; it is necessary, before

THE MURDER OF COLONEL PERCIVAL.

I say anything further of him, that I introduce you to another member of the family. My sister—my only sister she was, too—had married a gentleman named Strachan."

"Strachan, father?"

"Yes; but restrain your impatience, and you will soon know all. She was wedded, then, to Mr. Strachan some years before I married your mother, and this union was, as they thought, blessed by a son, who, at the time of the birth of my son, Job was ten years of age, so that that son is now about nineteen or twenty years your senior."

"Ah, then he is——"

"Captain Strachan."

"Good Heavens! then, father, that man is your nephew."

"He is, my child. He is my sister's only son."

"This is strange, indeed. But whence comes his inveterate hatred to you, my father?"

"You shall hear. At the age of seventeen or eighteen, this young Strachan, instead of being, as he ought to have been, the joy and comfort of his parents, was their curse. There was no description of vice in which he was not an adept, although, by an infernal tact and cunning, he always contrived to keep clear of the law, and to involve his unhappy associates in the consequences of the acts planned by himself."

"Alas! alas!"

"Well, my child, for a long time his parents put up with his terrible conduct; but at last his father died, and then his mother was compelled to call me in to aid her in actually escaping his violence. The father had left all his property, which was not much, to the mother, supposing that, by making Stephen, as this young Strachan was named, dependant upon her, he would make him, at least, respectful to her."

"Yes, father, I understand."

"That failed, however, and the mother died of a broken heart. When her will was opened, it was found that she had left all she possessed in the world to me, concluding by saying, 'I know my brother will be as kind as he ought to be to my reprobate son.'"

"How dreadful must have been his conduct to wring such a sentence from a dying mother."

"Dreadful, indeed."

"Go on, father—go on."

"Among the property so left, was this farm. But I had no intention to take advantage of the will. I yet only looked upon myself as a trustee, for the benefit of my nephew; but a circumstance occurred that made me feel that all lenity, all kindness, was thrown away upon him."

"What was that, father?"

"When the will was read, he flew at me, and struck me."

"Is that possible?"

"Yes, there was the unseemly exhibition of a fight between the uncle and the nephew, in the very room where my sister had breathed her last. I, in my roused passion, flung him through the window, which, fortunately, was upon the ground-floor, so that he was not hurt; but finding me, at that time, too strong for him, he stood at the window, and cried out—

"'It shall be the study of my life to be revenged upon you, and sooner, or later, if I live, I will bow your head in sorrow and in shame to the dust.'"

"Horrible!—most horrible!"

"With those words, he disappeared and, for some years, I neither saw nor heard of him. It was then, too, that my mind became occupied with the transgressions of my own son, Job; and too late I found that it was Stephen Strachan who had sought him out, and, taking advantage of his too ductile temperament, had made him what he was."

"The villain!"

"Yes, my child. It was a villanous act, for poor Job was as plastic in his hands as clay in those of a potter. He could make of him what he pleased, and that was the way he began to carry out his threat of usage, although I did not know till long afterwards who the bad associate was that had wrought Job such ruin."

"It is a sad story, father."

"It is, my child, it is."

"But there is more?"

"Ah, yes, there is much more. You shall hear all. I will conceal nothing from you. You shall hear how step by step the villain assailed me through my feelings and affections, and made me what I am."

"What you are, father?"

"Yes, a broken-hearted man!"

"Oh, say not that."

"It is too, too true."

"But, father, ought you to be broken-hearted while you have me to love you, and to look up to you? Ah, father, you wrong the fond affections of your poor loving girl, when you call yourself broken-hearted, for in her affections you ought to feel joy."

"I ought—I do, my Amelia. Come to my heart, dearest. I do, in your goodness and in your affection, find a consolation against a sea of troubles. I will not say that I am desolate while I have you to cling to, my darling."

CHAPTER LIX.

MR. REVIS CONCLUDES HIS STATEMENT TO AMELIA.

MR. REVIS was too deeply affected for a time to be able to continue his narrative to Amelia; but what he had already told her so strongly excited her curiosity to know the rest, that he felt it would be subjecting her to a world of mental uneasiness were he not to bring his statement to a conclusion.

Yet, notwithstanding she so ardently desired to hear all, she again begged her father to desist from continuing the narration if he found his feelings too vividly interested in it.

"No, no," he said, "as I have commenced this mournful tale, I will finish it. You shall know all, my child, and, perhaps, when I have told you all, I may feel somewhat easier in my mind."

"Then, father, I will indeed listen."

"I say, then, that I had not the least idea of the association that was between Stephen Strachan and my poor foolish boy Job, so that one day, about five or six years ago, when Strachan came down here to this place, and sent for me to a hotel, I went, little expecting that it was to look upon the man who had been the ruin of my son."

"Was Strachan in the army then, father?"

"No, but you shall hear what his object was in coming here at all. I did not know, when I went to the hotel, that it was my nephew, Stephen, that I had to meet, for he had merely sent word that a gentleman wished to see me."

"It was no wonder, father, that you did not imagine him under such a disguise as that."

"It was no wonder, indeed. Well, when I saw him, I hardly knew him, for he was much altered, and he spoke in a quiet, subdued tone of voice. I will tell you, Amelia, as nearly as I can, what took place between us upon that occasion, when he acted the hypocrite, and I was so completely taken in by his false professions.

"'Uncle,' he said, 'you have ample reason to have a bad opinion of me.'

"'I have, Stephen Strachan,' said I.

"'Well,' he added, 'I have seen the error of my ways, and I hope that, at my age, it is not too late to reform for the future, and repent of the past.'

"'No, Stephen,' said I, 'it is never too late.'

"'Then, uncle, believe me, that I have so reformed, and that I do so repent. You see me now an altered man, uncle; and if, at the sacrifice of my own life, I could bring my own mother from the tomb, and only have breath enough to tell how deeply contrite I am for my conduct towards her, I should be happier than I fear I shall ever be.'

"I was well pleased to hear this from him; and as he shed some tears, I thought him sincere, and I replied kindly, saying—

"'Nephew Stephen, as you are in this frame of mind, let me ask you what you are doing, and how you are living, so that I may see if I can be of any advantage to you.'

"'Dear uncle,' he said, 'I am sorry to say, that never having been brought up to any particular pursuit, I have contracted habits of idolence; and, in the first place, I am in debt to the amount of about three hundred pounds; and as you had all my patrimony, which was a very good thing, for if it had been mine it would have been squandered long ago, I have ventured to hope that you would aid me.'

"'Willingly,' said I; 'you shall have the money this day.'

"Well, my dear Amelia, upon this he pretended to be deeply affected, and to shed many tears; and, finally, I said to him, that I felt, as I always had felt, that I held his patrimony only in trust for him, and that as the total value of it had been about sixteen hundred pounds, including the value of the farm at that time, I thought he had a right to that amount from me."

"Did that noble generosity not move him, father?"

"It seemed to do so, indeed; but I doubt if it did so in reality. He was most profuse in his thanks, and I actually gave him, in the course of a few days, no less a sum than sixteen hundred pounds, which I had some difficulty to get together at the time.

"'Now, nephew,' I said, 'do not say that I had and have your patrimony, for there is the whole of it. I give you the value of Riversdale Farm, but I have become attached to the place, and wish to keep it. With the money, however, you can buy another place as good as it was when I came to it.'"

"And he was satisfied."

"He seemed to be. He embraced me—he shed tears—he positively knelt and called down blessings upon my head, and so we parted."

"Unfeeling monster! What next heard you of him, father?"

"The next I heard of him was contained in a letter from my son, whom I thought at the Cape of Good Hope, and that letter I will show to you, Amelia."

Mr. Revis opened a draw in his large old-fashioned writing table, and produced a letter, which he handed to Amelia.

The letter was as follows :—

"Limerick Barracks.

"Dear father,—You will see by this that I have not gone to the Cape of Good Hope, as you supposed I would do. The fact is, at the last moment, I felt a dislike to leave my own country, so I let the ship go without me.

"I had another inducement to stay, too, for a friend of mine—no other than my cousin, Stephen Strachan—wrote to me, and offered me help and assistance in England ; and as he is a capital fellow, and we are old friends, though you did not know it, I thought I would stay. It turned out, though, that poor Stephen could do nothing for me ; so, after my money was spent, he persuaded me to enlist in a marching regiment, and here I am in the fifty-fifth, stationed at Limerick barracks, though we expect soon to come to England.

"I enlisted in the name of Clinton, so that in the regiment, mind, I am known as Job Clinton.

"You will, however, be rather surprised when I tell you that Stephen Strachan has got hold of some money somewhere, and has bought a commission in the same regiment, and is, in fact, my officer. He tells me, of course, it won't do for us to associate together, but that when he can he will speak to me, and befriend me, and he says he has money enough to buy himself up in the service, and that he will be a captain soon.

"Now, of course, father, money is always acceptable ; so if you can send me any, I shall be very happy ; and, as Stephen says you had all his patrimony, I dare say you will be able to spare me some cash, to which, he says, I am very welcome, and begs that I will tell you as much.

"I can't say I like a soldier's life at all, for there's too much to do ; but it can't be helped now.

"Address to me, Job Clinton, barracks, Limerick.

"I am, dear father, yours ever and ever,
"Job."

"P. S.—Send the money as soon as you can. Stephen would lend me some, but he says just now he cannot get hold of a sum he has lent out at interest to somebody."

The letter dropped from Amelia's hands.

"I begin to see it now," she said, faintly.

"Yes," said her father, "I have no doubt in the world but that Stephen Strachan bought a commission, which, in war-time, is cheap, for the express purpose of continuing to be the evil genius of poor Job."

"He is a fiend, father."

"He seems more like one than a mortal man."

"Oh, go on—go on. I feel assured that the sequel of this tale is something worse than all I have yet heard."

"It is, my child, it is."

"Then you will tell that to me to-morrow?"

"No, now ; you shall hear it now. One night there came a letter to me from my poor son."

"Yes, oh, yes."

"I—I nearly fainted when I read it. Take it—take it."

From the same secret drawer, Mr. Revis took another letter, and placed it in Amelia's hands. It was a blotted scrawl, but she read, although with difficulty, the following lines :—

"Father,—If you wish to save me from death, you will make terms with Strachan. The fact is, I have robbed the military chest, and, I fear, killed a sentinel, and Strachan knows of it. He is the only man who does know of it. He has furnished me with money and means wherewith to fly from the regiment. He will be with you to-night. It is thought that I have deserted merely because I disliked the life of a soldier. Strachan alone can tell all or keep all secret.   "Job."

"And did he come?" said Amelia.

"He did."

Amelia drew a long breath, and looked fixedly at her father.

"Scarcely, my child, had I finished reading the letter, than he came and told me that he at once could accuse and bring to death my son. He asked a thousand pounds as the price of his secrecy."

"Ah, then, this is the secret of the bond?"

"Yes, this, as you say, Amelia, is the secret of the bond."

"Oh, father, why did you believe that man?"

"I can scarcely tell. He took me in the moment of my first terror. I saw in imagination the execution of my son, and my afflicted soul shrunk aghast from the awful spectacle. I agreed to any terms he chose to dictate."

"The worse than villain!"

"He left this place with me, and took me to that man Huncks, where the bond was drawn and such conditions were put into it, that I was almost prevented from paying the money at all. But then this farm would have been Strachan's."

"Ah, yes, I see it all."

"And you know how the last instalment was paid."

"I do—I do."

"I was mad to make the agreement at all; but having done so, although my soberer judgment told me it was illegal, I dreaded to refute it, and so I let it take its course."

"And Job?"

"I never heard of him from that time forth."

"Oh, father, it is all now as clear as day, that this Strachan has set his wicked head upon the persecution of you and yours for ever."

"It is so."

"And poor Arthur, too, he has come under the bane of his resentment, just because he thwarted him at the last moment about the money."

"Even so. Oh, I am, indeed, wretched!"

"And that man is my cousin!"

"He is—he is, Amelia. Heaven help us all."

Amelia rose, and lifting up her hand, she said solemnly—

"Father, *Stephen Strachan murdered Colonel Percival!*"

Mr. Revis shook like a leaf in autumn, as, in a choking voice, he replied—

"I have thought so—God, I have thought so! It is like him!"

"I feel that it is a truth," added Amelia. "That villain did the deed. He and he alone is guilty!"

"Hush! oh, hush!"

"Nay, father, I will make the truth heard, if I live to do so. I feel that he did the deed, and that poor Arthur is accused through his machinations solely. Oh, father, I thank you for telling me all this, for it has opened my heart to the truth, and it has had the effect of banishing hideous doubts. I tell you Arthur is innocent, and Captain Stephen Strachan alone did the deed!"

There was something solemnly prophetic about the tones of Amelia as she uttered these words, and her father looked at her with fear and trembling, and listened to her as though she spoke with a voice from Heaven, containing some revelation that it had not been permitted for mortal senses to comprehend.

"Oh, my child," he said, "I feel that it is the truth which you give utterance to. You give expression to the hidden thoughts of my own heart."

"You, father, you think him guilty?"

"I do—I do."

"We must be quite calm."

Amelia clasped her hands over her face for a moment or two, during which her father did not dare to interrupt her, and then when she looked at him again, he perceived that there was quite a stern expression upon her face, such as he had never seen it wear before.

"Father," she said, "there must be no more tears now—no more sighing and lamentation. There must be nothing but action—energetive action. Arthur Wilton must be saved."

"Yes, Amelia, yes. If—"

"I will admit of no doubt. He shall be saved!"

Mr. Revis looked in surprise at what had been the timid girl, but who was now the bold heroine.

"Yes," she added. "Everything is possible with truth, justice, and God upon our side, and surely we have all these."

"We have—we have."

"Then, father, we shall triumph; I feel assured that the truth will yet appear. I must go to the Abbey, now, father, and see Mrs. Percival again."

CHAPTER LX.

ARTHUR IS DEEMED GUILTY BY ALL BUT THOSE WHO KNOW HIM.

WE may now pass over a number of minor events that took place preceding the day when Arthur Wilton was to be brought before the magistrates of the county, to be duly and in all regular form committed for trial, for the murder of which he was so completely innocent.

We say he was to be committed, because that he would be so had quite ceased to be a matter of any doubt.

The impression of his guilt among those who knew him not had gained ground immensely during the week that had elapsed since that terrible morning when he was first accused of the fearful crime against gratitude, and against human nature.

Mankind are ever prone to magnify either the virtues or the faults of any one; and hence you have but to point the finger of suspicion at any individual, and you at once induce hundreds to believe that it is with abundant reason.

The circumstances that seemed most to tell against Arthur Wilton were talked over until everybody in the country would have seen him hanged forwith with great satisfaction, always excepting the judicious few who do not go with the stream of popular opinion.

The attorney-general, it was understood, would prosecute on behalf of the government, which took up the case, and the doom of the young soldier seemed to be all but settled.

The old court-house at Exeter, which since that time has been pulled down, was crowded to excess upon the occasion of Arthur Wilton, the murderer, as he was familiarly called, being brought up after his week's remand.

A dense and excited crowd had collected in front of the court-house, and its interior was packed to suffocation.

But despite all the public prejudice against him, Arthur was calm and tranquil. He had the assurance of his father —of Mr. Revis—of Amelia—and of the young barrister who had come from London to defend him, that they all believed him innocent, and that to him was everything. He had had, too, a hint from Amelia, that great doubts existed in the mind of Mrs. Percival as regarded the possibility of his guilt, and it was an exquisite gratification to him to think that she did not condemn him.

The feeling in the regiment, too, was all in his favour, for Corporal Steady and Cockles, after talking the matter over, had come to the fixed conclusion that Arthur was innocent, although the affair was so shrouded in mystery that they could offer no reasonable solution of it.

The popularity, and the respect in which Steady was held in the regiment, made many converts to his opinion; and as it was known, too, that Major Cuthbert was shaken in his idea of the guilt of Arthur, and that Doctor Smith had openly said upon parade, that if Wilton did it, he should never trust to an innocent countenance again, the feeling came strongly in favour of the prisoner.

Mr. Flummery, too, did his best with the villagers; but there he did not get on at all.

Amelia had merely said—"Mr. Flummery, Arthur is innocent,"—and that had been sufficient for him; but that could not counteract the evil influnce of mystery and ignorance.

Captain Strachan had got well very suddenly, as some people thought; but the surgeon combated that opinion, and hinted that some exceedingly judicious medicines that he had given him had had the almost increduous effect.

Now, Strachan was very near recovering his position in the regiment, and a popularity with the soldiers that he had never enjoyed at all before, by saying openly in the barrack-yard —

"Wilton and I have had some disputes; but for all that, I know enough of his character to feel as certain as I do of my own existence that he is not the man to commit a murder, and I will never believe it unless he is proved to have gone mad first."

It was on the evening before the day upon which Arthur was to to remanded, that Strachan called upon Mr. Huncks in quite a casual sort of way, and found that worthy engaged upon some papers in his study.

"Ah, captain," said Huncks. "How very well you do look. Why, your recovery is quite, really, an interposition of Providence."

"Peace—peace. Does all go well?"

"Pretty well."

"What do you mean by pretty well?"

"Why, that means quite well, although we are liable to litttle accidents. There is one thing to be guarded against, however, particularly."

"What is that?"

"Not to make the case against Wilton too strong. You cannot think what a mischief that does sometimes. We must keep back many little facts from the jury at the trial. There can be no doubt about his committal, and as there is evidence enough for that, why, that will do."

"But how does the criminal law stand in that respect? Can more evidence be produced at the trial, than is produced before the committing magis:rate?'

"To be sure."

"Then I perfectly agree with you."

"Yes. Any evidence will be received by the judge at the trial that is relative to the case in issue ; so let all the grand points that fill up the nice little story, be reserved till then. The attorney-general will, of course, call all the witnesses he can think of in the matter. The crown don't want to convict unless the man is guilty; so he will go into the case in full, without caring what comes out."

"I see."

"And in that way we shall get at all the little nice facts, you see, captain, and you must be particularly careful what you say. And now, captain, I have a word of advice to give you."

"What is it?"

"Could you not manage to be upon seeming good terms with the Revises?"

"No."

"But listen to me, man. It is a great point if you could; and I think that, under the present circumstances, they would be glad to shake hands with the devil himself, if he promised a good word in court for Arthur Wilton."

"You don't know them, Huncks."

"Yes, I do. They are human beings, I suppose."

"They are; but their feelings towards me are rather——"

"Well—well, I know what you would say; but yet I advise you to try it, captain. They can but say no to you; and it would be a good thing, in case of any little accident, that you should be found upon their side of the question, don't you see?"

"I know all that, but I tell you the thing cannot be done. Let me use what words of seeming sympathy I might, they would not believe them. They would just think that I had some covert motive in them, and I should meet with nothing but a rebuff. We cannot manage this case as we did the last."

"No. Then you made something of it."

"I did; and you will allow me to remark that so did you."

Huncks nodded.

"And if this story," he said this in a low voice, "that you tell me about the buried treasure that you took from the colonel be true, we shall not do amiss as regards this affair."

"You doubt it?"

"A little."

"Well, it is not in my power just now, without revealing the secret of the hiding-place of the jewels, and that I don't choose to do, to settle your doubts; but the time will come when you will acquit me of deceiving you in this particular. But stay, I have thought of something that may go some way towards the desirable condition of making you feel that I have told you the truth."

'What is that?"

"I will bring you a sample of the contents of the colonel's treasure."

"Do. That will be something like ocular demonstration."

"It shall be done, Mr. Huncks. To-morrow evening I will call upon you again with the sample. Good night. You will be at the court-house to-morrow, of course?"

"Yes. But stop. Once more I urge you to call at Riversdale Farm."

Strachan hesitated.

"It can do no harm if it does no good."

"If I thought——"

"What?"

"If I thought there was the slightest chance of their listening to me, I would go."

"Try it. Who knows but that the fair Amelia, now that the life of Arthur Wilton is at stake, may be induced to be just a little civil to one who can promise to befriend him? You can put on a look of great candour, you know, and recollect to say that you think him incapable of the crime he is charged with."

"Well, I will try it."

"Do. You may depend it is sound policy."

Captain Strachan, to tell the truth, had had some such an idea himself, and he was only wavering about it when he called upon Huncks; what that individual had said had had the effect of fixing him, and even while he affected to hesitate he had made up his mind to go at once to Riversdale.

One would have thought that after all that had passed in that house between him and old Mr. Revis, he would have shunned it with all the care in the world; but the same utter abandonment of all principle, and the same unblushing roguery that had enabled him to go there and to say and do such things as he had said and done, presented him with the necessary assurance to carry out the present visit.

To be sure, he had no idea that old Mr. Revis had communicated to Amelia the particulars of who and what he was, and the whole wretched story of Clinton, his half-brother, or he might have hesitated a little with the thought that after that it would be quite out of the question that anything he could say should have any effect in deceiving Amelia as to his real character.

It had been, in the first instance, rather a surprise to Strachan that Amelia knew nothing of the circumstances, for he found that she did not by her conduct to him. But he had a pretty good knowledge of his uncle's character, and he, after some reflection, attributed his silence to its right cause, namely a kind of false pride, which formed the underwork of Mr. Revis's character, and which influenced many of his actions, without his being aware of it himself.

It was merely the great danger of Arthur Wilton that had broken through all such faint barriers, and induced Mr. Revis to tell the tale he had told to his daughter Amelia.

But Strachan was playing a deeper game with the Revis family than he cared to let Mr. Huncks know of. He yet hoped that he would be able to work sufficiently upon their fears to induce the old man to make some terms with him about the farm, and it was in deep cogitation upon this point that he reached the gate of the flower-garden, and carefully opened it.

"Yes," he said, "I will see Revis alone first, and ——"

A deep growl struck upon the ear of Strachan, and induced him quickly to beat a retreat.

"That infernal dog," he said,—"I will be the death of that beast soon. It is ever in my way."

As he spoke, he took a small pocket pistol from the breast of his apparel, and seeing that it was in order, called—

"Prince! Prince! Prince! Hilloa! Poor fellow!"

Prince was not to be so easily coaxed as Strachan suspected, but while he was leaning over the gate calling to him, Prince got through a gap in the hedge, and, without saying a word about it, laid hold of his leg by the ankle.

The attack was so sudden and unexpected, that, Strachan's finger being upon the trigger of the pistol, he pressed it sufficiently to discharge the little weapon, and so was defenceless.

The sound of the shot brought Mr. Revis out into the garden, and he called out, loudly—

"Who is there? Who is there?"

"Call off the dog," said Strachan, "d—n him, he has got hold of me. Call off the dog, I say, or I will do him a mischief."

CHAPTER LXI.

CAPTAIN STRACHAN ALARMS MR. REVIS, BUT NOT AMELIA.

MR. REVIS had recognised the voice of Strachan in a moment, and now he advanced towards the gate; and, by the dim light, Strachan saw, to his alarm, that the old man had a fowling-piece in his hand.

"You are armed, sir," he said.

"Yes; and if you have injured the dog, I will avenge him."

"I have not—call him off, and you will find I have not."

"Prince! Prince!"

In a moment Prince bounded over the gate, and stood by his master, to the great relief of Strachan.

"You see that the dog is untouched."

"Yes, but you fired at him, I presume, for I heard the sound of fire-arms."

"Oh no; it was only an accident; but I don't see what necessity you have, sir, to come out to me with a gun in your hand. I came upon a particular, and, I hope, a friendly errand."

"You friendly to me?"

"Yes, strange as you may think it. I admit that my conduct has not been to you what it ought to have been; but I am here, Mr. Revis, and still there may be, even at the bottom of my heart, some remains of feeling that the present circumstances may have called into life and activity."

This was, indeed, a cunningly devised speech to entrap Mr. Revis, at all events, into a conference with him, and but that the old man was so thoroughly convinced of the villany of Strachan that he could not believe a word he uttered, except in its contrary sense, he might have answered him mildly enough, but, as it was, he said—

"Strachan, I have but one request to make of you."

"Name it, sir."

"It is, that you will forget me and mine, as I and they will forget, so far as we can, you. Farewell, sir."

"Now, uncle, you wrong me."

"Peace—peace! Go your way, and let us be, with our afflictions, in peace."

"Yet hear me, and if you feel that what I say does not concern you, or if you feel inclined to reject it after you have heard it, do so, and I will go in peace. It is possible, I suppose, even to your perception, that Heaven might touch even my heart, and make me strive to do one good act"

"It is possible."

"Open the gate, then, and keep the dog from me."

"No. If you have anything to say, say it where you are. We can hear each other well enough, and if that suits you not, go at once, and leave it unsaid at your pleasure."

"Well, perhaps, after all, I ought not to blame you, or even to feel hurt at these suspicions of me and my motives. I come now to warn you of danger, not from any personal advantage to myself. Your daughter, Amelia, and my very good half-sister, is in danger."

"From you?"

"No; I had not been here to warn you if that had been the case. But, I tell you, uncle, that an impression is gaining ground, and is growing into ominous whispers, that she is, in some measure, the accomplice of Arthur Wilton in the murder."

"Liar!"

"As you please, sir. After that, good night."

"No—no. Oh, God! Villain as you are, stay and tell me all. Let me hear the wretched fabrication out."

"Uncle, the discourtesy of your words is

THE MEETING OF THE LOVERS ON THE NIGHT OF THE MURDER.

such that I might well leave you, but, I tell you, my heart is touched, and I wilt not take offence if I can help it. What I have told you is the truth."

"No, it is a vile falsehood; it cannot be otherwise, for, inasmuch as Arthur Wilton is himself innocent, he can have no accomplice."

"Just so. But the unfortunate thing is that he is one of many victims. Did you never hear of an innocent man being convicted—ay, hung?"

"No—yes. I—I have."

"Well, if such be the case, I don't see why another who is equally innocent may not be suspected of complicity in the same offence."

"Villain! this is some hideous motive of your own to add yet another drop to my cup of bitterness and affliction."

"It is not so. I assure you that I am no friend of Arthur Wilton's, but the dreadful charge of which I cannot from my knowledge of the man bring myself for a moment to believe that he is guilty, has shocked me much, and made me think deeply. Perhaps I should not have gone out of my way to express all I felt for Wilton, but when the name of Amelia came to my ears, coupled with such expressions as I have heard, it made my heart tremble, and I came here in consequence."

"Vile expressions!"

"They say that Arthur Wilton was ambitious, and that he expected by murdering the colonel to get a large sum, with which he and Amelia would leave England, and live high and mighty in some other country. They say that letters passed between them upon some such subject, and that their designs were for grasping in some illegitimate way large sums of money."

"False! false!"

"As hell!"

"What say you?"

"Just what you say—false. That is my own opinion. Nay, it is not an opinion, it is a fact; for you, sir, and I know Amelia by far too well to need to form an opinion upon such a point. It becomes a fact with us that all such charges are false, and I think we know Wilton, too, well enough to say the same regarding him."

"We do—we do."

"To be sure, sir. But still I felt it to be my duty to come and arouse you and Amelia, so that you should be upon your guard."

"I shall go mad.'

"It is not for me, uncle, to intrude my counsel upon you; but I should venture, if I did give advice, to recommend——"

"What? oh, what? Speak!"

"Flight—instant flight for Amelia. I would not, were I in your place, tell her why. She will obey your orders, and I would make her leave England before the dawn of another day. Why should she be involved in the same hideous crime that has fallen upon the innocent Wilton? Surely one victim to the weakness and the fallibility of human nature is enough. Let her fly from England, sir, and from the secure haven of some foreign land, where she goes to I would rather not know, let her watch the course of events, and it may be that all may yet be well."

"Alas! alas! I know not what to think. I cannot send my child from me alone."

"Go with her, sir. What is to hinder you? I will take care of Riversdale for you; and when you come back, you will find I have been a careful steward. Oh, uncle, bitterly repenting the past, I come to you now, like the prodigal son, a pro-

digal nephew, to tell you that, in the time to come, I shall be a very different man."

"Strachan, you are either a devil, or—"

"Father, I will not go," said a calm, clear voice, and Amelia stepped to the side of her father.

"Amelia—my child?"

"I am here, father."

"I am glad of it," said Strachan, "for it gives me the opportunity of saying—"

"Nothing further, sir," interrupted Amelia. "I have heard all you have said already, and to-morrow morning I will repeat it to Mrs. Percival, who will communicate it to the council for the prosecution and for the defence of Arthur Wilton. Come, father; have we sunk so low as to converse with this man?"

"Allow me," said Strachan, "to——"

"Come, father. Oh, have not another word with that man."

"I have the pleasure, then," said Strachan, controlling his passion wonderfully, "to bid you good night; but not even the insults I met with here shall prevent me from doing all I can to save Arthur Wilton."

He darted off at a quick pace, for he dreaded that if he staid another minute, and heard Amelia say more, his passion would get the better of his prudence, and he would say things that would, as far as regarded the part he intended to play at the trial of Wilton, be much better unsaid.

It was when he got a quarter of a mile or so from the farm, that he raged and stamped his feet with wild passion, and yelled again with the pent-up rage that now burst from his breast.

"I will have all their lives!" he cried. "I will satisfy my vengeance only by the destruction of them all. Not one of them shall live to taunt me with the fact that they escaped. And most of all, Amelia, do I hate you, and bitterly will I be revenged upon you."

At great speed, Strachan went back to the barracks, and when he got there, he at once rushed to his own room, and taking a twenty-pound note from his desk, he enclosed it in the following letter, which he addressed to a well-known dealer in precious stones in London.

"Barracks, Exeter and Riversdale.

"SIR,—You will oblige me by purchasing, with the enclosed twenty pounds, as fine an emerald as you can get for the money, and transmit the same, as soon as possible, by post.

"I am, sir, yours, &c.,
    "STEPHEN STRACHAN, Capt."

Strachan went out and posted the letter

himself, at the village post-office, so that it would go in safety.

The emerald was for Mr. Huncks. That was to be the specimen of the colonel's wealth, with the existence of which, secreted somewhere, he, Strachan, wished so much to impose upon the attorney.

Strachan felt how dangerous a foe Huncks might be, and how excellent, because perfectly unscrupulous, a friend; and hence was it that he considered a twenty pound fee, in the shape of an emerald, to be very well laid out upon the attorney.

For once, Mr. Huncks had met with his match in cunning and devilry.

These were the events, then, that took place on the evening immediately preceding that day upon which Arthur Wilton was to be brought up to the court-house to be finally committed for trial.

We now proceed to that building.

At the hour of nine the magistrates took their seats, and the order was given for the production of the prisoner. The excitement among the crowd was intense, and when poor Arthur was brought in a coach to the court-house, the yells and shouts were terrific.

"Is it possible," said Wilton, "that the people think me guilty?"

"Don't know," said the constable who came with him.

Another yell, and a loud cry of "Hang him! Hang him!" convinced Arthur that he had become the object of popular excitement.

"It don't matter," said the officer; "never mind that."

"I don't mind them. I only pity them."

"That's the way to think of it. Some people is born to do things and to be scragged, and some isn't."

"Then, I suppose, you think me among the former?"

"Well, I suppose so."

"But suppose I am innocent?"

"Innocent? Oh! ah! Well, I—You own you are in custody, and all that sort of thing—so I—ah!—that is—hem!"

"I quite understand you. You mean that, after giving all this trouble, I have no right to be innocent. You have the idea that when once a man is taken up for any alleged offence, he ought to be considered guilty, rather than the police should be in the wrong."

"Well, I don't know."

"I do, though—and now, my friend, I pity you."

"Bother the fellow," muttered the con-stable; "I don't know what to make of him."

After this, the officers said no more to Arthur. They concluded, to use their own phraseology, that he was one too many for them; so they let him alone.

The idea that he was innocent, never for a moment crossed their imaginations as a mode of accounting for his behaviour to them. No; he was in custody, and that, to their apprehensions, seemed to settle the fact of his criminality; so that all he did and said that was connected with a contrary supposition, was just put down as the perfection of art.

But Arthur was not at all sorry to be left to his own thoughts, and, therefore, the silence of the officers was rather grateful to him than otherwise.

He shrunk from the eager gaze of the throng, though, that was about the court-house.

CHAPTER LXII.
SOME STRANGE DISCLOSURES TAKE PLACE AT THE BARRACKS.

THE officers got the prisoner within the building, where the magistrates were assembled, as quickly as possible, for they rather dreaded some expression of opinion upon the part of the mob; and Arthur was as glad as they to get out of the presence of a multitude that could not be in a position to judge either of his guilt or his innocence.

"Now," said one of the officers to him, "you had better take something before you go before the beaks."

"Thank you, I want nothing," said Arthur.

"Well, that's just as you like, you know, only you will please to recollect that we have done the civil thing, and asked you, so that's all we have to say about it."

"I presume I may see my friends?" said Arthur.

"Well, I don't know anything about it," said the officer. "You have got a lawyer, perhaps?"

"No—no; I merely want to see my father and friends."

It was at this moment that a message came from the court, requiring the attendance of the prisoner.

The officers hurried poor Arthur along several stone passages, and then, a couple of doors being flung open, he was at once ushered into the court.

So sudden had been the summons to appear in court, that Arthur had no time to think, and now he found himself confronted by some three hundred pairs of eyes, before he hardly knew where he was. No wonder that he shrunk, and felt abashed.

That action was noticed, and construed into the consciousness of guilt by many there present.

Oh, how cautious people should be in thus prejudging a fellow-creature! Accuse an innocent man of any crime—you look, and he, naturally enough, looks confounded—perhaps he changes colour; and it depends much upon his mind's organization whether he may not even tremble —nay, faint away; and people shake their heads, and say—"Ah! look at the guilty wretch!"

We would ask how many people are there with such command of nerves, and tones, and features, that they could hear themselves accused of a foul murder calmly, and go through the ordeal of a trial in a melodramatic way? Such things may do for the stage, but not in real life. Never condemn a man from appearances. Confusion may sit upon an innocent face, as well as a guilty one. Nay, it is much more likely to belong to the former than to the latter.

Indeed, the guilty man is much more likely than the innocent one to put a good face upon it, to use a common expression, because, from the fact of his knowledge of his own guilt, he is forewarned, in a manner of speaking, by being forewarned of what may likely enough occur with regard to him.

It took, then, poor Arthur Wilton, with all his consciousness of innocence—with all his real rectitude of character—with all the many noble and sterling qualities of mind that he possessed—some minutes before he could rally from the effects that the consciousness of having so many eyes upon him produced.

By a great effort, he did recover, and then he looked as steadily as possible upon the sea of faces before him.

There was a confused murmur of voices, and then he heard some one say, audibly—

"We have nothing further to urge at this present time, beyond what is already before the court. The prisoner is committed for trial upon the coroner's verdict, and, doubtless, you, gentlemen, will pursue the same course."

"Yes," said one of the magistrates; "this is a proceeding merely *pro forma.* Prisoner, you may say what you please, but you will be fully committed for trial; so that, perhaps, it will be as well for you to reserve your defence.

"I have no defence," said Arthur Wilton.

"No defence? Then do you admit your guilt?"

"Guilt! Oh, no. I can say nothing but that I am wholly and completely innocent; and that there is no more sincere mourner than I am for the death of Colonel Percival."

"We have nothing further to say at present," said a gentlemanly young man, rising.

"Who are you, sir?" said the serious magistrate.

"My name is North. I am a barrister."

It was at this moment that a hand was stretched over the bar, and clasped that of Wilton. It was his father. Mr. Revis, too, was by his side.

"My dear boy!" said old Mr. Wilton.

The tears were gathering in the eyes of Mr. Revis.

"Courage," said Arthur, with a smile; "you know and God knows my innocence of the deed."

"Oh, yes," said Mr. Revis, "we do. Mr. North, of whom I spoke to you, is here, you see."

"Yes," added old Wilton, "and he has brought with him a Mr. Anderson, an attorney, who, he says, has great skill."

"You appear, then, as council for the prisoner, Mr. North?" said one of the magistrates.

"I do."

"Very well; then you will understand that he is fully committed for trial for the wilful murder of Colonel Percival."

"I presume I may have a copy of the depositions?"

"Every possible facility shall be given to you, Mr. North, by the clerk of the peace, to prepare the defence of the prisoner. Heaven knows that we all here have but one desire, and that is that justice should be done."

"I am as certain of that, sir," said Mr. North, "as I am of my own existence."

"Make way!" cried a voice at the door of the court at this moment—"make way, there. Way for a witness."

There was a great commotion and stirring among the crowd, and the magistrates had to interfere to preserve order in the court. After some difficulty, a couple of soldiers and an officer made their way to the bench, and the officer said, in a tone of respectful deference—

"I beg to apologise, if this be an intrusion; but some discoveries have been made in the barracks only a few hours since, which bear very strongly upon the guilt of the prisoner at the bar."

"The prisoner is committed," said the magistrate, as he glanced at Mr. North. "I don't know whether, now, anything extra had not better be delayed till the trial. The sessions are so close at hand, that the probability is, the prisoner will be tried this day week."

"If this is an appeal to me," said Mr. North, "I say let us hear this gentleman. We have nothing to fear. Every revelation based upon truth connected with this affair must be in our favour."

The officer shook his head.

"Well, sir," said the magistrate, to him, "we will hear your evidence. Let the gentleman be sworn."

The officer, who was but slightly known to Arthur Wilton, was sworn, and he said, in a calm, clear voice—

"What is called the common-room, or reading-room, of the officers' quarters at the barracks, is cleared out of waste-paper and other matters once a week, or thereabouts. It so happened that that process was gone through this morning by these two soldiers, and they found, among the waste-paper upon the floor, a pocket-book, with the prisoner's name in it."

"Have you it with you, sir?"

"Yes, it is here. There are certain memoranda in its pages, bearing strong reference to the charge for which the prisoner is here to-day."

The officer handed the pocket-book to the magistrate. It was the same one, of course, that the villain, Strachan, had prepared and entered certain suspicious memoranda in, for the express purpose of being found as it was, and adding a piece of damning evidence to the various circumstances that already seemed strongly to bear against Arthur Wilton.

The magistrate glanced at the writing in the pocket-book, and then he handed it back to the officer, saying—

"You will oblige the court, sir, by reading what is there written, and then we must get evidence of the hand-writing."

While this was going on, poor Arthur Wilton looked from the magistrate to the officer, and from the officer to the magistrate, in mute wonder, and the expression of his countenance was more like that of a man in a dream than anything else, while the officer, in rather a low tone, for he regretted that his duty mixed him up in the matter, read as follows from the pocket-book:—

"Best route to America.—Go to Hamburgh, or Amsterdam. Stay there a week, under assumed name, and then embark in American trading vessel for any port in United States."

"If any jewels in box, get rid of them in Holland.—Query: Any Jews in Holland?"

"Send for A. in short time, and persuade her—it won't require much, after what has passed—to leave old R. When a girl has bidden adieu to her virtue, she don't want much asking to follow the man of her choice."

"Memorandum. Try to think on what would be most likely to fix the affair on S. That would be glorious.",

"Is that all?" said the magistrate.

"That, sir, is all the connected writing that I can find in the pocket-book; but the name of Arthur Wilton is written carelessly in a number of places."

There was a pause, now, of some few moments' duration, and then the magistrate said—

"Did you find this book yourself, sir?"

"No. It was handed to me by those two soldiers."

"Let them be sworn, then, as to the finding it."

The two soldiers were duly sworn, and their evidence just amounted to the fact that they were clearing out the officers' common or reading-room, and finding the pocket-book, they took it to the officer who had then produced it in court.

"This can be added to the depositions," said the magistrate. "If the prisoner has anything to say to this new fact, he can now say it, if he should be so inclined."

The glance that the magistrate gave towards Mr. North, as he uttered these last words, was quite translatable into—"He will be very ill-advised if he says a word;" but the young barrister rose, and said at once—

"It is quite impossible that the prisoner can damage himself, unless he wishes to commit suicide. Being innocent, he cannot say anything that can possibly prejudice himself in any way."

"I have only to say," said Arthur Wilton, "that I have no pocket-book, and never had one, and that I never till this day saw that which is now produced in court."

"Can any one here speak to the hand-writing of the prisoner?" said the magistrate, as he glanced round the court.

"I can," said old Mr. Wilton, stepping forward, but looking so pale and wan, that the magistrate, not knowing the relation in which he stood to the prisoner, thought that he was some sick man who, only with the wayward fancy of illness, thought he knew something that probably he had no opportunity at all of having any knowledge of.

"Are you sure that you can speak to that fact, sir?" said the magistrate, "for, if you are not, we will not trouble you, as you seem rather indisposed."

"I am sure."

"Very well. Let this gentleman be sworn. Now, sir, who are you?"

"The father of Arthur Wilton."

The magistrate looked shocked, and consulted with his colleague; but there was nothing in the fact of the relationship to prevent the evidence of old Mr. Wilton being taken, and the pocket-book was handed to him.

"The writing," he said, "is marvellously like the writing of my son. It is an excellent imitation——"

"But yet an imitation?" said Mr. North.

"Decidedly so."

"Upon what do you ground that opinion?" said the magistrate.

"I am so very intimate with his style of writing, that I can see little discrepancies that would escape the eye of another. I swear that this is not the hand-writing of Arthur Wilton; yet, as I said before, it is marvellously like it. Oh, gentlemen, there is some awful villany at work in this affair. God help the innocent! God help my boy!"

CHAPTER LXIII.

ANOTHER PIECE OF EVIDENCE IS PRODUCED AGAINST ARTHUR WILTON.

As old Mr. Wilton uttered these words, he fell back fainting into the arms of several of the spectators.

"Father! father!" cried Arthur.

There was a general commotion in the court; but by the aid of a glass of water the old man was revived, and he declined to leave the court; and, by the indulgence of the magistrate, he was allowed to remain close to his son while the proceedings continued.

"Our duty," said the magistrate, "is painful, but we must do it. The crime, as against the prisoner at the bar, will be by no means prejudiced by having this evidence added to the deposition, as the question regarding the identity of the writing in the pocket-book can be fully and carefully entered into at the trial."

"We can have no possible objection," said Mr. North.

"Then the prisoner is committed, and——"

A note was handed to the magistrate at this moment by one of the officers of the court, and after glancing at it, he handed it to Mr. North, without a word. That gentleman looked at it, and then said aloud—

"More evidence? Let us hear it, by all means. Who is this Mr. Grey, and where is he?"

"Here," said a voice, from near the door of the court, a pompous man made his appearance with some difficulty through the dense throng, and all eyes were bent upon him. No one looked with more intense anxiety upon these proceedings than Arthur Wilton himself. It seemed to him as if the agents of another world had entered into some dreadful conspiracy to try to prove him guilty of that act which had never even crossed his imagination, and which he would have tried to prevent another from committing.

"From this note that you have handed up to me, sir," said the magistrate, "it appears that you have something to say in the case. Pray what is it, and who are you?"

"My name is Grey, and I am a clerk in the Steam Packet Office, in London. I came here by direction of our manager, who received a note, which I bring with me, and which bears upon this case."

"It is the manager, then, and not you who should have come," said the magistrate."

"He thought, sir, that I was the proper person, as I had first received the note, and opened it in the usual way of business."

"Oh, very well. In that case, then, we can take your evidence; but what induced you to think, or to suspect that it had anything to do with this case?"

"Seeing a report of the case in the newspaper, sir."

The man handed the note up to the magistrate, who read it aloud as follows:—

"Barracks, Riversdale, Devon

"To the Manager at the General Steam Packet Company Office.

"Sir,—Can you be so good as to inform me, provided I arrive in London any morning by an early hour, by what route I can most expeditiously make a Dutch Port? Is Hamburgh open to English visitors? Please to address as above.

"I am, sir,

"Yours faithfully,

"ARTHUR WILTON."

The reader will not fail to recognise this note as the one which Captain Strachan had written as part of his plan for the purpose of aiding in fixing the weight of his own guilt upon poor Arthur Wilton.

The sensation that the reading of this

note produced was very painful, indeed. There was a general movement among all the spectators in court, and those even who were most favourably inclined towards poor Arthur, looked at each other as much as to say—

"After all, then, this man must be guilty!"

As for poor Arthur himself, he was so astounded at this strange accumulation of evidence against him, not any of which had the remotest foundation in fact, that his bewildered look increased each moment, and it would have required a very unusually powerful intellect indeed to stand out against such matters, so far as to believe that they could, by any possibility, be real.

"I have but one hope," said Arthur to himself, "and that is, that I shall not go absolutely mad."

"Do you swear," said the magistrate to the witness, "that you received this letter by the post?"

"I do, sir."

"And did you answer it?"

"Yes, sir."

"Can any one say what has become of that answer?"

No one spoke.

"Well, the letter must be added to the depositions. Does the prisoner or his counsel wish to say anything concerning it?"

"Yes," said Wilton. "I never wrote such a letter."

"Very well; then, I presume, we may now consider that the proceedings are over. Perhaps it is all the better, for the purpose of truth in this inquiry, that such matters as we have heard to day have come out so fully."

"It is so, sir," said Mr. North, "I feel—speaking, of course, for the prisoner at the bar—that it is far better he should know the full extent of the frightful plot in which he is encircled, than that there should be anything yet to learn, although I suspect that there may yet be some other stroke of duplicity to become apparent."

"Of that we know nothing," said the magistrate; "our duty is to commit the prisoner to a jury, and he stands committed accordingly."

"Stop!" cried a voice.

"Who is that?"

"Me!" shouted Mr. Flummery, making forward with a little canvas bag in his hand. "Me!"

"Who are you, sir?"

"Flummery is my name. He didn't do it. Not he. I tell your worships he ain't the sort of man to do it; but to put an end to any further bother, I've come to be the bail for him, so that he may go home comfortably with his poor old father, and Mr. Revis, and Miss Amelia, as he ought to do."

"My good man, this is not a bailable offence," said the magistrate, mildly.

"Oh, we will soon see that; perhaps you think that I haven't got enough; but look there!—look there!"

Giving the canvas bag a shake by one corner, Mr. Flummery rolled out of it, on to the table in front of the magistrates, a variety of coins, consisting of gold, silver, and copper, of every kind and description.

"Look there," he added. "Twenty puns, and no mistake—twenty puns. Take it all, and let Mr. Arthur go, for, I tell your worship, he no more did this here murdering affair than I did."

"My good fellow, you don't know what you say," said the magistrate, kindly. "Pray take up your money and go."

"Oh, do—do take it."

"We cannot."

"Then, who will? Oh, Mr. Arthur, do take it—I beg that you will take it."

Arthur shook his head.

"Will any lawyer take it, and do all the good he can for Mr. Wilton? It can't be ill-bestowed, then," sobbed poor Flummery.

"My dear friend," said a voice, "I will."

"Oh, thank you—thank you—the devil!"

Mr. Flummery had suddenly grasped the extended hand of Mr. Huncks, who, finding that twenty pounds were a-begging, as it were, could not resist the temptation of trying to bag them upon his own account.

"My dear Flummery," began Huncks, "I——"

"Hold your row. I don't want to have anything to say to you, you wagabone!"

"What did you say?"

"You wagabone!"

"I don't know whether that isn't actionable, and if it is, I'd advise you to look out, Mr. Flummery, for I shall get your twenty puns, as you call them, after all. Hem! of course, I shall be happy to take a fee from either side—hem! Mr. F."

"Get along with you," said Flummery; "you know Mr. Wilton didn't do it—you know that well enough."

"Ha—ha! Who did, then?"

"Why, your friend the captain—Strachan did it. You and Strachan did it between you, you know that well enough. I don't know how you did it, but perhaps I shall find out."

"A libel! A horrid libel!" cried Huncks, lifting up his hands. "A dreadful libel! Upon my reputation, a formidable libel! Ha! Now, Mr. F., I have you on the hip—hem! The twenty *puns* are as good as gone."

The magistrates had risen while this little interlude between Mr. Flummery and Huncks proceeded, and one of them said—

"Who is this Strachan that was spoken of?"

"I can tell you, sir," said Major Cuthbert, who was sitting upon the magistrates' bench.

"Then come and dine with me, major, if you pease."

"With pleasure; but I promised to take something with Captain Grant of ours, so I'm afraid——"

"Bring him with you. This case now is done with, so far as I am concerned, and I may hear anything I like about it, or express what opinion I please, you know. I have done my duty, and sent it to be investigated before a jury, without in any way pre-judging it; so now I am a free agent in the matter. Mr. Flummery?"

"Yes, yer *washup*?" said Flummery.

"Call at my house in the evening; and, in the meantime, take care of your twenty pounds."

Arthur Wilton was removed from the bar, and strongly guarded as he was taken back to the prison. Mr. North and Mr. Anderson, as his legal advisers, claimed the right of accompanying him, so they went in the coach with the officers and their prisoner. Mr. Huncks had his feelings so lacerated by Mr. Flummery, that he quite reeled into the thick of the crowd, crying out—

"A libel! A most atrocious libel! Hem! I will bring an action. Huncks *v.* Flummery—special jury case—damages one thousand pounds. A most scandalous and horrible libel."

"Why, that be Huncks, the lawyer," said a countryman.

"To be sure," said another. "He took my cow and a calf last week, for tithes due, he said, to the vicar, as he's the vicar's agent for that sort of robbery, you see."

"Drat him," said another, "he put me in prison in Exeter, all along of a rabbit, that he would have was a hare."

"Why, good gracious, Lawyer Huncks," cried another. "How dost thee do, man—eh?"

"Get out of the way, bumpkin!"

Bang! went the broad, flat hand of a poacher upon the top of Mr. Huncks's hat, and, in a moment, it was down to his chin, and his nose nearly wrenched off in the process.

"Don't pump upon him!" said a voice.

In the market-place, close at hand, the town authorities had only recently erected, over an ancient spring, a very large and elegant pump, and now, with a shout of approval of the suggestion, half-a-dozen of the sturdy countrymen lifted Mr. Huncks off the ground, and carried him towards the pump.

It was in vain that Mr. Huncks shouted "Murder!" it was exqually in vain that he brought to his aid the cry of "Fire!" His assailants only laughed the more, and Mr. Flummery kept calling out—

"Oh, my eye! what a shame to pump upon old Huncks. What a shame for two or three to hold him under the blessed spout while two more pump away like mad! What a shame to turn him round and round like a piece of meat a-roasting, that you wants to brown nicely! Oh, ain't it a shame to keep on at it till he can't move at all! Oh, lor!"

"Murder!" shouted Huncks, as the first deluge of cold water came upon him, and then he fell into the sink of the pump, and for three minutes a fearful shower of water come upon him.

"That will do," said Flummery. "Lots of ale to-night at the Blue Lion. I'll spend one of the twenty puns."

The mob dispersed rapidly, leaving Mr. Huncks half dead in the sink of the town pump.

CHAPTER LXIV.

THE MYSTERIES OF ARTHUR WILTON'S POSITION INCREASE INSTEAD OF DIMINISHING.

MAJOR CUTHBERT, Captain Grant, and the surgeon of the regiment, dined with the committing magistrate.

When the major, with the magistrate, left the court-house arm-in-arm, they met Captain Grant with the surgeon, and the major said—

"Grant, Mr. Bathurst, here, has been so kind as to ask me to dine, and likewise to add how much pleasure he would have if you would join us, and I know you will."

"Certainly, with great pleasure."

"This gentlemen is your surgeon, I presume?" said the magistrate.

"Yes, sir."

"I hope, sir, you are disengaged, and will do me the favour of joining me?"

"With pleasure," said the surgeon.

STRACHAN ESCAPING FROM THE ROOM OF THE MURDERED COLONEL.

"We were just talking about that poor fellow, Wilton, and wondering whether we really thought him innocent or guilty; for our minds are in a painful state of turmoil in this matter."

"I should like to talk over the matter with you all, gentlemen, after dinner," said the magistrate, "for, now that I have nothing further to do with it in a judicial sense, I feel myself at liberty to use my judgment and my tongue like any one else upon the matter."

The three gentlemen then dined with the magistrate, and after the cloth was removed, and the magistrate's lady and her sister, who had sat at the table, had retired, the magistrate said—

"Now, gentlemen, is it, or is it not, quite plain to you as impertinent upon my part, to say—who is this Captain Strachan of your regiment, who was, by a man in court to-day, madly accused of the murder of your late respected colonel?"

"You may say a nything you lie, sir, of Captain Strachan, without giving any offence to me," said the major; "the only unhappy thing is, that he does belong to the regiment ; but after what has been intimated to him, I may say, by every officer in it, he cannot long disgrace us by his presence among us."

"I hope not," said Captain Grant. "Confound the fellow, I wonder how he could stay an hour after what the colonel said to him."

"He is a very great rogue, no doubt," said the surgeon; "and yet it is surprising what ability he has—ay, and candour, too, in any affair that does not interfere with him or his plans."

"How do you mean?" said the major. "You talk of Strachan's candour ? Upon my life, doctor, that is something new."

"Yes," said Captain Grant, "I think that is a dose the doctor won't persuade us to swallow."

"Not a bit of it."

"Well, but stop, now," said the surgeon, "and listen to me. Strachan has been very ill."

"Agreed, as you say so."

"Well, of course, I came into contact with him ; and I will say that the medicines I gave him did wonders, and he expressed as much in—in—the—a—a—"

Both the major and the captain burst into a peal of laughter, and then the former called out—

"This is capital. Strachan has found out the weak side of Esculapius. Ha ! ha !"

"Decidedly," said the captain. "He has clapped an emollient plaster on the feelings of the doctor."

"And," added the major, "made him swallow a sedative to his profound endowments."

"Take flattery, two ounces."

"Gammon, half-a-pound."

"Lies, *quantum suff.*"

"And cram the dose down the doctor's throat, after gammoning him well with adulation."

"Ha—ha—ha!"

"Go it, gentlemen," said the doctor, "go it. You do it remarkably well; but I still persist that Strachan's was a wonderful cure, and that the way in which he expressed as much would have been very gratifying, if it had come from any other man."

"My dear doctor," said the major, "you are the best fellow that ever lived ; but you are no more a match for the rascality of such a fellow as Strachan, than I, in strength, to Hercules."

"Oh, well—well——"

"But," said the magistrate, "when did this illness begin?"

"Just a day or two before the murder."

"Then he was not in a good state to commit it, even if he had felt the disposition to do so."

"A good state !" said the surgeon. "I can assure you, sir, that he never left his bed during an interval of two days before the murder of the colonel, and two after it."

The magistrate looked thoughtful.

"And this very—very bad man," he said, "would really, if he had been about, have stood a good chance of being suspected."

"He would," said the major. "My opinion of Strachan is such, that I could as readily believe him guilty as I do Wilton innocent."

"You believe Wilton innocent, major?"

"I do."

"And I don't know what to think," said Captain Grant.

"Nor I," said the doctor. "It wasn't Strachan, and, therefore, we are all abroad in the matter, and it may be anybody. If he had only been out and about, I should have thought that yet something would have come out to implicate him."

"Yes," said the major. "I saw his face when poor Percival spoke to him as he did, and desired him to quit his regiment; and if ever the glance of a fiend came forth from human eyes, such was the look with which Strachan regarded our lost friend."

"Just so," said Grant. "I saw it, too."

"Gentlemen," said the magistrate, "I am free to confess that, in all my judicial experience, I never met with a case that gave me so much real uneasiness as this. The convictions seem to blow hot and cold. Evidence is piled upon evidence to prove the guilt of Arthur Wilton ; and yet the whole of that evidence appears to be flatly contradicted by the words and manner of the man himself. I do most sincerely hope that from out all these painful complexities the truth will at last come."

"Amen!" said Major Cuthbert, "and I believe it will, too."

"You are quite sure, doctor," added the magistrate, "that Captain Strachan did not leave the barracks that night?"

"The thing was impossible. The man was completely prevented by severe illness. He could not have killed a fly."

"And, besides, sir," added the major, "it is quite out of the question that he could have left the barracks for five minutes without the guard at the gate being aware of it."

"Oh, true—true !"

"You see, we are perfectly satisfied in that respect. The sergeant of the guard has to enter in his order-book the name of any officer going from the barracks after gun-fire, as we call the hour when the gates are shut upon the out-of-door world. This is not done as any check upon the officers, for they go out and come in as they please, but it is a part of the regular duty of a guard to know who passes its post, and if the commander-in-chief were the person, his name and rank would be entered just the same as mine or Grant's."

"Just so," said the captain.

"Then Strachan is as clear," said the magistrate, "as I am from even the shadow of a suspicion. He could not leave the barracks, and, ergo, he could not commit a murder some mile or two off."

"That is it."

"By-the-by, doctor," said Captain Grant, turning to the surgeon with a curious look, "you were out that night for some time. Did you see or hear anything suspicious?"

"I?"

"Yes; you were out between twelve and two, you know."

"I out—out of the barracks on the night of the colonel's murder, between twelve and two!"

"To be sure you were."

"I beg to assure you, Captain Grant, that I went to bed at eleven o'clock on that night, and slept uncommonly sound till I was awakened by the drums in the morning!"

At this rather startling announcement, under the circumstances, upon the part of the surgeon, Captain Grant and Major Cuthbert sprang from their seats, and the magistrate dropped a walnut that he had been carefully peeling, and looked very much surprised indeed.

The surgeon himself looked rather taken aback at these tokens of astonishment regarding his movements.

"Why—why," he said. "What do you mean by all this? What are you all staring at?"

"I am surprised at the actions of your friends," said the magistrate, "for I know nothing about this affair."

"Come—come," said the surgeon, "I am quite surprised, Major Cuthbert, that you can make such a jest upon so serious a subject, as anything connected with the death of our unfortunate and deeply lamented colonel must be."

"I make a jest of it?"

"Yes, to be sure. What else?"

"You mistake me very much, doctor. I never was more serious in all my life."

The order-book of the guard was brought to me at my own particular request on the morning of the murder, and there is an entry that you left the barracks about twelve, and did not reach them again until nearly two or thereabouts—I won't be positive as to the hours but I am quite positive as to the fact, and you shall see the book yourself.

"It is as Cuthbert says it is, doctor," said the captain, "I have seen the entry in the order-book, and there can be no mistake about it."

CHAPTER LXV.

CAPTAIN STRACHAN ASTONISHES MR. HUNCK'S WITH THE EMERALD.

THE magistrate listened to this discourse of the officers with the greatest possible interest, and availing himself then of a pause in the conversation, he said to the doctor—

"Pray pardon me, sir, for putting the question to you in so positive and apparently rude a manner, but I would ask is it possible or not that you may be mistaken?"

"Mistaken?"

"Yes, sir. I hope there is no offence?"

"None in the world; but allow me to say that the idea of my being mistaken as to whether I was in bed and asleep or out of the barracks on the night in question is too absurd. I have not been out at night since the arrival of the regiment recently, and so, once for all, I beg to say that the statement in the order-book is false."

Major Cuthbert looked at Captain Grant, and the captain looked at the major. The magistrate felt very uneasy, for he did not know what to make of the affair. It was by far too complicated and enveloped in mystery for him just then to be able to come to any conclusion upon it. Still there was a strange suspicion in his mind that in some way it had a relation to the fact of the innocence or guilt of Arthur Wilton, and he made up his mind that it should not rest there.

The officers made up their minds to the same purpose, and so did the surgeon, who cried out—

"Presume that I was out of the barracks on the night in question, and I will let you arrest me on suspicion of the murder."

"Oh, stuff," said Major Cuthbert. "That is not the question at all, my dear fellow. The extraordinary thing is, how the fact came to be recorded in the order-book."

"But it ain't a fact."

"Well, the mistake, then."

"Yes, that is nearer the mark, and I don't mean to rest till I have sifted that matter to the bottom."

"Nor I," said the captain.

"Nor I," said the surgeon, rising, "and I am sufficiently anxious about it to propose that, if our hospitable and kind host will not think that we are putting any slight upon his hospitality by so doing, we will go at once to the barracks, and look into the affair without further loss of time."

"I am both ready and willing," said the magistrate.

"So am I," said Major Cuthbert. "Will you, sir, make our apologies to the ladies for this seeming rudeness, and we will then go to the barracks at once together?"

"I will do so," said the magistrate. "I will tell them that we shall return in a few hours at the utmost."

The magistrate ordered his carriage to be in readiness as soon as possible, and then, after briefly explaining to his wife that business called him out for an hour or two, and that the two officers would go with him, they started for the barracks, to try to follow up this first clue to the guilt of Captain Strachan which had been obtained, although they had no suspicion at the time that it was such a trail that they had got upon, for they only felt what a mystery they were enveloped in, without being able to come to any satisfactory explanation concerning it.

The magistrate's coachman saw that his master was anxious to get to the barracks, so the well-kept horses were put to their mettle a little more than usual, and the distance was soon traversed.

"You see," said Major Cuthbert, as the great gate of the barracks was opened to allow the carriage to pass in. "You see, by even our daylight arrangements here, how utterly impossible it is for any one to pass in or out without ample observation."

"I do," said the magistrate; "but permit me to say, that such a caution only increases the mystery of the whole transaction."

"Just so," said Captain Grant; "for, as the doctor did not go out, why the odd thing is that he should be reported to have done so."

"Now, you see," said the surgeon, as they crossed the barrack-yard, "it is possible enough that there might be an omission to record the fact of some officer leaving the barracks. I say such a thing might occur, although, with habits of military discipline, it is not likely; but no carelessness, no neglect could induce a man to open a book, and make an entry of a circumstance that never happened."

The magistrate acknowledged that there lay the difficulty in the case; but they all soon reached the major's room, and then that officer said—

"Now we are come here, let us sift this matter thoroughly. It may, or it may not be of importance to do so; but still we cannot help feeling that even the remotest circumstance that took place on the night of poor Colonel Percival's death is worth consideration, and may be the key to the most important results."

"That is true," said the doctor; "so now I consider myself as upon my trial in this affair."

"No—no," said everybody.

"Oh, but I say yes," said the surgeon. "I have to prove that I did not leave the barracks on the night in question."

"Pardon me, sir," said the magistrate. "Do not fancy that you have to prove any such thing. It is others that have to prove you did do so; and then, when it is proved, I can't say that I see the bearing it has upon the colonel's murder."

There was a flush upon the face of the surgeon, as he said—

"Unless I did it."

"Come, come," said the major, "this is nonsense. As a matter of curiosity let us find out the truth in this matter."

The major rang for his servant, and ordered that the officer on duty on the night in question should come to him.

That officer was a young man named Hoilton, and he at once attended the major.

"Now, Hoilton," said the major, "we want the sergeant who was on your guard on the night of poor Percival's murder, and we want all the men. Can we get at them at once?"

"To be sure, major."

"And the order-book, too?"

"Yes, I will set about it."

"Don't say what we want with them, Hoilton; but the fact is, we want to know who left the barracks on that night."

"No one passed my guard but the surgeon."

"But I did not pass your guard, Hoilton," said the surgeon. "I assure you, my good friend, that I was in bed, and asleep by eleven."

"Did you see him?" said the magistrate. "Did you yourself see the doctor, Mr. Hoilton?"

"No, sir; but the sergeant came to me and said—'the doctor has gone out, sir;

shall I enter it in the order-book?'—and I said—'To be sure.'"

"But I——"

"Now be quiet, doctor," said the major. "There is some mystery in this affair which we shall, I dare say, succeed in unravelling yet. Hoilton, go and get the men and the order-book."

The young officer went upon his errand, and in about ten minutes there was heard the tramp of a guard, and he re-entered the room, carrying the regimental order-book.

"They are all here," he said, "and here is the entry."

There it was, sure enough, and the surgeon himself stared at it in amazement, and did not know what to make of it.

"Do you walk in your sleep?" said Captain Grant.

"Oh, no—no."

"Well, let us hear the sergeant of the guard," said the major.

The sergeant was called in, and respectfully saluted his officers.

"Did you see any one pass your guard, on the night of the murder of Colonel Percival?" said the major.

"Yes, your honour. The doctor."

"You saw him?"

"Yes, your honour, I did."

"Are you sure of that?" said the surgeon.

"Oh, yes, sir. Quite sure."

"How was I dressed?"

"Your own uniform coat, sir, and your cocked-hat as usual, sir, at night, if you please."

"Very well," said the major; "now let us hear the sentinel."

The soldier on duty was called, and distinctly stated that the doctor had passed his post.

"Good gracious! did you speak to me?" said the surgeon.

"No, sir."

"Very well," said the major. "Did any other of the guard see him, can you tell me?"

"Yes, sir. Private 202, White, saw him, and spoke to him, after he came back, or as he went out."

"The devil, he did!" said the doctor.

"Hush—hush! Send 202 here."

Now this 202 was the man who had stopped Captain Strachan in the barrack-yard, and said to him that he was no better; and when he was called before his officers, he deposed, with all the calmness in the world, to this fact; and turning to the doctor, added, in the most provoking way in the world, to that amazed practitioner—

"I am better now, sir, if you please."

"Go to the deuce!" said the surgeon. "I never met you at all, nor asked you anything at all."

"Beg pardon, sir; it was I who asked you."

"You can go," said the major.

The room was clear again; and then the major said, in a voice of great surprise—

"I don't know what on earth to make of this, doctor. Can any one of you favour me with a hypothesis upon the subject? for I declare that I am all abroad. You see, there is no other officer wears such a hat as our surgeon, and he is, in fact, well known to all in the regiment; and that the guard think they are right, there can be no doubt at all."

"I'll tell you, major, what my opinion is," said young Hoilton. "I have listened to all that they said about it, and you know the night was dark and stormy, and it is quite clear they all went by the hat and coat."

"That's it," cried the surgeon. "Somebody has been out of the barracks, and borrowed my hat and coat. Why, it's the easiest thing in the world to do so. They are both in the common room. That's it—that's it."

The magistrate nodded; and Major Cuthbert, as he drew a long breath, said—

"That must be the explanation, and now we are all thrown abroad to find out who it was."

"Doctor," said young Hoilton, "have you examined your hat and coat since?"

"I?—No. It's an old coat that I have not had on for weeks, and there it hangs in the corner now."

"Get it, doctor," said the major, "I don't know how it is possible it may do so, but yet it seems as if that coat were so mixed up in this mystery, that it is worth the looking at."

The doctor rushed out of the room, and came back with his hat and coat in a minute.

"There they are, both of them," he cried.

"Allow me," said the magistrate, "gentlemen, if you please, to examine these articles well. I am, of course, used to judicial investigations, and may be able, with more art than you can bring to bear upon the question, to inquire into the affair."

As he spoke, the magistrate took the coat, and laid it upon the table, and they all looked at it with intense interest.

"Here is a piece of the skirt gone," said the magistrate, "and another piece just hanging by a few shreds. Ah! here is gravel upon it, and here a piece of moss sticking to one of the buttons. The whole front of it is discoloured and rubbed, as if it had been pressed against a brick-wall with violence. Here, too, is a layer of caked mud upon one of the sleeves."

They all looked at each other aghast, and the surgeon said—

"I tell you what it is, gentlemen, that is my coat, but how it came into that condition, I no more know than the man in the moon ; but I mean to say that there is evidence sufficient to empower you to take me into custody for the murder of Colonel Percival. So you may do so, if you like, and get me hung upon circumstantial evidence."

CHAPTER LXVI.

CAPTAIN STRACHAN FEARS THAT EVERYTHING IS NOT QUITE RIGHT.

THE manner of the surgeon, as he made the remark we have closed our last chapter with, was so ludicrously serious, that although none there present, were in any laughing mood, they could not forbear smiling at him.

"This is nonsense," said the major. "Here is a mystery, that is all, and it requires clearing up. What, sir, have you to propose?—(to the magistrate)—for I need not say that we feel ourselves all at your disposal in this most troublesome and intricate matter."

"Have you any objection, gentlemen, to going to the Abbey?"

"None in life."

"Then let us go there, and take the coat with us. What I want to see is, if the various stains upon it, and the bit of moss that sticks to the buttons, correspond in any way with the garden-wall at the back of the Abbey, over which Arthur Wilton says that, to the best of his belief, the assassin took his way."

"Come on," said the surgeon. "Commit me, all of you, do. I shall be hanged for this coat yet, I see. Indeed, I don't, myself, at all perceive how you can avoid it."

"We will manage to do so," said the major; "but I do, in good truth, think that you and your coat, doctor, will have more to do with the affair than you or any of us at first supposed."

They all got into the magistrate's carriage now again, and drove off to the Abbey; but just as they went out at the barrack-gates, who should be coming in but Captain Strachan in his undress. He drew himself up, and saluted the major, who stiffly returned the salute, and the magistrate took an eager and searching look in his face. Suddenly the colour forsook it, and Strachan looked as white as a sheet.

His eyes had fallen upon the surgeon's coat, which the magistrate had upon his arm very carefully.

Whatever the magistrate thought he kept to himself just at that time, but it was clear to them who were with him that his mind was very much pre-occupied with something, for he hardly for some time said a word; but at last he rallied, and requested that they would tell him all they knew of Captain Strachan.

The request of the magistrate was complied with, and if Strachan did not come out of the examination very creditably, he certainly could not blame any one but himself, for his brother officers rather took an indulgent and candid view of him and his actions than an ill-natured one; and so they reached the Abbey.

We need say nothing further of the proceedings at the Abbey than that the whole party were quite satisfied of the fact that the surgeon's coat had been on the back garden wall, and then they were all at fault, and could go no further.

We now return to Captain Strachan.

The sight of the surgeon's coat, although it could not tell him exactly the amount of his danger, at once convinced him that something was amiss, and that those who would spare neither pains nor expense to arrive at the truth, had struck upon a clue, which, if they could but follow it, would end in his destruction.

Hence was it that, with all his natural effrontery, the coward's colour fled from his cheeks at the moment that he saw the coat, and he felt as though he were going to faint.

The carriage had passed on, and was out of sight before he rallied sufficiently to enter the barrack-yard.

Then it was that Captain Strachan felt most fearfully his isolated position in the regiment. There was not one person of whom he could venture to ask a question; and although he felt the most intense anxiety to know what had been the cause of the visit of the magistrate to the barracks, he was compelled to endure all the tortures of suspense upon the subject.

As he passed a group of soldiers, he just caught the words, "But the doctor says he wasn't out at all," and he fairly staggered as he heard this, for they at once sufficed to let him know that, by some cross accident, the question of whether or not it was the doctor who had passed the barrack-gate upon the night of the murder of Colonel Percival was agitated.

Captain Strachan felt that his evidence would not have the belief of any one, and he made the best of his way to his own rooms.

When there, his first act was to lock the door, and then with a deep groan he flung himself into a seat, and sat for nearly half an hour without uttering a single word.

At length he did speak, and it was but to give utterance to the many fears that were tugging at his heart.

"What does it come to?" he said. "What is now the amount of the danger? Let me think—let me think!"

Resting his face upon his hands, so as to shut out a perception of all external objects, while he consulted his thoughts upon the perils of his position, he strove to take one of those kneen mental glances at all the risks and chances by which he was surrounded, which would either at once let him know what he had to fear or convince him that as yet he stood safe even from the shadow of suspicion.

Captain Strachan, though, like all really guilty persons, reasoned rather differently from what he felt.

His fears would not be dictated by his colder judgment, and he shook with apprehension while he assured himself of his safety.

"What can it all come to?" he said. "At the very worst, it comes to this, that the doctor declares some one has been out in his coat. Well, will he, in the face of his own knowledge of my state of seeming severe illness, so far stultify his judgment as to say that person was myself? Oh. no—no—no!"

Captain Strachan said "No," but still he was in a terrible fright for all that.

"All will be well," he said. "Quite well. Let the worst come to the worst—that the affair should be found so enveloped in mystery as to make it impossible for any jury to convict Arthur Wilton. Well, his acquittal is not my conviction. Oh, no—no. Who's that? No—I didn't do it. Hold! God! what is that?"

A sudden knocking at the door of his room had given him a terrible fright, and, pale and haggard, he rose from his seat, and laid his hand upon his sword.

The knocking continued.

"Who is there?" cried Strachan, in the best assumed voice he could assume. "Who is there?"

"Orderly sergeant, sir."

"Oh, come in."

The latch was tried, but Strachan had turned the key in the inside, so that the sergeant could not get in. Strachan saw the difficulty, and striding to the door, he unlocked it and flung it open.

"Oh, sir," said the sergeant.

"What's the matter?"

"Worse?"

"What do you mean? How dare you stare at me in that way?"

"Beg your pardon, sir; but you don't look so well as you did. I fear, sir, you are bad again."

Captain Strachan caught at the excuse for his look of ghastly apprehension, and seating himself, he said, faintly—

"Why—a—yes, sergeant. I think I went out and about rather to soon. Perhaps you will have the goodness to tell the surgeon that I am not so well as I hoped to be."

"He has gone out, sir, with the major; but as soon as he comes back I will tell him, sir."

"Thank you—thank you. What is that you have—a letter?"

"Yes, sir. A letter and a little parcel by the post for you, sir. Both paid, sir. I will tell the surgeon when he comes back, that you wish to see him—shall I, sir?"

"If you please, sergeant—thank you."

Strachan was alive again. He eagerly tore open the little parcel, and found a letter to the following effect :—

"SIR,—We duly received your favour, and beg to forward you an emerald, according to order, with which we hope you will be pleased. Hoping for the favour of future commands, we are, Sir,

"Your very obedient servants,

"SIMPSON AND HILL."

In a little pasteboard box that just held it and a roll of fine wool, was an emerald of considerable beauty.

Strachan drew a long breath.

"I had forgotten all about this," he said. "It is that rascal Huncks's fee; and now I am more than ever anxious to bind him to my interests. I will take it to him at once. It will be a relief to me to speak to even him."

Strachan destroyed the jeweller's letter, and the receipted bill that it contained, and taking the emerald loose in his purse, he set out from the barracks to pay a visit to his friend, Mr. Huncks, the lawyer.

The orderly sergeant, who happened to be at the gate of the barracks, looked rather surprised to see Strachan, whom he supposed to be very ill, indeed, going out; but, of course, he said nothing, and Strachan could not afford to attend to so trivial a matter as the surprise of the orderly sergeant.

At a rapid pace, Captain Strachan passed in the direction from the barracks to the house of the attorney, and pushing open the garden-gate, he walked up to the window of the room in which Mr. Huncks usually sat, and tapped at it with his fingers.

No answer was returned.

Strachan then went to the door, and rang loudly at the bell, and that summons produced the old woman who acted as servant of all-work to the attorney.

"Is Mr. Huncks within?" said Strachan.

"Bless me, sir, yes ; he is, and he isn't."

"What do you mean by that?"

"Why, Mr. Soldier, you must know as he's very bad, indeed, and has took to his blessed bed, Mr. Soldier. He ! he ! he !"

The old woman looked quite delighted at the idea of Mr. Huncks being obliged to take to his bed.

"Never mind," said Strachan, "I must see him upon business of importance, and you had better go and tell him so. What is the matter with him?"

"Oh, nothing but rheumatics in all his limbs and his back, that's all ; but he gives way to it."

"Oh, indeed?"

The old woman went to inform Mr. Huncks that he was wanted, and as she had an idea that it gave him great pain to move, she greatly exaggerated the message of Captain Strachan, and made Huncks believe that something very serious had occurred ; so with many groans he got up, and completely encased in flannel, with a nightcap with long lappets of the same material, and over all, an immense wadded dressing-gown, Mr. Huncks crept, nearly bent double, down stairs, to see his visitor, whom he found seated by the fire.

"Oh, oh, oh !" said Huncks.

"Why, what the devil is the matter with you now?"

"Oh, oh, oh !"

"Well, I don't come here to listen to your complaints ; I want your advice. I suppose, as long as there is life in you, you can give that?"

"My dear sir, there is not much—oh!—life in me—Oh!"

"What has happened?"

"Don't—don't ask. Oh—oh!"

"Yes, but you were well enough a day or so ago. What on earth has put you into this state, Huncks?"

"I—oh—yes ! Oh, Captain Strachan,

were you ever—oh—oh—my back—m legs !—oh, were you ever pumped upon?

"Ever what?"

"Pumped upon?"

"How dare you ask me such a question You scoundrel, what do you mean by the insinuation?"

"Oh, it is not an insinuation, I assur you. I only wish I had been pumped upo by insinuation. Oh, dear, my back—m legs—my neck ! Oh—oh !"

"I tell you what it is, Huncks," sai Captain Strachan, with calm serenity "my opinion is that, for some purpos of your own, of which I know nothing and concerning which I cannot pretend t guess, you are acting a part."

"Oh, indeed?"

"Yes ; you fancy that it will answe some object of yours to be very bad. I may deceive the world, but I know you to well, old friend, to be taken in by any suc flimsy practices, I assure you.'

CHAPTER LXVII.

MR. HUNCKS THINKS HE HAS HIS FOR
TUNE IN HIS GRASP.

CAPTAIN STRACHAN accompanied thes words that he uttered to Mr. Huncks b such a deriding kind of laugh, that th lawyer, who was really suffering from a acute attack of rheumatism, fairly groane again.

"Oh, go on," said Strachan ; "you do it very well, indeed. It might impose upo another, but not upon me."

"Oh! oh! oh!"

"Upon my life, Huncks, you are a good actor."

"An actor—I an actor? Do you think that I would adopt any such low calling? Why, you might as well call me an author, if you want to insult me."

"Good—capital ! Where is the principal pain now, my dear Huncks? Is it in your back, or in you conscience—eh?"

"If people's consciences, Captain Strachan, gave them pain when they go out of order, I really cannot help thinking that yours would be in a continual stat of agony."

"Indeed?"

"Precisely so ; and now I revert to my original question of — Were you eve pumped upon?"

"And I tell you, that if you ask tha question again, I will pull your nose for you."

"For which indignity," said Huncks, "I will forgive you on the morning of your execution for the murder of——

THE DISCOVERY OF THE MURDER.

"Hush! idiot!"

"Ha! ha!"

"Say no more. This is folly, indeed. For us to quarrel is positive madness, when by hanging together we——"

"Stop, you go too far there, noble captain. We shall not hang together. If there is to be any hanging in the case, you may depend upon it that I will take care you shall have it all to yourself."

"No, Mr. Huncks," said Captain Strachan, savagely, "if there is to be any hanging in the case, you shall be with me in the process; for I will then declare your cognizance of the murder !"

"After the fact."

"That will do equally well."

"No, it won't. I am a solicitor."

"You don't mean to say that you are any the less of a rogue on that account, surely, do you?"

"Not at all; but my story is very simple. You came to me as a client, and whatever you tell me is confidential, even if it go the length of a confession of the fact of your guilt of a capital felony. My dear captain, I am very safe—very safe. But you need not look so blank, for that is all in your favour, as it enables me, upon being properly remunerated, to aid you better by far than as if I were in any way implicated in the consequences of your guilt."

"Huncks?" said Captain Strachan. 'Huncks?"

"Strachan — Strachan?" said the lawyer.

"How are you now?"

"A little better."

"So I thought. We won't quarrel, Huncks. And now tell me why you thought proper to imitate being in this condition?"

"It is, unfortunately, real. The mob, for no cause that I can tell, got hold of me outside the court-house at Exeter, and —and pumped upon me, till I had hardly a spark of life in me. I am, unfortunately, of a rheumatic tendency, and the consequence has been such an accession of pains, that I don't know, at times, how to move or breathe in consequence of it."

"I pity you."

"Oh, thank you. Don't trouble yourself. I hope, by the aid of such medicines as I know of, to be soon better; but at present it is no joke, I assure you. You come with some news, I suppose, captain?"

"I do—I do."

"Well, is it good or bad?"

"Bad."

"Ah, well, things do not always turn out quite as we wish them. Are you, then, really at last suspected?"

"Oh, no—no. Do not think that. I should hardly be so calm as I am if I were suspected; but the fact is, a little circumstance, my good friend, has happened, which has given me much uneasiness."

The captain then related to Huncks the story about the great coat, adding at its conclusion:—

"I don't know that I ought to apprehend anything from the circumstance, but still it looks as if our enemies were on the right scent, and so it is uncomfortable."

"Just so."

"What would you advise, then, Huncks?"

"Captain Strachan?"

"Well?—well?"

"Advice gratis, all over this mortal sphere, has been generally agreed to be of very, very little use to anybody, besides not being at all profitable to him who gives it. I am quite sure, Captain Strachan,

that as a man of sense and judgment, you can appreciate the sentiment."

"I understand you; but I am out of funds."

"Hem! There are the jewels and the little etceteras of the colonel, deceased, which you say are buried in the wood."

"They are—they are."

"Hem!"

"But, Huncks, I assure you you shall have a moiety of whatever is there; and if I had only known that you would not be satisfied to wait a little, I would have taken some of the jewels at once and brought them to you."

"Ah," said Huncks, "if you had done that now, one might have said something to this affair. Not only would it have put one's mind at ease as to the correctness of your memory, my dear sir, regarding the fact of burying such a treasure at all or no, but it would have been satisfactory in another way."

"Well, I admit all that; but the fact is, in my hurry, all I took was one jewel from a small bagful. It dropped out, and I picked it up, and put it in my pocket. I don't know whether it is of any value or not, for I am not a judge of such things."

"Oh, indeed. Why don't you show it to me?"

"I will do so with pleasure; and not only will I show it to you, but I will give it to you if you like, as an earnest of what you are eventually to have, my good friend."

Mr. Huncks half-shut his little pig-like eyes, and peered in the face of Captain Strachan, as if he would have said—

"What excuse now will you make for backing out of this apparently frank offer, I wonder?"

Strachan took out his purse.

"This is the only specimen, I may say, that I am able to produce," he remarked, "of the wealth that lies buried, awaiting the ownership of yourself; and if this be of any value, I should say that what is there is worth a thousand times as much; but, as I say, I am no judge of these things."

The emerald was duly produced, now, and handed to Mr. Huncks, who took it eagerly in his hand and glared at it.

"Green," he said.

"Yes, very green," said the captain.

"Eh?"

"I only said green. It is green."

"Oh, oh! Then pray, captain, what do you take it to be?"

"Emeralds are green, I believe, though

really, I don't know a bit of glass from a precious stone."

"It looks the thing. There is a working-jeweller in the village, and I dare say he would know what it was worth."

"If anything at all," added Captain Strachan, carelessly; "and yet it don't seem probable that such a man as Colonel Percival would have little bags full of such stones of different colours and sizes, and put them by so carefully, if they were worthless."

"Oh dear, no. Bags full—bags full?"

"Yes. I should think that at the storming of some Indian principality, do you know, Huncks, he must have lit upon such a treasure. What, suppose now they were to turn out to be worth ten times what we fancy! Perhaps he even did not know the value of them."

"Perhaps not."

"Or, if he did, perhaps he dared not produce them."

"That, too, is possible; but you will give me this stone, captain?"

"Cheerfully."

"Very good, then. I will think over carefully what you have said to me about the great coat, and it is likely enough I may think of a plan to counteract any ill effects from such a circumstance. At all events, be quite sure of one thing, and that is, that your best policy is just at present to be quiet. If anytning serious should happen, throwing direct suspicion upon you I will then adopt a bold line of conduct that will have a good effect. Leave me alone for a nice little plot, and—and—Oh—oh! that pain again. Oh!"

"This illness of yours, Huncks, is very unlucky."

"It is—it is."

"You must try to get the better of it as soon as you can."

"Trust me for that; and when I do get the better of it, those who are mixed up in the affair shall not hear the last of it for some time, I can promise them. Oh, dear—oh, dear! If they had only kicked me, it wouldn't have been near so bad—or—or horsewhipped me. I have been caned, and kicked, and horsewhipped, but I never was pumped upon till this time, and I don't like it at all. Good-day, captain; I must go to bed again, for I feel in the most intolerable pain."

Captain Strachan left Mr. Huncks, quite satisfied, in his own mind, that he had thoroughly awakened all his cupidity, and put an end to all his doubts of the genuineness of the colonel's treasures, by the production of the emerald.

That circumstances might occur, in which he might need an unscrupulous friend, such as Huncks, Captain Strachan dreaded; and now he considered that he had fully secured him. After the whole affair was done with, he, Captain Strachan, cared nothing for the effect that Huncks's disappointment might have upon him; and, in fact, he really chuckled to himself at the prospect of the agony the lawyer would be in at finding that the story of the colonel's treasure was but an empty delusion.

The moment Captain Strachan had left his house, Huncks called to his old servant, saying—

"Go to Mr. Brown, in the village, and tell him the kitchen-clock wants looking to. Ask him to come at once, as I want him to look at my watch, likewise, will you?"

"Ah," said the old woman, "it's true enough the kitchen-clock wants looking to, and it has wanted it for I don't know how long, and I have told you of it till I am tired. However, it's a good thing you have thought of it at last."

The jeweller and clock and watch repairer of the district was soon at the cottage of Mr. Huncks. The kitchen-clock was out of order, and Mr. Huncks's watch wanted repairing. As he spoke to Mr. Brown, Huncks contrived to knock off the chimney-piece the emerald, and Mr. Brown, as Huncks was so bad with the rheumatism, picked it up for him.

"Why, Mr. Huncks," he said, "what have we here?"

"It's a stone that belonged to my great aunt," said Huncks. "The old lady used to think a great deal of it."

"And well she might," said the jeweller, as he breathed upon it, and then held it up to the light. "It's a very fine emerald."

"Oh, yes, it's an emerald."

"It is, indeed, Mr. Huncks; there is no mistake about that. I wonder you don't take more care of it."

"Oh, it is safe enough. What is it worth, do you think?"

"Well, I can't say to a pound or two; but twenty, or thirty pounds, would be wanted for such a one; I can tell you."

"So I thought about that sum. You will do the watch as soon as you can, Mr. Brown?"

"Certainly, sir. Good-morning, Mr. Huncks."

"Ah," said Huncks, as he held the emerald up to the light when he was alone; "twenty or thirty pounds, eh? and there are bags full of them. Bags full—hundreds of such things. Others, perhaps, worth ten, ay—twenty times the money that this is. What a prize! I must have them all—all. I—I will leave England for ever with such a treasure. I will set up as a German Baron. A baron, do I say? I can go and buy a principality in Germany, and be the Grand Duke something. His Serene Highness of Kicknoicklesburgh, or some such name—or Coburg and Gotha, or some such stuff. Bah! it is stuff. A German Prince! I'd better stay and try to be an English gentleman. Yes, I'll stay here, though I will go abroad to change my jewels into cash. I shall be rich at last—rich!—rich!"

CHAPTER LXVIII.

THE DAY OF ARTHUR WILTON'S TRIAL ARRIVES AT LAST.

No man in all the world could now be more perfectly satisfied than was Mr. Huncks, with the idea that he was on the high-road to that wealth and that power which wealth in this country gives. The emerald had completely dazzled his eyes, and he considered that all he had to do was to stick to Captain Strachan until he had got possession of the secret of where the remainder of the jewels were hidden.

No man could be much better satisfied than was Strachan of the fact that he had bought the best services of the lawyer in case of need, and as he heard nothing further of the coat business, his mind calmed down regarding that, too; and he hugged himself with the thought that Arthur Wilton was, indeed, and in truth, a doomed man.

The reader, now, will find it necessary thoroughly to understand the position of all the parties in this singular drama, before proceeding with the events which the strange trial was so prolific of.

The actions and the motions of Captain Strachan are as plain and clear as daylight, and it no longer remains any mystery why it was that he persecuted old Mr. Revis, and how it was that he came to have such a power over him. The affection of the old man for his profligate son had been the source from which Strachan had plucked the poison to wound him.

There can, at the same time, be no doubt but that Strachan, in his own vitiated mind, thought that in the way in which the property, which he had fondly hugged himself into a belief would be his own, had been disposed of, he had good ground for quarrel with Mr. Revis. The reader, however, who, from the statement of the old man to Amelia, is in possession of the real facts of the case, cannot fail to see that Strachan had been treated with a liberality that he was far, very far, indeed, from deserving.

We may say, now, that among the converts to the opinion of the entire guiltlessness of Arthur Wilton, might be ranked Mrs. Percival. Her mode of life before her marriage with the colonel had had the effect of giving her much self-reliance, and of inducing her to depend much upon her own reason, so that when the first shock—and a dreadful one it was—of the murder of her husband was passed, and she had had a second interview with Amelia, she could no longer permit herself to doubt but that the murder of the colonel was involved in the greatest possible mystery, and that that mystery was not to be properly solved by any supposition of guilt upon the part of Arthur Wilton.

It was an immense consolation to Amelia to find that Mrs. Percival was in this frame of mind.

And here, indeed, we may say, that scarcely an hour had passed since the arrest of Arthur Wilton, upon the terrible charge, without witnessing some converts to the fact of his innocence; and although in real truth the evidence—the circumstantial evidence—as against him, remained just where it was, the opinion that he was guiltless had so increased, that men shuddered at the idea of being placed in such a situation as to be compelled to say "Ay," or "No," upon the question of life or death to him.

So strange a combination of circumstances regarding a man charged with so horrible an offence, was surely never before presented.

All the circumstances were against him, and all the opinions in favour of him. What will be the result of this most singular combination of events, we shall soon see, for the day of trial came at last, and expectation was on tip-toe as to the result.

The excitement that the trial of Arthur Wilton for the murder of Colonel Percival created throughout the whole of England, was immense, and the influx of strangers into Exeter, the day before, was such as had never been equalled in the memory of that remarkable person, the oldest inhabitant.

From all the surrounding towns—from London, and in some instances from places still further removed from the scene of action—strangers had arrived in numbers, so as to be present, if possible, at the trial.

It was quite clear that no court-house in England would suffice to accommodate one tithe of the number of people who came to Exeter to be present at the trial, but still they poured into the city thick and three-fold.

The number of military officers who sought the spot was immense. The benches were full to overflowing, and you met in the streets, go where you would, with eager little groups, whose air and carriage at once bespoke their professional pursuit.

And none the less attractive had that trial been to the legal profession, for hosts of lawyers came from London for the purpose of being present and studying all the minute points of the evidence that might be produced, *pro* and *con*, on the trial.

The magistracy from the several surrounding counties made their appearance, and the judge who was to preside at the trial looked really rather alarmed at the concourse of people who hemmed him in upon all sides.

The excitement lasted until past midnight on the night before the trial, and then for a few short hours only Exeter seemed to sleep.

At the hour of six in the morning the friends of the prisoner sought the prison in which he was confined, and by virtue of an order, which had been procured from the judge, had a long interview with him. These friends consisted of Mr. North, the young barrister who had charge of his defence; Mr. Anderson, his attorney; his father, old Mr. Wilton; Mr. Revis, and Amelia; for no persuasion could induce her to stay away upon the occasion.

In answer to her father's anxieties upon that subject, she had replied—

"Father, if all goes well, as it surely will do, with Arthur, I ought to be there, so that I may know as much without the delay of a minute; and if all goes ill, I ought to be there to comfort him, and to tell him that I still know and feel that in the sight of God, if not in that of his fallible mo tal judges, he is innocent; so do not ask me to stay away."

To this Mr. Revis did not feel that he could oppose any course of reasoning, and so Amelia went to Exeter with him.

Arthur met his friends in an apartment of the prison where the prisoners usually had interviews with their legal advisers; and he smiled as he saw them all; and then, after shaking hands with them, and letting Amelia's hand linger in his awhile, he said—

"Will you not all congratulate me to-day? This should not be a day of dread to any of us, for it ought to be the day of emancipation. Surely a careful inquiry cannot end in a mistake?"

"No, Arthur, no, it ought not and cannot," said Amelia. "You are innocent, and so this day, before all the world, you must, and will be declared so."

"We will hope so," said Mr. Revis. "What say you, Mr. North? I know that you have been giving the matter the most anxious consideration, and, no doubt, you have formed an opinion."

"My opinion," said Mr. North, "is that everything that can possibly take place that we don't know of, must be in our favour. All the little accidental circumstances and facts that are sure to creep out in the course of a solemn judicial investigation, are with us, in consequence of the one great fact of the innocence of our friend, Wilton; and, therefore, I am hopeful."

"But the evidence?" said old Mr. Wilton.

"Is," added Mr. North, "certainly circumstantial; and such as it is, if it can be believed, is all against us."

"But it is all false!" said Amelia.

"Not all false," replied the barrister, "but it is pregnant with falsehood, and it is so artfully constructed, and one fact is so dependant upon another, that the least accident will bring it all down together in one ruin, and then Arthur Wilton is saved."

"Good heavens!" said Mr. Revis, as a roaring sound, like the surging of the waves of the sea, came upon their ears, "what is that?"

"Now, gentlemen, if you please," said an official of the prison. "It's time to go. The breakfast-bell is ringing."

"But what noise is that we hear?"

"Oh, that is the people collecting to see the prisoner brought out of the jail, you see. Why, the crowd extends all the way from here to the court-house. I never saw such a blessed kick-up as this here trial has made, in all my life."

"And yet the accused is innocent."

"Eh? What did you say, sir?"

"I say that he is innocent."

"Oh—ah! that may be. Of course, if the jury finds him innocent, he is; and, of course, if the jury don't, he isn't."

The man looked so completely satisfied that he had said rather a clever thing, that Mr. Wilton did not think it worth his while to say another word to him upon the subject.

It would have been quite out of the question for any of the friends of Arthur Wilton to have forced their way into the court, late as they would have been, if they had had to go to it by the ordinary mode of entrance. But such was not the case; they were allowed to go by the route which connected the prison with the court, and by which the accused was conducted to his trial. So they avoided the dreadful scrambling and pushing for an entrance to the building which many, for the gratification of their curiosity, had to go through.

The officers of Arthur's regiment attended in a body, with the exception of some one or two, to whose turn the barrack duty had come, and who, consequently, could not leave that duty which was no doubt very much to their chagrin.

The anxiety of Captain Strachan to know how the affair progressed was so great, that he could not possibly have staid away; and although when he found himself so wedged into the body of the court that, let what would happen, escape was out of the question, he felt a pang of alarm, yet he soon reassured himself with the idea that it was quite impossible anything could occur to effect the disclosure of the secret guilt that was only known to himself and to Mr. Huncks.

It did not increase the comfort of Captain Strachan, though, to find that Mr. Flummery would pertinaciously keep close to him, and he muttered curses upon him between his clenched teeth.

The scene in the court-house within a quarter of an hour after the doors were thrown open was positively terrific, and if the witnesses had not been all allowed entrance by the judge's private door, no trial would have taken place that day, for not one of them would have found his or her way into the building.

The frantic efforts of those within the court to resist the frantic efforts of those without to force their way in, created a war that threatened at one time the entire demolition of the place.

The judge, with the high sheriff of the county, and a number of magistrates and others connected with the administration of the law, came into the court at nine o'clock precisely.

The scene presented at that moment baffles description, and the judge stood for a moment looking around him, though quite baffled to know what to do or say.

Those who were with him, too, looked equally aghast as they saw the roaring, tearing, shouting, fighting throng of apparently infuriated people in the court-house.

"Mr. Sheriff," said the judge, "we cannot go on in the midst of all this."

"I am afraid not, my lord."

"But what is to be done?"

"I will speak to the chief constable, my lord. He is a man of great experience, and may suggest some course."

"Do so—do so. Dear me, they will pull each other to pieces, I'm afraid."

The chief constable was sent for, and appeared with his coat torn right up to the nape of his neck, and without his hat and wig.

"Why, Mr. Brown," said the sheriff, "what is the meaning of all this?"

"I don't know, sir. I don't know, really; but the constabulary are quite, I beg to assure you, insufficient to cope with such a mob. The people are mad, I do think, and unless you will give me leave, sir, to deceive them to a certain extent, I am afraid you will never get to-day any quiet in the court-house."

"Confound them all," said the sheriff, "you may deceive them as much as you like, providing you get rid of them."

"Very good, sir. Will you be so good as just to say to my lord judge that what I am going to say is only to get rid of the crowd?"

"Yes—yes."

Upon this, the chief constable sprang upon the barristers' table, and called out in a loud, clear voice—

"The trial of Arthur Wilton for the murder of Colonel Percival is traversed till next sessions, to be here holden in——"

The remainder of what he said was quite drowned in one loud and angry roar from the people; but the effect was quite magical in the clearance of the court. The mob rushed out and dispersed through the city with such speed, that in a little time the only persons who remained were the witnesses, the officers from the barracks, the officials, and those of the assemblage who, even in leaving the court, were resolved to let the more unruly of the mob precede them by a great way.

"That will do," said the judge. "Now close the doors, and don't open them again on any account. It is quite a mercy to have got rid of that wild and boisterous ocean of people."

CHAPTER LXIX.

THE TRIAL OF ARTHUR WILTON COMMENCES.

THE officials of the court were quite delighted at the success of the little stratagem of the chief constable, and the sheriff gave him an approving nod, as though he would say—"That is the way to do it. We are all very much obliged to you."

The judge took his seat on the bench, and the court was finally opened.

At first the announcement of the chief constable had taken the friends of Arthur as much by surprise as it had done the indifferent multitude, who only came to satisfy a morbid curiosity from the details of a horrible crime; but they soon found how the court was cleared by such means, and that it was only a *ruse* upon the part of the constable for that specific purpose.

Captain Strachan, too, remained, and so did Mr. Flummery, who still would keep close to him.

Notwithstanding the great clearance, however, that had been effected, the court was quite as full as it ought to be. Indeed, it was what under ordinary circumstances would have been called crowded; but with a recollection of what it had been only so short a time before, nobody could feel very well inclined to call it such.

There was now a death-like stillness for a few seconds, and then it was broken by a scuffle of feet, and a couple of constables made their appearance, and stood one on each side, while Arthur Wilton, with a calm and steady step, passed between them, and took his place at the bar of justice.

Poor Arthur! He was very, very pale, indeed—paler, much, than he had been only a short half-hour before; but, probably, the excitement of finding that so many eyes were upon him, produced that effect, and in some constitutions paleness is the result of excitement, while in others the face flushes.

In the former the blood retreats to the heart—in the latter it rushes to the surface, partially surcharging the small blood-vessels immediately under the skin.

This preternatural paleness, however, did not last very long, and Arthur's face in a few minutes assumed its wonted colour, and much of its usual expression.

Amelia scarcely dared to look at him.

Old Mr. Wilton buried his face in his hands, and seemed to be engaged in prayer; but there was one pair of eyes that, beneath their overhanging and corrugated brows, were looking with hatred and devilish spite at Arthur. They belonged to Strachan.

"My victim!" were the only two words that Strachan whispered to his heart, when he saw Arthur Wilton standing in that dock where he, Strachan, should have stood.

From the moment of the prisoner's entrance into the court, the stillnes within it seemed to be awful and solemn. People appeared almost to suppress their breathing, and all eyes were fixed upon the youthful-looking person who stood there, with so clear, and open, and handsome a countenance, to answer to his fellow-men upon a charge which the expression of every feature of his face so strongly belied.

At a nod from the judge, the clerk of the arraigns rose, and in a confused gabbling voice read the indictment, which charged the prisoner at the bar that he did, with deadly malice aforethought and instigated thereunto by the devil, and in contravention of the power of our sovereign lord, the king, kill and slay one John Percival, for the which deed he stood there that day arraigned.

It was quite in vain that Arthur strove, amid the monotonous gabble of the reading, to catch a single intelligible sentence; but the purport of the charge he knew well, and, therefore, it did not matter whether he heard the pure legal jargon in which the charge was couched or not.

When the reading of the indictment was over, he was asked—

"Prisoner at the bar, do you plead guilty, or not guilty, to the charge laid against you this day?"

"Not guilty!" said Arthur Wilton, firmly: but without any theatrical display of the sentiment, or affected pronunciation of the words.

"That's true," said Mr. Flummery.

"Silence!" said the crier of the court, "si——lence!"

"Who was that?" said the judge.

"He won't be quiet, my lord," said Flummery, pointing to Strachan. "Here he is. He won't hold his tongue."

"I?" cried Strachan. "I did not——"

"Silence, sir," said the judge, directing a sour glance at Strachan, who he believed was the delinquent. "Another word, and I will commit you."

Strachan bit his lips, and if at that moment a wish would have annihilated Mr. Flummery, why, certainly, annihilated he would have been.

The jury were duly sworn, and the proceedings were all arranged in due form; and at a quarter past ten o'clock, after a whispered consultation with the other counsel retained for the prosecution by the Government, the attorney-general rose to state the case to the jury for the crown, which prosecuted in this case, as Colonel Percival was decidedly an officer of the crown.

Every sound was hushed, and the most painful attention was given to the first few sentences uttered by the attorney-general, as those who pretended to know a great deal of such matters affected to be able to tell, by their tone and manner, what impression he, the attorney-general, had upon the matter.

The attorney-general commenced as follows:—

"My Lord, and Gentlemen of the Jury—

"The prisoner at the bar, Arthur Wilton, stands charged, as you have been informed by the indictment this day brought forward against him, with the wilful murder of Colonel Percival, an officer in his majesty's army.

"There is another indictment against the prisoner, framed upon the proceedings of the coroner's jury; but it is not the intention of the crown to proceed with that, as the same facts in substantiation of it could only be produced that occur to the prosecution in favour of the first indictment.

"It will be my duty, without exaggeration, and without favour or affection to any party or parties concerned in this most painful inquiry, to detail to the jury such circumstances as have come to the knowledge of the prosecution, and which tend to point to the fact of the criminality of the prisoner at the bar; but in detailing those circumstances, I wish most particularly to guard the jury against supposing that I, as an individual, from them deduce any conclusion whatever.

"It is not my province to do so. I do not appear here to-day as an advocate for or against the prisoner at the bar of this court.

"No, gentlemen of the jury; my functions are purely ministerial in this case. As the law officer of the crown in such matters made and appointed, I am here to see, if possible, and so far as human evidence may go, justice done between the prisoner at the bar and the subjects of the crown, and my duty, therefore, plainly resolves itself into this—that I have to state the facts as given to me in evidence, and which, by that same evidence, will be substantiated to you, and leave you to draw your own inferences therefrom.

"If the witnesses who shall depose to those facts be such as you find you cannot give credit to, it will be your duty to acquit the prisoner at the bar.

"If the facts themselves appear to you too loose a material for the purpose of fixing upon him so fearful an offence, you will likewise acquit him. But if, on the contrary, you believe the witnesses, and you think the facts conclusive of his guilt, I am sure that, consistent with your oaths, you will not scruple to pronounce him guilty.

"The prisoner at the bar, then, gentlemen of the jury, is named Arthur Wilton, and is, I understand, the son of a respectable yeoman in this county. There are certain circumstances, with which we have nothing whatever to do, which induced him to accept the bounty of twenty pounds, and enter in the seventy-second regiment of the line, now stationed in Exeter and its immediate vicinity, and occupying now, as then, a large building as a barracks, in the immediate vicinity of the village of Riversdale.

"Colonel John Percival, the murdered man, concerning whose mode of death and by what hand we are here met to inquire, was the colonel commanding that regiment, and a most distinguished and gallant officer. He had served with distinction abroad, and had been present in many engagements. As a man and a soldier, we shall rarely find his equal."

A murmur of applause ran through the court.

"Gentlemen of the jury, Colonel Percival was distinguished by his kindness to every man under his command, and it appears that, finding the prisoner at the bar to be a young man of education, and of a respectable station in society, and knowing that his enlisting was from peculiar circumstances not at all to his discredit, he took the most kindly notice of him, and made him his private secretary, by virtue of which he was relieved from the ordinary duties of a soldier.

"This state of things continued for some time, during which, however, it seems that the prisoner at the bar made various representations to the deceased colonel concerning conversations between him and a Captain Strachan of the same regiment, which were of so strange a character, that the colonel thought fit to withdraw his confidence from the prisoner at the bar.

"After a time, though, the colonel again placed him in a confidential position about him, in which he continued till the lamentable catastrophe which has induced this inquiry.

"The expressions said by the prisoner to have been used by Captain Strachan to him were to the effect that it would be a good thing to cut the colonel's throat, and take away his brass-bound box, in which it was believed there were rich treasures.

"Now, gentlemen of the jury, Captain Strachan will be called before you this day to deny upon his oath that he ever uttered such expressions to the prisoner at the

ARTHUR APPREHENDED FOR THE MURDER OF COLONEL PERCIVAL.

bar, and then the only inference we can draw from the circumstance is, that the shadow, so to speak, of the dreadful crime since committed was even then haunting the soul of the unhappy man at the bar of this court."

It was with great difficulty that Arthur Wilton, at this juncture, could restrain himself from an indignant repudiation of what was attributed to him; but he felt the necessity of so doing, and was silent.

"After this, gentlemen of the jury," continued the attorney-general, " we come to the particular circumstances which have produced the present inquiry. The regiment was ordered from Riversdale for a short time, and during that time the colonel treated the prisoner with confidence and esteem. The regiment came back to Riversdale, and as it was probable his stay in these quarters would be considerably prolonged, and as the colonel expected his wife to join him in this part of the country, he rented an old mansion known as the Abbey, in this neighbourhood, where the crime in question was committed.

"It appears that Colonel Percival left

all minor arrangements regarding his removal to the Abbey from the barracks in the care of the prisoner at the bar, and among other articles removed and placed in the colonel's bed-chamber was the brass-bound box to which allusion has already been made. A sergeant's guard took possession of the domestic affairs at the Abbey, and on the night of the murder the persons within that building consisted of the gardener and his wife, an aged couple, who attended to the premises; the sergeant's guard; the prisoner at the bar; the colonel; and two persons who made their appearance in the middle of the night, but whose appearance there can be satisfactorily accounted for.

"The prisoner at the bar had a bed-room afforded him close to that of the colonel's, and, moreover, a sitting-room, or secretary's-room, was ceded to him on the ground-floor of the house, looking into the garden at the back of it. The sergeant's guard occupied what was called the great kitchen : one sentinel was placed in front of the house, and one in a lane running at the back of the garden-wall.

"Such, then, gentlemen of the jury, was the disposition of affairs at the Abbey upon the night of the murder, and early on which night it appears that Colonel Percival went to bed.

"Now, the guard states that there were two alarms in the course of that night. First, a corporal named Standy, and a drummer named Cockles, both belonging to the regiment, arrived, and said that they had exceeded their time of leave out of the barracks, and preferred stopping at the Abbey and getting the forgiveness of the colonel to throwing themselves upon the mercy of their captain, who they did not expect to be merciful.

"Secondly, gentlemen of the jury, the prisoner at the bar made an alarm that there was some one in the garden at the back of the house, and then it appeared that the prisoner had never retired to rest upon that night at all, although there was nothing to keep him up but his own free will to be up.

"And now with regard to the alarm of a man being in the garden; it will be for you, gentlemen, to decide whether it was a false one or not, from the evidence that will be brought before you. You will hear witnesses who saw a man, and you will hear witnesses who think that if there had been one they must have seen him. You will exercise your best judgment in striving to arrive at the truth.

"One thing, however, is certain, and that is, that if there was a man there, we may be led to believe he was the murderer solely on his own account, or that he was the accomplice of the prisoner now at the bar."

CHAPTER LXX.

THE ATTORNEY-GENERAL FINISHES HIS STATEMENT OF THE CASE AGAINST ARTHUR.

AFTER a slight pause, the attorney-general proceeded.

"Gentlemen, a chase was made after this real or supposed man, which ended in nothing but meeting with a young lady, named Revis, who, it appears, is much attached to the prisoner at the bar, and who, strange to say, had risen in the middle of the night to go to him at the Abbey, and warn him of a somebody or something which does not clearly appear.

"Heaven forbid, gentlemen of the jury, that I should say a word against the innocence or the purity of that young lady; but it is strange that upon the night of the murder at the Abbey she should get up from her bed, and go to seek the prisoner at the bar. I will not suppose that she had any distant idea that the notion of committing the dreadful deed that was that night committed was hovering about his brain, and that she could not rest until she had gone to him to dissuade him from it—that would be a very horrible supposition; but yet it is one which will force itself upon the consideration of every thinking man, as within the range of possibility. Perhaps that young lady, when she appears upon her subpoena as a witness this day, will be able to tell us something to do away with that terrible impression.

"Well, gentlemen of the jury, the alarm subsided, and the real or supposed man who was in the garden was not captured. The whole party returned to the Abbey, and then some one suggested the propriety of arousing the colonel, which was ignored by the prisoner at the bar, who still would not go to rest.

"The hours to the morning soon passed, and Major Cuthbert reached the Abbey on horseback to see the colonel respecting some matters of military discipline. Then it was that, surprised at the non-appearance of the colonel, who was an early riser, the major insisted upon entering his chamber, and found him lying dead in his bed, and weltering in his blood.

"The regimental surgeon was at once sent for, and other officers came from the barracks — a magistrate, too, attended; and then, gentlemen of the jury, a knife was found in the room below, which the prisoner had occupied, and upon the hilt were the initials, rudely scratched, of ' A. W.,' meaning Arthur Wilton. Traces of blood were found from the room of the colonel to his own—the handle of the door had been grasped by bloody fingers—the prisoner appeared confounded at the charge, and denied it, but the magistrate thought it his duty to give him into custody on suspicion.

"From that time, gentlemen of the jury, to the present, facts have accumulated against the unhappy man at the bar.

"It appears that clearing out a room, in the barracks, on the morning of a day in the past week, a pocket-book was found, evidently belonging to the prisoner, with such memoranda in it as foreshadows the dreadful crime for which he is arraigned.

"It appears further, gentlemen, that he wrote and posted a letter to the agent of a steam-packet company in London, begging to know his best and shortest route to the continent.

"It is for you, gentlemen, to say if all these circumstances combined lead you, or lead you not to a conclusion that he is guilty. Let me now, as briefly as may be, place these circumstances before you in the order in which they seem to have taken place.

"The prisoner at the bar endeavours to get up a prejudice in the minds of others against a captain in the regiment by reporting that he suggested the murder of the colonel, and the appropriation of his supposed treasure. I would suggest to you the glaring improbability of that captain so far committing himself, to an avowed enemy, too, unless he were insane.

"Then we have the mysterious sitting up of the prisoner on the night of the murder at the barracks—the false alarm respecting a man in the garden — the hidden knife, with his initials upon it—the blood traced from the colonel's room to his; and then we have the letter to the steam-packet agent in London, and the pocket-book found at the barracks.

"Heaven forbid that I should positively assert that even all these circumstances may not be compatible with innocence, but they wear an awfully suspicious aspect. With regard to the part that Miss Amelia Revis appears to have played in the transaction, I do not wish to say one more word.

"Now, gentlemen of the jury, I have taken you through the case as concerns the prisoner at the bar, and I may tell you, therefore, that I am informed there are some mysteries connected with the whole affair that seem to baffle all inquiry. It will be for the able advocate that the prisoner has retained for his defence to point out to you what those mysteries are, if he should in his judgment think that they bear sufficiently upon the case in hand to warrant him in doing so."

"At all events, I am quite certain that in such a matter as this the court will award to that gentleman the greatest possible latitude of speech.

"For myself, I can only say, that it is my earnest wish and prayer that from out of all these observations, the truth, and only the truth, may be evoked."

The attorney-general sat down.

Now certainly the case as stated looked rather ugly against poor Arthur Wilton, and there was no one in the court who did not feel how very difficult it would be, notwithstanding the purely circumstantial character of the evidence, for him to do battle with it with any degree of success.

As regarded Arthur himself, he had listened to the speech of the attorney-general with quiet calmness, inasmuch as he knew the utter fallacy of the deductions attempted to be drawn from the facts detailed; but what cut him to the soul was to have, even by innuendo, aspersions cast upon the innocence of Amelia.

Up to that time he had thought that he alone had to bear the heavy weight of that false accusation; but now he saw how subtly the plot had been woven, for it had involved her with him in its terrible construction.

And yet, what could he do or say? There he was, speechless, even at the moment when she whom he loved better than all the world was so maligned. Oh, it was indeed a heart's bitterness to poor Arthur to know that!

The hum of conversation that had arisen in the court was now stopped, as in a loud, harsh voice the crier called out—

"Captain Strachan, first witness."

Strachan stepped forward, and got into the witness-box. His appearance was truly awful. Every particle of colour had left his face, and his lips, through being so perfectly bloodless, had the most frightful aspect that could be conceived.

All eyes were bent upon this man, and even the counsel whose duty it was to examine him, paused, and regarded him with a fixed and earnest gaze before he spoke, as though he were in some strange manner fascinated by his dreadful looks.

The monotonous tones of the officer whose duty it was to administer the oath to the witnesses first broke the stillness of the court, and Strachan started as he took the sacred volume in his hand, and hurrie ly pressed upon it the Judas-like kiss.

The counsel recovered from the strange effect that the appearance of Strachan had produced upon him, and said—

"Your name, I believe, sir, is Strachan?"

"It is. You will probably perceive that I am very ill?"

"You look so."

"I have only partially recovered from a dangerous illness, as the surgeon of my regiment can depose to, and nothing but a strong sense of duty would have induced me to come to this court to-day."

"Very well, sir. Of course, we will trouble you as little as possible."

"The witness may be seated," said the judge.

"I thank your lordship," said Strachan; "but I dare say I shall be able to go through my evidence in the regular way; but should I feel faint, I shall avail myself of your lordship's kind indulgence."

"Well, Captain Strachan, what do you know of the prisoner at the bar?"

"Simply that his name is Wilton, and that he is, or I should say was, for I understand he is dismissed from the army, a soldier in my company."

"Now, sir, attend to me. Did you or did you not ever say to the prisoner at the bar, that it would be a capital thing to cut the throat of Colonel Percival, and plunder him of his brass-bound box, or words to that effect?"

"Never. I am not insane, sir."

"Very good. How long have you been ill?"

"About a week before the melancholy end of my friend, the colonel, I was taken sick, but I have such a dislike to lay-up, that I said nothing about it, which I found the imprudence of, for I was compelled at length to do so, and was in my bed the day before the murder, and for some days afterwards. I think the melancholy intelligence very much retarded my recovery, for I was deeply affected by it."

"Do you know the prisoner's handwriting?"

"Certainly not sufficiently to swear to it."

"Very well, sir. I have nothing further to ask of you."

Captain Strachan would have left the witnses-box, but Mr. North, the counsel of Arthur, rose and detained him.

"One moment, if you please, Captain Strachan."

"Certainly, sir."

Mr. North certainly had a bad opinion of Strachan, but he little knew the real devilish subtilty of the man he had to deal with, or he would not have attempted a cross-examination of him. The fact was, that it was for this cross-examination by Arthur's counsel that Strachan had reserved all his cunning and all his powers. He well knew that the counsel for the prosecution could have but one question to ask of him, and that was with reference to the words repeated by Arthur Wilton to the colonel; but for the defence, he knew that there might be much asked him, and to answer all he was fully prepared.

"Now, Captain Strachan," said Mr. North, "had you and the prisoner at the bar any ground of quarrel?"

"Yes."

This answer took the counsel rather by surprise.

"What was it?"

"It is a private matter, sir; but as I think, upon a review of my whole conduct in the matter, that I, under the impulse of that passion which obscures all our judgments, treated the prisoner unfairly, I will, although it costs me a pang to do so, tell you."

"Well, sir?"

"We both were attached to the same young lady—Miss Amelia Revis—and as I had reason to think the prisoner the favoured suitor, I felt that I had that ground of quarrel with him, if it can be called such at all."

"And that prompted you to revenge?"

"Oh, no. But he had the same ground of quarrel with me, and I don't know what it might have prompted him to. The man who could commit a murder, and such a murder as the one under investigation, is capable of anything."

"We don't want your reflections, sir, upon possibilities, for it happens that the man is innocent of the murder, and that we have still to find the man who committed it, and who, consequently, is capable of anything. Do you still deny that you uttered the words you have denied uttering to the prisoner about cutting the colonel's throat, and carrying off his brass-bound box 'for the sake of the treasures it might contain?"

"Most indubitably I do."

"Have you never uttered threats against the prisoner?"

"Very likely I have; I was angry for the reason I have told you; but all that has dissipated, and now I can only pity him."

"Very well, sir. Now, did you not have some words with Colonel Percival about a false charge you brought against this young man at the bar for deserting the regiment?"

"Yes."

"Oh, you admit that?"

"I do, sir. I deeply regret that, seeing all his actions through the jaundiced eye of jealousy, I should form a wrong estimate of them. I was clearly wrong, and it is a great satisfaction to me that Colonel Percival and I made up our differences thoroughly before his death. I know I have been unjust to the prisoner at the bar, and I am glad of this public opportunity of saying so, for we are no longer rivals. The young lady is no longer an object of my ambition."

"And so, you were in bed on the night of the murder?"

"I was."

"Have you any witnesses to prove that?"

"Yes. The 72nd regiment, I presume, would be able to prove it, for I was in barracks, and extremely ill, indeed."

Mr. North was baffled. What could he say to the man who so candidly confessed his errors, and who with such a simple appearance of truthfulness denied nothing that was trivial, and glossed over all that was important?

CHAPTER LXXI.

THE EXAMINATION OF THE WITNESSES CONTINUES.

Mr. North was evidently much vexed at the issue of the examination of Captain Strachan, but it was evidently useless to pursue it any further, and he sat down, saying as he did so—

"We may want this witness again."

"I shall not leave the court, sir," said Strachan.

"Call Corporal Steady," said the attorney-general, after a glance at his brief.

The corporal was in the witness-box, and duly sworn within the course of two minutes, and then he stood in an attitude of attention.

"Your name is Steady?"

"Yes, sir."

"Do you know the prisoner at the bar?"

"No. 227, private, Captain Strachan's company."

"Very well. Now tell me what you know of the events at the Abbey on the night of the murder?"

"Cockles and I had been out, but the rain came on, and we lost our way, and so overstaid our leave. We didn't like to go to barracks, so we stopped at the Abbey, intending to ask the colonel to let us go clear in the morning. We thought that the best plan. We found the guard in the kitchen, of course, and we made ourselves as comfortable as we could, considering all things."

"Well, we don't want to hear that. You will be so good as to proceed now to the moment when you first got the alarm that something was going on of an unusual character at the Abbey."

"Yes, sir. We heard the report of a musket."

"That was the first alarm?"

"It was, sir. Of course, that aroused us all, and we hurried to the direction whence it came from, and there we found Mr. Wilton, who told us that there was some one in the garden."

"Did you see any one?"

"I shouldn't like to swear I did, but I thought I did see a shadowy-looking figure, too."

"What happened next?"

"We pursued this figure, if figure it was, but it escaped us, and then we met Miss Revis and Mr. Flummery, and after that we came back to the Abbey."

"Why did you not awaken the colonel, or how was it that you were not rather surprised he did not awaken?"

"I was surprised; but Mr. Wilton said that possibly a cannon fired at his ear would not then awaken him."

"Did you hear the prisoner make any remark to Miss Revis, or she to him?"

"She said 'Thank Heaven, you are safe,' or something like that."

"Do you know to what she alluded?"

"No, sir."

"What happened in the morning?"

"Major Cuthbert came, and then the death of the colonel was discovered. I have told all I know about it."

"Very well. I have nothing further to ask of you. Perhaps my learned friend who appears for the prisoner has."

"A word," said Mr. North. "You say you would not like to swear you saw a figure in the garden?"

"I have said so, but I don't know why I ought to hesitate about it, for there certainly was a shadow as of something—I think I really may safely swear that I did see some figure in the garden."

"In fact, you will swear it to the best of your belief?"

"Yes, I will do that—I do that."

"That is all the court requires of you. Of course, all human testimony is liable to error. We can only depose to things to the best of our belief. You are, I believe, personally acquainted with the prisoner at the bar?"

"I am, sir."

"Then you know something of his disposition, and habits, and modes of thought, and from that knowledge you can come to some judgment as to the fact of whether he is a likely man to have done such a deed as he is charged with?"

"Sir," said the corporal, "I believe that Mr. Wilton is as innocent of the death of the colonel as I am; and if the colonel is looking down from Heaven on this day's work, he knows it, and pities the man who is wrongfully accused."

"You can go down, corporal."

"Call Cockles, a drummer," said the attorney-general. "Cockles, I think, is the name."

When Cockles found himself in the witness-box, he looked about him in such a comical manner, that the spectators, notwithstanding the serious character of the inquiry that had commenced, could hardly forbear laughing; and when he made a movement with his hands as though he were beating his drum, there was a general titter.

"What is this witness about?" said the judge.

"Nothing," said Cocklee. "Row-de——oh, nothing."

"Now, witness, who are you?" said the attorney-general.

"Cockles I is, and Cockles I were."

"Were you with Corporal Steady——"

"Sergeant, now."

"Well, well; were you with Steady at the Abbey?"

"In course I were."

"Have you heard his evidence?"

"I is."

The judge had to pretend to cough to cover a laugh.

"Well, we want you to tell us your version of the affair at the Abbey, on the night of the colonel's murder."

"My what?"

"Your version of the incidents."

"Can't do it."

"You can't do it? What do you mean?"

"Not in my line, sir. Never made any verses in all my life. No use to try."

"Good gracious me! I don't wan't you to make verses. I wish to know if you agree with Corporal Steady?"

"Agree with Steady? To be sure I do. Why didn't you say that before? Why, Steady is the best tempered man in the whole regiment; and a feller would be a pig to disagree with Steady. There never was two people as agreed better than me and Steady."

"But has he sworn to the truth? Can you corroborate upon your oath all that he said?"

"Can I what?"

"Corroborate his statement."

"I should be very sorry to *conglomerate* anything as Steady said, 'cos he's sure to be right; and I'm quite surprised that you, a gentleman in a white wig, and come to your time of life, can ask me to do it."

Despite the gravity of the occasion, the irrisibility of the audience was too strongly affected to stand this, and there was one roar of laughter through the court from all but those who were too deeply interested in the fate of poor Arthur to join in it.

"This is most indecorous," said the judge. "If the counsel have nothing important to elicit from this witness, I would suggest that his evidence be dispensed with. He has counteracted the corporal already. Of course, I have no desire to dictate to counsel."

"Thank your lordship," said the attorney-general. "We can do without Mr. Cockles any further for the prosecution."

"I have no questions to ask but one," said Mr. North. "Cockles, did you, or did you not, see any one in the garden when the alarm was given by the discharge of the sentinel's musket?"

"I did: I saw a man."

"Did you know him?"

"No. He flewed away like a streak of lightning, and he went over the wall like a hot pea in a shovel, and the last I saw of him was his leg going away like the French when they catch sight of an English bayonet."

"That will do."

"Call private John White."

Private John White was sworn, and the attorney said to him—

"Were you on duty on the night of the murder of the colonel?"

"I was, sir."

"Relate what took place."

"I was on duty at the back of the garden-wall of the Abbey, and suddenly a voice called out from the garden, 'Fire!' or 'Stop him, and fire!' or something like that; but there was the word fire; and so I discharged my musket at once, and then I saw a man run at full speed down the lane."

"You are sure you saw a man?"

"Quite sure."

"And that is all you know about it?"

"That is all, sir."

Mr. North had no questions to ask of this witness, as he had clearly and distinctly deposed to the only fact which, from all the witnesses, it was impossible to get at, namely—that some one was, upon the night of the murder, about the premises, and, consequently, that he, and not Arthur Wilton, might be the murderer of the colonel.

The sergeant of the guard now gave similar testimony to that which was deposed by Corporal Steady and by Cockles, and as one after another of these witnesses were examined, the fact that there had been some one in the garden of the Abbey, at all events, became more and more apparent, and beyond all dispute. Indeed, to do the counsel for the prosecution justice, they took as much pains to establish the fact as Mr. North did, so that by this stage of the proceedings it became an agreed-upon fact, however mysterious it was, and utterly destitute of everything in the shape of satisfactory explanation.

Major Cuthbert was now called, and gave his evidence in a candid, straightforward, open manner, strictly confining himself to facts; and when anything in the shape of an inference was wrung from him by counsel, he took care it should be in favour of Arthur Wilton, of whose total innocence he by this time became quite assured, although he could no more undertake to explain the events of that terrible night at the Abbey than he could have jumped over the building.

Such a witness, of course, Mr. North had nothing in the world to say to.

The surgeon of the regiment was the next person examined; and he, with professional precision, described how he found the body, and the nature of the wound which caused the death of the colonel.

Then came the soldier who had found the knife in the room where poor Arthur Wilton had passed the night at the Abbey, and the fatal knife or dagger—for, from its shape, it might be called either, as a civilian or a military man spoke of it—was produced in court, and created an universal shudder.

The doctor was recalled.

"Look at that knife or dagger, sir."

"I do."

"Would that weapon produce the sort of wound that you found had caused the death of Colonel Percival?"

"Precisely so. I have made a *post mortem* examination of the body, and I am able to swear positively that this was the weapon that the deed was done with."

This produced a sensation

A soldier then swore to the marks of bloody fingers upon the door-handle of Arthur Wilton's room, and upon the footing of the window; and as this soldier was evidently an intelligent man, Mr. North thought it worth while to cross-examine him.

"Pray attend to me, if you please," he said. "How many stories high is the Abbey where this deed took place?"

"Only one, sir."

"Then there is, I presume, a flight of stairs leading direct from the hall or basement to the chamber where the colonel lay?"

"Yes, sir; there is the hall, which goes right through the house, and opens to the garden at the back again; from that hall there are some half-dozen doors, and the last one on the left-hand as you go in was Mr. Wilton's room. The staircase commences about eight feet from the door of that room."

"Very well; and above?"

"Above there is a long landing, from which opens no less than eight rooms, one of which belonged to the colonel."

"How is that landing lighted?"

"By several windows, sir, looking into the garden at the back of the house."

"Are there any trees close to those windows?"

"Yes, sir; there is one in particular, that every time you open the window pushes its branches right into the house. It is a tall, strong tree."

"Then would it not be possible for any one tolerably active to get into the garden—climb that tree, and so get into the Abbey—murder Colonel Percival, and go down the staircase then, and place the dagger where it was found, and so escape by the front window of Mr. Wilton's room into the garden again, fancying Mr. Wilton to have been asleep while that took place?"

"Very possible indeed, sir."

"Very good. I have nothing more to ask of you."

It was strange how Mr. North, in putting what the court looked upon as the hypothetical case, had hit upon the exact mode by which the murder was really committed by the villain Strachan.

At this moment there was a cry of—"Air! air! A gentleman has fainted!"

———

CHAPTER LXXII.

AMELIA IS COMPELLED TO BEAR UNWIL-
LING TESTIMONY AGAINST ARTHUR.

THE confusion that now took place in the court was immense, and when, after some trouble, it was ascertained who it was who called for air in so peremptory a manner, it was found to be no other than Captain Strachan.

The real fact was, that the suppositious case put by the counsel for Arthur Wilton had come upon him like a blow, and for the moment so truthful was it, that he could not persuade himself otherwise than that his whole villany was now discovered, and that up to that period the lawyers had been only playing with him.

This feeling, combined with his previous agitation, and the fact that he could not get out of the court even to run for his life, if he had been ever so inclined to do so, had completely, for the moment, overcome him, and he had called out in the way we have described.

With the sound of his own voice, though reason and reflection had come back to him, and he felt how forgetfully indiscreet it was of him to throw away a chance in such a way, for after all it was but a supposition on his part that the counsel spoke from any foreknowledge of the real facts of the case.

The people who were close to Captain Strachan, with the exception of Mr. Flummery, who would have nothing to do with him, supported him, and a glass of water was handed from the barristers' table to him.

In a few minutes he was so far recovered that he was able more fully to feel his great indiscretion, and when the judge said—

"Let that gentleman be removed carefully from the court," he managed to reply—

"Oh, no—no, my lord, I am better now. My recent illness has weakened me, that is all, and I am particularly desirous of staying till the end of the trial, as I wish to speak to the good character of the prisoner."

"Very well," said the judge, "you can stay, of course, if you feel yourself able to do so; but the court cannot be interrupted in this way by the obstinate perversity of a sick man in staying where he should not stay by any means."

Captain Strachan took no notice of this remark from the judge, although he and every one else knew quite well that it was intended for the purpose of making him leave the court.

A slight appearance of bustle and anxiety was now perceptible at the barristers' table, and the attorney-general suddenly said—

"It can't be helped. I am sorry for the necessity; but we cannot get on without the witness."

Then he added in a loud tone—

"Call Miss Amelia Revis."

At the sound of that name there was a general sensation in the court, and poor Arthur looked dreadfully distressed. The idea that his Amelia, of whose purity and innocence of all unworthy thoughts or actions he felt so well convinced, should be subject to the annoyance of appearing in a court of justice upon such an occasion, gave him a pang of the acutest anguish; but he was powerless to save her from the ordeal that she was ordained to go through. He could only suffer!

Amelia was sitting with her father and Mr. Wilton; but at the sound of her name she rose with so pale a face, that it was like looking upon some fair sculptured image to gaze into that face.

"Be firm," said Mr. Revis. "Be firm, my child."

"I am, father."

"Oh, that I could spare you this!" said Mr. Wilton.

"Heed it not," said Amelia. "They want the truth, and why should I shrink from that? I am quite ready."

With a soft and gentle movement she got into the witness-box, and placing aside the veil that had straggled over her features, she stood calm and still, prepared to answer any questions that might be asked of her.

The little ceremony of swearing her to tell the truth, the whole truth, and nothing but the truth, gave her time to still further nerve herself for the duty she had to do, and she waited for the questions which the counsel for the prosecution might think proper to ask her.

The attorney general spoke to her with a tone of mildness and deference, and showed evidently a disposition to spare her as much as possible in the examination.

"What is your name?" he said.

"Amelia Revis."

How sweetly the gentle tones of that young girl fell upon the ears of all present! They went direct to the heart of Arthur Wilton, and he had to grasp the dock for support as the idea crossed his mind that he might, though innocent, be condemned to a sad and fearful death, and

ARTHUR WILTON IN PRISON.

so be deprived of the joy of calling her his, and leave her but the legacy of despair, and the thought of his murder—for a murder it would be—to weigh her down prematurely to the grave.

It was, in truth, no wonder that the young spirit felt half maddened at the situation in which it was placed.

"It is with great reluctance," added the attorney-general, "that I feel myself compelled in the course of my duty here this day to ask you questions which I would willingly have refrained from mentioning; but I cannot help it."

"I will answer you, sir."

"Very well. Is there or is there not an attachment subsisting between you and the prisoner at the bar?"

"There is."

"In point of fact, we may look upon you as engaged to be married to him. Is it not so?"

"It is so."

"Did you see him on the night of the murder of Colonel Percival?"

"I did."

"Describe to the jury what passed upon that occasion, and state, if you please, why it was that you saw him upon that night."

"I had no thought of seeing Arthur on that night; but I had a fearful dream, and it pressed so much upon my imagination, as dreams will when night has not fled, and when the brain is heated and excited, and thrown off its balance by a disturbed sleep, that I could not rest until I went to the Abbey to see that nothing had happened to him. I took with me a person named Flummery."

"That's me," cried Mr. Flummery.

"Silence!" said the judge. "Turn that man out if he speaks again.

"Pray go on, Miss Revis," said the attorney-general.

"When we got to the Abbey we heard a confused noise, and Prince was evidently impressed with the idea that there was some danger."

"Who did you say was impressed with that idea?"

"I beg your pardon, sir. I should have mentioned that a favourite dog of my father's, who is much attached to me, was with me likewise. His name is Prince."

"Exactly. Pray proceed."

"The tumult increased, and suddenly a man plunged from among some trees to the right, and from the direction of the Abbey, and attempted to pass us; but the dog made a bound at him, and I think caught him, but if he did so, the man broke away again and escaped."

"Did the dog follow him?"

"No. The dog acted in a manner that much surprised me, for he neither followed the man nor came with me, but turned and went homewards at his utmost speed. A few moments after that, Mr. Wilton and some of the soldiers from the Abbey visited the spot, and that is all I know."

"What did you say to Mr. Wilton?"

"I said, 'Thank Heaven you are safe!' or words to that effect."

"Are you aware that something like that has been already sworn to by a former witness?"

"I am, and he is quite correct."

"You then returned home?"

"I did, at once."

"Was the manner of the prisoner at the bar in any way confused or embarrassed upon that occasion?"

"Oh, no. Why should the manner of an innocent man be confused or embarrassed?"

"Well, Miss Revis, it is quite clear that you think the prisoner at the bar to be innocent of the crime imputed to him. Now, on your oath, did he ever propose to you to go abroad?"

"Never."

"He never spoke of leaving England with you, and living in some other country if he had means enough so to do?"

"Never."

"Had you any correspondence with him?"

"Yes."

Amelia shook like an aspen leaf, and twice she tried to speak before she could manage to utter the one word, yes. It was evident that she was in a state of the most acute mental suffering, and her situation excited the commiseration of everybody in court. It was after a pause of some few moments' duration, that the attorney-general said, in a solemn voice—

"Amelia Revis, you are upon your oath here, and I charge you, by the duty you owe to God and man, to answer me truly what I am now about to ask of you. In the course of your correspondence with the prisoner at the bar, was there anything which in any way, more or less, could shadow forth the idea of the awful crime with which he is now charged?"

Amelia fell fainting into the arms of a couple of constables of the court, and Arthur Wilton cried out—

"Save her—oh, save her!"

Some water was given to her, and she partially revived. A chair was placed for her, upon which she sat, and then, as she so sat, she looked like a corpse, so pale and wan was she.

"Amelia," cried Arthur, "answer them at once, and say 'No.' Say that it was impossible any letter of mine could shadow forth a crime that my heart never sanctioned, and that my whole soul abhors."

"Arthur—Arthur!" she gasped, "I—I cannot!"

A copious flood of tears now came to her relief, and it was some minutes before the attorney-general spoke to her again.

"I must press the question," he said, "much as I commiserate you, and admire the noble sincerity of your disposition. I feel that you will tell the truth. Say no, and I will not press this part of the examination further."

There was a death-like stillness in the court.

"Oh, God! what is it you would have me say?" said Amelia.

"Did you receive any letter from the prisoner at the bar that hinted in any degree at the commission of this crime, directly or indirectly?"

There was another awful stillness, during which Amelia turned her tearful gaze to Arthur, and then she said, in an agitated voice—

"Arthur, forgive me!"

"God of Heaven!" said Wilton, "I know not what this means."

"We wait your answer," said the judge.

Amelia clasped her hands, and then, in a low voice, struggling with a world of emotion, she said—

"I did.—I did receive such a letter!"

Arthur Wilton drew back a step in amazement, and there was a visible sensation in the court.

"This is heroic virtue," said the judge, in an under tone, to the sheriff. "I never knew such a case."

"She is a noble girl, my lord."

"She is, indeed. We shall hear the truth from her."

"Can you produce that letter?" said the attorney-general.

"I can. It is here. There is but one. He wrote it to me from Exeter. God help me if I am doing wrong, but here it is."

"You are not doing wrong, Amelia," cried Arthur. "The truth is never wrong. I did write to you from Exeter."

"Oh, Arthur—Arthur! why did you so write?"

Amelia, with a trembling hand, took the letter from her bosom—that letter which the villain, Strachan, had himself written and substituted for the one that Arthur had really indited, and handed it to the attorney-general, who, as he held it in his hand—his hand shook a little as he so held it—said, in an anxious tone of voice—

"My lord, and gentlemen of the jury, I feel myself bound to state to you, and likewise to the counsel for the prisoner, that I received an anonymous note, putting me in possession of the fact of the existence of this letter I possess, and urging the questions concerning it which I have put to the witness. There is the note. I desire no concealment in the matter, and my learned friends on the other side can make what use of it they may think fit."

The anonymous note, which the reader will have no difficulty in understanding came from Strachan, ran thus:—

"To the Attorney-general.

"SIR,—In the case as against Arthur Wilton, for the murder of Colonel Percival, you are requested by a friend to justice to ask of the witness, Amelia Revis, the production of any letter or letters written to her by the prisoner that may contain statements having a bearing upon the case.

"There may be such letter or letters that may contain expressions to show that the idea of the murder of the colonel was a fixed and floating one in the mind of the prisoner. The girl may or may not perjure herself upon the occasion.

"I am, sir,
"A FRIEND TO JUSTICE."

It was not at all likely that Mr. North should be able to make anything out of such a note, written, as it was, in the disguised hand that Captain Strachan had taken care to write it; and it, therefore, only added yet another mystery to the many in which the case was involved, and yet another perplexity to those which had made it beyond all mortal power to unravel.

Alas, poor Amelia!—Alas, poor Arthur Wilton!

CHAPTER LXXIII.

THE EVENTFUL TRIAL OF ARTHUR WILTON CONTINUES.

AMID the breathless stillness of the court, the attorney-general read the following letter:—

"Exeter.

"MY OWN DEAR AMELIA,—I cannot help writing to you again, although I have so very recently done so. My situation is none the better. Pray excuse my apparent inconsistency between this note and my last, as I really don't know what I said in it, except that I love you as truly as ever. That I can never forget.

"Oh, my Amelia, the colonel has a small chest in which there is gold enough, they say, to make any one for life. If you and I only had it—Well, well we will say no more about that. I am not familiar with even the thought of crime, and it makes me shudder to think of it.

"I hope your father is quite well. I hope, too, that all our friends in the happy little village are kind to you and to yours. As regards Captain Strachan, I feel that I owe him so much evil that it would serve him well if I were to play him the worst trick possible—namely, make him suffer for the crime of another person. But I will say no more upon this head to you. You are too good and pure, after all, to enter into the conditions and the heart-burnings of crime; so farewell, and may Heaven hold you in its special keeping.

"I am yours,
"ARTHUR WILTON."

This epistle is not at all new to the reader. In it he will recognise the one that Captain Strachan had sent to Amelia, and which was so close an imitation of the handwriting of Arthur Wilton, that up to that moment in court, where he was upon his trial for his life, and where it formed so fearful a link in the evidence against him, she had never once thought of questioning the authenticity of it. There it was, to her apprehension, a thing not to be doubted, but to be deeply deplored.

It may be asked, with some degree of reasonableness, now, how it was that, with such a letter in her possession, the genuineness of which she had not doubted, she could feel so confident as she did of the innocence of Arthur? But to that we can only reply, that, without attempting to unravel the seeming inconsistency, she did feel so confident.

It is possible enough, too, that if she thought deeply upon that part of the subject at all, she came to the conclusion that the death by violence of the colonel, after Arthur had written such a letter, was but a coincidence of a darkening character, but by no means a proof of his guilt.

Of the damaging influence of that letter, though, upon other minds not so well acquainted with Arthur Wilton, she had shown, by the mortal struggle she had had to produce it, a full and certain appreciation.

Every one in court listened to that letter with the most marked and painful attention; and when the attorney-general ceased speaking, every one looked at him as much as to say—

"That has done it. He is guilty !"

The judge half shut his eyes, and leant back in his seat to think, and Amelia wept bitterly.

But if that letter surprised some and afflicted others, what kind of effect was it likely to have upon Arthur Wilton, who for the first time had heard its contents, and became aware of why it was that Amelia had shrunk so much from its production ?

His impression, as it proceeded, was that he must be, after all, in some dream, and that, since that letter purporting to come from him to Amelia was so unreal, that every other circumstance connected with the awful situation in which he found himself could be but of the same complexion.

He looked rather wildly about him for a moment or two, and then he said, in a low tone—

"Where am I?"

"Rouse yourself," whispered an officer by his side. "Come, come—don't give in yet, whatever you do."

"It is real, I suppose?"

"Real enough."

"My lord, and gentlemen of the jury," began the attorney-general, in a grave and rather saddened voice, as he felt that he must make the necessary comments upon the letter—"My lord, and gentlemen of the jury, it is with pain that I——"

"Hold, sir !" cried Arthur Wilton, in a voice that rang through the court like the sudden blast of a trumpet. "Hold, sir !"

The judge proudly rose from his seat, and every one in court turned with agitated gestures towards Arthur, who lifting upon both his hands above his head, shouted out—

"I swear by the great God above us, that I did not write that letter !"

A shriek of joy burst from the lips of Amelia.

"I swear," added Arthur, "that until this hour in this court, I never heard of such an epistle, and that not one word of it is mine !"

"Arthur ! Arthur !" cried Amelia ; "you have lifted a mountain from my heart. Oh, joy, joy ! He did not, even in a moment of thoughtlessness, write such a letter. He did not—he could not ! Oh, shame upon me for dreaming for one moment that he could. The shadow is off my soul ! He did not write it !"

Disdaining all obstacles—in the joy of her heart caring nothing for the large concourse in which she stood, Amelia sprang forward, and leaning over the dock, she clasped the hands of Arthur in both her own.

"Amelia," he said, "and did you think that I was guilty ?"

"Oh, no—no?"

"And yet you put faith in that letter?"

"Arthur, forgive me !"

"I do—I do. Blessed and pure spirit, you have been deceived."

The attorney-general looked rather pale as he said—

"My lord, with such interruptions as these, it is impossible that I can do my duty."

"Witness," said the judge, "paying, as we feel inclined to do, all possible regard to your feelings, we cannot permit this irregularity. You are under examination by the prosecution, please to recollect."

"Yes, my lord, I do. I am ready."

Amelia, with a bright flush of happiness upon her face, now, took her place again in the witness-box, for she thought, in the innocence and simplicity of her heart, now that Arthur had said the letter was none of his, that it could have no further weight against him.

The attorney-general held up the letter. "You received this, I see, by post?"

"Oh, yes; but Arthur wrote it not."

"Did you not think it a most extraordinary letter to receive from him?"

"I did indeed; but that is now accounted for. I ought from the first to have known that it was none of his. Oh, how foolish I have been!"

"How comes it that, when you mentioned it to him after his return from Exeter, he did not then at once repudiate it as he has done to-day?"

"I never mentioned it to him. I forgot it till the dreadful death of the colonel gave it a fearful coincidence. I might then have burnt it; but with a faith which is rewarded in the innocence of Arthur Wilton, I would not."

A murmur of applause ran through the court, which the judge would not even try to suppress, for in his heart he fully concurred in it.

"Take the letter in your hand, Miss Revis, and look at it well, and say upon your oath, is it or is it not in the handwriting of the prisoner at the bar?"

"Of course it is not," said Amelia, innocently. "Has he not said it is not his letter? How can it be in his handwriting?"

"Yes, that may be satisfactory to you; but it is very essential that the court should have some other argument than the assertion of the prisoner, that this letter was not written by him to you."

"I understand you now, sir," said Amelia, as she took the letter, and then she said, after gazing at it for some few moments, "it is marvellously like; and yet, now that I come to scrutinize it, it is not his writing. It is a different shape, and he does not use the kind of A that is here at the commencement of the name, Amelia. No—it is a forgery! Oh, God! who can have been so wicked as this?"

"This letter, gentlemen of the jury, is fearfully important to the prisoner at the bar," said the attorney-general. "We must have witnesses who know his handwriting well to look at it, and it must be well compared with other letters indubitably written by him. With your lordship's permission I should like so to proceed."

"I will sit here for a year," said the judge, "rather than any injustice should be done to the prisoner at the bar, or any one."

"Who is there now present in court," said the attorney-general, "who is well acquainted with the handwriting of the prisoner at the bar?"

Both Mr. Wilton, senior, and Mr. Revis, rose, and Mr. North said, in a clear, loud voice—

"If this letter be forged, as it clearly appears that it is so, then the letter to the Steam Packet Company agents in London is forged, and the memoranda in the pocket-book found in the barracks are forged, and there is some plot against the prisoner at the bar of so awful a character, that it is a shock to human nature to contemplate its possibility."

This speech produced a most extraordinary sensation, and Arthur Wilton called out—

"All forged, so help me Heaven! I never had a pocket-book—I never wrote or dreamt about writing to a Steam Packet Company. It is one frightful tissue of horrible duplicity from first to last."

"How is Captain Strachan?" cried a loud voice among the crowd, and on the moment Strachan uttered a scream, and stood shaking like a man with the ague.

"Find the person who used those words," said the judge, "and bring him before me, officers."

The greatest exertion was made to find the person, but it utterly failed, and Strachan said, in a tremulous voice—

"I think I will go—I am very unwell."

"No you don't," said Mr. Flummery. "If you attempt to go, I will collar you, and, let the blessed consekences be what they may, I'll say I seed you do the murder yourself."

Strachan looked like a ghost, but he did not attempt to go. Surely if that bad man had had no other punishment than the horrors of that day, he would have suffered a great retribution for his crimes.

Mr. Wilton got into the witness-box.

That this was the father of the prisoner at the bar was well known to many in the court, but not to all. Those who did know old Mr. Wilton felt the greatest possible sympathy with him on the present occasion, and those who for a few moments only remained in ignorance of who he was, yet keenly felt that they looked upon a man bowed down by sorrow.

The oath was administered to the old man, and there was a breathless stillness in the court, which was only broken after a few moments' continuance by the attorney-general, who said in a low voice—

"Your name is Wilton, sir?"

"It is."

"You are the father of the prisoner at the bar?"

The old man turned an affectionate glance towards Arthur, as he said in a voice that shook with emotion —

"That is my boy, sir—my innocent boy. God bless him!"

A murmur of sympathy now ran through the court, for all knew then who the aged man with the white hair really was.

"Well, Mr. Wilton," added the attorney-general, "I assure you that it is not willingly I call upon you to give any testimony in this affair, but as the father of the prisoner at the bar, and as one who I am quite sure will respect his oath, you are desired to look at this letter, and to say if it be in the handwriting of your son or not."

"I will, sir."

The letter was handed to old Mr. Wilton—that letter which only so short a time ago had seemed as if it would be so fatal a document against poor Arthur. It was with difficulty that old Mr. Wilton could see it at all through his tears; but at length he did manage to clear them from before his eyes, and to look at the document.

"Well, sir, what is your opinion, to the best of your judgment and belief, upon your oath, concerning the handwriting of that letter?"

"Sir, it is like my son's hand."

"But can you swear that it is in his hand?"

"No. How can I?"

"Will you swear that it is not?"

"Yes."

A long breath of relief came from almost every one in the crowded court, and old Mr. Wilton added—

"Gentlemen, my son has said that he never wrote such a letter as this, and I know that he speaks the truth, for he never did otherwise than speak the truth; therefore I can safely say that this letter is a forgery; but if it be desired to procure impartial testimony upon this head, I would say, compare this letter carefully with others that he will avow having written, and concerning which there can be no doubt."

"That is a very good suggestion," said the judge. "Has any one such letters at hand?"

"I have," said Amelia, and from the bosom of her dress she tremblingly produced the other letters of Arthur Wilton, and held them towards the attorney-general.

CHAPTER LXXIV.

THINGS TAKE RATHER A BAD TURN FOR CAPTAIN STRACHAN.

OH, how little it had ever entered into the imagination of Arthur Wilton when he wrote those letters, or of Amelia Revis when she received them, that they would ever be thus produced publicly in a court of justice!

But yet there was nothing in them that could cause either the blush of shame, or the dread even of misconception, or the perception of guilt.

It is no doubt true, as we have very many facts of daily occurrence to prove as much, that the letters of lovers to each other sound singularly uninteresting and foolish to other persons; but with regard to Arthur Wilton's correspondence, it had about it an air of manly, good sense, which greatly relieved it from such a reproach.

The attorney-general took the letter that Amelia handed to him first, and then he said—

"I believe I am able to say that there is a gentleman now in court who is connected with a government establishment, and who has made it the study of his life to compare handwritings, so that he is able, from signs, and tokens, and minute differences that would escape the attention of ordinary observers, to pronounce with great certainty upon subjects of that nature. I may state that that gentleman's evidence has been repeatedly received as regards the disputed signatures to bills—bills of exchange, and other important documents, and that whenever subsequent circumstances have thrown any light upon the matter, they have signally confirmed his views."

"If the counsel for the defence," said the judge, "see no objection to all this, of course, I do not."

"Certainly not, my lord," said Mr. North. "Everything that tends to the elucidation of the truth, is in our favour; and feeling, as I do, that my learned friend, the attorney-general, if he will permit me to call him such, does not come here for the purpose of attempting to prove a conviction, but solely that the truth should be elicited, I cheerfully assent to any course that is at all likely to achieve that object."

"I can assure your lordship," said the attorney-general, "and likewise my learned friend, Mr. North, that no one in this court would more unfeignedly rejoice at the fact of the prisoner's entire and undoubted innocence of the present charge being established. I do not come down here to try for a conviction—God forbid that I should do so."

"Very well, Mr. Attorney-general," said the judge. "Let us have this witness, then, who can speak to the handwriting."

"Yes, my lord. Mr. Williams is in court, I believe."

"Mr. Williams!" cried the usher.

An elderly gentleman stepped into the witness-box, and bowed to the court. He was duly sworn.

"Now, Mr. Williams," said the attorney-general, "what are you?"

"I am chief clerk in the Office of Public Records."

"Very well, sir, and you have devoted your time and attention very much to the comparison of handwritings?"

"I have."

"You feel that you can, with some degree of exactitude, say upon your oath, having two documents exhibited to you, whether they are or are not written by the same hand?"

"I am, by experience, encouraged to say so with certainty, so far as human judgment can at all go in any matter."

"Very good, sir. Here are two letters. We will trouble you to say upon your oath, to the best of your belief, whether they are or are not written by one and the same hand."

"It would be quite as well, if there be no objection upon the part of any one," said the judge, "to let us hear the letter read which the prisoner avows. There is something, although not much, in the style of composition."

"That may be easily imitated, my lord," said Mr. North, "where there was the disposition to do so."

"Granted," said the judge. "I do not press it."

"We have no objection, my lord, whatever, to the letter being read, our only objection consists in the inference that any seeming similarity of style between it and the one we avow to be genuine should lead to a belief that they are both so."

"I beg the jury will take no such inference from me. Let the clerk read the letter now produced and avowed by the prisoner at the bar."

"I beg pardon," said Arthur Wilton. "I have not avowed it yet, I believe, my lord?"

Poor Arthur might well have his doubt, now, and be suspicious of any epistle being fathered upon him after the audacious forgery that had been read in the open court as coming from him.

The letter was now, therefore, handed to him. It was that which he had really written to Amelia from Exeter, and which Captain Strachan had striven in vain to get from the post-office, for the purpose of substituting another for it, and failing in which he had let go, on the chance of its containing nothing important, and had sent his own as well.

"Do you acknowledge that letter?" said Mr. North.

"I do."

"You wrote it to Miss Revis?"

"I certainly did, and posted it myself one evening at Exeter. I remember it well."

"And have you no objection to its being read in court?"

"None in the world. I may state that it was written under the influence of much mental depression, consequent upon the attempts which Captain Strachan was making, and in which he was then partially succeeding, in alienating from me the good-will of Colonel Percival. With that explanation of the gloomy tone of the letter, it may be read."

The clerk of the court now took the letter to read, and no one in the court listened to it with a deeper interest than did Captain Strachan, who was rather anxious to see how far it contradicted or tallied with the epistle that he had sent to Amelia in the name of Arthur Wilton so shortly after it.

The letter was as follows, and no doubt will be recollected by the reader:—

"Exeter.

"MY OWN DEAR AMELIA,—It is night—nearly midnight; but I feel that I could not sleep until I had written to you, if it were only a few lines, to tell you that I still live, and that I still hope that we may be happy.

"The colonel, after being so very kind to me as he was at the first time of my appearance in the regiment, now evidently suspects me, and treats me with coolness, for which I have to thank Strachan—that arch villain.—I thought when I sat down to write, that I should have been able to give you in detail some of the circumstances that now surround me, but my heart fails me as I think of them. Oh, Amelia, if I were but free from the army, and, with a small amount of means, able to call you my own, how happy we should be in the quiet and serenity of some cottage home, with free hearts and consciences at ease, and nothing but the season's difference to cost us a thought.

"But for the present, Amelia, such thoughts are but dreams, and should not be indulged in. Let it suffice that I feel my fortunes are upon the verge, as it were, of some crisis, and what may be the result I cannot even guess; but I dread it, Amelia. Do you, however, my own dear one, keep up a good heart, and expect to hear from me soon again; and in the meantime believe me to be

"Your own, ever and ever,
"ARTHUR WILTON."

A breathless stillness followed the reading of this letter for a few moments, and then the attorney-general said, in rather an embarrassed tone, as if the contents of the letter had been a little different to what he had expected—

"Well, Mr. Williams, pray compare that letter with the one you have in your hand, and let us know the result."

"Yes, sir."

Every eye in the court was fixed upon Mr. Williams, the man who was pronounced to be so cunning in handwritings, while he carefully examined the two letters by placing one upon the other, and sliding it gradually down line after line.

Captain Strachan, fancying that all persons were too intent upon noticing the witness to attend to him, and noticing that Mr. Flummery, too, with his mouth open, was glaring at Mr. Williams, made an attempt to wriggle his way out of the crowd; but Mr. Flummery noticed him, and immediately trod upon his toe with his heavy-nailed boots, with such a force that made Strachan cry out with the pain it gave him.

"Be quiet," said Flummery, "will you?"

"Silence!" cried the usher of the court. "Silence!"

"Don't you come that there again," said Mr. Flummery. "I don't mean you to go, so there's an end on it."

Captain Strachan was boiling with rage. It was so essentially absurd a thing that he should be detained in court without his leave, and by such a person as Flummery, that it was enough to drive him wild to think of it. Nothing in the world but a consciousness of his own guilt, and a positive dread that Flummery would proclaim it aloud, although without proof of the fact, kept him from making a disturbance upon the occasion.

Oh, what a thing is guilt! There was Captain Strachan, with all his rank, with all his angry passions, and with all the consciousness of the danger he was in, detained from seeking the present safety of flight by a village constable, who had not even a right to say that he was formally in custody.

But Mr. Williams has finished his examination of the two letters, and looks at the attorney-general with an expression that implied as much.

"Well, sir," said the attorney-general, "what is your opinion regarding those two letters? Are they written by one and the same hand?"

"Decidedly not!"

Amelia uttered a shriek of joy at this positively uttered confirmation of the truth, and a general clapping of hands ensued in the court, which all the exertions of the officers could not put a stop to for some moments.

The attorney-general looked at the judge, and the judge seemed more flushed about the face than he had been; but he did not say a word. He had from that moment, though, his own firm opinion upon the case, although it was not the time to state it.

CHAPTER LXXV.

SOME IMPORTANT EVIDENCE MAKES ITS APPEARANCE FOR THE DEFENCE.

AFTER this declaration upon the part of Mr. Williams that the letters were not written by one and the same hand, an expression of great ease of mind came over the face of Arthur Wilton, and as he looked at Amelia, the shadow of a smile of hope that yet all would be well played about his lips.

Captain Strachan turned paler than before.

Mr. Williams still remained in the witness-box, and the attorney-general spoke to him as though he had been the advocate for the defence instead of for the prosecution.

"Have you any doubt upon the point, Mr. Williams?" he said.

"None whatever. The one letter is an imitation of the handwriting of the other, and it is a very good imitation; but yet there are little discrepancies easily discernible to those who have made it the study of a life to look after them."

"Does your art, sir, enable you to state which is the original of the two letters and which the forged?"

"Why, one can hardly be called an original, because one is not a copy of the other; but this letter that has been only a short time ago read in the court is a genuine and not a disguised hand. The other is an imitation of that hand, and, although generally well done, it has failed completely in some half-dozen places."

"Then you deliberately swear that, to

COLONEL PERCIVAL'S STRANGE RECEPTION AT LADY TODGERS'.

the best of your belief, these two letters were not written by one and the same hand?" said the judge.

"I do, my lord."

The judge leant back in his seat, and the attorney-general, with a slight inclination of his head to Mr. Williams, said—

"I need not trouble you further, sir. The counsel of Mr. Arthur Wilton, perhaps, may have something to say to you."

"Nothing," said Mr. North.

It was noticed by all in court that the attorney-general called Arthur by his name now, instead of styling him the prisoner at the bar. The change was not important, but it was significant of the effect which the evidence of Mr. Williams had had upon the mind of the attorney-general.

"My lord, and gentlemen of the jury," he said, "that is the case for the crown on the part of the prosecution. I have no one else whom I think proper to take up the time of the court by calling."

With one sweep of his hand, which certainly might have been only accidental, but which some present judged to be otherwise, the attorney-general then sent the brief and papers connected with the case on to the floor under the barristers' table.

Mr. North wrote hastily upon a slip of paper the words—

'Arthur is saved."

Then he gave the slip, doubled up, to an officer of the court to hand to Mr. Wilton, after which, he rose to address the jury, or rather to call witnesses for the defence, for, after all, he had not much to say, and he felt that it would be quite out of the question to commit Arthur for the murder under the present circumstances.

If, though, the jury thought that, putting out of sight all the affair of the letters, they ought to commit him, Mr. North felt quite satisfied that the judge would save him.

"My lord, and gentlemen of the jury," began Mr. North, "I think myself justified in stating that the question in the minds of all intelligent men now present in this court is not whether or no the prisoner at the bar be guilty of the offence imputed to him, for that I do believe is settled in the negative, but who really did the deed?

"Gentlemen of the jury, we have the clearest possible evidence of the fact that a foul, barbarous, and most iniquitous murder has been committed, but as this inquiry has proceeded, it has had done of the most remarkable effects that any inquiry of this nature could possibly have—that is to say, it has, instead of adding to our knowledge of who is the party guilty of the deed, denied that knowledge, inasmuch as it has tended to exculpate the only person towards whom, by a collision of fortuitous circumstances, the finger of suspicion has been pointed.

"My lord and gentlemen, there is an awful plot ! A plot having two phases—two objects. One of those objects has been frightfully and fatally carried out. The other will be defeated.

"The object that has been carried out consisted in the murder of Colonel Percival !

"The object that will be defeated consisted in the casting upon the head of the innocent Arthur Wilton the onus of that terrible crime !

"Now, gentlemen of the jury, and you, my lord, let me beg that all that licence which is awarded to the advocate of the accused will be accorded to me while I endeavour to clear up some of the complexities in which this case is involved ; and, in the first place, allow me to state what I think I have gathered to be the string of points as against the prisoner at the bar.

"It is alleged that—first, he enlisted from a romantic feeling to do a great good to the family of his betrothed. Then, that finding Colonel Percival had a box in which was presumed to be certain wealth, he conceived the idea of murdering the colonel for its possession, and that, co-existent with that idea, he likewise projected casting the guilt upon a certain Captain Strachan.

"This state of things is implied, gentlemen of the jury, from the assumed fact that Arthur Wilton went to the colonel, and told him that Captain Strachan had proposed his murder and robbery.

"Now, gentlemen, either Captain Strachan did say to Arthur Wilton, 'It would be a good thing to cut the colonel's throat and rob him of the contents of his brass-bound box, or he did not ; but it is quite certain that the prisoner at the bar reported that he did so, however strange it may appear.

"Well, gentlemen, if the prisoner reported so in the wrong of Captain Strachan, the inference that he contemplated the murder, and sought to implicate Strachan in it, is fair and just ; but that proposition holds quite equally good as regards Captain Strachan !"

The jury looked at each other at this point, and the judge closed his eyes to think. It was quite clear to all that Mr. North was, in all but direct terms, accusing Strachan of the murder.

"Well, gentlemen of the jury," he added, "after this I have to account for the time and the occupation of my client from the last moment Colonel Percival was seen alive at the Abbey to the first moment when he was found murdered in his bed. That is easily done.

"Arthur Wilton did sit up all night, or, rather, he fell asleep in a chair in the room which had been assigned to him by the colonel, at the Abbey, and the first he knew of anything being amiss consisted in the fact that he saw a figure at the window of that room. Now, gentlemen, it is established beyond a doubt, by the concurrent testimony of several witnesses, that there was some one about the Abbey and its gardens on the night of the murder in question.

"The question is, who was that? The inference is that he, whoever he may be, was the murderer of Colonel Percival.

"Gentlemen of the jury, it remains to us, as an anxious duty, to discover who that man was; and although it does not follow that, in order to acquit the prisoner at the bar, we should be able to lay the onus of the murder of Colonel Percival upon the person who really did it, for that may, perhaps, never be known; yet it would be a very ready mode of absolving him from all appearance of guilt in the transaction if we could do as much.

"The mere fact that a man fell asleep in a chair instead of going to bed is not sufficient to convict him of a murder. The mere fact that another person had ample opportunity to do such a deed, and to conceal the weapon with which he did it in the room so recently occupied by the prisoner at the bar, is likewise not sufficient to commit him of the murder, and specially when we find that one portion of the circumstantial evidence against him has exploded in the singular manner it has done in court to-day.

"I allude to the letters that have been produced as being both in the handwriting of the prisoner, but the only one from which any guilty inference could be drawn being the one which seems to be a forgery.

"Well, gentlemen, an unknown person committed the murder. That unknown person was seen in the Abbey-garden, and he fled from the spot. Now, I have to draw your attention to a very singular train of circumstances, which would tend to show that some mystery was going on at the barracks where the regiment of the prisoner is located, and which seems to have some sort of bearing upon this case.

"Naturally, it was believed that if the prisoner at the bar did not commit the crime, some other person, as well acquainted as he could be with the habits of the colonel, and the expected plunder to be derived from the commission of the deed, had done it. Acting upon this idea, the officers of the regiment instituted an examination, to ascertain who was absent from the barracks on the night in question.

"Well, my lord, and gentlemen, it came out that the surgeon of the regiment, a gentleman of skill, and much respected by every one who knows h'm, had left the barracks before the murder, and returned after it, being absent just during the time it might have taken him to go to the Abbey and do the deed and come back again.

"It will be shown to you upon evidence that the sentinel at the barrack-gate saw, or rather, I should say, thought he saw, the surgeon pass out, and remain out for a time quite long enough to do the deed, and then come back again; he being out between the hours of twelve and half-past one.

"Now, this implicates the surgeon; but —but, gentlemen, we have evidence, all of which I shall lay before you, to prove that an ensign in the regiment being,

'Troubled with a raging tooth,'

at a quarter before one got up and went to the surgeon's room, to ask him to extract it; but found that gentleman in so quiet and sound a sleep, that he would not awaken him, but left him and went to his own room and to bed again.

"So you see, my lord, and gentlemen of the jury, that there is evidence that the surgeon left the barracks, and that there is is evidence that he did not leave the barracks.

"What is the inference to be drawn from this? I would ask what is the only natural inference we can draw from such a circumstance? Why, just that some one left the barracks *disguised as the surgeon* upon that night, and did the deed for which the prisoner at the bar now stands arraigned!"

An extraordinary commotion was visible in the court at this statement of Mr. North; and the truth of it—for, after all, there is a certain something about truth which, like the ring of a true coin, at once makes it pass current—appeared to come home to every heart.

"Let me say something further upon this point," added Mr. North, after a slight pause.

"Gentleman of the jury, you will be told by the sentinel at the barrack-gate on the night in question, that the means by which he knew, or thought he knew, that he saw the surgeon pass his post, were just that he saw his cocked hat and great coat. The guard within the gate will tell you the same—a soldier who stopped the supposed surgeon in the barrack-yard to say something to him, will tell you the same; so that it is a coat and a hat we have to trace and contend with.

"Well, then, gentlemen, it appears that there is a room in the officers' quarters where that coat hung, and where that hat hung, and where both were accessible to anybody within the barracks. It is as clear as anything need be, then, that under cover of the surgeon's hat, and under cover of his coat, the real murderer of Colonel Percival went from the barracks—walked to the Abbey—did the foul and despicable deed—and in the same disguise came back again.

"Gentlemen, the coat has mud, gravel, and moss upon it—moss that has been proved to have come off the top of the garden wall at the back of the Abbey— that very wall over which the figure that was seen in the garden on the night in question made its escape; and further, gentlemen, that coat has a rent in it, and has lost a piece.

"Gentlemen, the rent has been made by the teeth of a dog. A dog did stop, for a moment, the murderer on his flight from the Abbey, after the deed of blood had been done! All that will be proved to you this day."

As Mr. North proceeded thus to unravel the horrible plot by which poor Arthur Wilton had been made to seem guilty, when in reality he was so innocent of all complicity even in the dreadful deed that had been laid to his charge, the colour came back to the cheeks of Amelia, and her eyes recovered their brightness; for she felt that a happier day was dawning for her and for all who loved her.

The conviction upon the minds of all who heard the counsel was, that he knew much more then he gave utterance to, and that there was yet something to come of an overwhelming character to assure the world of the fact of Arthur Wilton's innocence.

This was a mistake; for, after all, Mr. North was detailing all he knew; but it was an idea and a mistake that was shared in by Captain Strachan as well as by many others.

It was with the utmost difficulty that the officers of the court could prevent some powerful demonstration of the public opinion upon the occasion.

Perhaps curiosity to hear what more could be said upon the occasion had more to do with the suppression of the people's applause than anything else.

CHAPTER LXXVI.

CAPTAIN STRACHAN MAKES YET ANOTHER EFFORT TO ESCAPE FROM THE COURT.

THE effect of all this upon the imagination of Captain Strachan may, as the newspapers are wont to say, be better imagined than described. He felt as if he were going mad.

One by one he saw all the flimsy supports, by which he had thought himself held up in his fancied security, struck from under him, and in the results of the patient, calm, and persevering professional scrutiny which the whole affair had undergone, he read his ruin and destruction.

There was but one chance, he thought, now left him, and that was to escape—to mount his horse, and fly from the place for ever—to take with him what money he had, and reach the coast, and leave England before some other horrible revelation took place to further point him out as the murderer.

"I must escape," he thought. "Oh, fool, fool that I have been not to be satisfied by hearing all this from a safe distance instead of coming here to take the chance of all the cross accidents that might take place to mar my plans!"

In casting his terrified gaze, now, round the court, being as yet undecided how he was to make the attempt to escape, he encountered the gaze of his friend and partner in villany, Mr. Huncks.

The face of that sage expounder of the law looked anything but in a pleasant style of expression. There was a look of alarm upon it, that certainly did not have the effect of diminishing the growing terror in Strachan's breast.

"Ah!" he thought, "Huncks, too, sees that the game is lost, and that I am in great danger. He, too, sees it. What shall I do?"

Mr. Huncks managed to find his way to the side of Captain Strachan.

Before, however, that rascally pair could say anything to each other, the counsel for Arthur had resumed his address to the jury.

"Under these circumstances, gentlemen of the jury," he said, "I do not see how you can, with any safety, do anything but acquit the prisoner at the bar; and however painful it may be to consider that the truth as regards this terrible affair has yet to be evolved from out the complication of circumstances which envelopes it, yet we will hope that some accident may yet throw sufficient light upon it to enable us to find out who it was who left the barracks on the night in question in the surgeon's coat and cocked-hat. I will now call that gentleman before you."

The surgeon appeared in the witness-box, and after being sworn, the attorney-general said to him—

"You are the surgeon of the regiment of which the late Colonel Percival was the colonel?"

"I am."

"Were you out of the barracks on the night in question?"

"I was not."

"Is this hat yours?"

"Yes."

"And this coat?"

"That is mine likewise."

"Where do you keep them?"

"The fact is, that they were all but cast-off clothing, although, in bad weather, I did still occasionally wear them. They were kept hanging on the wall of a room in the officers' quarters, to which all had access."

"Very good, sir. Now, did you attend Captain Strachan from illness in the barracks?"

"I did."

"What was the matter with him?"

"His complaint seemed to consist of a low fever, and he seemed very much prostrated in strength."

"When did you see him last on the night of the murder?"

"Rather late in the evening. He appeared very unwell."

"Can you take upon yourself to say that he would not be able to leave his room or the barracks?"

"I can, unless I was very much deceived."

"How do you mean as to being very much deceived?"

"I mean, unless the debility and some portion of the illness had been feigned."

"Exactly. Now, are you able positively to say that it was not so?"

"I am able, positively, to say that there was illness, but, of course, any medical man may be, to some degree, deceived by a patient regarding symptoms and the existence of debility."

"Are there medicines which would give an appearance of great illness, without such being the case in reality?"

The surgeon was silent for a moment or two, and then he said—

"There are such drugs, and—and—confound it——"

"Confound what, sir?"

"The appearance under which Captain Strachan laboured might easily be produced, and then a little clever acting would do all the rest."

"Permit me," said the judge, "to ask if counsel intends by this mode of procedure to accuse Captain Strachan of the murder?"

"Yes, my lord!" replied Mr. North, in a voice that rang through the court again.

The commotion that ensued was perfectly terrific, and amid it all the voice of Strachan, raised to a perfect scream, could be heard, crying out—

"A lie! A base lie! A lie!"

The judge rose.

There was a temporary lull in the noise to enable them all to hear what he should say.

"I shall order the officers to take into custody any person they may observe, by word or gesture, interrupting the proceedings of the court."

"I will not," cried Strachan, "remain here to be subject to the insults of counsel. I leave this court confident that no English judge will permit an officer and a gentleman to be vilified."

"Officers," said the judge, calmly, "keep the doors, and suffer no one to leave the court till further orders."

The judge gave this general command to the officers, but everybody understood that it was special, as regarded Captain Strachan; and he himself felt it to be such. He shrunk back, and clutched the arm of Huncks with a force that made that worthy say—

"Oh, the devil! You will pinch me black and blue."

"Eh?"

"Be quiet, captain. Hush—hush!"

"Huncks?"

"Well, what?"

"I rely upon you. Remember the treasure."

"I do; but—but——"

"But what? Do you doubt?"

"Not at all; but, my dear friend, allow me to suggest, that if things do go wrong with you, it is far better to let a friend like me know where the treasures lie buried, than leave it to be found by some clodhopper by chance."

"I don't think so."

"Come, now, tell me?"

"No. If I die, I carry the secret to the grave with me. Exert your cleverness and save me, and you have your half."

"But really, now——"

"It is in vain. Say no more about it, Huncks."

"Then I abandon you."

"Go to the d—l!"

"I mean, that if you don't tell me now at once where the colonel's jewels are hidden, I abandon you and your cause for ever."

"Do so, and if things go wrong, I mention where a certain emerald that forms part of the plunder may be found."

"My dear captain!"

"My dear Huncks!"

"Well, well. We will do the best we can. Did you think that I would desert you? Oh, no!—Curse him!" he muttered, "I have shown the emerald to that jeweller in the village, and where any stir made about it, he would be sure to blab; so I must just stick to Strachan."

"Call Ensign Hargrove," said Mr. North.

A young officer stepped into the witness-box, and was sworn, and Mr. North then said to him—

"Sir, had you a toothache on the

night of the murder of Colonel Percival, and if so, what did you do thereupon?"

"I had a severe toothache, but I felt, as I suppose most persons feel, repugnant to have it extracted."

"Just so, sir."

"Nevertheless, I was so tortured by it on the night in question, that I rose with a determination to seek the surgeon, and to get him, notwithstanding the lateness of the hour, to extract it."

"What was the hour?"

"Half-past twelve."

"Are you quite certain of that, sir?"

"Oh, yes. My watch was upon the dressing-table in the room, and I looked at it, and considered for some few moments whether it really would not be too bad to disturb the surgeon at such an hour; and at last, with the idea that he might possibly be up and awake, I sought his apartment, carrying with me a very small hand-lamp. I found his door open—that is to say, on the latch merely."

"Where you surprised at that event?"

"No. The surgeon has repeatedly told all the officers that he never fastened his door at night, in case he should be wanted on an emergency, and there might be a difficulty in waking him, as he is a very sound sleeper."

"Very good, sir. Go on."

"When I got into his room, I found that he was in a deep sleep, and I felt ashamed to rouse him up, and perhaps by so doing disturb his night's rest on my own account. The pain, too, of the tooth had got better. I had left my bed, and the great fever that it had put me in had subsided, so I stepped lightly out of the room again, without disturbing the surgeon, and closing his door, I went back to my own quarters."

"Now, sir, are you certain that you saw the surgeon in bed at the hour you mention?"

"Quite certain. I am as certain as I am of my own existence."

"Very well, that will do."

Mr. North glanced at the attorney-general, who said—

"No—no. I don't mean to question any of your witnesses. I beg to state that I am very happy to hear the testimony of this gentleman."

"Very good," said Mr. North. "I will now call a Mr. Flummery, who was with Amelia Revis when she left her home to go to the Abbey. Mr. Flummery!"

"Mr. Flummery!" shouted the crier of the court, but there was no answer. Mr. Flummery had gone, and to the great surprise of Arthur Wilton and his friends, no

shouting, either within the court or without it, could make him answer to his name.

"My lord," said Mr. Huncks, advancing to the barristers' table, and bowing to the judge. "My lord!"

"Well, sir," said the judge, "what do you want?"

"As the professional adviser of Captain Strachan, my lord, I wish to ask whether that gentleman is to consider himself in custody or not?"

"No."

"Very good, my lord. Then it is a high breach of the liberty of the subject for any one to interfere with the progress of my client when he may please to go. Captain Strachan, as you are very much indisposed, from your recent illness still hanging about you, you had better go home."

Strachan bowed, but an officer laid his hand upon his arm, and said—

"The doors are closed, sir."

"Hilloa—hilloa!" cried Mr. Huncks "what is the meaning of all this? Hilloa —hilloa! The liberty of the subject in danger! My lord, they won't let him go!"

"Very likely," said the judge. "I think that I ordered that the witnesses should be detained for the present."

"Oh, indeed; and pray, my lord, what for?"

"For the ends of justice."

"The ends of justice? Oh, dear, me! Well, my lord, I beg to state that it is quite illegal to detain my client."

"If the court is interrupted further by you," said the judge, "I shall give you into custody, and order you to be kept in the common jail till the end of the assizes."

Mr. Huncks made a low bow, and then retreated behind his highly respectable client, Captain Strachan.

"No go," he whispered.

"I am lost," said Strachan.

"Hem! No—I will swear that I saw such things on the night in question, that will not only save you, but convict the others."

"What others?"

"Wilton and the doctor. You have no objection, I suppose, to getting him into the scrape?"

"None in the least. Get anybody you like into it, so as you get me out of it."

"Just so; that is the very answer I ought to have expected from you, my dear Strachan. And the—the jewels. Come, now, you will tell me, in case of accidents, where they are?"

"No; but you shall have two-thirds,

instead of half, if you do what you say. I promise you that, upon my word."

"Hem! Well, say that I shall have twenty thousand pounds certain, or two-thirds, according as I may choose."

"Done! Be it so—I agree."

"Very good. Here goes, then, for hit or miss—hem! Now for it."

Mr. Huncks sprang into the witness-box, to the surprise of everybody in the court.

CHAPTER LXXVII.

MR. HUNCKS VOLUNTEERS SOME IMPORTANT TESTIMONY FOR THE PROSECUTION.

THE judge looked at Mr. Huncks, and the jury looked at Mr. Huncks — the attorney-general put up his double eye-glass, and took a good stare at him, and the counsel who sat at the table devoted to their use, all looked at him with intense curiosity.

Arthur Wilton, too, regarded that man with a look of great mistrust, for he fully expected that some great master-stroke of villany was about to be perpetrated.

Captain Strachan looked askance at him, and perceptibly shook, notwithstanding all the confidence he had in the cunning of the rascally attorney.

In the midst of all this Mr. Huncks put his handkerchief to his eye, and shook his head, as though he were deeply affected at something.

"What do you want, now?" said the judge.

"My lord, I proffer myself as a witness in this distressing case. I have with a painful, I may, indeed, go so far as to say with an agonised interest, watched the proceedings, and as I have done so, a new light has dawned upon me, and I see that something I thought unimportant is important—I see that it would be the hindrance of public justice that I should longer keep silent — I see that the time has come when I ought to speak out, let the consequences be what they may; and here I am to do so, although my heart beats with emotion, and I deeply regret that I——"

"Silence, sir, and come to the point," said the judge.

"With great pleasure, my lord. I tender evidence for the prosecution."

The attorney-general looked annoyed.

"Yes," added Mr. Huncks, "I tender evidence for the prosecution which I thought of no moment before, but which the course of the evidence produced in this court this day has convinced me is important; and I may say that my feelings are so much af——"

"We don't want to hear that," said the judge. "Mr. Attorney-general, I suppose, as we have been going on, you will feel it incumbent upon you to examine this witness?"

"Yes, my lord. We have been receiving volunteer testimony, and, therefore, I will examine him. Now, sir."

Mr. Huncks bowed very low, and then blew his nose with a noise like an immense trumpet.

"Who are you, sir?"

"Jeremiah Huncks."

"And what are you?"

"Attorney at law."

"Certificated and in practice?"

"Yes, both."

"Swear him, crier."

Mr. Huncks was sworn, and then he proceeded as follows; and inasmuch as he had made himself remarkable for his verbosity a short time since, he now was as remarkable for the clear and concise manner in which he told the frightful lies he had hatched up to save Strachan, and to destroy Wilton and the surgeon, whom he, without the slightest degree of compunction, mixed up in the affair.

"On the night of the murder of Colonel Percival," said Mr. Huncks, "I sat up preparing a will for Farmer Maddox, who is the tenant of the Low Farm Estate, as it is called, in the immediate vicinity of Riversdale. As I proceeded in my work, I found some inconsistencies in the instructions I had received, and I thought I would go at once to my client and get him to explain them.

"Without looking at my watch, I hastily put on my coat and went out, thinking that it was not nearly so late as it was in reality; and I had proceeded about half way, when I heard a clock strike the hour of twelve, and I was immediately struck with the impropriety of waiting upon my client at such an hour, so I turned to go home again.

"Thinking, then, that I would take a near cut through the little wood that lies between Riversdale and the Abbey in which Colonel Percival was murdered, I left the high-road and lost my way. The night was a very violent one, indeed, and I had my hat pressed down over my eyes, so that I went on in rather a blundering fashion, till I was startled by a light close at hand, although some trees and bushes hid me.

"Upon creeping close to that light, I saw standing in a rather clear spot of the little wood, two men."

Mr. Huncks paused, and dabbed his eyes with his handkerchief.

"My lord," he said, "I have mentioned this to Captain Strachan, and his noble and manly reply was—'Mr. H., say nothing about it. Let the prisoner at the bar escape if he can. Heaven may bring him to repentance yet;' but—but my duty —the sense of——"

"Go on, sir, with your story," said the attorney-general.

"Thank you; you are very kind. I will. I see you wish to spare my feelings as much as you can. Hem! I saw two men, and as I hid behind a sycamore tree, I heard one say to the other—

"'South America, I should prefer.'

"'Should you?' said the other. 'Well, I don't know; but we can easily talk about that afterwards. You will have no difficulty in getting over the wall, and you will find me in the room I mentioned to you.'

"'Very good,' said the other. 'You go back now at once, and I will follow. We shall easily get the thing done, and then our best plan will be to——'"

"Well?" said the attorney-general, as Mr. Huncks came to a dead stop at this point of his circumstantial lie. "What then?"

"Why, then I got alarmed, and likewise I thought that it was not a gentlemanly thing to listen to them, so I turned and left the spot, and got into the high-road, and so home again."

"Is that all, then?"

"It is."

"Who were the two men that you say you saw?"

"I have sworn I saw them."

"Well, that you have sworn you saw?"

"One," said Mr. Huncks, with great composure, "was Arthur Wilton, the prisoner at the bar, and the other was the surgeon of his regiment, who has given his testimony here to-day."

The sensation in the court upon this was immense, and Arthur cried out in the indignation of the moment—

"Liar! monstrous liar!"

"You unwarrantable scoundrel!" cried the surgeon. "How dare you tell such an unnatural falsehood?"

"Oh, dear," said Huncks, "I expected all this. Oh, of course, they don't like to hear; but, my lord and gentlemen of the jury, what a merciful and yet what a beautiful thing it is to think that in some mysterious and inscrutable way of its own, Heaven always permits the dreadful crime of murder to be found out sooner or later."

The attorney-general sat down, and then glancing at Mr. North, he said in a low tone—

"I have nothing to say to that man or to his testimony."

"I have," said Mr. North, as he rose. "Now, Mr. Huncks."

"Sir?"

"Now, sir, look at me."

"I do, sir. You are a very young man, and rather indiscreet; but I hope you will get on at the bar. It is not always talent that succeeds best, so you have a chance."

"Why did you not mention this before?"

"I did not think it important."

"And you a solicitor, too?"

"A solicitor, too, as you elegantly express it."

"Come, come, Mr. Huncks, you know that this is from first to last a cool deliberate falsehood, invented to get your friend and client, Captain Strachan, out of the awkward position in which he finds himself."

"Indeed!"

"Pray, sir, have you heard the testimony of the young officer who had the toothache, and who saw the surgeon in bed at the time you mention?"

"Oh, dear, yes, poor young man. His toothache must have been bad, indeed."

"Why so?"

"Because it made him see things that were not there to see."

"But still you have, in a very extraordinary manner, kept back this evidence?"

"Well, to tell the truth, I feel deeply for the prisoner at the bar, as well as for the Revis family, and so did Captain Strachan, and, therefore, there was a reluctance to say more than was necessary."

"Now, sir. Did you ever practice in London?"

"Yes."

"Where did you reside?"

"In Gray's Inn."

"Were you not in a kind of partnership with one of the greatest rascals that London could present, of the name of Sudds, and engaged in the practice of money lending, and did not one of the judges threaten your partner with a prosecution for practising as a solicitor, and you with being struck off the rolls?"

"Quite a mistake, sir. The judge always complimented me and Mr. Sudds, who is a very respectable man, indeed."

"What has become of him?"

"Oh, poor man, I rather think he went abroad."

"Was he transported?"

"Well, they did say so."

"Here he is! Hurrah! here he is! I

AMELIA'S JOY ON ARTHUR DECLARING HIS INNOCENCE.

thought as he was the wery uncommon witness as we wanted—so here he is, and I wouldn't for the sake of twenty *puns*—"

"Silence! silence!"

Mr. Flummery made a rush into the court with Prince on his back, and the huge fore-paws of the dog over his shoulders. In Prince's mouth was something that looked like a ragged piece of cloth. Following Flummery, came Major Cuthbert, Captain Grant, and a file of soldiers, with a bundle.

"What is all this?" said the judge. "Really, this is——"

"All right," said Flummery. "Oh, la! oh, la! My lord, just hold this twenty puns for me, while I speak. Oh, you won't? Well, never mind."

"Can anybody explain this?" said the judge.

"To be sure," added Flummery, "I can, and this is it. Miss Amelia and me and Prince went out, and we met, on the night of the murder, in the wood, a man a running like mad, all which is sworn to already, and Prince he tooks a hold on the hind-quarters as never was, and grabs him tight, but the man he runs off, and Prince he runs to his blessed kennel, and me and Miss Amelia then we meets Arthur Wilton, as never was; and to-day I thought, as Prince had something to do with it, I ought to bring him to the court, and I went to his kennel, and he wouldn't come out, and I upset the blessed kennel, and along with all the straw, out came these here torn bits of cloth, and Prince then takes 'em in his mouth, so I takes Prince on my back, and here he is, and I met the major at the door of the court, and he has got with him a coat of Captain Strachan's, and a pair of what's-his-names, and the doctor's great coat, too, and—and—Hilloa! where's my twenty puns? Oh, gracious, where? Ha! ha!—here they is, in my hand all the time. Why what a *hass* I are !"

"Let me go!" cried Huncks. "Let me go!"

"No," said Major Cuthbert, advancing "My lord, here are clothes we have now taken from the room at the barracks, which belong to Captain Strachan. They have upon them the marks of gravel and moss, and there is a piece torn out of a coat, and out of a pair of trowsers. My lord, the hand of Heaven is in this affair. This dog has now in his mouth the pieces that belong to the surgeon's great coat—to Captain Strachan's body-coat, and to his trowsers. Since the night of our poor friend Percival's death, this dog, with some singular instinct, has secreted these rags in his kennel. They are here now to confound the murderer ! to set free the innocent ! Captain Strachan it was who, in the disguise of the surgeon's coat, left the barracks and murdered the colonel. Behold the evidence in these portions of his apparel torn from him by the dog in his flight from the scene of blood!"

Captain Strachan uttered a shriek, and began to try to fight his way out of the court.

The judge rose.

"Secure that man !" he said. "Secure that murderer !"

Half-a-dozen officers flung themselves upon Strachan, and he was placed in irons in a moment.

"Good-day," said Mr. Huncks. "I— that is—oh, dear me ! Good-day, my lord. Bless me, I——"

"Take Mr. Huncks into custody," said the judge.

Huncks dropped to the floor ; but the officers picked him up again, and then he cried out—

"I tender my evidence for the crown as against Captain Strachan, the murderer of Colonel Percival !"

"And there," shouted Strachan, as he pointed to Huncks with his manacled hands, "there stands the instigator of the crime. There stands the man who, from first to last, was equally guilty with me. But I will be now revenged."

Prince made but one bound, and caught Strachan by the throat, and they both fell together.

CHAPTER LXXVIII.

THE CONCLUSION.

A SMALL pocket-pistol, with which, no doubt, it had been the intention of Strachan to take the life of Arthur Wilton at that last desperate moment, exploded as the dog bore him to the ground, and, luckily, did no one any injury.

The bullet buried itself in the oaken panelling at the side of the dock in which Arthur still was.

The confusion and the excitement in the court now exceeded all possible description. Neither the judge nor the officers were at all capable of stilling the wild roar of human feeling and human passion which the groans and startling attack of the dog had given rise to ; and yet the judge stood in attitude deprecatory of the tumult, and imploring silence.

Out of respect for him—after Strachan was effectually prevented, by his hands being now handcuffed behind him, instead of as they had been in the ordinary way, from doing further mischief—the crowd stilled itself, and then the judge was able to speak.

"Let Arthur Wilton," he said, "be removed from that bar. I feel that the jury have already acquitted him."

"Not guilty !" roared the foreman of the jury with a very red face. "Not guilty, my lord, of course."

A general clapping of hands ensued, and Arthur Wilton was fairly lifted over the front of the dock. His father fell upon his neck in a passion of tears ; and then Amelia, with a shriek of joy, clasped him in her arms, heedless of the assembled hundreds.

Arthur could not speak. His heart was too full.

"Hurrah !" cried Mr. Flummery, and he then very imprudently flung up his twenty *puns* in the little bag he had them in, and they went right through the skylight of the court, and lodged upon its roof.

"Oh, lor! my twenty puns!" cried Flummery, as he rushed out to try and recover them, "my twenty puns! Stop them!—stop them! Twenty puns!"

"Don't let that singular man in again," said the judge.

Major Cuthbert now came forward, and bowed.

"My lord," he said, "I have something to say yet which will still further place this affair in a clear light."

"Speak, sir," said the judge. "We hear you with pleasure."

"I have a witness, my lord, who saw Captain Strachan return to the barracks on the night of the murder."

There was quite a sensation at this.

"Yes, my lord, he is here. Job Clinton, advance!"

"No!" yelled Captain Strachan. "Don't call up the dead to appear against me. He is dead—dead!"

"They have got a Habeas Corpus, and had him up out of the quarry," groaned Mr. Huncks. "Oh, dear!—oh, dear!"

An emaciated figure stepped into the witness-box, and holding up its hands, said—

"I swear, by Heaven and its Great Master, that I saw Captain Strachan on the night of the murder close to the wall of the barracks, with the surgeon's hat and coat on!"

"Who are you?" said the judge.

"My son!—my son!" cried Farmer Revis. "My erring son!"

"Not so erring, sir, as you think," said Major Cuthbert. "He has been the victim of the villain Strachan. I have procured him a pardon for the past, and his discharge from the regiment."

Clinton, or rather Job Revis, as he ought to be called, fell down in a fainting fit, and was consigned to the care of his father and Amelia.

There was now a bustle at the door of the court, and a gentleman in an undress military uniform made his appearance, and bowed to the court.

"This," said Major Cuthbert, "is General Brotherton, the commander of this district."

"I have that honour," said the general. "I am in possession of all that has passed this day; but I should not have appeared but that affairs have taken the turn they have. Lady Percival sent to me, stating her strong opinion that Arthur Wilton was innocent, and I rejoice at the full and complete confirmation of that opinion. Where is Mr. Wilton?"

Wilton advanced with great agitation, and the general shook him by the hand, as he said—

"Mr. Wilton, your friend, Major Cuthbert, is now colonel of your regiment."

"It cannot have a better soldier, general, nor a better man."

"I believe you there, Mr. Wilton. And now, here are two papers—one is your discharge from the army, the other a captain's commission. I must own that I would rather you took the latter, and joined your friends, the officers of the regiment in which you are so much respected."

"Do, Wilton," said Major Cuthbert. "Let us have you for a brother officer."

"Amelia," said Arthur, "do you speak."

"Arthur, you shall follow the path of honour open to you. I will be the captain's wife."

"Well spoken," said General Brotherton, as he kissed her hand. "And now, Captain Wilton, come with me and dine. This is a happy day for all of us, I hope."

*　　*　　*　　*　　*

Our story has now reached its climax and its conclusion. We have but briefly to state what resulted from the deeply interesting day's proceedings at the Exeter assizes.

Captain Strachan was tried for the murder of Colonel Percival, and duly convicted and executed for the crime. He vowed he would not confess, and he kept his word, and no one heard him utter a word from the moment that he declared he would not.

Mr. Huncks was transported for life, so that he had again an opportunity of cultivating the acquaintance of his old partner in iniquity, Sudds.

Job Clinton, as he called himself, went home with his father to the farm, and from that time was the joy and comfort of Mr. Revis's declining years, and became, in time, one of the most respected of the yeomen of Devonshire.

Amelia and Arthur Wilton were married within a week after his acquittal of the dreadful charge brought against him. General Brotherton gave the bride away, and all the officers of the regiment attended upon the occasion.

So gay and so truly happy a wedding had not taken place at Riversdale in the memory of the oldest inhabitant.

Mr. Flummery found his "twenty puns" again, and the officers of the regiment added among them a hundred puns to it, so that he was enabled to take a small dairy farm, and got on uncommonly well, with the good-will of all who knew him.

Prince, the faithful dog, lived to an unprecedented old age in the history of dogs, showing how kindness will lengthen the life of an animal, and to the last being the grateful and attached attendant of Amelia wherever she went.

Corporal Steady, as a sergeant, and as holding several other offices in the regiment, passed a tranquil and respected life; and Cockles came in time to be drummajor; and when the regiment entered a town, the boys thought him a much finer fellow, with his immense silver-topped staff of office, and his gorgeous costume, than the colonel, in his plain blue frockcoat.

Arthur Wilton rapidly rose in his profession; and the recruit who, for the sake of the twenty pounds' bounty, entered the army, and was nearly destroyed by the villany of Captain Strachan, became a general in the service, and an honour to his country.

Arthur and Amelia always loved Riversdale and the old garden; and as often as they could they would come there and pass a week with old Mr. Revis, and Job, and Prince; and upon these occasions Mr. Flummery would come to the farm to see what a grand officer Master Arthur had become, and sometimes Cockles would be asked; and when Flummery would comment upon the good fortune of the drum-major, the latter would say—

"No, Cockles I were, and Cockles I is, and nothing less, nothing more. Don't be a flattering a fellow afore his face."

It was a sad thing that Colonel Percival was numbered with the dead while all this happiness went on; but when we come to think, we shall see how out of what seems to be evil springeth much good.

The murder of Colonel Percival certainly had a great and startling effect upon the fortunes of many persons; and we will hope, that after passing from this life to eternity, through the pang that the knife of the assassin inflicted upon him, his noble and gentle spirit, in another and a happier world, would be gratified to find that in its mode of passing from mortal life to eternity it had been productive of so much happiness to others.

Mr. North, who had so ably defended Arthur Wilton in his trial, from that moment might date a rapid rise in his profession.

The judge who presided upon that occasion, and who was one of the most able, and one of the most intelligent and honest upon the bench, took the young barrister by the hand, and showed him the road to an honourable career. He, too, was a frequent guest with General Wilton in after times, when the judge's ermine became to him a fair possession; and the two men of rank and station would often discuss of that wondrous day at Exeter, when right and innocence triumphed over villany.

———

Thus, then, ended this

"Strange eventful history,"

in the course of which we may truly see how criminality, however it may seem to have framed itself round with the most cunning devices to save it from the consequences of its acts, never is able wholly to provide against some little cross accident, which at once upsets all its deeply-laid calculations, and drags forward to the light of day its most hideous and glaring iniquities.

It will be seen, too, how a patient and an undeviating course of virtue, although it may be exposed to many trials, will at last confer upon those who practise it an enduring reward; and, indeed, it is a tolerably well ascertained fact in the history of individuals, that, even while apparently suffering much, and greatly depressed by circumstances that all seem to be adverse, those who feel and know that they are right endure far less than the guilty, even in their hour of greatest seeming triumph.

"Thrice is he armed who hath his quarrel just,
And he but naked, though locked up in steel,
Whose conscience with injustice is corrupted."

THE END.

PRINTED BY E. LLOYD, SALISBURY SQUARE, FLEET STREET, LONDON.